FANTASTIC AMERICANA

STORIES

ALSO BY JOSH ROUNTREE

Can't Buy Me Faded Love

FANTASTIC AMERICANA

STORIES

JOSH ROUNTREE

FAIRWOOD PRESS
Bonney Lake, WA

FANTASTIC AMERICANA
A Fairwood Press Book
August 2021
Copyright © 2021 Josh Rountree

First Edition

Fairwood Press
21528 104th Street Court East
Bonney Lake, WA 98391
www.fairwoodpress.com

Cover image © Elena Vizerskaya
Cover and book design by Patrick Swenson

ISBN: 978-1-933846-16-3
First Fairwood Press Edition: August 2021
Printed in the United States of America

For Beckett and Gibson,
assorted adventures

CONTENTS

CHASING AMERICA

1. Go West, Young Giant — 1837

I T TOOK LONGER THAN EXPECTED, CROSSING THE ATLANTIC on clouds. Paul wished for a storm front to stretch out like a rumbling gray road beneath his feet, a pathway straight through to the New World. But he was accustomed to trials, and was content to pick his way from cloud to cloud, searching for the perfect westward drift, hoping one wouldn't dissipate before he found another. And driven by innate stubbornness and fear of the world he left behind, Paul found his new home.

After a period of careful searching, he determined that beanstalks were hard to come by in the New World. But he found a forest of tree-tops piercing a low-hung blanket of stratus, and decided one method of descent was as good as another.

A short climb later and Paul stood in America.

The forest surrounding him was quite unlike the ones he'd played in as a boy. The woods of Albion were shadow-drenched places of bent oak, wych elm and boxwood, so choked with history that you couldn't help but search the undergrowth for boggarts and goblin teeth, enchanted jewels and the bones of ancient barbarian kings. Every hidden grove gave solace to witches and whistling thieves, wolves with unsure motives and broken men who'd murder a child for the touch of copper against their palms.

But this American forest was unspoiled. Pines rose straight and stout, and they seemed to hold up the sky itself. Grasslands rolled away from the tree line, spilled into a busy valley that teemed with life. Horses pulled huge felled timbers, coaxed on by men in checkered shirts and woolen caps. Laughter and smoke poured from scattered wooden buildings. A white-capped river cut a path through the camp before disappearing beyond the valley's edge, and Paul imagined its continued progress. Beyond the valley stood a seemingly endless stretch of majestic forest, and beyond that, mountain peaks topped with snow, bathed in sunlight that chewed away the clouds.

There was room to live here. How easy to get lost in such a land, and easier still to evade the Jacks. They'd never find him.

Paul stepped boldly into the valley, drawing stares from the workers. A bent man with a drawn face and patchy beard approached and turned a bemused gaze upward. "Where the hell did you come from?"

"Albion," Paul said, as if that explained everything.

"Big fella, ain't you?"

Paul shrugged. "Big as I need to be, I guess."

"Can you handle an axe? Or a saw?" The man offered Paul an axe but the giant waved him off. He wrapped his arms around a skinny pine and pulled it from the soil with a few sharp tugs.

"Name's Charlie Blade," the man said, watching Paul lower the tree to the ground with a mixture of fear and admiration in his rheumy eyes. "I'm the foreman around here. You looking for work?"

Paul wasn't looking for work, but he *was* looking for a new home. The men here seemed content. And there would be plenty of time to get lost in the endless world beyond the mountains if the need arose.

He shook the foreman's hand, and the legend of Paul Bunyan was born.

*

Paul might have lived in the logging camp forever if Charlie Blade hadn't been crushed by a log spill. Paul loved the camaraderie a rough day's work fostered in the souls of working men, and he never grew tired of the quiet evenings, the sounds of work calls and blades on wood banished to the morning, when endless night crossed the world like the shadow of God. This was a land where all men were giants. And true giants like Paul? Well, they were something *more*.

In Albion, giants were accused of hoarding gold, stealing women and stomping houses beneath booted feet—a ridiculous notion. Paul was small for a giant, but the largest of his kind stood no taller than a ship's mast. Those stories were the product of fear and insecurity. The Americans wove their tales from the twin threads of admiration and respect, spreading wide a blanket of belief that anything was possible in a world so new and fine. There were no limits to what men could do, and Paul understood their need to express this. When they shared tales of how his footsteps created lakes or how he kept a giant blue ox for a pet, he'd simply smile, shrug and return to his labors. These men worked hard, and they deserved their indulgences.

On the night before his death, Charlie Blade crowded the cook stove, rubbing his bony hands together to stave off the brutal cold. "So damn cold out tonight, the lantern light's liable to freeze solid."

Paul chuckled, rattling the bunkhouse and causing a few of the snoring loggers to stir beneath their blankets. "If it did, I'm sure they'd find a way to give me credit for it. Zeb Walton asked me this morning if it was true I punched a hole through the mountains to clear a path for the railroad."

"Well, you're stronger than a grizzly bear, but I doubt you have that kind of might." Charlie gave Paul a thoughtful look. "You're good to go along with all that. They ain't just teasing you, you know. They think highly of you."

"I know."

"This is a hard life and men need to know great things are possible. Just a little hope, you understand?"

Paul nodded. Hope was the reason he'd crossed the ocean.

There was no peace left for giants in Albion. The Jacks saw to it that they were always on the move, afraid even to rest easy in the ancient cloud cities for fear the Jacks might one day organize and topple their entire existence. When Paul first came to the camp, he'd asked Charlie if there were any loggers named Jack. There'd been only one, a stone-faced, unhappy man named Jack Pierre and Paul had kept a close watch on him from day one. There was no fool-proof way to tell if Pierre had murderous intentions, for not all men named Jack were giant killers. But all giant killers *were* named Jack, and as a result, Paul had long since given up the luxury of sleep.

"You look tired, Charlie."

"Long day. Gonna be a longer day tomorrow. Got to get them logs ready for the river." Charlie went to bed and Paul left the bunkhouse, eliciting a chorus of shouts when the howling north wind carried into the room. Paul shut the door behind him and took a seat near the river's edge. The temperature had no effect on him; the cold night smelled like ice and pine needles, and the wind whispered forgotten stories of the forest, tales left behind for those who would hear them of a time before men walked the woods.

It was the most perfect place on Earth, the only place Paul had ever found peace, and he wanted to absorb every second of the experience.

He remained by the river until light blossomed in the east and bunkhouse doors creaked wearily open, once again releasing men into the world with their coughs and laughter, banging pans, axes on whetstones. The misty air carried the logging camp smells of fried ham and morning urine, unwashed bodies and bitter black coffee. And within minutes they were hard at work again—Paul with them—whipping horses into action, bucking logs, working them toward the dump. Spring had come, and soon the river hogs would ride the shipment downriver.

Paul was helping some men choke a log when the ruckus started—panicked shouts, a low rumble, then a terrified scream truncated by horrible silence. Paul released the choke cable in his hands and leapt away from the rumbling logs. By the time he regained his feet, men were already lifting away the massive lengths of pine that had scattered like spilled matches. Paul heaved the logs away, one after another, no doubt giving birth to a hundred more stories. But it didn't matter, there were men trapped beneath.

They found seven dead in all, including Charlie Blade. Paul cried when he saw the old man's grizzled face, and he pulled the limp body from the timbers. But his sadness turned to a fear when he saw Jack Pierre standing just beyond the edge of the insanity, watching Paul with his smoky eyes, smiling. He held a cant-hook at his side like a medieval pike, and his breath came in malignant white clouds. There was no mistaking the man's cool malice.

Paul would have taken revenge on a normal man. But not a Jack, no matter how much he wanted to.

Paul was no fool.

He didn't wait for Charlie Blade's burial. That night, he chose the largest log and rode it downriver. And so it was that Paul began his life on the road.

2. A Giant Keeps His Back to the Wall — 1876

Paul tossed back another nickel whisky and studied the cards in his hands. A pair of sevens to go with a mixed bag of nothing. Luck was not on his side.

The man seated across from him, however, was the luckiest son of a bitch he'd ever met. He'd introduced himself as Bill Hickok, and Paul recognized that name from the newspapers. He couldn't rein in all the details, but Paul knew one thing for sure. The man took his gambling seriously.

"So, you came here for the gold?" Bill tossed a couple of poker chips into the center of the table, then glanced back toward the door. He'd done this often enough during the course of the afternoon that Paul assumed he was waiting for someone. The saloon was filled with raucous men who smelled of earth and sweat; heavy drinkers, card players, and those who simply had nothing better to do. Women in nightclothes and stockings wandered from table to table, laughing and planting lipstick kisses on dirty foreheads, drumming up business for Swearengen's brothel. Bill and Paul had claimed the last unused table, far in the back of the room where they were mostly ignored by a bored-looking bartender who waged a losing battle for a clean countertop with a whisky-soaked rag.

"No. Had enough of that madness back in California." Paul matched Bill's ante. "I don't like watching what gold does to people."

"Then why in the hell did you come? Ain't nothing here *but* gold." Bill leveled a curious stare at Paul, and the giant met his gaze. The gambler's eyes looked to have soaked up every ounce of virgin wildness the West had to offer, and they provided a frank glimpse into Hickok's soul. This man had stared down the barrel of a Henry rifle at a doomed Sioux chief, bested the famed John Wesley Hardin in Kansas, and followed Buffalo Bill around the country in his Wild West show. Hickok was the weaving, wandering spirit of America and Paul realized they were very much alike.

"I like to wander," Paul said. "Deadwood is just another place on the map. I spent time in a logging camp over in Minnesota, got tired there and headed out for Oregon. You ever been there? Trees big around as houses. I've been all through the Rockies, I lived a while in Texas, and I already told you about California. It was a lovely place to be until the prospectors came."

"Forgive me for saying, but you don't look old enough to remember California before the gold rush." A slanted smile broke beneath Bill's bushy moustache, the kind a man might use to humor a harmless drunk.

"I'm older than I look," Paul said. If Bill knew how old he really was, the gambler might choke on his whisky. Paul was aware he was sharing too much of himself, but he'd never held his alcohol well. Normally, he was very circumspect about his heritage, and especially his comings and goings. With the Jacks always on his trail, it was simple common sense. But Paul felt a kinship for the man they called "Wild" Bill; they were kindred spirits.

"You'd have to be a damn sight older."

Paul didn't reply. He folded another losing hand and waited for Bill to shuffle the cards.

Bill raked in a mound of chips. "In my experience, most men who say they're wandering are on the run from something. That the case with you?"

"Yes, it is."

"What did you do? Kill someone?"

"No, nothing like that."

"Then why are you running."

"Because I'm a giant."

Bill dealt the cards, chuckling at Paul's revelation. "You damn sure are. I wasn't going to say anything, but as long as you brought it up, how tall are you? Ten foot easy, I reckon."

Paul shrugged. "I never measured."

"So, what about being a giant caused you to be on the run? You escape from a circus?"

Paul let the unkind comment slide. "No, it's just the way giants are. We're restless. It comes from looking over your shoulder your whole life."

Bill glanced at the door again. "Speaking of that, you mind if we switch seats? I never like to sit with my back to the door. I got a lot of people in this world that don't like me. Keeping my back to the wall has kept me breathing a lot of years."

"Sorry. I have the same policy."

Bill nodded, looking only mildly put-out. "I understand. It's just that sitting this way irks the hell out of me."

"I'll watch your back."

"Guess that'll have to do."

They played for a time in silence. Bill won most hands, but occasionally Paul managed to get some of his money back. When it was Paul's turn to deal again, Bill poured another shot of whisky, slid it to Paul, then fixed another for himself. "I gotta know. What's so scary it keeps a giant on the run?"

"The Jacks." Paul drank the whisky and held out the glass for a refill. The drink was steering the conversation into dangerous waters, but he didn't care. His adopted homeland was wide and untamed, more far-reaching that he'd ever imagined. But it was also lonely. Paul sensed that Wild Bill was a man who understood that.

"Who're the Jacks?"

"Giant killers."

Bill laughed, then cut it short when he realized Paul was serious. "My grandma used to tell stories about a kid named Jack who went around killing giants, stealing their gold. Stuff like that."

"They aren't just stories."

"You're telling me there's a bunch of kids running around trying to cut off your head?"

"They're not kids. The old stories have been twisted. They're regular men, but they've got something in their blood that makes them hunt us."

"Something in their blood? Like it's carried down from father to son."

Paul shook his head. "More like a disease. You can't tell who they are by their family or how they're raised. The only thing they all have in common is they're named Jack. It's an ancient struggle, creatures of magic versus those who would banish us from the Earth. And I've never found a reason for what they do beyond simple blind hatred."

"Men don't always need a good reason to kill." Bill skipped the shot glass and drank straight from the bottle. "Damn. I must have drank more than I figured. I actually believe what you're saying."

"I'm just telling the truth." Paul dealt the cards. The noise and smoke were giving him a headache, but he wasn't ready to leave the game. It was rare to find a man like Hickok with whom he could share his troubles.

"Seems strange to me you'd run from these Jacks if they're just regular men. You're big enough. Why not just whip their asses?"

"Quite a few giants have tried. But it's never ended well. The Jacks are lucky. I'd say fate was on their side, but what does that say about my kind?"

"Fate pisses on everybody with the same stream. You just got to learn to keep out of the way." Bill discarded a single card and grinned. "I'll take one."

Paul was about to lose some more money. He slid a card across the tabletop, hoping it wasn't the one his companion was looking for. When he pulled back to study his own cards, he noticed the man standing a few feet behind Hickok and the .45 revolver he had aimed at the table. Paul's eyes widened and Bill was savvy enough to react. He was on his feet, gun in hand and beginning to turn when the assassin's bullet tore into the back of his head. Another bullet followed and Bill dropped his gun. He fell back into the chair and collided with the table edge. A pair of aces and a pair of eights slipped from the dead man's hand.

A group of men tackled the shooter and wrestled away his gun, but not before Paul recognized him. Jack McCall—a buffalo hunter he'd crossed paths with a few years back in Wyoming. He struggled against his captors, shouting about murder and giants, but his ravings meant nothing to the clientele of Saloon #10. Everyone in the room had seen him kill Wild Bill Hickok, and that was the only fact that mattered. Only Paul understood those bullets were meant for him; Bill's lightning-fast reflexes had propelled him into the path of the gunfire, and into frontier legend.

Paul didn't wait for the trial.

He left Deadwood before sunset.

*

3. This Land is Jack Land — 1937

A roiling cloud of brown dust chased the battered flatbed Ford truck through the panhandle. Paul had a firm grip on the truck's bed, knees pulled up to his chest to keep his legs from dangling over the edge. The truck lurched at every pit and pothole, but Paul managed to hang on. Sand stung his eyes and settled as a fine layer of grit between his teeth. It rode the wind, a voracious brown cloud that chewed away sunshine and distance, swallowed families and dreams, feasted on jobs and land and lives. Paul huddled in the belly of the beast, desperate to be anywhere but Oklahoma, and he prayed the sand wouldn't follow them forever.

It wasn't the only truck leaving Oklahoma. For months Paul had seen them hurtling down the highways, ferrying dirty, beaten people away from wind and misery, and if the rumors were to be believed, toward a rich bounty waiting in California. Paul knew California wasn't the answer, but it suited him far better than waiting around to be buried in dirt. Besides, he'd stayed in one place long enough.

Two other men shared the truck bed with him. The first was a rangy man with nothing but a guitar case and a paper bag full of sandwiches who'd introduced himself as Woody. He seemed unconcerned that they might fly off the back of the truck any moment. One hand rested on his guitar, the other on his sandwich bag, and he watched the world recede with a weary smile, like he'd never seen anything at once so glorious and so heartbreaking.

The second man was gray with middle age and much less calm. His clothes were patched and a size too small, and he kept inching closer to the middle of the bed, shifting and groaning with every bump in the road. He hadn't volunteered his name yet, but in his mind, Paul had nicknamed him Jumpy.

"You comfortable yet?" Woody asked, flicking a cigarette butt over Jumpy's head and into to brown void.

"No, I'm not," Jumpy said, missing the sarcasm. "Do you think he's going to drive this fast all the way to California?"

"Hope he does. The quicker we get there the better."

"Assuming we get there alive."

"If we don't, that's just one less thing to worry about." The truck lurched and Woody put a hand on his floppy hat to keep it in place. Jumpy endured a second of terror before settling down again.

"So, what's your story?" Woody asked. He shot Paul a quizzical look, as if he'd just noticed the giant was sitting next to him.

"What do you mean?"

"How'd you end up here? You don't exactly look like a native Oklahoman."

Paul considered the question and found no answer he was willing to share. Woody stared at him with probing eyes, but it didn't make Paul uncomfortable. From a normal person, he'd shun such close inspection, but he could tell Woody was studying him the way all great artists do. Soaking in the detail, saving it for a book, a song, a painting. Woody's connection to the realm of music was as visible to Paul as the man's weather-creased hat or the thin trails of dirt on his palms. The music whirled about him like a shower of gold dust caught up in a tornado, and Paul knew this was no ordinary guitar picker. He was bound for something more. Woody scrutinized him for several more heartbeats, then nodded his head, unconsciously storing away everything he could remember about his giant traveling companion. Paul knew the man would write a song about what he'd seen some day. It wouldn't be a song about Paul Bunyan, roving frontier giant, but a song about everything he loved and feared. The vast majesty of America; man's desire for freedom and wide-open spaces; the pain of watching the last, lonesome places between the oceans shrink beneath cities, highways, fences, factories.

In short, the way the Jacks were ruining the country.

"I just left home, and this is where I ended up," Paul said, answering Woody's question and yet offering no real insight.

"Well, you ended up in the wrong place. Smart you're getting out."

"You think life in California will be better?"

"Can't be worse," Woody said, munching on a sandwich. "Supposed to be plenty of farming jobs for those willing to work. And I am. Plus, I figure somebody might want to pay me to play guitar. Better chance of that happening there than here."

"So, you're a professional musician?"

"No," Woody grinned. "But I will be."

And Paul knew that was undoubtedly the case.

"Why are *you* headed to California?" Paul asked, inviting Jumpy into the conversation.

"I'm not really *headed* anywhere," he said. "I just like to keep on the move."

"How come?" Woody gave Jumpy the same stare-down he'd given Paul.

"Because if I stay too long in one place, the Germans will get me." Jumpy cast a searching look out into the dust storm as if his enemies might be lurking by the side of the road, waiting to take him out with a canister of mustard gas. Paul got the distinct impression that the man was crazy, though he knew people would draw the same conclusions about him if he went around saying an ancient order of giant killers was hell bent on his destruction and willing to wrinkle the very fabric of America to get to him.

"And how come the Germans are after you?" Woody asked.

"Do you remember that pilot they had back in the Great War? Richthofen? The one they called the Red Baron."

"Course I do," Woody said, indignantly. He seemed insulted someone would think he didn't know who The Red Baron was. "What's he have to do with you?"

"I'm the one who killed him. The damn Germans have been out for my head ever since."

There were a quiet few seconds when all that could be heard was the hum of tires on the highway and the enraged howl of the relentless wind. Then Woody began to chuckle. It grew into a hearty laugh and Paul couldn't help but crack a smile. Jumpy didn't seem upset that he was being mocked. Instead, he just nodded his head as if he'd been expecting this reaction all along.

"See? That's why they'll get me some day. Because no one will ever believe me."

Paul's grin vanished and a sudden chill stole its way up his spine.

"You know some Canadian flyer shot down the Baron, right? They say it was either that or some Aussie ground gunner. Which one are you?" Woody tore one of his sandwiches apart and gave some to everyone. Paul could tell he was feeling guilty for making fun of Jumpy, but it was just too hard to resist.

"Neither," Jumpy said, taking the offered sandwich and sniffing it like it might be poisoned. "I'm a born and raised American, and I'm the one that killed him. No matter what the papers say. Why else would the Germans be after me?" As if this circular logic verified his every claim, Jumpy shoved the sandwich in his mouth and began chewing.

Paul and Woody exchanged amused glances, then Woody offered his hand to their traveling companion. "Well, I guess you did the free world a service then. What's your name?"

"I prefer to keep that confidential," he said, shaking Woody's hand. "You understand."

"Sure, sure. Best not to make it too easy for them." Woody winked at Paul. "You can tell me *your* name, can't you?"

"It's Paul."

"Not Paul Bunyan?" Jumpy's eyes grew wide and bits of sandwich flew from his mouth.

Paul was disturbed that this stranger knew his name, but he nodded. No sense lying. If Jumpy was a Jack, he already knew the truth. "How'd you know that?"

"You being a giant sort of gave it away. I mean, everyone knows who you are. My mother used to read me a book when I was a kid that told all about you. Shit, you're really *the* Paul Bunyan?"

"I suppose so." Paul hadn't known someone had written a book about him and it distressed him mightily.

"Did you really put out a forest fire by pissing on it?"

Woody choked with laughter. Jumpy's eager eyes stared at Paul and he could tell the man wanted the story to be true, even if it wasn't. It was no different than his obviously fabricated tale of killing the Red Baron. And Jumpy was no different than the loggers Paul had known nearly a century ago. For the first time in years, he thought of Charlie Blade, and he remembered the man saying that sometimes men just need to know great things are possible. Paul watched Jumpy squirm in his rag clothing, caked with grime and beaten flat by the world, making up stories to give his life some color. If ever a man needed hope, it was Jumpy.

"Yes, I did," Paul said, and Jumpy hooted like a kid who'd just stumbled across Santa Claus filling his stocking with candy. "Good thing I drank a couple of lakes that morning or I'd have never been able to douse it all."

"Paul Bunyan! Can you believe that? I'm riding to California with a real live legend."

Woody's knowing smile was so wide it looked like his face would split in half. "Well, hell. I didn't know you was a celebrity too. Tell us what else you done, Paul."

"Yeah! And tell us about Babe!"

And so, Paul did. He spent the next hour recalling every fantastic thing he'd supposedly done, allowing Jumpy to steer him toward the stories he'd forgotten. He spiced up the narrative with a few new twists that drew sparkling smiles from Woody and childlike laughter from Jumpy. He spoke of the water palaces that used to hang in the skies of Albion and how the sun drew golden sigils on the wings of visiting angels. He described the peculiar scent of memory, and spun tales of the faerie lands, destroyed centuries before by the absence of true belief. He even told them about his constant flight from the Jacks and the way they had started to organize in hopes of rooting out the last known giant in America. Pulling together to trample on the world he loved just because they could.

His companions didn't know the truth from the tall tales. Jumpy swallowed it all and Woody didn't believe a word of it. Yet they both seemed immensely satisfied when Paul's narrative drew to a close.

"See, this land was made for anyone who wants it. And I'll be damned if I let those bastards take it from me." Paul ended his speech with a bow of his head, and his companions broke into applause.

When night came, loneliness settled back into Paul's soul and he knew all his talk of fighting back against the Jacks was empty bravado. They seemed to have their hand in every aspect of the world—he wouldn't have been surprised to find they'd caused the dust storms just to flush him out of his comfortable life on the plains. They'd come so close to killing him on so many occasions, he found himself sometimes wondering if it would just be better to give up. But always there was a new horizon. And with it hope. He just wasn't sure that would be the case much longer.

"Nice stories," Woody whispered. Jumpy lay asleep on his back, hands folded across his chest like a dead man.

"Not all of them were stories," Paul said.

"Near enough, I guess," Woody said. "Not that it matters anyway. It's hard to tell the truth from the lies sometimes."

Paul simply nodded. Woody's statement encapsulated his entire existence. The giant closed his eyes and kept them that way, not wishing to dwell on the dying frontier that he'd once found so ripe with possibility.

When he opened them again, he saw California stars.

*

4. The Spirit of the West — 1950

Paul sat in the corner of a rumbling boxcar, trying to remember what magic was like. The memory of it lined his throat like the aftertaste of cheap beer and lingered in the air like the mostly forgotten scents of childhood. How long since he'd seen the brilliant threads of light that connected this land to the land of magic? How long since he'd heard the conversations of ghosts?

The Jacks had done their job well, squeezing it out with industry and urban sprawl, keeping Paul forever on the road, running, trying to cling to the last embers of enchantment that still flickered in the hidden wild places.

A plain-faced man dangled his feet out the boxcar's open door, watching nighttime rise above an endless stretch of unspoiled farmland. Unshaven and ripe with the stench of travel, the man spoke to himself in a persistent, frantic whisper like air leaking from a car tire. His hands were in constant motion and sweat poured down the back of his neck despite the cold temperature.

Paul watched him nervously. The guy probably wasn't a Jack, and he certainly wasn't *the* Jack who'd been on his tail in recent years. But paranoia kept Paul alive.

The man suddenly climbed to his feet, like he'd just remembered something he'd forgotten to do. He whirled to face Paul, focusing his bloodshot eyes on the giant for the first time since he'd hopped the train in Wyoming. One hand rubbed absently at his belly, the other pointed at Paul like the accusatory hand of God. "You like the lonely places, don't you?"

Paul found the stranger's statement to be both the most random and most trenchant observation anyone had ever made regarding his character. He watched the man sway back and forth in anticipation, then answered. "Yes."

"Yes, yes! I knew it! I could tell it by your eyes. Point 'em out the door and take a look. That's the last of it we'll see in our lifetime. The last dying hunk of the old lonely West, turning belly up right before our eyes. People like me and you, we appreciate that. Nobody else gives a shit this country's beat. But you understand, don't you?

"This used to be a land of possibilities. Ideas! Oh, man I got ideas popping in my head. Can't even keep up with all of them. I don't care if she's dying, I want to see every inch of this bitch before they bury her. You dig that don't you? Yes! Yes! Aw, shit. Even if I could live forever I couldn't do it though. She ain't got that many days left."

Paul would have jumped into the one-sided conversation, but he might have drowned in the stream of consciousness.

"One thing she's still got is *magic*. See it out there?" The man crossed to the door and pointed out across a field of tilled earth, and beyond that to the snowcapped peaks that surrounded Denver. "Gorgeous, man. You can taste that shit." The stranger plopped down and dangled his legs again. His dialog had seemingly run its course, but his head still bobbed constantly like he was listening to music the rest of the world couldn't hear.

Paul remembered the days when he could hear that kind of music, and he wondered if the man really was tuned in. Several of the old stories told about mortals who'd found various ways to connect with the magic of creation, and it never ended well for them. For a time, it was wonderful—seeing colors freshly escaped from the dreams of the gods, feeling the core of your soul touch every spot in the universe at once, and best of all, the music. The sound of every living thing striking a single endless chord, whispering and howling, crying and whistling through branch and flesh and stone. But the human mind could only cope with that type of glory for a short time. The magic would overcome them, twist their thoughts into obsessions, color their sight with unknowable visions and turn the sweet symphony of life into the shrill, painful wail of burgeoning insanity. Paul had never seen a mortal who'd stumbled upon the magic. But the wild-eyed man in his suit of rags might be the first.

It was as if he'd reached into Paul's mind and yanked out his thoughts—possible, perhaps, if they both shared a connection to the magic. Yet Paul's connection had dwindled over the years; the absence of magic haunted him like a missing limb. But if this man still felt it, then maybe it was still alive. Attainable. Maybe Paul could find it again.

He sat down next to the stranger in the boxcar's open doorway. His legs should have touched the rapidly passing ground, but he noticed they were hardly longer than the stranger's. In fact, he was only a foot taller than the man; he'd been shrinking right along with the rest of the country.

"What makes you think there's magic out there?"

"Man, how couldn't there be? Aw, it's not any of that fairy tale stuff; this is home-grown American magic. The stuff of freedom. Yes! Yes, it is. That old kind is gone, and this kind is fading fast, but you can still see it if you stare out at the mountains long enough. Look out there, Paul! Take a whiff of your own history."

"How'd you know my name?" Paul asked, but he was pretty sure he already knew the answer. No doubt, this guy was hooked up to the other plane, and his straight-through connection to Paul's mind meant the giant hadn't entirely lost touch with the land of creation.

"American magic! Best goddamned stuff there is! Aw hell, and I know you're worried about it, worried the Jacks are going to tear all of it away and leave the country naked and broken. Shit, man, that's their job! Of course that's what they're going to do. So quit worrying about it. Take a peek from another direction.

"You *are* magic. They can't kill it all as long as you're still on the move, one step ahead, fighting hard and pissing on their plans. You're a living breathing tall tale. A creature of the West. I got a friend who says the West just takes you over. And then you become it. That's you, man. You're the spirit of the goddamned West. That's me too. That's everybody that ever watched Kansas pass by from a train car or stood out in a summer thunderstorm with his thumb in the air hoping to hell somebody would pluck him up off that deserted road and *talk* to him for a while. That magic reaches farther than you think. There's a little of it in all of us. But you? You're the wellspring. The Jacks keep draining the creek and you keep filling it back up."

Paul stared in amazement at this boxcar prophet. Paul could feel him digging around in his head, working his brain like a lump of clay, trying to reshape it into something that resembled hope. He'd always felt like a coward, running from the Jacks but never actually doing anything to stop them. But if what Neal (the name popped into his head of it the prophet had left it there for him to find) said was true, the mere act of staying alive stoked the embers of the American fire.

"Neal? Do you travel a lot?"

Neal nodded vigorously. "Yes, yes. I know what you're wondering. Do I know the fellow keeps following you from place to place, from one end of the country to the other? Guy named Jack? You figure he's on the hunt."

"Isn't he?" Paul's heart thundered in his chest. The way Neal could pick up his thoughts was spooky, and it was more frightening still that he knew the man who'd been chasing him. Paul had almost written it off as paranoia. But here was the proof.

Neal smiled. "Guy's name is Kerouac. Sometimes he calls himself Sal for no goddamned reason. Beatest cat I ever saw, but he's a friend of mine. He ain't one of the one's on your tail; he's just another restless soul like you and me. We all have the spirit in us. As long as we keep moving, it keeps on pumping through the country's veins like fresh clean blood. Once we slow down then entropy sets in. America starts to wind down. It's plain to see that there ain't too many movers left in the world."

Neal patted his shirt pocket, sweat pouring down his face, life popping like firecrackers in his wide eyes. "Say, you got any tea? I'm fresh out."

Paul shook his head. "Sorry."

"Ain't no problem. Once we get to Denver, I know a guy who

grows it in his garden. He's got a place near downtown not too far from the train station. Oh man, just wait till you see the bop cats they got in Denver. Yes, yes! Places open all night and if they don't have something to make you jump, we'll commission a car and head out to Frisco. That's the real shit out there! You're getting off in Denver ain't you?"

"Actually, I think I'm going to keep moving."

Neal nodded sagely. "Yes. You do that. I think you understand it now. I'm getting off in Denver."

Paul would miss this frantic, enigmatic citizen of the road like he missed all the other transitory people in his life, but he was used to being alone.

"Freedom's a lonely road," Neal said.

Paul didn't answer.

5. The Giant and the Knoll — 1963

Paul leaned against the back of the picket fence, trying to be as inconspicuous as possible. He kept his rifle hidden under a heavy wool trench coat—hot as hell for Texas, even in November, but it served its purpose. Beyond the fence, green grass tumbled toward Elm Street, and a number of excited onlookers buzzed like honeybees in the crisp fall sunshine.

By now, that crazy loon Oswald would be setting up shop in the School Book Depository, relishing the task at hand. The man approached murder with a failed military mind and a misplaced sense of patriotism. Paul wished for the hundredth time that he'd never met Oswald, never fallen in with the Cubans. They knew exactly what to promise. His dreams, served up on a platter for the taking. And yet, he was starting to think the price was too high.

Paul looked at his watch and pressed his transistor radio to his ear. The motorcade was crawling down Main, and they were about to turn onto Houston. Paul had a very serious decision to make in the next thirty seconds.

Paul had taken Oswald for a kindred spirit. The guy was always on the move—Russia, Mexico, Dallas, New Orleans. Paul couldn't help but accept the invitation to Florida. It was one of the few places in America he'd never visited. But he hadn't been expecting the meeting with the Cubans, and he damn sure hadn't been expecting them to know all about the Jacks.

Paul looked over his shoulder to make sure nobody was around before loading his rifle. Through a clutch of low-hanging tree branches that still held their leaves, Paul saw a convertible Lincoln Continental turn onto Houston Street. The crowd below cheered. Parents raised kids up on their shoulders, a couple of cops clapped; one man followed the car's progress with an 8mm camera.

Was he being used? The president had the right name, but how could he know the man was really a Jack? The Cubans had their own reasons for wanting the man dead, but they'd done a good job of building Paul up to the task. They'd spoken of magic and the fey folk—los niños de la tierra. They knew about Paul's connection to the source. And they knew the Jacks wouldn't rest until they'd killed every giant, paved over every enchanted glen with concrete and severed every string between this world and the other. How could they have known these things if they weren't telling the truth?

And yet, Paul couldn't help but feel he was nothing more than a disposable weapon. Oswald might relish that role, but he did not.

The motorcade turned right onto Elm Street and drew closer to the kill spot. Paul raised his rifle, pressed the stock against his shoulder and notched the barrel in a crook between two pickets. The Lincoln crawled closer. The president and first lady waved at the onlookers from the back row of seats. He wore a polished smile; she wore a pink dress and a pillbox hat. Another couple occupied the next row of seats—presumably the governor and his wife—and a pair of secret service agents sat in front.

Paul stared down the rifle's scope and found the president's head. The man he was supposed to kill. Paul's hands trembled; the crosshairs leapt from the president to his wife, then back again. If Paul decided to pull the trigger, the target had less than three breaths left. No more saber rattling at the Russians, no more space initiative, no more hobnobbing with Marilyn and Frank. Just a lifeless body that may or may not have belonged to an immensely powerful Jack. Tears welled in Paul's eyes.

When the sudden bark of gunfire broke the peace, he was just as shocked as everyone else.

Paul met Oswald at the Texas Theater in south Dallas. He slouched in his seat, staring blankly at the Audie Murphy flick that played to a nearly empty room. Oswald leaned toward him, reeking of sweat.

"I'm surprised you came," he said.

"Why? We agreed to meet here afterward."

"Yeah, but you chickened out. I figured you'd already be in Mexico by now."

Paul bristled. "I didn't chicken out. I changed my mind."

"Same damn thing. Why the hell didn't you shoot?"

"The more I thought about it, the more I figured those Cubans were just using us."

"Of course they were. You're just figuring that out." Oswald shook his head and snorted. "Hell, I knew all along they were using us. But what does it matter if everybody wants the same thing? They wanted him killed, we wanted him killed. What's the problem?"

"I'm not sure I wanted him killed."

A look of frustration crossed Oswald's gaunt face. "It's a little late for that."

Paul closed his eyes and listened to the projector clatter behind him. "I'm not even sure he's a Jack."

"Of course he is. You told me what they're trying to do. Look at all he's responsible for and tell me he ain't a Jack."

"That's just it. He hasn't really done anything."

"Aw, he's done plenty. He just doesn't let the media get wind of it. It's all under the table stuff, see? That man was running this country into the ground."

Paul wasn't convinced, but he nodded to shut the guy up. What had he been thinking? Even if the president was a Jack, he knew better than to try to kill him. That sort of thing never ended in a giant's favor. And if he was innocent, then killing him would make Paul no better than his enemies. Either way, the man was dead, and Paul was glad he hadn't been the one to pull the trigger. A minor consolation, but it couldn't assuage his guilt.

"If he was a Jack, they're going to be hunting you."

Oswald laughed. "They won't have to look far. I'll be in jail. Speaking of, you better get moving. You don't want to be seen with me. I think I killed a cop."

"I'm serious," Paul said, rising to his feet. "Watch your back. The Jacks won't forget something like this."

"Sure thing," Oswald said, grinning. Paul knew he'd never believed any of the tales about Jacks and magic. He wondered what line the Cubans had used to snare *him*.

Paul left the theater and stood for a few seconds in the blinding sunlight, wondering where to go next. Unsure what else to do, he started down the sidewalk, hands stuffed in his trench coat pockets. Police sirens wailed in the distance, and a minute later, two cruisers sped past, lights flashing. People stopped to watch and speculate about where the cars were headed. Paul kept his head down until he reached the bus station, then he bought a ticket for the next one leaving town.

Paul spent the next few hours watching America speed past his window, listening to news of Oswald's arrest on his radio and wondering what would happen to the man. He kept expecting to hear himself named as an accomplice, but it never happened. As the sun began to set, Paul clicked off his radio and pressed his head back against the bus seat. He fell asleep wondering if he'd ever really know the truth about Jack Kennedy.

The next day, Jack Ruby answered his question.

6. A Jack by any Other Name — 2007

Paul waited in the terminal, one hand clutching his boarding pass. The plane to Heathrow was scheduled to board any minute and he looked forward to his departure with a mixture of resignation and nostalgia.

When he'd first crossed the clouds from Albion, he could never have imagined going back. But the American Jacks had proven even more horrible than their old-world counterparts, and Paul was ready to admit defeat. There was nothing left of the untamed nation he'd grown to love nearly two centuries ago, and his foes had taken on new identities.

The Jacks weren't always named Jack anymore.

This startling revelation had occurred to Paul after nearly a decade without encountering one of his ancient enemies. Yet a Jack by any other name could still slay giants. Giants like Paul and giants like America. No more boundaries existed to slow their ambition, no magic to allow the wide-open spaces to flourish. No memory of better days when the world was large enough to get lost in. That sort of freedom had been driven from the country years ago.

A lady with a faux British accent informed the swarm of passengers it was time to board. Paul took his place in line, mobbed by the incessant chatter, the harsh ringing of cell phones, the droning newscaster on the television monitor, the coma-inducing Muzak. The greasy odor of fast food and bath-deprived humanity assaulted his nose, and he fought the urge to run screaming from the terminal in hopes of escaping the throng. He kept his composure, and ten minutes later, Paul was in his seat.

He buckled his seatbelt—a perfect fit. Paul had shrunk along with the rest of the world and he doubted he'd ever regain his former stature. America, however, might still have a chance. Paul whispered an apology to his adopted country as the plane taxied down the runway. What might she have become if he'd stayed in Albion? If he hadn't led the Jacks across the ocean?

Leaving this place might give the Jacks reason to leave it too. It could be they no longer cared enough about giants to follow him, but his presence had fueled their destruction for far too long. His departure might be too late to change anything, but it was the only avenue of hope left to walk. Great things might still be possible.

Paul wouldn't linger long in Albion—she had her own share of Jack troubles—but he would continue on until he found some untouched land, a place where Jack boots had not yet soiled the earth. If the Jacks followed, then America would be allowed to thrive. And if they didn't, at least Paul would have a new home in which to wander.

The plane left the ground with a lurch and hurtled skyward. Paul gave a gasp when it punched through the clouds and emerged into a world of pure sunshine. It had been so long since he'd seen the land of his fathers that tears formed in his eyes and trailed down his bristly cheeks.

The plane leveled out and turned toward Albion.

And so it was, The Spirit of the West left America for good.

THE GUADALUPE WITCH

THE WITCH HUNTER CAUGHT UP WITH ME ALONG THE BANKS of the Guadalupe River. He was barely old enough to grow a moustache, and I figured my husband had paid him half of what he would've paid someone with more experience. Ellard was always tight with money, even when it came to important things like killing the mother of his dead son.

I was fixing candles to the prow of my keelboat with horseshoe nails and lighting them one by one with a kitchen match when I heard him approach. I had unhitched the horse from the wagon I'd used to haul the boat here and left her to chew at the autumn weeds. The sound of boots slipping down the steep banks sent her trotting away. I watched the man approach, the setting sun burning at his back.

"Mrs. Anderson?"

"Used to be."

"I don't take your meaning."

"I mean I don't answer to that name anymore."

He was familiar, but I couldn't place him. Someone from back in New Braunfels, to be sure. Maybe someone from Ellard's church or a worker in his mill. Not someone old enough to have ridden with Ellard back in his Indian-killing days, which was the type of person I would have expected. This was just a boy, hungry or desperate enough to follow a supposedly dangerous witch into the wilderness. He wore a long coat against the cool evening, and one hand rested on the pistol at his hip, as if he had any intention of using it.

"Your husband sent me."

"Well, if you plan to kill me, then get on with it. I have a schedule to keep."

I stood knee-deep in the shallows, the hem of my dress unfurling over the surface of the water. The river ran quick and cold against my legs. Hackberry leaves traced unhurried paths from overhanging limbs, down to the water where they drifted away. I held one hand on the boat to keep it from following just yet. A brass bell hung from the stern, and I tested it one last time to make sure it could ring freely.

The boy watched me with growing discomfort. His boots reached the edge of the water, but he'd yet to draw his pistol or make any move to capture me.

"What did you think was going to happen here?" I asked. "You'd take Ellard's money, show up, and put a bullet through me? Easy as that? You don't look like your blood's that cold."

Satisfied that the boat was ready, I climbed inside. The few belongings I'd brought with me when I left New Braunfels were bundled in a grain sack. I checked one last time to make sure my grandmother's book was safe, then used the long setting pole to shove the boat from the river's edge and out into the flow.

The boy splashed into the water and grabbed the side of the boat just as the river took hold and began to pull. It had rained hard the day before, and the river was too strong for him. He struggled to keep the boat in hand but soon enough he'd have to let go or be drawn along behind.

"I'm sorry, you can't go."

If I was the monster so many of them believed me to be, I'd have mumbled some words and the boy would have bled out through his eyes. Maybe I would've snapped every bone in his body with my laughter.

I would surely have killed my husband long ago.

I was never that person, no matter how hard Ellard and so many others tried to turn me into her.

But this boy had come to kill me.

He seemed to consider his diminishing grip on the wooden gunwale and the pole I still held in my hands. It would be an easy matter to swat him down with it and let the river pull me away.

With a grunt, he hefted himself into the boat.

We pitched precariously; then he was aboard, crouched down near the stern, and the river grabbed hold again.

"It would have been easier to shoot me," I said. "What are you going to do now?"

His wide-brimmed hat was pushed far back on his head, framing the worry in his young face. Whatever plan he'd devised during his pursuit was unravelling like poor quality cotton, and he hadn't yet figured out how to stitch it all back together again. Autumn wind raced along the water, and he was already shivering in his wet clothes. He pulled that long coat tighter around him and glared at me in my thin linen dress.

The cold didn't cut me.

"We're just going to follow the river until it takes us into New Braunfels," he said. "I can hand you over to Mr. Anderson there."

"We aren't going that far," I said. "Besides, wouldn't my husband be mad if you brought me home still breathing?"

"He said dead or alive, ma'am."

"Well, it for sure won't be alive."

We were many miles upriver from New Braunfels, along the stretch of the Guadalupe that wound like a snake through the Texas countryside. If we continued on long enough, the river would run right into the heart of the place I'd fled several nights earlier. If Ellard got his hands on me, I wouldn't escape again.

Long before I married Ellard, people came to me for medicine to cure their aches. For simple spells to ensure good luck in raising crops and children. Harmless, helpful magics. Ellard might not have understood, but if nothing else, he indulged my talents as a frivolous affectation. Something that would vanish when I devoted myself to the important matters of raising a family.

He never understood my magic wasn't a hobby.

It was my blood and my soul.

I hadn't realized what sort of man Ellard was until we'd been married for a time. Until he'd tried all manner of cajoling to get me to abandon my magic and finally decided to try beating it out of me. By then I was pregnant, and options for escaping Ellard's reach disappeared in a hurry.

I'd tried leaving more than once since my son's death, but Ellard always found me. The last time he said he'd kill me if I ran off again, and I was inclined to believe him.

That was fine with me.

I had no plans to go on living, with or without him.

"What's your name, boy?"

"George."

"Not George Emerson?"

"Yes, ma'am."

"I didn't even recognize you It's been a long time. You were friends with my son, weren't you?"

"Yes ma'am. Me and Frank used to run around together when we was kids. Before. Your Frank was the only one could beat me up a tree. He could climb like a squirrel. I'm real sorry about what happened to him."

"Not so sorry, I don't think. You're happy enough hunting down his mother."

"Well, it ain't like that."

"What's it like then?"

He didn't have any answer for that. I put the book in my lap and flipped through the pages, reading by the light of the candles as the last rays of October sunshine vanished. I had come here for a reason. And though George wasn't part of my plans, my mind wandered across the pages and I began to wonder if maybe he could be.

George had taken the setting pole and was working to keep the boat centered in the river as the current gained speed. Huge cypress trees hugged the shorelines, their exposed roots like fingers working to catch the boat. Rocks jutted up in the darkness, and candlelight scattered across the surface of the water like runaway lantern oil.

"You're good with that pole," I said. "Lucky for me you came along when you did."

"You act almost like you expected me."

"The world whispers to you if you listen. Problem is, no one does. You can find out a whole lot of things if you shut your mouth long enough."

"So, what they say is true? You're really a witch."

"I am a witch. Not sure what they say is true, though."

"You ran away from home, and now you're heading back the same direction you come from. It don't make no sense."

The way he said *ran away from home* made it sound like I was a child who'd snuck out after dark, gotten lost in the woods, and cried until her parents found her. But my leaving had purpose. Laboring under our son's memory for so many years had bent me beyond repair. And I knew one way or another, Ellard would kill me eventually. He had killed so many Indians in his youth that he'd developed a taste for the violence. I could read the hunger in his eyes every time he looked at me. I should at least make my death worth something.

I'd spent too long already trying to sort out at what point everything had gone so wrong.

Now it was time to make things right again.

"It doesn't have to make sense to you." I found the page I was searching for in my book and placed a hackberry leaf between the pages to save my place. "Besides, I told you I'm not going that far."

"Then how far are you planning to go?"

"Only as far as I need. You just settle in and we'll be there before long."

"Ma'am, I hope you know I can't let you run off. Wherever we stop, I'll have to take you into custody."

I laughed. "You a sheriff now, George?"

"You know I ain't."

"Then what you mean is, you'll take me to Ellard so he can kill me."

"I don't believe he really plans to kill you. Anyway, I wouldn't let him hurt you none."

"Well, that's kind of you."

"He's just mad is all. He doesn't seem like a killer to me."

"You might want to study him a little closer."

I put my hand in the water and let the cold take a bite.

I imagined Frank, forever ten years old, so eager to please the father who'd never wanted much to do with him. Waving back at me as they rode away together, bound for the river. Frank promised me he'd have fresh trout when they came home, but Ellard rode back alone and Frank remained at the bottom of the river, held under with ropes and rocks.

I didn't even need to listen to the world to learn the truth of what happened. Ellard had told me, bold as day. But he wasn't ready to give up on me. I was like a wild stallion that he was determined to tame. Killing me would be a failure. But he'd decided that he wouldn't be responsible for another generation of witches. And besides, Ellard had never been fond of his son. I believe he saw too much of me in Frank's manner.

The hard truth was, Frank had no magic inside him. But he died for it anyway.

"Are you married, George?"

"Yes, Ma'am. Just this summer."

"No children yet, then. I expect you'll have some soon enough."

"Probably will."

"You'll die for your child if you have to. You might not understand that now, but you will."

"I reckon I would if I had to."

"Can you feel the night growing thin, George?"

The air around us had quieted, like the darkness was holding its breath. The river had advanced to the point where limestone cliffs stretched along the western riverbank. Candlelight capered along the surface of the stone, creating the unsettling sensation that the river had entered a subterranean cave.

"All I feel is cold."

"Are you tired of steering yet?"

"No, I'm doing fine."

"Have you figured out why your pole has gone silent?"

George plunged the pole into the water for another push, and the wood broke the surface without a sound. He punched at the water again with the same result. He drew the pole into the boat, as if afraid the third time might bring about some calamity.

"You really are a witch, then."

"I already told you I was. Listen here, George, that's nothing but a sign that conditions are in place for what I mean to do here tonight."

"And what's that?"

"What would you say if I told you my husband killed Frank?"

"Well, I wouldn't believe you."

George looked like an overgrown child, huddled at the rear of the boat. He sunk deeper into his coat and pulled the pole up against his chest like a shield. He was the one with the gun. He was the one who'd forced his way onto my boat and into the middle of something more dangerous than the job he'd been hired to do.

"Whether you believe me or not doesn't figure into any of this. Ellard killed him. I'm going to bring him back."

"You're evil."

"And you're a lumbering, foolish boy who should have stayed home with his wife."

I opened my grandmother's book and began to read passages aloud. Every word drew the night in close as a corset, and the boat creaked as the spell tightened around us. Tension gathered in the air. George began breathing like a locomotive, as though he felt a change had taken place but wasn't able to understand it. I kept reading.

What I was doing was anything but evil.

Being a witch was no curse. It was a life planted in the earth by a mother and tended by her daughter. It was a chorus of ancient voices, singing the secrets of our souls. It was a responsibility that could not be cast aside. Those voices wouldn't grow quiet just to please my husband.

I wanted to tell all of this to George, but I knew he wouldn't listen any more than Ellard had.

Men must be shown things.

The air grew so still that only the cliffs and the riverbank passing by gave any indication that we were still moving. Silence wrapped around us like a shroud.

Then the bell started ringing.

"I want out of this boat." George sat forward on his knees, rocking us from side to side.

"You could swim, I guess. Though I wouldn't recommend jumping in the water just yet."

"Oh, hell."

Hands sprouted from the surface of the river like flowers from fertile soil. First one, then a dozen, then a thousand of them, in all directions. Fingers flexing, palms reaching from another life back into this one. These were the last hours of October, when the already thin line between worlds could be breached. With the right words and the right intentions, wrongs could be undone.

One of those hands belonged to my Frank.

Tears welled in my eyes. I read the rest of the words, snapped the book shut. The bell kept ringing.

George drove the pole into the water, trying desperately to steer us to shore, but the boat was caught up in something stronger now.

"Ma'am, what's happening?"

"We're going to figure out which one of these hands belongs to my boy, and we're going to pull him up into the boat. Just be careful not to grab the wrong one. No telling who you'll be bringing back, and you have to pay the price whether you get it right or wrong."

"I'm not grabbing any of them!"

"Hush now, George. I need to concentrate."

Hands slapped against the side of the boat as we cut through that current of souls all eager to return. Life stories flickered around me like summer fireflies—faded images of bluebonnets fanning out around a churchyard wedding; children laughing, their faces lit by the sun. Saddle leather creaking as hands worked at it with hammer and awl; a weathered man astride a plodding mule and the sound of hooves on granite. An old woman on her knees, howling, pulling at her gray hair in grief. Faces bent with jealousy. Eyes bright with hope. All of these experiences and more appeared before me, rising and falling and fading away. I watched every one. I listened for the sounds of who they'd been in life, absorbing the grief and disorientation and cold memories in silence. Searching for the one soul I would recognize in an instant, no matter how many years had passed.

George's face reddened with fear, and his body grew wispy around the edges. Now I knew *his* stories too. Whispered intimacies between husband and wife. Playful arguments over what they'd name their children, when they had them, and real arguments about why George would accept Ellard's money to hunt down his wayward wife. But Ellard issued demands, not requests. And the money, while not a huge bounty, was enough to give them options. Now George was terrified and wishing he'd never left New Braunfels. He'd never really believed he was chasing a witch. He'd been more afraid of Ellard than of a runaway woman old enough to be his mother. Now he'd learned otherwise.

Faint music slipped through from the other life, gray and somber.

Then it was Frank's story on the breeze, his voice as familiar to me as my own. His upraised hand still flexing while all the others grew still.

"*Ma? Help.*"

"I'm right here!"

Frank's fingers were spread wide, his hand only a dozen feet ahead and off the bow. When the boat drew close, I grabbed his wrist with one hand, his arm with another, and pulled. He was waterlogged, nothing but dead weight, and the current pulled against me, nearly prying him loose from my grip. His cold skin was slipping from my fingers, and I heaved harder, but it was like trying to uproot a tree. I would never let him let go, but I couldn't make any progress. And then George was with me, nearly capsizing the small boat as he lunged to take hold of Frank's arm. Something below the water pulled back, the other life eager to keep its dead, but we were stronger. Together we held firm and pried my son loose from the current.

Frank's head broke the surface, hair overgrown and tangled as it had always been, wet strands covering his eyes. His mouth hung open, and his skin was the color of mesquite ash. I thought for one terrible moment that we'd managed to bring him back from the dead but not truly bring him back to life. Then he gasped, drawing the night air into his lungs, and I knew my son had really returned.

Together, we hauled him into the boat.

Frank was the same boy he'd been. No older than the last day I'd seen him, bone-thin and delicate. He hadn't opened his eyes, but his breathing steadied, and I realized he was peacefully asleep. I could feel the slow steady beat of his heart and the hammer of my own. Color began to leak back into his face, and he whispered quiet words I couldn't understand. His body felt warm, as if the life running back inside him had kindled a fire in his chest. I drew him tight against me to feel that warmth, and to smell the musty, little-boy scent of his hair that had remained the same as ever, no matter where he had been. No matter what he'd endured.

Frank's eyes darted about behind his closed eyelids. He was dreaming. I wondered if his dreams were of the place he'd been, or places he might go with a second chance. I knew it would take a few hours for him to shake the other life entirely, and by then he might be alone, so I whispered in his ear all the things I wished I'd told him before he left those many years ago.

Who can say if he heard me?

"Is he alive?" George sat close, breathing heavy with panic. "Is that Frank? He hasn't aged a day."

"He's alive. And he's still a little boy. You're seeing what you're seeing. He'll wake up in a little bit, and he can tell you himself how he died. You might believe more of what I'm saying then."

"I believe you now, I think."

"Well, that's a relief to me." I offered him the thinnest smile, and he accepted it with great enthusiasm.

"Ma'am, I hope you know I never would have killed you. Your husband runs my livelihood, you understand?"

"I understand, George. Why don't you take that wife of yours and leave New Braunfels? Find a better situation for yourself."

"Well, I've never lived anyplace else."

"Might be time you did," I said. "Ellard won't appreciate you coming home without me."

"I don't know where else I'd go."

"Someplace better, George. Just pack up and leave."

The hands in the water began to thrash. Those near the boat slapped at the wooden hull and grasped at the gunwales.

George plunged the pole into the water again, but we weren't going anywhere yet. "They're liable to sink us!"

"We pulled Frank back," I said. "Now somebody has to take his place."

When George had climbed into my boat, it had occurred to me I might be able to have my child back and also keep my life.

I stared at the man who'd come to capture me.

I stared at the man who wanted nothing more than to raise a family with his new wife, preferably somewhere where Ellard's shadow didn't reach.

"Have you ever been to Galveston?" I asked.

"What? No."

"Big city. Plenty of work for a young man. It would be a good place for you to raise your family."

"We need to get out of this boat!"

"Frank always used to talk about how he wanted to see the ocean."

"Ma'am, they're going to sink us."

I held my son close, stroked his wet hair away from his face and kissed his forehead.

"Here's what you're going to do, George. You're going to take my book and give it to Ellard. Tell him you killed me, if that's what he wants to hear. He knows I'd never part with that book, so he'll believe you. Take his money. Then you and your wife go somewhere else. San Antonio, or Galveston, or New York City. It doesn't matter. And you take Frank with you. You were friends once, and he's going to need someone to look after him."

The boat lurched, then tilted astern. The gunwale plunged beneath the water, and the boat started to flood as those hands began pulling it under.

I gave Frank another quick kiss, then handed him to George. He held my son close in one long arm while he balanced himself against the rising prow with the other, trying to keep both of them from falling into the water.

"I don't understand what you're doing!" he said.

"You won't give my boy to Ellard?"

"No, never."

"Thank you, George."

I leaned toward the water, let myself fall overboard and into the river.

The boat righted in an instant. I bobbed in the still water, close enough I could have climbed back aboard. Then every hand released its hold on the boat, and the river came alive again in a rush, like it had just remembered its own nature. The hands fled beneath the water as the boat glided away, caught up again in the sudden current.

Something held me in place, floating.

I could feel the border between the living and the dead grow taut as a bowstring.

Impenetrable.

I watched them float away, the young man in the flickering candlelight with my son in his arms, calling out to me, until darkness obscured him from my sight. Fragments of their life stories—days they'd already lived, and those still to come—rose up from the waters, burned bright, pushed back the darkness.

Gave me one last reason to smile, before the dead claimed their payment and pulled me under.

VERONICA

PETER MORNINGSTAR ARRIVES TO ESCORT VERONICA TO THE far side of whenever wearing the magic coat they nicked from Lady Jenna's pirate lover when they were both still children. Peter hasn't lost a day of his youth and he tells Veronica he forgot to grow up. How neat is that?

Veronica knows more about growing up than we do, but she hasn't forgotten about popsicle swordfights. Remember those? You always wielded the grape, but Veronica preferred the less traditional sour apple for her weapon. You'd circle and slash, opening sticky purple and green wounds on each other's arms. Then Peter would drop from the treetops or burrow up from the earth and disarm you both with his silver tongue. At least that's what Veronica says happened.

You never saw Peter, never even believed in him.

Not until later.

But Veronica's belief in the kid must have been enough to sustain him because they'd have long conversations about the time they shipwrecked on an island in the South Pacific and had to live on bugs and coconuts for a month while dodging cannibals, or the horde of stampeding apes that had trashed Lady Jenna's parlor right before Veronica's mother's second wedding reception, the ones they'd eventually trained, outfitted with tutus and sold off to the circus. They used the proceeds to buy bubble gum. And on darker days, when gray storm clouds chased them inside, they'd huddle in long shadows and whisper about Veronica's father and what it must feel like to choke on mustard in a trench in France. They could never quite figure out how a person could die from mustard, but Veronica's father certainly had. Regardless, she always refused to eat French fries out of spite. And who could blame her?

Peter takes Veronica's hand, and you feel it too, the rasp of her worn flesh against your palm and the too frail bones beneath. How kind of Peter to let you share. There's no family doting on her, just a bothered nurse who smells like menthol cigarettes and a doctor who looks barely beyond his teens scribbling on a clipboard with a leaky pen. Ink smears and he scratches out what he's written.

No one notices the skinny kid with the freckles and golden hair. He's protected by the magic coat. It looks like simple gray wool with tarnished brass buttons, but when Captain Stag was drunk, he'd tell stories about how it was made from the gathered skins of all his vanquished foes and how it could make you invisible, make you fly, deflect weapon blows, and bring you back from the dead. You and Veronica never believed more than half of what that old man said. Lady Jenna had poor taste in companions.

The doctor glances at the clock and Peter slips the pen from his hand. He doesn't seem to notice, just walks out of the room and the nurse follows, her shoes squeaking on the tiles. Peter writes HELLO QUEEN VERONICA in the air in drippy inky letters. Veronica doesn't open her eyes, but she smiles, and she speaks.

"You've come again, have you Peter?"

"Of course," he says, still clinging to her hand. "It's been boring without you. I stuck matches between Grandma Corker's toes while she was dozing on the back porch. Still had a half-shelled sack of peas in her lap, and when she jumped up yelping, they spilled out all over the ground and Stag's alligators snapped them all up. Lord, she was angry. Wish you'd have been there to help me hide from her. You always had an eye for good hidey holes."

"You always gave us cause to need them."

Peter holds Veronica's hand in silence as the sun passes away and the only light left is the dull glow of hospital machinery. Tubes and lights and hoses surround the death bed like remnants of Her Majesty's Brass Battalion, though with admittedly less stench and scalding steam. You were not there when Peter and Veronica battled on the shores of the Sapphire Sea, but you've heard their tales so many times you envision yourself as part of them. To this day there is still a question as to whether Peter's automa-squid army prevailed or if it was Queen Veronica's forces that won the day, so you decide not to bring it up. In the end it didn't matter anyway. Lipsy toppled the churn of ice cream that was supposed to go to the winner and licked it clean while they were busy fighting over it. It's still a sore subject.

"Has autumn arrived yet?" asks Veronica.

"Nope, not even one yellow leaf," says Peter. "It's always summer."

"Peter. You know I don't really care for summer."

One image that will never leave you, no matter how diligently you work to scrub it from your memory: the play of moonlight against the surface of the lake, as viewed from below by a soon to be corpse. You've mercifully forgotten if it was Peter or if it was Veronica who suggested the midnight hunt for lemur bones. After all, lemur bones only reveal themselves in the dead of a summer night and then only to children who've made a blood pact never to reveal their location, and even then, they can only be found along falls of stone that hang like hammers waiting to crash against the glass surface of an enchanted lake. That's common knowledge.

Less common knowledge was the fact that you never learned to swim, and that falls of rock tend to shift and fall again when pressed by the bare feet of little children.

Lesson learned.

Veronica was still very young when she shoved her magic to the back of her sock drawer to jostle among banshee teeth, poison apples, and other oddments from adventures that no longer seemed worth remembering. And she folded Peter up like one of Grandma Corker's afghans and slid him into a drawer too, right beside the threadbare Navaho blanket that Chief Yellowhair had given her for safekeeping, the one with the last great village of the People woven into its creation, waiting to be released by the teardrops of one truly honest man.

Lipsy yipped and tugged at Peter's folds, but Veronica shooed the pup away, pressed the wrinkles from Peter's skin with her fingertips, then closed the drawer.

You weren't invited to Veronica's wedding, but you came all the same. She ignored you, but that's understandable. A bride has a million things to contend with on her wedding day. There's little time for reminiscing about hiding out from vampire bats in tree house forts or how difficult it is to find saddles for giant salamanders, what with the way they burn right through most of them. Still, it was a nice wedding, as weddings go.

The new husband missed the Great War, but he was just young enough when the next one came around. Veronica had given birth to Jimmy Junior by that time, and though she didn't know it yet, we knew that Leslie Ann was already in her belly, plotting and planning on how to escape from the troll cave so she could find her sword and get back to ridding the countryside of boggarts and green faced witches.

Veronica was sitting in the parlor in the house that had been Lady Jenna's before her death, reading a telegram with some very bad news when she finally decided to acknowledge Peter again. She didn't remove him from the dresser where she'd stored him, but he was there nonetheless, and you were there, and you remember those glassy eyes and the clatter of Jimmy Junior's fire engine as he raced it around her ankles.

Peter held out his hand, but she shied away from it, pulled Jimmy from his play and into her lap.

"You have suffered a tragedy," said Peter.

"Not the first one," she said. "And likely not the last. I know why you're here. Don't think I don't see you haunting my every step. I hear your whispers every day, and if you love me at all you'll keep them to yourself. I don't want to hear about all the fun you're having with Lipsy or Lady Jenna and her damned old pirate, or any of them. My place is right here in this house, in this world."

"Don't be stupid," said Peter, grinning. "It's easy enough to come along. Remember the old chant? Twice up the hill, then back down the valley. Travel on foot or saddle up Sally. Close one eye and—"

"I know I can go!" said Veronica. Jimmy was struggling to get free from her grip and whining for his truck. "I don't *want* to go."

"Suit yourself," said Peter, then disappeared in a huff.

He confided to you later that Veronica was just a stupid girl and he didn't want her to come back and play with him anyway because all the really neat ideas for adventuring were his and it was a lot of work dragging her around and pulling her out of scrapes in the first place.

You just nodded and nibbled on one of the honeycombs Peter had nicked from the bee people. You knew he was just trying to sound tough. He wanted Veronica to come back even more than you did, and you wanted it a *lot*.

Besides, he was wrong. It was Veronica who always thought up the best adventures.

*

Peter Morningstar has spent years trying to coax Veronica to join you on the far side of whenever, but she is stubborn in her desire to persevere. It is one thing of many that you love about her.

But it is her time to go. You don't need Peter to tell you that. And if she doesn't go with you, she'll go to some other place and there's no hope of finding her after that.

She's still holding Peter's hand. That's a good sign.

"We can make it autumn if you like," says Peter. "I'm sure we could. We can hunt Mr. Giant Pumpkin Head again, or toss rotten apples through the windows of the old Prater house and see if we can wake up whatever that thing is he has chained up in the attic. If you come, I'll even eat one of those caramel covered apples you like to make, and you know how much I hate apples."

"I don't make those anymore."

"Well, you could."

"Are there many children there?"

"Loads of children! Almost nothing but."

"Is it where *all* children go?"

"Not all of them."

"Then how can I know I'm going to the right place?"

We know where children go when they leave the world, don't we? We know all the places they choose to hide out and ride the slow decay of the universe toward its inevitable end. And though the place we've chosen is just about the neatest place a kid could conceive, not every child is so lucky. Not every child has an imagination like you and Veronica, and certainly not like Peter. Not every child is even old enough to choose for itself.

You never understood why Veronica would only speak to Peter from the depths of grief, particularly since Peter is more interested in wringing the most possible fun out of every living second than in wasting one of those seconds to mourn for a lost husband. Or a lost child.

Peter was wearing a King's crown tipped merrily to the side and a red velvet cloak with leopard skin lining when he took form in Veronica's bedroom. He tapped his scepter on the bed three times, hoping to rouse her from beneath the sheets that clung to her feverish body in wet clumps, hugging her like the funeral shroud that we all knew she longed for.

"Awake, Queen Veronica," said Peter. "Your chariot awaits. With me, m'lady. To the land beyond all others!"

"Leave me alone, Peter!" Veronica said.

"We've come to rescue you from this vile place," he said. "This is no fit world for a queen. Why, we've goblins to hunt and even now the hounds snap at their leashes. What a merry chase it shall be! We'll dine on goblin steaks tonight, m'lady, or I'll forswear my oath to the Realm and melt my crown into pennies."

"This is not a game!" Veronica threw back the sheet and sat up in bed and you realized that she was naked, and you couldn't help but turn away. But you still haven't forgotten the sight of her. Thin and see-through pale, hair clipped in a short shag and a patina of weariness that transformed her once sharp features into the image of a sickly creature that bore little resemblance to the girl you still pine for. There was weariness in her bones and sickness in her soul, and her arms were crossed over her stomach as if feeling for the life that had grown there until just that morning.

Part of you still remembers the blood on the sheets and how some of it still clung to her legs, but only a small part. Mostly you remember the sheer horror in her expression as she howled at Peter and the arrival of her mother and the doctor in response to her screams. She stared right through them, refusing to take her eyes off Peter as he continued his campaign of luring her away from this hell to the place she was really supposed to be.

It was obvious that this world of hers was no place for someone as special as Veronica. But no matter how badly you wanted her to come with you, you found yourself wishing that Peter would take the ridiculous crown off his head and just leave her alone.

"I've had enough death in my life to suit," says Veronica. Her eyes are still closed but she hasn't let go of Peter's hand yet. I can tell he still thinks that's a good sign. Peter is nothing if not persistent.

"Ah, but this isn't death!"

"Maybe not. But it's not life either, is it?"

"No, not life," says Peter. "But near enough."

"You're either alive or you're not," says Veronica. "There's no in between."

You and Peter left her alone for a while, but something called you back. When you arrived, she was having dark thoughts that you wish you weren't privy to. They still give you nightmares. Lady Jenna's parlor was ice-box cold and each time Veronica exhaled it reminded you of that trip to the ice dragon's cavern. February wind buffeted the curtains through open windows that she'd simply not had the will to shut, and her bare feet were blue against the hardwood floors.

She wore a dingy patterned dress pulled down to her ankles, legs apart so that the dress made a makeshift basket, and in that basket rested a gun. She stared at it like she was waiting for it to take control and do for her what she didn't quite have the nerve to do. It wasn't a fit and polished Martini-Henry like the one they'd seen H. Remington Hookstratten use to fell an elephant from five hundred paces, or a long barreled six shooter gleaming with high noon sunshine and eager for a fight. It was a hard, ugly little thing that her husband had given her before going to war, just something to fend off burglars. She'd never even shot it.

"Neat gun!" said Peter. "Let's play war. You can be the good guys and I'll be the Huns and we can pretend the war is somewhere other than France."

You wanted nothing more than for Peter to stop talking but you didn't have it in you to say anything. It was so obvious to you that Veronica needed to leave her life behind. Who wants to live in a world that can take your father, your husband, the baby in your belly, and still have enough evil left to snatch away the only thing in your life worth living for with something as innocuous as a bottle cap? Veronica's mind was empty save for thoughts of the gun, and images of Jimmy Junior turning as blue as her feet while she beat on his chest with both hands as his little fists and heels kicked at those same hardwood floors. You did everything you could not to share that memory, but it was no use. You'd come along for this even though Peter had warned you to stay behind, and now you were in the thick of it.

"Go away, Peter," she said.

"You've got to come with me this time," he said, looking downtrodden. He'd thought for sure she'd come this time without argument. Peter couldn't imagine a reason she'd want to stay here, and neither could you.

"I'm leaving," she said. "But I'm not going with you."

The gun wasn't in her lap anymore, and you knew exactly what she planned to do with it. Peter didn't seem to understand, and he began rattling off a list of all the neat and wonderful things they'd do if only she'd take his hand and take her last breath and just give herself to the whenever. He didn't even stop talking when she pointed the gun at him and pulled the trigger.

Lady Jenna's prized mirror shattered into a million pieces. You couldn't believe she'd shot it. It was the enchanted mirror that Captain Stag had brought back from the island of ghosts, and if you knew who owned the mirror's twin, you could look into it and speak with whomever was on the other end. They'd spent days at a time staring into it and making funny faces, hoping someone would appear and tell them all about the ghost islands, even the stuff the

Captain said was too scary for children. But looking at it then, you
noticed for the first time how tarnished and dented the old thing
was. Bits of glass clung to the frame like dragon teeth, and it was
evident that if the mirror had ever possessed any magic, it had fled
long ago.

"That's the spirit," said Peter, emboldened by Veronica's actions. He dropped into a crouch and adjusted the helmet that had
appeared on his head. "I'll get you back, Yankee scum! You'll never take this trench!"

When Veronica dropped her gun and fell from her chair, you
naturally assumed she was playing dead, felled by imaginary Hun
bullets. But when she didn't respond to Peter's antics, when finally,
Peter frowned and faded back into nothing, you were left alone
with her and you know that something else had happened.

Veronica had left her world, and she'd gone where you couldn't
find her.

Veronica was still there physically, and you remained by her
side even when Peter wasn't in the mood to keep her company.
Her doctors said she was sick, but whatever she had wasn't like
any of the diseases you could recall. Veronica couldn't be cured
this time by a liberal application of peanut butter to the forehead
or a piping bowl of chicken soup laced with giggle berries. Veronica's *brain* was sick, and never in any of your games had you
imagined a brain doctor.

She spent more years in that same room with those same care-
takers than you can even count, and you can count to eleventy million and one. But you can count the number of times Peter came to
see her during that time on one grubby hand.

Peter claimed that sometimes he could see her in your world,
but never for more than a single second before she faded back into
whatever enchanted bog or ancient forest he'd been playing in. He
said she was a little girl again, and he was almost certain she was

smiling. You never saw her there, but then you spent most of your time with the real Veronica. Still, you hoped it really was her. You liked the idea of Veronica turning the tables on Peter, secretly hiding out and spying on him just like he'd been spying on her for so many years.

Veronica grew very old, and though she began to resemble many of the witches that she'd vanquished in her youth, you knew she was still a force for good. You tried some half-remembered chants and a few horrible looking potions, hoping one of them would stop her from aging, but it was useless.

Veronica was old, and even Peter couldn't change that.

Queen Veronica has forgotten many, many things in her life. But she has never forgotten Peter. And she has never forgotten you.

Veronica lets go of Peter's hand and you know she's going to refuse him again.

"You are worse than the devil, Peter Morningstar. And I will listen to no more of your temptations."

Her words break your heart as surely as they do Peter's. Her time has come, whether she's ready for it or not, and she's just chosen eternity without either of you. Veronica has signaled an end to the games, and you have little choice but to grant her wish. You slip your arms free from Peter Morningstar, that old familiar costume that's ready made for horseplay and grand adventure, the one that's starting to feel a little tight, and if it were a jacket or a pair of pants, you'd have already picked out a new one long ago. Peter pools around your ankles and you step free, not bothering to fold him because you know he won't be there long. Another child will come along, and Peter will fit that child perfectly and away they'll go to the tops of Nepalese mountains in search of snow monsters, and to the center of the Earth to mine fire jewels for the Stone Prince's crown.

But these are pursuits for the very young.

For the first time that day, Veronica opens her eyes. She sees *you*, puts her hands together and smiles. "There you are. Finally."

"Yes, here I am."

"We have places to go together."

"Yes, I think maybe we do."

She takes both of your hands, and for the first time she's the one inside *your* head. She sees Lady Jenna sipping iced tea on her great wraparound porch and Lipsy gnawing at the cuff of Captain Stag's frilly shirt as he snores away in a hammock strung between two straining cedars. Granny Corker chases brownies out from under the front steps with a broom, shoos them back to the howling forest. A storm of autumn leaves pours from the sky, and as the low, fat sun falls gently into twilight, the shadows grow claws and make one last attempt to keep you both there. But you are too quick for shadows.

In the background, barely visible so late in the day is a freckle faced golden haired boy who can't entirely hide his smile, no matter how much he'd like to. He waves, and you wave back.

"Tell them goodbye," you say.

"I already have," she says.

And then you follow Queen Veronica, like you always have, into the spilling folds of the universe. Creation is limitless, and so are the places where children go to hide when they leave their lives but have no guides to lead them though the whenever. You will search these places, one by one, and you will find the true desires of Veronica's heart. The heart of a little girl, the heart of a woman in love, the heart of a mother.

I envy you, little one.

Because, you know, Veronica always thinks up the best adventures.

REWIND

MONDAY

T HE DUST BIKER COMES INTO THE VIDEO STORE THAT AFTER-
noon looking for slasher flicks. He heads straight to the horror section, not bothering to remove his breathing apparatus, and
pulls a couple of classics from the shelf. *Friday the 13ᵗʰ Part III* and
the original *Halloween*.

"You like this kind of stuff?" I ask when he hands the tapes to
me for checkout.

"Yeah, so?" His voice is a mechanical whine and the desert
winds have rendered his gray body suit smooth and practically
transparent. I can't see his eyes through the scored surface of his
goggles, but I can feel the edge in the way he's staring at me.

"I like them too," I say. "I've seen hundreds of them. Slasher
flicks, I mean."

"Yeah, so what's the best one?"

I don't even have to think about it. "You ever seen *Sleepaway
Camp*?"

His neck makes a stretching, leathery sound as he shakes his
head side to side. "No."

I sprint to the back of the store, pull the sun faded VHS box
from the shelf, and add it to his pile. "On the house. Just let me
know what you think when you drop it off."

"You aren't charging me?"

"No, just a favor from one fan to another."

He might be smiling but I can't see through the grill of his mask. He looms there like Jason Voorhees, silent and unreadable. Dust rides the creases of his suit and he reeks of illegal petroleum. He's a seven-foot shadow come to life, an abstract artist's rendering of torn metal and melted rubber pooling along an endless broken highway. He exhales heavily and it sounds like the rattle of failing pistons.

"Do you have a bag?"

I bag up his tapes and he grunts his thanks on the way out the door. The front wall of the store is made of glass and I watch as he starts his bike and speeds away toward the shimmering red horizon.

I hope he likes the movie.

TUESDAY

Gandy catches me goofing off again.

We have a small television and VCR set up in the store that constantly runs movies, and I'm planted in front of it in one of those old style director's chairs, watching *Raising Arizona* for roughly the ten thousandth time, so I don't notice his approach from the back office until he's standing over me, his pen tapping against a clipboard.

"Jeff, what are you doing?" he asks.

"Sorry, just taking a quick break. I straightened all the boxes on the shelves and checked in the returns."

Gandy heaves a sigh that could reach from one end of the store to the other. He's a late middle-aged guy with a thin moustache and not much hair. A *Rewind Video* nametag is pinned to the chest of his purple oxford, and GANDY is spelled out in big block letters. I don't know if Gandy is his first name or his last name, but I've been working here too long now to ask.

"You're not getting paid to watch movies," he says. "The store's not in good financial shape. We need to be working hard to keep it afloat."

I think about telling him that we haven't had a customer all day and nothing I do in the store will help attract them, but I don't want to lose my job. Gandy likes to fret about the store being in trouble, but he hates when anyone else acknowledges it. This place is his life. Literally. The guy has a cot and a hot plate in the back office and he never leaves. I think he bathes in the sink.

Wind pushes against the front windows and the glass squeals like it wants to break. Gray smoke boils outside like it's being heated in a pot, and it's so thick you can't see more than a few inches through it. Silvery shapes dart in and out of the murk, and I'm pretty sure I saw a nest of tentacles lash against the glass a few hours ago, but I'm not telling Gandy that. His eyes are fixed on the front windows now and I can smell the sweat coming off him.

"I can run the vacuum again?" I say. "Gandy?"

"Yeah, thanks Jeff. That would be great."

Gandy returns to the sanctuary of his office and the rattle of an adding machine confirms that he's back to business. I vacuum the cheery lime green carpet for the second time today, then drop back into the director's chair and press play on the remote.

WEDNESDAY

I've barely flipped the CLOSED sign to OPEN when the first customer of the day walks in, slips off her protective body sheath and floppy hat, and dumps them in the corner where they sizzle for a few seconds before going quiet. The woman underneath is wrapped in layers of rough leather and her boots leave blackened prints in the carpet as she walks deliberately to the Musicals section.

"Anything I can help you find?" I ask.

"There's a musical I saw once that I liked but can't remember what it's called." She turns and I see the scar bisecting her face.

"Is it the movie starring that guy who was in that other movie with that one girl?" I ask.

She smiles, and her teeth are crooked in just the right way. "Might be."

I help her dig through the shelves, rattling off suggestions, but she keeps shaking her head. An oiled machete hangs from her left hip, and a one-handed chainsaw is strapped to her back, bits of unknown viscera still caught in its teeth. She plucks box after box off the shelf with torn and bruised fingers.

"Are you a hunter?" I ask.

"Most days," she says. "But even the stuff I kill doesn't like going out in this kind of weather."

The sky outside is green and twisty, and acid rain falls in sheets.

"What do you hunt?"

"Whatever they pay me to," she says. "Apelings and the undead mostly. But I'm certified for bigger game if needed."

"You need a partner?" I ask.

"I work alone," she says.

"No, I was just kidding. I like it here. Hey, you know this one, right?" I put *Singing in the Rain* in her hand.

"I've heard of it, but I haven't seen it."

"Well, since we can't find what you came in for, this would make a good alternative. Classic Hollywood. Hard to beat Debbie Reynolds."

"Sure, okay."

"Hey, so . . . if you want you can just watch this here? We have a TV. We can watch it together. Maybe the rain will pass by the time it's over."

The rain roars against the roof, and the stench of it sneaks in through the building's crevices, making the place smell like a high school chemistry class. The hunter's fingers tap against her machete blade and she studies my face with cold, unreadable eyes.

"I'm not looking for a date," she says.

"I wasn't asking for one. Just saying you could watch it here. Sometimes it gets old watching movies by myself."

"Okay, well that's not the worst idea then."

I offer her the director's chair and sit beside her, cross-legged on the floor. We consume the rest of the day with a procession of musicals, and while she loves *Singing in the Rain,* we get lucky and realize that *The Music Man* is the movie she'd originally been hunting. She hasn't seen it in years but remembers the words to some of the songs and we sing together about River City and pool and brass band parades. Gandy pokes his head out from the back office a couple of times but he either no longer cares that I'm goofing off or doesn't want to come down on me in front of a customer.

When night arrives, it chases away the rain. The hunter, who by now I've learned is named Cutter, and who once upon a time wanted to be either a veterinarian or a social worker, stands up and checks her weapons. She studies the empty sky, and then dons her protective sheath and hat just in case. The smile she's worn for hours flattens and her face hardens like clay in a kiln.

"Thanks, Jeff," she says. "That was fun."

"Come back sometime. We'll watch *Paint Your Wagon.*"

Cutter nods, pauses for a few seconds with her hand on the door. It's past closing time, but I don't mind.

She can stand there as long as she needs.

THURSDAY

Bryce comes into the store to show off his latest exoskeleton. "So what do you think?"

I'm sure it's the newest and coolest and most amazing exoskeleton that money can buy, but it's still just a shiny metal suit that makes him walk like he can't quite bend his legs in the right places, and if I told him he reminded me of Robocop he'd probably start to sulk, so instead I just say, "It's pretty cool," and try to sound like

I mean it.

"Bro, pretty cool?" he says. "It's better than that. Check this out."

He holds up what looks like an unlabeled soda can, gives it a gentle squeeze, and his suit deconstructs into a swarm of nano-mites. They make a few laps around the store, knocking a couple of VHS boxes off the shelf, then squash their way into Bryce's tin can, which seals itself with a satisfying click.

I have to admit, that part was more than pretty cool.

"It's a Trimm-Henderson 42LX Klingwrap. You can't even buy one of these babies yet. Company has me testing it out. Nothing gets through this thing. Dino claws, bullets. A trash scavenger took a pot shot at me yesterday and it didn't even tickle. Supposedly it will stand up to gamma cannons too, which I guess I'll get to test out soon enough because the extraterrestrials are forming up on the south side of the vapor waste again and the company can't sit by and let them get a foothold. Bad for business, you know? Why don't you come with me? The company pays way better than this dump and you know you want one of these suits."

I'm running a pair of tape rewinders that hum pleasantly, thinking that maybe we need to get more of those stickers that read BE KIND, REWIND and wondering what the dirt biker thought of *Sleepaway Camp*.

"I like working here."

"What for? Jeff, bro, we've been friends since we were kids, but the difference is I grew up. Hey, I like movies too. I've seen *Armageddon* like five times. But you need to start living in the real world."

"I met a girl," I say.

"You went on a date?"

"Not really a date. We just watched some movies together."

"What's her name?" he asks.

"Cutter," I say.

"That her first name or last name?"

"I forgot to ask."

"Well I guess it's a start," he says, "but working here is still a dead end, Jeff."

Bryce's tin can makes a clattering noise. The lid pops open and within seconds the nanomites form an exoskeleton around him again. He snaps his head to the side and watches a blue shaft of light tear though the gloom, coming to ground somewhere in the distance, beyond the hills. "Green freaks are beaming down a team already. Look, Jeff, I have to go. To be continued, yeah? Time to seize the day buddy."

"Sure."

"Hey, can you put back a copy of *Red Dawn* for me? I'll swing by later and pick it up."

"Will do."

"And pack a coat this weekend. The company scientists are predicting ice. No telling what that means."

"Coat. Check."

"Later, bro."

Bryce lumbers though the exit and is lifted up by a squadron of hovering drones that carry him away, presumably to defend the profits of innocent shareholders.

I finish rewinding the tapes, then settle into the director's chair for a screening of *Close Encounters of the Third Kind*. I've seen it a bunch of times, but it's still a really good movie.

FRIDAY

When the lizard man comes into the store the air turns as hot as a tropical jungle. Squat leafy trees erupt from the carpet behind him and slinky vines drop from the ceiling like streamers at a middle school dance. Fireballs fall in lazy arcs outside, like rocks hurled by angry volcano gods. The lizard man's tongue licks in and out, tasting the stale air-conditioned air and turning up the heat even more in protest.

I know better than to offer my assistance. Lizard men are sin-gled-minded, and he wouldn't have come if he didn't know what he wanted already.

Turns out his movie of choice is *The Great Escape*. He places it on the counter and pushes a pile of gemstones toward me with a three fingered claw.

"This is one of the best movies ever made," I say.

The Lizard man presses his thoughts into my mind and makes me aware that he's a huge Steve McQueen fan and that he's pleased that I agree the car chase in *Bullitt* is the best ever filmed otherwise he would be forced to take exception with me, and that would lead to the likelihood of a gruesome death by beheading or vivisection. He also makes me aware than his name is Alvarado, and that is nei-ther his first name nor his last name, but simply his name.

Gandy comes to the front of the store with his clipboard, no-tices the vines dangling from the ceiling, and casts a nervous look around the store like he's expecting Tarzan to come swinging in. Alvarado looks at him and Gandy freezes like he's been spotted by Medusa. Something passes between the two of them. One tear streaks down Gandy's face and lingers on his chin. A lot of peo-ple have problems with the fact that lizard men can project their thoughts, read minds, and alter the surface of reality, but I can take it in stride. Gandy isn't as easy going as I am. He makes a military about face and hustles back into the office, slamming the door in his wake. A worn poster for *Lethal Weapon 2* hangs on our side of the door, one corner unpinned and drooping forward.

"You've seen *The Getaway*, right?" I'm digging though his pile of gemstones, trying to find one that I can accept to cover the rental fee.

Alvarado makes certain that I'm flooded with embarrassment because of course he's seen *The Getaway*. How could he call him-self a Steve McQueen fan if he hadn't seen that one? My fingers clench around a handful of jewels and I lean forward on the counter to support myself against the onslaught of emotion that he forces at me. Eventually he senses my regret and he relents.

"Hey, so these jewels are probably worth millions and your rental fee is $4.32. I can't make change for that."

He gives me another mental push and makes it known that he doesn't require any change, that material things have no value to lizard men, and these are only baubles to dangle in front of humans so they will dance and caper like the uplifted monkeys that they are. I may keep the entire stash, and what's more, if the fear radiating off of my master is any indication, they are sorely needed because *Rewind Video* has a limited life span, like a wolf-man with its head caught tight in the maw of a hungry pterosaur. Furthermore, he informs me that his videocassette player is on the fritz and he will require one of those as well, if we have them for rental.

"Sure, VHS or BETA?"

Instead of invading my mind, he gives me an exhausted look and flicks his tongue.

"Kidding," I say. "We don't rent too many BETA tapes."

Our transaction concluded, Alvarado leaves clutching the VCR and his copy of *The Great Escape*. The temperature begins to cool, and the vegetation becomes momentarily spectral before disappearing altogether. As sometimes happens, the lizard man left some of himself in my thoughts, and for the rest of the day I have the power to turn the lights on and off without touching the switch, and to float VHS boxes from one side of the store to the other like a flock of birds. I'm not sure if it's really happening or if my brain just tells me it is, but it's a lot of fun either way.

SATURDAY

Bryce was right about the weather. The ice comes in the after-noon, dropping in huge chunks so that it feels like being in an air raid, and within minutes the parking lot is a solid shimmering mass. I remember the jacket I left at home as I turn the thermostat from AC to heat.

The stuff is two feet deep in some places by the time the woman and her children arrive, and I have to chip away at the frozen bits around the door in order for them to make it inside.

"We have five minutes," she says, "so pick something quick. We still have to go to the grocery store and get Lydia's chamber recalibrated before we go home. Don't dawdle, Junie."

Junie is a hyperactive little girl who runs for the Children's section like goblins are at her heels. There she commences to yank down box after box and toss them to the floor, screaming that all she wants to see is *The Little Mermaid* and how this is a terrible place because we never have a copy. The woman's second child, presumably Lydia, is encased in an iron chamber shaped like an egg. The chamber skitters around maniacally on spider-like legs, knocking over the director's chair and nearly toppling the TV along with it. When it approaches, I can see the baby inside—a hairless kid with too many eyes and not enough noses. I'm stuck wondering what's worse, sheets of ice or the mutative effects of radiation, when Gandy walks up and puts the store keys in my hand.

"I'm leaving," he says. "Lock up or don't."

"Where are you going?"

"Do you have a copy of *The Little Mermaid*?" The mother sidesteps Lydia's chamber as it attempts to climb the checkout counter. "We can't find it on the shelf."

The only thing remaining on the shelves in the Children's section is Junie, who hangs from the highest one like she's trying to rip it off the wall.

"It's checked out," I say. "I can put you on the waiting list."

"Are you serious?" She looks mildly terrified.

"Yeah, sorry," I say.

"Store is going to have to close," says Gandy. "You were a pretty good employee, all things considered. You'll be fine. Me, I don't have any other options, so I guess that's that." He slips a tan windbreaker over his shoulders and tosses his GANDY nametag on the counter. I don't understand at first what's happening as he heads toward the front door. The prospect of Gandy leaving the building is something I've never considered. Junie finally breaks the shelf and tumbles to the ground screaming. A red light starts flashing on Lydia's chamber and it's accompanied by a siren that's just a few decibels shy of a departing jumbo jet. The mother and her children spin around me in a vortex of chaos, and I stand frozen in the middle as Gandy climbs out onto the ice and begins walking in no particular direction. I realize that for Gandy, this is a form of suicide. He might have hung himself in the office with his bed sheet or guzzled down a gallon of the cheap blue toilet cleaner we keep in the back, but instead he's chosen life beyond these walls, whatever that might be.

The woman and her children leave without a movie, and I trace their progress along with Gandy's as they navigate the surface of the ice. A wall of sleet pushes in and clatters against the windows, causing me to lose sight of them all. It's only then that my brain settles down and I remember a couple of things.

We have two copies of *The Little Mermaid*.

Also, Alvarado's pile of jewels, which I estimate to be worth about eight million dollars, is still piled neatly on the counter by the cash register.

SUNDAY

The ice has melted, and the trees are on fire again.

Customers rarely enter the store on Sundays. Instead they drop their tapes in the return slot like spies on a secret mission, eager not to get caught. I hear the clatter of tapes as they come into the receptacle, but when I look up to see who's dropping off, they're gone like ghosts.

In the morning's returns I find our other copy of *The Little Mermaid*, and all of the slasher movies the dust biker checked out. He's scribbled something in magic marker on the cover of *Sleepaway Camp*.

THIS WAS PRUTY GOOD. THK YOU.

I spend most of the afternoon in the director's chair watching *Groundhog Day* on repeat. I slip in and out of sleep, wondering if I have enough of the lizard man's mojo still inside me that I can warp reality. Maybe I could rewind to Monday, start the week again. Do it over and over and over, not so that I can get it right but so I can just keep living. I'm happy in this place. I'm not ready for it to end. I've always loved *Groundhog Day* and the quiet, happy way it manages to be relentlessly melancholy.

I don't hear Cutter enter the store until she shakes my shoulder and says, "Hey, wake up."

"Cutter? You dropping off your movie?"

"I didn't rent a movie. Remember?"

"Oh yeah, right." I stand up, flatten my hair down with my hand and generally try to look like I wasn't asleep on a Sunday afternoon at work.

"So, Jeff. I came in to ask if you want to go do something. After you get off work."

"Like go on a date? You said you weren't looking for a date."

She's swapped her chainsaw for a sawed-off shotgun, and a leather strap loaded with shells crosses her chest like she just stepped out of a spaghetti western. She shakes her head and gives me a grin that seems to ask just how big of an idiot I can be. "All I'm saying is we could go do something fun. Together. At the same time."

"I'd like that," I say.

"Great," she says. "So what do you want to do?"

"We could go to a movie," I say. "In a theater."

"Okay," she says. "It's a plan. What time do you get off?"

"I don't really have a boss anymore, so I guess now?"

"Then lock up," she says. "We can get something to eat first. My treat."

"I wanted to ask you something. Is Cutter your first name or your last name?"

"It's my last name," she says. "I just go by Cutter at work. My first name is Stephanie."

"Nice to meet you Stephanie."

I eject *Groundhog Day* and put it back on the shelf without rewinding it. I can pick up where I left off tomorrow.

Right now, I'm looking forward to a movie I haven't seen before.

GONE DADDY GONE

D IG.
    Moon Doggie's never seen so many feathers, and he knows straight away that Priscilla finally took her jacket back. He stands there in the ruins of their living room, listening to the hiss and fizz of rain on cinders, trying to wrap himself in the solemn comfort of northeastern gloom as he considers the cold abandonment that's become his future.

He's a husband without a wife.

A man without a woman.

And he doesn't know how to be that cat anymore.

Looks like somebody bombed an aviary, nothing left of the house he and Prissy share in the burbs but charred bits of particle board furniture and sizzling curls of orange shag carpet lifting up in the wind. And the feathers, thousands of them, millions of them. Moon Doggie knows she left them there for a reason. She wants him to follow her.

A carpet of them stretches out in all directions from what he's now thinking of as the *blast site*, looking very much like a flow of white lava that has erupted from the crater of their lives.

A block to the west, one lone feather skitters across the street. Beyond that, another one.

West.

Moon Doggie grins, feels the warmth of life flow back into him, like he's bathing in pure grade desert sunshine. He will be soon enough. No mystery where Prissy is headed. Everybody who runs away winds back up in the same goddamned place eventually.

Home.

Prissy is going to California.

The garage has been mercifully spared.

Moon Doggie tosses his seafoam green Stratocaster into the backseat of the Thunderbird. Straps his splintering surfboard to the rusted roof rack. He won't need much else.

He takes one look back at what's left of their home and then he's history.

He remembers Priscilla in the surf with her sisters. That image will never leave him no matter how many miles she runs, Prissy wearing not a stitch, gold hair plastered to her back as she paddled the surfboard out far enough to catch the big waves, and then the turn of her head and the silent laugh at something one of her sisters said and Moon Doggie could just make out the silver glint of her eyes and that was it, done deal, he was in love and there was no turning back.

Six leather jackets lay sunning on the rocks. Moon Doggie braved the crashing waves and found the one he knew was hers. Still couldn't say how he knew but he *knew*. Snatched it up, took it back to his T-Bird. It smelled like the earth and the sky. The leather was cracked and ancient.

Moon Doggie watched them throughout the afternoon. He felt a shiver and a sudden queasiness when they finally started swimming for shore, surfboards abandoned to the sea. They saw him, all of those silver eyes, but kept their distance. Wet arms slipped into jacket sleeves. An eruption of euphoric smiles and then they were airborne, lifted up in a sudden storm of feathers.

Moon Doggie wasn't the least bit surprised.

The youngest one approached him with the inevitability of sunset. Her sisters circled overhead, calling out with the voices of eagles. Moon Doggie tossed her a blanket from his back seat and gave her his jacket. Hers was already locked up in the trunk.

"What's your name?" he asked.

"Priscilla," she says, drying her hair with the blanket.

"Priscilla, I think I love you."

She nodded with all the enthusiasm of a corpse, then climbed into the passenger's seat of the T-Bird. Moon Doggie got behind the wheel. Revved the engine.

"Well, you caught me," says Priscilla. "What's your next bright idea?"

Moon Doggie knows it's the place he's supposed to be the second he spots it. A diner shaped like a giant Airstream trailer, a blinding sliver of silver slicing through Midwest monotony. Jerky neon sign that simply reads EAT, gravel parking lot that snaps and pops under his tires, probably nothing on the menu but coffee and pie but that's just swell with Moon Doggie.

The middle-aged counter man is sporting bloodshot eyes and sallow jowls. His apron is stained with what Moon Doggie sincerely hopes is cherry pie filling, and a lone eagle feather sticks out from his paper hat.

"So she's been here," says Moon Doggie. The pie is okay, but the coffee is better.

"The bird lady?" says the man. "Oh yeah, she's been here. You looking for her?"

"She's my wife."

"Uh huh."

"She burned down half our house."

"Well, that's to be expected."

"How's that?"

The man refills Moon Doggie's coffee, smears the dust of

ages back and forth across the counter with a moldy rag. "You can't expect to keep a woman like that. I've seen this play out a million times. There ain't much special left in this world. So, people get a little of it in their hands and they can't help but squeeze. They hold on so tight it just crushes all the mystery out of the thing. You understand what I'm saying? This ain't her fault, it's yours."

"I can dig it," says Moon Doggie. "But she loves me. She didn't at first, but she does now."

"That she does," says the counter man. "Else she wouldn't have left you this." He plucks the feather from his hat, hands it to Moon Doggie. It's as beautiful as the sky on the day he met Prissy, all the rich hues of sunset swirled together into one perfect color.

Moon Doggie shoves the feather in his hip pocket, leaves some cash on the counter, and heads for the door.

The counter man calls after him. "Things won't be the same as they were before. Even if you find her. You know that, don't you?"

"Things are never the same," says Moon Doggie.

"Truer words," says the counter man.

The bell over the door heralds Moon Doggie's return to the amber waves of truck stops and low rent motels and mostly forgotten small towns that haven't changed a lick since 1959.

"You know, that ain't necessarily a bad thing," says the counter man, but Moon Doggie is already gone.

Moon Doggie recalls the soft curve of her hips and the way they'd spend most Saturday mornings laughing in bed, and most of all the way she really, truly loves him. He questions a lot of things, but never this.

"I would have come with you anyway," she told him one morning, her ear against his chest. She liked to listen to his heartbeat; she had none of her own. "You didn't have to steal my jacket."

"I know," he said. "I'm sorry."

"It would have been better if you hadn't," she said. "Maybe then I could have stayed. Not forever. But longer."

Moon Doggie sat up, took gentle hold of her wrist, terrified she meant to leave right then. How the hell had he ever let himself get so attached to someone? There wouldn't be much left of him if she split.

"Calm your nerves, Daddio. I'm not going today. But someday."

"When?"

She shrugged and kissed his neck. "Someday."

"We're married. You can't leave."

"We can only pretend like this so long," she said. "Like we're a normal couple. This is unnatural. Haven't you noticed how nothing ever seems to change? You gotta be hip to that, Moon Doggie. This isn't just about us, it's about the world. There's an order to things, and much as I love you, you broke it. I'm not supposed to be here. One day the sunset is gonna come calling again and I'm not going to have any choice but to go to it. You dig?"

"You can't. I have your jacket." Shame took him the moment he said it and he began searching for an apology, a way to redirect the morning that had suddenly taken a left turn into Shitsville.

But Priscilla only smiled. It was sad and far away and pained Moon Doggie in ways he couldn't understand.

"I wouldn't stop you," he said. "I'd want to, but I wouldn't. Not anymore."

"I know," she said. "That's why I love you."

Moon Doggie laid back again, wrapped her in his arms. "Where will you go to? When it's time."

"East of the sun, west of the moon."

"What kind of bullshit answer is that?"

"No bullshit. That's my home."

"Then I'll go with you," he said, chasing after hope he knew he'd never catch.

"You can't go." Was she crying? "Not there."

"I'll follow you anyway."

"I know you will," she said. "But it's not gonna matter."

Nothing on the AM anymore but Miles Davis and a thousand bands playing Willie Dixon songs, and Moon Doggie is beat with all of it, so he turns off the radio and dwells in the hypnotic world of humming tires and angry wind gusts as he steers the Thunderbird higher into the mountains and straight across the Continental Divide. He figures it'll make him feel different somehow, coming back this way, but he's wrong.

A black man with his thumb out stands almost knee deep in snowdrifts. He waves a feather in the air and Moon Doggie brakes. Offers him a ride.

"Guess this is yours," says the man, handing over the feather before Moon Doggie's even had a chance to put the car in drive again.

"Guess so." This feather's dark and leathery, stained with old earth and ageless scars, just like Pricilla's jacket. Moon Doggie puts it in his pocket with the other one.

His new passenger has a handsome face. Young and friendly, if a little forlorn. His hair's dusted with snowflakes. He rubs his hands together and holds them out to catch the heat emanating from the dashboard vents.

"So, what's up, Jack?" he asks.

"My name's Moon Doggie."

"So it is. Mine's American Sky."

"For real?"

"Close enough."

"So I guess you saw her too," says Moon Doggie.

American Sky whistles. "You bet I did. You messed up bad when you locked that one up, didn't you?"

"I didn't lock her up."

"Might as well have."

"She could leave when she wanted," says Moon Doggie. "And she did."

"But you didn't encourage her none," says American Sky. "You've noticed maybe that not a goddamned thing has changed in this country since you plucked that bird out of the surf?"

"Plenty has changed," says Moon Doggie.

"No, things have just become . . . *more*. That make sense to you? It's like everything you loved about that one beautiful day on that beach, but revved up right past the point of safety. Speaking of which, you mind slowing the hell down on this ice? I'd like to see the other side of these hills alive."

"Sorry."

"Uh huh. Well, things can't stay the same way always. They gotta change. This ain't the fifties anymore."

"Sure it is," says Moon Doggie, knowing full well he's full of shit.

"To you and her maybe, but to the rest of us? No, we'd just as soon move on if you catch my drift. This decade's a drag and it's like there's a corner out there, waiting to be turned and you're the one with his foot on the brake." He grabs the window knob with one hand and puts the other one against the dash. "Seriously, man. Slow the fucking car down."

Moon Doggie slows the car, cranks up the heat.

"All right," says American Sky. "That's better."

"I don't know why you're complaining to me," says Moon Doggie. "She's free now. That gig's over."

"Nothing's over," says American Sky. "So long as you're still on the hunt. You saying if you find her you ain't gonna try to catch her again? Cause that's nothing but a lie and we both know it. You have to find her, for your own sake, but when you do then you have to leave her be. Let the world start turning again. Let freedom ring!"

Moon Doggie knows a thing or two about freedom. He grew a goatee once. He's read Kerouac. He doesn't see what the hell that has to do with Prissy. Nothing wrong with the world they can't fix if he can just catch her before she flies back to the world she came from.

"Look here," says American Sky. "You're scaring the shit out of me. I think I'd rather take my chances with the snow."

"Suit yourself." Moon Doggie pulls the car over and American Sky steps out into a swirl of flakes.

"So, what am I supposed to do with these feathers?" asks Moon Doggie.

"Shove 'em in your pocket, I guess." American Sky slams the door and by the time he's out of sight in the rear-view mirror Moon Doggie is cruising through another world altogether.

By the time Moon Doggie reaches the desert, the road has become a snake. Not some metaphorical snake designed to illustrate the twists and turns his life is taking but an honest to God *snake*, a sheet of gray scales writhing beneath his tires and stretching out before him in a series of sharp curves that circle the scrub-covered dunes and lead him that much closer to the end of the continent.

Things, as they say, are going downhill.

The stars spin circles overhead until they're nothing but a great shining smear on the canvas of night. Lizards and night owls flash their golden eyes at him as pellets of rain strike the car and the snake. The scales are becoming slippery and Moon Doggie's afraid he'll never see the other side of this place.

Not like Prissy didn't warn him.

"We aren't living where you think we are," she'd told him only a week ago. They'd been holding hands and staring across the still surface of the lake near their house. It was within walking distance and Prissy insisted they visit it at least once a week. Moon Doggie never cared for it. When Prissy approached water, she did so with an unhealthy intensity. Moon Doggie never let her hand go on these occasions. He was afraid she'd leap in and keep on swimming forever.

"According to the number on the mailbox, we are."

"That's not what I mean," she said. "This isn't your world anymore. Not completely, anyway. My world is creeping in."

"Tell me about your world." Moon Doggie had asked her this a thousand times in their years together and never received so much as a hint in return.

She gave him a coy smile. "You'll see it soon enough."

"What do you mean?"

"I mean I'll be going soon, and you'll follow me."

They stood in uncomfortable silence, watching the leaves tumble from the trees and settle on the lake. Moon Doggie squeezed her hand tighter.

"I can't live in one place like this much longer," said Priscilla. "My spirit will burn out if I do. I need to roam. I need to be free from all this."

"You want freedom? You want to roam? Shit, let's get in the T-Bird and drive to Vegas. We can move there if we want. Or anywhere. Maybe to the beach again, huh? The real beach, not this ice cold drag of an ocean they got out here. We're free. We're Americans. We can do whatever we want." It wasn't the kind of freedom she was talking about, and he knew it. But he was desperate to change her mind.

Priscilla shook her head. "This ain't really your America anymore, Daddio. This is the spit-shined, dry cleaned idealized version that you made up in that thick head of yours." She jabbed him in the forehead with her finger to drive the point home. "You fell in love with that one perfect day by the sea; barely a couple of years into a whole new decade and you're done with it all. But that day ain't everyone's idea of perfect. There's a lot of stuff that's supposed to happen after this. The future's not so bad. You might actually dig it."

She pulled her hand from his, kicked off her shoes, and walked ankle deep into the water. Moon Doggie held his breath, resisted the urge to grab her.

"What kind of stuff are you talking about?" he whispered.

"Good stuff. Bad stuff. Stuff. That's why I'm gone any day now, you dig? Your world has to get back on track. And besides, my world's come looking for me. You notice how the sky's a pink mist half the time and the fish are telling dirty jokes to one another?"

Moon Doggie nodded. He'd noticed.

"So, there you go. I keep playing house with you and pretty soon there won't be any of this. I'm not long for this world, Doggie."

"How soon," he asked, barely able to voice the words.

"Too soon." Prissy splashed from the water and put her hands on his cheeks. "But I have one more surprise for you before I go. A good one."

The roar of thunder yanks Moon Doggie from his memories, and he takes firmer hold of the steering wheel, terrified of sliding off the snake's back and into the roiling whirlpools of burning sand.

Priscilla had a surprise for him, all right.

But burning down the goddamned house wasn't what he'd had in mind.

And then the desert is gone, and Moon Doggie can see the ocean.

It's just like he remembers it, and he half expects to see Prissy's sisters bobbing in the surf, waiting for that one perfect wave before calling it quits for the day. The sun hangs fat in the western sky, threatening to fall, but Moon Doggie knows it'll keep its cool until their business is done.

The last feather is the perfect silver-blue of ocean waves, and the man holding it stands bare-chested and tan. Sun-bleached hair covers his shoulders, and he's carrying the longest surfboard Moon Doggie has ever seen. The cat is tall, and he's grinning. He hands Moon Doggie the feather and claps him on the back.

"You made it!"

"Guess I did," says Moon Doggie. He takes all three feathers, places them on the hood of the parked T-Bird.

"Well, you been through the fire and lived. I guess you've earned your way here. You know what to do now?"

"No, but I'll figure it out."

"That's the spirit," says the overgrown surfer. "Look, pal, my work's done. I'm gone. Gotta catch a wave."

"Don't we all."

The surfer laughs and then sprints toward the waves. Moon Doggie watches him paddle out past the largest breakers until he disappears into the horizon, then he grabs the guitar from his back seat and starts to pick some Dick Dale licks, quietly at first, and then with more spirit.

"Where are you, Prissy?" he asks when the last chord dies in the crash of surf on the rocks.

He plays another song, a quiet one this time, because he's not sure what else to do.

The night before Priscilla blew the house up and ran away, she'd slept in Moon Doggie's arms. He'd sung her to sleep with one of the songs they both loved, the one about a place where they could be together forever, waiting for them just beyond the sea.

Neither had noticed the other one crying.

When the song is finished, when *that* song is finished, he spots Priscilla in the ocean. The guitar slides to the sand and his fingers begin fumbling with the rope binding his surfboard to the car roof. Then it's loose, and Moon Doggie dives into the water, fully clothed, and paddles the board toward the rapidly fading sun.

And then she's in front of him, straddling her board. Moon Doggie touches her hand and knows it's really her. She's wearing a yellow two-piece and her jacket, of course. He knows she can change anytime she wants and then she'll be gone someplace he can never follow. She's wearing a backpack, ready to leave for good.

"Hey, Doggie," she says.

"I came for you."

"I knew you would."

She smiles at him and he's more in love with her than ever. Her eyes are shards of silver, hardly human anymore.

"You're going away," he says. "I don't know why I even came."

"You came because that's the way these things go. You're human. You've got to make these wonderful grand gestures even when you know they're never gonna amount to anything. You did it for love and you did it to find out what your surprise is. I don't think you're as scared of the future as you think you are."

"You burned down the house. You have something more surprising than that?"

She laughs and the sound of it breaks what's left of his heart. It's not a normal laugh. Not her laugh. It's the most unnatural thing he's ever experienced.

"I didn't burn the house down," she says. "I told you my world was coming for me. Well, it came. Not very subtle, is it? But when the mystery reaches out and levels half your house, well that means it's time to put away your toys and come in for dinner. You dig?"

"Yeah, I dig."

"I'm glad you caught me, Doggie."

"I'm glad I caught you too."

The waves surge and he struggles to keep her close. She reaches behind her, to her backpack, pulls out a baby, and damned if it ain't the last thing Moon Doggie ever expected to see. She hands him the kid, the boy. His eyes are like hers, and Moon Doggie can't help staring into them.

"Take care of yourself, Daddio," says Priscilla.

Moon Doggie looks up and she's an eagle, circling overhead with her sisters, and he gets one last glimpse at the love of his life before she's gone, east of the sun, west of the moon.

Darkness follows in her wake and Moon Doggie catches a wave, the squealing boy in his arms. It's a monster wave, the king of waves, and it sets them back on shore with the gentle touch of a mother.

The world turns again and Moon Doggie heads up the coast. Word is, there's a future, and he can do any damned thing he wants with it. The boy lays flat in the front seat, holding three of his mother's feathers and listening to the endless collision of ocean and earth. His very own lullaby.

By the time they reach San Francisco, Moon Doggie has named his son American Sky.

A BETTER PLACE

CLAYTON NEVER FORGOT THE DAY HIS BROTHER CROSSED THE cotton field and left the farm for good. Russ had always been given to wanderlust, and when the sand man said he could take him to a better place, the boy didn't give his old life another thought. Now, as Clayton sat on the front porch in his dusty green coveralls, watching an approaching sandstorm turn the wide western sky a dismal, smoky brown, he wondered what would have happened if he'd gone to the better place too.

Rigs thundered by on the highway, loaded with gasoline, frozen chicken, and foreign cars. Gone were the graying Ford trucks that carried laughing farm hands to their day's labor, only to return in the afternoon pulling trailers loaded with bails of hay, the men tired and yearning for supper. Everything was bigger now.

His back hurt, like it always did, as he half-heartedly smoked his cigarette. He hated the things, but he was set in his ways. *That's just a polite way of saying weak willed*, he thought before taking another drag. Russ would have been able to quit. That boy did whatever he pleased and there was no way he'd be willing to let anything control him. That's what had given him the strength to take chances, and Clayton often imagined his brother, living in a dream world, reaping the bountiful harvest of his decision.

Clayton tipped his sweat-stained straw hat a bit lower to block the sun as he stared out across the endless rows of cotton. A lone green tractor, choking out foul emissions, crept toward him. His only son, Harold, sat behind the steering wheel, a look of intense concentration on his face. Keeping a tractor running in a perfectly straight line was not an easy skill to master, and one he decided Harold never would.

Harold was ill suited to farming, always bitter about his lot in life and sure he was meant for better things. In many ways, Clayton understood and agreed with him, but he was from an age when you accepted the life you were given and if that wasn't good enough for you, you lived with it. Clayton wished he could tell his son he was sorry. This was life and there was no getting around it, no easy solution. But of course, that would be a lie. Russ had found a way.

Not far from the rumbling tractor, Clayton's grandson hacked away at random weeds with a hoe. Young and energetic, head bopping beneath tiny headphones, shirtless in spite of the blazing sun. Watching John work always made Clayton smile. The boy couldn't be more unlike his father. Though not yet twenty years old, he'd achieved a peace in life that neither his father nor grandfather had ever felt. Farming was what he aspired to and he was too young to think he would ever need anything else.

The sandstorm moved fast. The whirling, raging wall of dirt reached the end of the west field, and the tiny green tractor was no longer visible. The smell of loose earth rode the wind and tickled his nose, causing him to sneeze. He wiped his nose with a worn handkerchief and shoved it back into his pocket. Soon he'd be able to feel the dirt like grit between his teeth, and his watery eyes would turn a brilliant red. Such was life in West Texas.

Blown loose from miles and miles of farmland, the incoming sand moved as a single entity. Clayton never failed to be amazed when he witnessed such storms, creeping ever closer, seeming to devour the land and its inhabitants. Watching his fields disappear always reminded him of Russ, and the day he'd chosen to leave with the storm.

*

Russ had been much like Harold. The boy had a longing for the city that couldn't be satisfied by the occasional trip up to Lubbock, and he'd often sit on the back porch, staring west and telling Clayton how he'd leave some day. Maybe move to Dallas or New York, or maybe to Los Angeles so he could be in the movies.

"Anywhere's better than here," he said that day. His white shirt had been clean and tight with starch that morning, but was now wrinkled and dirt stained, tail hanging lazily over the back of his pants. He sipped a bottle of root beer their mother had let them buy on the way home from church, and he handed it to his brother.

"Here ain't so bad," said Clayton. He took a deep swallow and felt the gas bubble instantly begin to form in his stomach.

"Farming ain't for me," said Russ. "I want to live where the dirt ain't always blowing and they let you sleep past four. You know what I heard?"

"What?"

"I heard them movie stars sleep till ten o'clock. And why not? They don't got chickens and pigs to feed, or cotton to pick or nothing."

"Ten o'clock? Why would you want to sleep that long?"

"Because you can. Nobody's your boss."

Clayton had become used to his younger brother's flights of fancy over the years and he worked hard to keep the boy grounded. "Sandstorm coming," he said, not bothering to point over the west field. They always came from the west.

"Course it is," said Russ, scowling. "Can't have a day without sand, can we?"

"Suppose not," said Clayton dryly, handing the bottle of root beer back to Russ.

Neither of them spoke for several minutes, content to watch the quietly approaching sandstorm. The wind that carried it spun the blades of the windmill in an endless circle, producing a lonely squeal. Two spotted cows lapped water from opposite sides of a rusted trough. By the time the brothers had finished their root beer, the wall of sand had hidden the cows from sight.

"Look there," said Russ, nodding his head toward the hazy brown horizon. "Where'd he come from?"

Clayton held his hand over his eyes and saw a tall, well-dressed man approaching. He wore a suit of pale brown fabric that flapped merrily in the stiff wind. He moved toward them with an easy grace, leather shoes reflecting the sun's brilliant light despite his path through the tilled earth

"Looks like he's coming from church," said Clayton, but he knew that wasn't the case before he finished speaking. He'd never seen anybody sitting in their chapel's polished pews with clothes so fine. He studied his own Sunday clothes; littered with patched holes and stains so old he'd forgotten how they got there.

"Church is the other way," said Russ. He rose to his feet to get a better look. "Ask me, he's coming to sell something. Nobody but salesmen dress like that, except maybe movie stars. You figure he might be a movie star?"

"If he was, what would he be doing here? You see any movies made here lately?"

"No, but he might be," said Russ, defensively. "I didn't say he was for sure. Probably just a salesman."

"Probably."

A group of thin chickens with filthy white feathers searched the ground for seeds. When the man passed them, they raced off with a chorus of irate clucks. He was nearing the front of the house, so the brothers decided to stand and greet him.

"We already got a Bible," said Russ, nudging Clayton with his elbow. "So if you're selling Bibles, we ain't buying."

"Young man, I'm not here to sell anything. Everything I have to offer is free of charge." Now that he was close enough to really study, Clayton noticed his teeth were as shiny and well kept as the rest of him. His blue eyes were deep and friendly, and he couldn't resist shaking the man's hand when it was offered. Russ stared up at the man, eyes narrowed, the top of his head even with his shoulders.

"We already got religion too," said Russ. "That's the only thing I ever seen anyone give away for free."

Clayton noticed a gold watch chain dangling from the stranger's vest pocket, a sure sign he wasn't a preacher. He'd never known a preacher that could afford a gold chain.

"Religion is wonderful, but that's not why I'm here either."

"Well, Daddy and Mama are in town still. So you'll have to come back." Russ shoved his hands in his pockets, signaling the matter closed.

"I didn't come to see them. I came to see you."

"What for? You ain't a movie star, are you? I've seen lots of movies and you weren't in any of them."

"No, not a movie star. But I know some."

That got Russ's attention. He dropped his resistance and gazed at the stranger with newfound admiration. "Movie stars! Which ones you know?"

"Oh, lots of them. There are more than a few where I come from."

"Hollywood? Lots of stars there."

"No, someplace better."

"Where?"

"Nowhere in particular."

"You're just pulling my leg, ain't you?" Russ's shoulders dropped and Clayton thought he looked like a dog that had been offered a bite of rib eye but instead got a kick in the flank.

"Listen," said the man, his smile never wavering. "I heard you saying you wanted to go someplace better than here. That's true, isn't it?"

"Yeah, so?"

"Well, I'm here to take you."

Clayton wasn't sure he liked the tall stranger and he attempted to stand as straight as possible, so the man might know he was a bit older and wiser in the ways of the world. "Take him where?" he asked, wishing their parents would get back from town.

"A better place," said the man, as if that explained everything. The sand had moved in, causing Clayton's eyes to run and his nose to itch, but the stranger seemed unaffected.

"But where," said Clayton, becoming exasperated.

"A better place. A place where movie stars live next door and you don't have to feed chickens. A place where there's oceans and mountains and not a single grain of sand. A place where the cotton jumps right off the plant and onto the truck."

"What else?" Russ stared directly at the man's eyes, as if he were trying to see the place he was describing.

"What's you favorite thing to eat, Russ?"

Clayton did not remember telling the man their names and when he spoke Russ's, a nervous lump settled in his stomach beside the gas from the root beer.

"Peach cobbler. But the kind mama makes, not the kind Old Lady Grubb brings to the church lunches."

"Well, that's wonderful," said the man, looking genuinely pleased. "*Everything* where I come from tastes like peach cobbler."

"Even the vegetables," asked Russ, hopefully.

"They would, except we don't have vegetables."

Clayton didn't believe what the man was saying, but the place was starting to sound pretty good to him anyway. The fields and the animals were no longer visible, and now the three of them stood alone in a world of soft brown light. Clayton reached back and grabbed the porch rail, needing a bit of reality to hold onto as the man spun his lies. He wished the sandstorm would go away and take the stranger with it.

"And you don't have to wear your Sunday clothes," he continued. "And though you may not appreciate it now, you never have to worry about anything. You have all the money and medicine you need, and you can buy anything you want."

"Can I sleep till ten o'clock?" asked Russ, testing the man.

"You can sleep until eleven if you want. Nobody's going to wake you up. We don't worry about chores there."

"Where is this place?" asked Clayton. He was becoming worried about the far away look in his brother's eye.

"No place in particular, just past the sand."

"Let's go," said Russ. "That sounds like the kind of place I want to be."

"You can't go there, Russ. There ain't no such place." Clayton's heart was pounding in his chest. He felt nervous and lightheaded in the thick, sandy air, and he gripped the porch rail tighter, afraid he might suddenly feel compelled to leave too.

"You're wrong about that, son," said the stranger. He didn't seem to mind that Clayton had called him a liar. His smile widened and he crouched down so that he was looking up at the boys. "Why don't you come along and see. You're both welcome, and you can come back any time you want. You just have to blow in with the sand."

"I don't think Daddy would be too happy to come home and find out we ain't here."

"Well, nobody's going to keep you there. You get tired of bumping elbows with the movie stars and riding in rocket ships, you come on home."

"Rocket ships!" said Russ, bursting with impatience. "You stay here if you want, Clayton. I'm going."

"Shall I lead the way?" asked the stranger, rising to his feet and shaking the sand from his suit jacket.

"You bet," said Russ.

Without another word, the stranger began walking away, Russ in step right behind him. Clayton wanted to say something, wanted to grab his brother and tackle him, hold him there until he saw reason. But he did none of these things. He watched the brown cloud envelop his brother as he followed a stranger in search of something more. Before disappearing entirely, Russ's voice called back. "I'll be home soon. I just want to have a look."

It was the last time Clayton had seen his brother.

*

Now, nearly seventy years later, Clayton sat on the same aging porch, watching the sand approach, wondering what became of Russ. He still pictured him as he'd looked that day, hands and face burned an earthy brown by the unchallenged Texas sun, hair a rusty blonde, headstrong and young in his wrinkled church clothes. After decades of consideration, Clayton preferred to believe the happiest of all possible scenarios. Russ had found his better place, a place of eternal youth, free from hardship and the unwieldy weight of adult responsibility.

The sand reached John, causing him to put down his hoe and tie a blue bandana over his mouth and nose. Satisfied, he went back to work and soon vanished from Clayton's sight. Clayton smiled, recognizing one of the reasons that made him happy he'd stayed behind that day. Sometimes life was expensive, but damned if it didn't pay you back one hundred-fold.

Clayton rose to his feet and clenched the worn porch rail with one thin hand. He felt the warm air whip the sand around him, returning him once again to that world of dull, brown light, and a childhood memory of singular circumstance. He closed his burning eyes, wondering as he always did if Russ would blow in with the sand, busting with tales of peach cobbler and other sources of adolescent bliss. Maybe when he opened his eyes, he'd see his brother. Maybe Russ and the sand man would be standing there, ready to offer him one more chance to come along.

Clayton was pretty sure he'd still have to pass.

HER SOUL,
A DARK FOREST

W HEN MY MOTHER WAS YOUNG, SHE DID SOMETHING THAT surprised everyone. She walked willingly into the mesquite forest. Everyone in our town knew then, and knows now, what a bad idea that is. When she came out, she was cold, and she was pregnant, and she was diminished. Her hair was knotted with twigs and thorns, and she'd chewed her fingernails to bloody nubs. For weeks, she spoke only in a language that nobody recognized. When she regained her English, what she had to say drove even her family away.

I asked many times what compelled her into the woods, and the closest I ever got to an answer was when she leaned close to my ear and whispered, "Happiness is wherever you go looking for it."

She worked as a grocery checker when I was in elementary school and rented a two-bedroom house outside of town, close enough to the mesquite forest that you could hear the clackety sound of the wind moving through those trees from our back yard. I would twine my fingers through the chain links of our low back fence, shaded by bedsheets and threadbare towels that swayed from a nylon clothesline. From there, I would watch the mesquite forest as it lay along the horizon like a great sleeping animal, the wind stirring its limbs, causing the forest to breathe. I could smell the ancient, turned earth odor of the place, and hear the faint creep of unsettling music. Things that might have been coyotes lingered in the undergrowth, yellow eyes watching me back.

My mother had a boyfriend named Kelly who lived with us for a while. He had long sandy hair and a Glen Frey moustache. He used to take me for rides in his primer gray Mustang, and he'd crank up the Molly Hatchett 8-track that he kept lodged permanently in the tape deck. He must have been about twenty-three, my mother's age at the time. Less than half the age I am now.

Kelly grew weed in our backyard shed, and when his friends would visit, they'd lounge in the aluminum lawn chairs out back and smoke for hours. I'd carve roads in the dirt for Hot Wheels, listening to them talk about bass boats and football. I think I would've been content to live in the slow crawl of those afternoons for the rest of my life, but one day Kelly got up from his chair, tossed down a half empty can of Pearl, and ran out through the back gate into the fields that separated our house from the mesquite forest. He'd spotted my mother, moving slowly toward the trees in a T- shirt and cutoff shorts, feet bare.

The forest glistened black like an oil slick.

Kelly caught up to my mother, positioned himself between her and the forest. When she moved to go around him, he grabbed her arm. She yanked loose and slapped him in the face.

The forest screamed, but no one else seemed to hear it. Kelly's friends laughed, and one of them blew out a mouthful of smoke and said, "Damn, kitten's got claws."

Kelly or my mother shouted something; they were too far away for me to know who spoke. Then Kelly walked back to the yard, gathered his friends to leave, and said, "Man, I'm sorry kid. I think your mom is losing it."

I wanted to chase after him, but I was afraid to look away from my mother for fear that she'd disappear into the forest. She waited at the edge of the tree line. Creatures lurked just within the gloom, but heat rose up from the field in shimmery waves and it obscured them in such a way that I couldn't determine their precise shape.

Kelly's Mustang came alive with a rumble and a cloud of gasoline smoke.

My mother stayed close to the forest until the sun was nearly down, then she came home. We lived afterwards like Kelly had never been a part of our lives.

When my mother worked evenings, my grandmother would babysit. She read me fairy tales about what happened to little boys who wandered into places better avoided. We stayed inside, never went into the backyard. She fretted around the house, asking me who my mother was seeing, and picking through our junk drawers as if she might find some residue of wrongdoing.

My grandfather came with her one evening, a tool bag slung over his shoulder. He worked at the kitchen faucet with a wrench, trying to tame a leak. All the while, he kept looking out the window in the direction of the forest, talking to himself about how mesquites aren't supposed to grow that high or knot together so tightly. How unnatural it is for a woman to live alone, and so close to that terrible place.

His eyes grew wet and he wiped them with the back of his hand. "She's ruined. There's no undoing any of this."

When he finished with the sink, he dug into the fridge and went to work on a six pack of beer. My grandmother and I sat at the kitchen table, eating a bowl of too salty popcorn while my grandfather drank the beers one by one, flattening each empty can in his fist before tossing it in the trash. The window air unit chugged like a freight train but didn't do much to cut the summer heat. My grandfather put the last can of beer up against his cheek and pressed the cold into his skin.

"Hey, has your mother ever told you who your daddy is?" he asked. "She damn sure never told us."

My grandmother hissed and stood up in a fury. "That's enough of that." She took his arm and pulled him into the living room. My mother arrived home a few minutes later, and I don't recall my grandfather ever visiting our house again.

When my mother joined me at the table to finish off the popcorn, we didn't talk about what my grandfather had said. It was an old conversation. I'd heard whispers about my mother's month away in the woods since kindergarten. Was she pregnant before she went into the mesquite? Was she driven there by the shame? Or worse, did some unholy thing get her with child while she hid herself away from the world? She told me plainly the first time I asked that she simply didn't remember being in the woods, and that was enough answer for me. A lot of other boys had fathers who treated them poorly, and I was quite content living without one.

When I was in middle school, my mother married a man named Mitch who worked as a driller on an oil rig. He made decent money, and we could have moved into a nicer house somewhere in town, but my mother refused to leave our two-bedroom. She gave in to Mitch on just about everything else, but she dug in her heels about the house. Working in the oil patch, Mitch would be gone for weeks at a time, but when he was home, I lived in his shadow.

When my mother was at work, Mitch staked out a place on the couch and expected me to play quietly somewhere else. Usually that meant outside. I'd listen for him to yell if he needed a beer, or if he needed me to bike up to the convenience store to get him a pack of Marlboro Reds. Otherwise, I'd keep my distance.

Out by the fence, I'd lean against the hot wind racing across the flatland, listening to it bend the brush and the long spills of prickly pear. I'd bite back the dust and watch the forest come alive.

Something always revealed itself.

Sparks of golden light illuminated the fringes of the forest. Shapeless figures and curious animals gathered in the deep foliage, breathlessly still, as if eager to draw me in, but anxious not to frighten me away. That music carried, always, and I knew it played for my mother, and maybe for me. Everyone in town still avoided the place, but from superstition, not from understanding. They had never been touched by the mesquite forest, so they only knew to fear it.

One evening, Mitch came to the back door and watched me try to carve a bit of tree branch into something resembling an arrowhead. I moved my pocketknife in smooth, easy strokes, always pushing away from myself. Every few seconds, Mitch took a drag from his cigarette, the world gone so quiet that I could hear the crackle of the tobacco and paper burning with each puff. He wore nothing but jeans and flip flops, his hands sun browned and worn, the rest of him muscled and white as milk.

"How come you're always out here playing by yourself?" Mitch was a big man, and his bones cracked when he walked. He stepped out into the back yard, letting the screen door slam behind him. "Don't you have any friends?"

"A few," I said.

"Well I ain't never seen one."

"They don't play over here. Mostly I see them at school."

Mitch knew I didn't have many friends, and he knew why the ones I had weren't allowed to play over here. Sometimes he just figured I was having too good of a day and might need reminding how unloved my mother and I were in this town. To a lot of people, the memory of who she used to be was so much better than the person she'd become. They never really tried to understand the woman who came out of the forest.

And they had no idea what to make of me.

"You shouldn't be out here all the time by yourself, staring at them mesquite trees."

I didn't remind him I was out here all the time because when I was inside, he looked for reasons to be mad at me. The only thing he liked less than me seemed to be the mesquite forest, and that's just because he thought it might one day take my mother away from him.

She had a habit of walking out there most evenings and standing near those trees, like she was working up to leaving again. She always came home, but it still had a way of making the rest of us feel like we were worth leaving behind.

"I should get a can a gasoline and burn them trees down," said Mitch. "Solve that problem real quick."

Mitch was building up to something. He was aching for a fight. Usually, it would be him railing on my mother about how lucky she was that he'd taken a chance on someone like her, after the way she carried on. She'd yell back and I'd find some dark place to hide out and wish that wherever my real father was, he'd come get me and take me there. More than once I considered walking into the forest just like my mother had. The way Mitch looked tonight, like a gray sky gathering storm clouds, I considered running for the forest might be my best option.

"Cat got your tongue?" he said.

"No."

"How about we burn all that down, you and me?"

"I don't think that's a good idea."

Mitch smiled. "You mean your Mama wouldn't have nothing to hold over my head anymore, isn't that right? What is it that draws her out there?"

I knew to keep my mouth shut, but the words leaked out before I could stop them. "She says happiness is wherever you go looking for it."

Mitch flicked his cigarette away with the same motion he used to thump me on the skull when I was irritating him. "You think she ain't happy here? With me."

"That's not what I meant."

Mitch came across the yard, grabbed my arm and lifted me roughly to my feet. He pushed open the gate and pulled me into the field, moving at such a pace that I stumbled, and for a second he dragged me along behind him like a sack of potatoes. Then I got my feet under me and jogged to keep up.

"That forest is such a happy place, how about you go live there?"

Mitch stopped a few yards from the tree line, and I knew he was afraid to go any closer. He shoved me in the back, and I stumbled forward, fell to my knees there in the sand, closer to the mesquite forest than I'd ever been. A raw sort of wildness called to me from the place. Whatever mystery lived within latched on to something deep inside me and I wanted nothing more than to crawl forward into the cool shade of those branches and disappear from a world that never had much use for me anyway. Something pleasantly feral possessed me, and the notion of taking my pocketknife and driving it into Mitch's stomach was suddenly appealing. It had nothing to do with any particular dislike of Mitch, or any desire for violence, but was more of a need to let go of my worldly norms and give in to the chaos of the place. I turned to look at him, and something in my expression drove Mitch back.

"You and your mother are both more trouble than you're worth."

He left me there by myself, in thrall to the mesquite forest, and I stayed there until my mother came home and found me on my knees with my fingers dug into the earth. She of all people understood the pull that place could have, and she locked her arms around me and held me there until I regained some of myself.

"You don't belong there," she said.

It wasn't long after that that Mitch packed up his things and moved out, leaving another man-shaped hole in our house that I was in no hurry to fill.

My mother began to grow distant during my high school years. Her yearning for the forest stole her ability to be present, to live solidly in the world. She stopped eating altogether, no longer able to stand the taste of food, yet somehow, she continued to live. She grew thin and her face sank in on itself, but the life never left her eyes, no matter how haunted, no matter how drawn to the forest they remained.

It was only a matter of time.

She married a kind man named Roberto, though I don't believe she ever really loved him. This was my senior year of high school, and I think she married him as some last attempt to tether herself to her life here. Roberto had two grown children who didn't live with us, and though he was well intentioned, I was on the edge of adulthood myself and didn't need another stepdad. I do believe he loved my mother, though certainly he didn't know who she really was.

They were married for only a few months when my mother returned to the mesquite forest for good.

I stood with her by the forest when she'd made her decision, knowing better than to try and stop her. There was something inside those trees that she'd always yearned for, something nobody could give her. I'd grown up understanding that she'd leave some day, but it had been so far in the future that I'd never really concerned myself with how alone I'd be without her.

The forest music was mournful, and my mother put her hands on my cheeks, looked me in the eyes, and put me ahead of that place for a few more seconds.

"I'm sorry I have to go," she said.

"I can't come with you," I lied.

She smiled. "I know that. This isn't your place. You'd never be happy here. All through my childhood, I wanted to be here. I knew it's where I belonged. And of course, everyone told me this is the one place I must never go. But I was never very well behaved."

"Good thing, I guess."

"I don't know what happened while I lived among these trees, but I know I was happy here. I know I never should have left. I stayed with you as long as I could."

"It's okay, Mom."

"I do love you."

Then she was gone. She didn't step into the forest, but simply dissolved into its cool shadows.

I considered my mother's life when she was my age. A childhood spent pretending to be happy, punctuated by an unshakable longing that nobody else cared to understand. Like a girl with a pocketknife, she carved away all the best parts of herself, hoping to reveal a shape that would please everyone. But it was never enough. No matter how much she cut away.

So, she'd done something about it.
She cut everything loose and went looking for happiness.
And I hope, maybe, that she found it.

FEBRUARY MOON

SOMETHING KILLED OUR ROOSTER AND THREE OF OUR BROWN hens during the night. Thin ice crusts the ground, and it breaks in delicate patterns as I step toward the scattering of feathers and bones. Blood lies dark against the earth. It rarely snows here in the winter like at home. Only ice and gray rain that settles on the trees and pulls their limbs toward the ground like they've lost the will to fight for their own lives. These are gnarled, fearful trees, nothing like the commanding black forest of my youth, but their shadows still grow long enough to hide monsters.

The chicken coop door has been pulled from the hinges, and the splintered remains stand evidence to the force with which it was removed. If I were a stupid or fearful woman, I might convince myself that a rawboned coyote was to blame; they forever haunt these hills with their hunger. But I'm neither of those things, and I know how a wolf attacks.

I've lived among them my whole life.

Gretchen is already busy with breakfast preparations when I come in from clearing away the carcasses. There's a pot of water not yet at a boil, and I scrub the blood from my hands as Peter pulls on his shoes and his coat, in a hurry to milk Klara and get the rest of his work behind him. He's eight years old, two years younger than Gretchen, and I expect tears from him when I tell him about the hens, but he only nods with the air of stoic acceptance that he learned from his father.

Another day of cold survival stretches before us all. In the nearly six months since my husband and eldest son have been gone, we three have learned to face our days one at a time, placing them each after the next like bricks in a road that we hope will lead to somewhere better.

"Mother," says Gretchen. "We're nearly out of flour."

"I'll make a trip into town today."

"Were there any eggs?"

"They were destroyed," I say.

"Klara is safe?" asks Peter.

"Yes, thankfully," I say. "We'll have milk at least."

The smell of the sausage that Gretchen is frying is a harsh reminder that we're almost out of meat too. My husband always kept us full of venison and small game, and I would be angry at him for how he left us on the edge of hunger were I not largely to blame for his absence.

"Peter, I need you to take the rifle this afternoon and bring back some dinner. And be careful. Whatever killed the chickens might still be about."

My children are not fools, and they almost certainly know what killed the chickens, but neither of them argues and Peter won't show any fear. Sending him alone beyond the threshold and into the frozen hills summons old guilt from deep inside me, but what else can I do? It's no job for Gretchen, and if I don't travel into town we won't even be able to make bread.

When the din of morning chores gives way to the quiet advance of afternoon, I shove a crust of bread into Peter's coat and put the rifle in his hand. Even in his wool hat and mittens, he manages an eerie impression of his father. His jaw chews at the cold, and a still confidence nests in his blue eyes. I admonish him to be careful, and above all, to return before nightfall.

My children have spent so much time living with terrible realities that I'm afraid they no longer take the world's dangers seriously. I wish for them to simply be children, and for myself to be burdened with nothing more than a mother's routine fears for their safety. Gretchen should not lie awake at night listening for monsters, and Peter is certainly too young to be the man of the house. Yet here we are. Hugging him is like hugging a warm corpse, and when I release him, he trudges into the cedar line without a farewell.

Gretchen leads our horse from the barn and wraps me in one of the extra saddle blankets like I'm her newborn babe. She named the horse Herr Butter when she was younger, though the animal is brown as mud. Gretchen waves as I ride away. Wind tugs her hair into an unruly blonde mess, and she retreats indoors. I pray that I won't return to find my children torn bone from bone. I will be racing nightfall myself, and the moon is never far away at this time of year.

Travel into town on horseback takes over an hour. In the spring-time the ride is pleasant enough. Tall willowy grass rides the breeze and thorny cactus patches erupt with red buds. Bluebonnets pour down the sides of every rolling limestone hill like spilled paint. The air is birdsong and honeysuckle and the electric touch of approaching thunderstorms, and I can almost imagine myself happy here.

But spring is still weeks away, and winter refuses to relent. The landscape around me is the color of bone and rot. Was it any better in my birth country? I remember the warm sweet taste of my grand-mother's strudel and the long afternoons we spent among the trees together, listening for the forest's secrets. But I remember blood too. And I remember feeling helpless.

The town of Broken Oak has less use for me than I do for it, and I'm thankful that few people are about when I ride into its rutted streets. German immigrants have settled this part of Texas in large numbers, yet Mattias saw fit to plant us near this thoroughly American town, where my poor English brands me an outsider and worse, unintelligent. I can understand conversations well enough, but when I try to summon the proper response in English, the words don't always come. I want to scream at these people. *You don't know my mind. I can quote long passages from Aristotle and sonnets from Shakespeare. I can compose symphonies in my head. Because I cannot yet explain these things to you in your language, you think you're smarter than I am? You're no better than me.*

I lash Herr Butter's reigns to the post in front of the mercantile and hurry up the wooden steps, eager to complete my errand and return to my children. The heat inside the store is immense. Fire rages in the belly of a fat woodstove, and men are gathered around it, rubbing their hands and talking in low voices as the flames paint unsettling masks on their faces. The stove is poorly vented and mesquite smoke clings to the ceiling.

The mercantile belongs to Mr. Starling, and he stands behind the counter in a stained leather apron with a weary air about him, like spending his days hawking frayed rope, horseshoe nails, and penny candy is too large of a burden for any man's soul. Sweat trails down both of his temples, and he smells vaguely of stale tobacco.

"Well Frau, what are you doing out today?" he asks. "It's near froze solid out there."

I produce a weak smile and open my coin purse. What I would like to say is "Children must eat, Mr. Starling, whether it is warm or whether it is cold," but what I say aloud is, "Flour for bread, please."

"Oh yes ma'am," he says and begins rummaging through the shelves behind him.

As I wait, two men separate from the pack surrounding the stove, drawn by the scent of what they consider weakened prey. Mr. Grandly is a grizzled, silver haired goat farmer whose boots always smell of manure. His companion, Mr. Elder, is handsome if a little on the thin side, with preposterous lamb chop whiskers and a voice like a ruined preacher. They position themselves on either side of me, close enough that their shadows join on the counter.

"Hello, Frau," says Grandly.

"Hello."

"How are your children?"

"Very well."

He nods his head. "Glad to hear it. Now listen, you need to be careful up there by yourself, you understand. Your husband ain't come back, has he?"

Mr. Grandly knows very well that my husband has not returned. They presume me a widow. A woman with hungry children and some modest acreage. They covet all of what I have and are ill equipped to hide their sin. Mr. Elder is particularly forward with his desires, and he inserts himself into the conversation with an odious bark.

"Grandly, you know he's not come back, else we'd have heard. No reason to hound the poor woman."

"Well, I ain't hounding her," Grandly says.

Mr. Elder smiles. "Frau. You must be home before dark, you know? There are certain to be Indians about."

"Red savages," Grandly says.

"A fat white moon drives the Comanche into a frenzy," Elder says. "They'll be on the prowl for several nights."

"They killed a family over near Fredericksburg last night," Grandly says. "Tore off their faces. Took a little boy's feet with them too."

I think of Peter, alone in forest, hunting for dinner, and my heartbeat quickens.

Mr. Starling places a bag of flour in front of me and hisses through his tumbledown teeth. "Enough of that talk, with a lady in the room."

Mr. Elder places a hand on my back and leans close enough for me to feel the heat of his breath when he speaks. "I will accompany you home to make sure you arrive unharmed."

"No, I am fine."

"Then I shall ride out later to ensure that no savages are lurking. We were just discussing a night hunt wherein we might encounter and kill some of them. It will be no extra trouble."

"I have a rifle. We are fine."

Mr. Elder removes his hand and withdraws the bulk of his animal mass. The smell of his sweat and his lust remain close, but I refuse to be overwhelmed. I place some coins into Mr. Starling's outstretched hand, snatch up the bag of flour, and leave Mr. Grandly and Mr. Elder standing at the mercantile counter. They call after me like yapping dogs, encouraging me to hurry home, to lock tight my doors, to shutter the windows and to listen for strange noises in the night.

I don't require their counsel. I will do all of these things and more. Mr. Elder is right about one thing. There are terrible things in the world that grow bold when the moon is fat. I know them. If he intends a night hunt, then he should pray it is only the Comanche that he finds.

Peter is not home for the evening meal.

We dine in silence, Gretchen and I, unwilling to voice the fear we share. Afterward, she practices her arithmetic, scratching figures on a slate, erasing, starting again, a ritual to occupy her mind. I seat myself in the rocking chair on the front porch, and even outside I can hear the click clack of her chalk and the tuneless humming sound she makes when she's deep in thought.

The wind is cold enough to burn, but I can't countenance the thought of Peter alone in the darkness without anyone to share his misery. Colder still is the guilt I feel. Leaving Gretchen alone in the cabin so I might hunt for Peter in the night would simply trade fear for fear. Yet Peter's father and older brother would be hunting for him even now if not for my actions.

The moon is a raging white fire in the sky, and I can feel the way it pulls everyone and everything towards it. Herr Butter and

Klara moan and stomp from within the barn, victims of the moon's spell. My hands fidget with the arms of the rocking chair and my jaw clenches to the point of pain as I work to bite back the cold chatter of my teeth while I stare off into the tree line.

Something emerges from the nearest stand of wind-beaten cedars. Hulking and slow, it proceeds apace toward the house, and when I rise from my seat and lift up my lantern, a weak yellow light paints the gloom and I can make out the form of my son.

"Peter!"

A small doe lies across his shoulders, and he struggles beneath the dead weight of the animal as he trudges toward the porch. Blood soaks his shirt and breeches and lies thick on his face. When he greets me with the thinnest of smiles, he looks like a child who's just dug his way out of his own grave.

That night I dream of home.

I am young and dancing and surrounded by trees so massive that they banish the daylight. So tall that their tops pincushion the low winter clouds. Snow-covered branches form a white canopy overhead, and I pretend I'm a guest of some Nordic prince in his grand ice palace. The air smells of pinecones and frost and dainty sugar candies and I'm desperate to remain in this beautiful dream forever, but I can feel the call of the path at my feet.

An outsider would never even notice it, but I've lived in this forest all my life and I know the ways in and the ways through. Heel and toe I follow the memory of my own footsteps deeper into the maw of that great forest, drawing closer to my Grandmother's cabin, a place I love far more than any prince's castle; a place warmer than any mother's arms.

But Mattias is there before me. He is always there.

A grim harbinger of what my life will become, he sits on the stoop of the cabin, awash in blood, an axe nearly as tall as I am laid across his knees. He is no prince, but he will become my husband one day. On this day he is winter pale from blood loss, and the world's largest wolf lies dead at his feet. The cabin behind him is too quiet, flooded with darkness, and when Mattias lifts his eyes to mine I see the reflection of my grandmother's death. Mattias has slain her killer, but vengeance does not raise the dead.

His shredded shirt reveals several ragged channels where the dead beast took a taste of him, and the woman I grow into will spend many nights tracing those scars with her fingers and considering how foolishly easy it is for young girls to fall in love with men simply because they are strong enough to slay monsters.

The dead wolf shudders, and my younger self screams.

But there is no wolf; not anymore. There is only a man, naked and bloody, with his skull split wide by my hero's axe.

Then the whole forest shudders, and the icicle ceiling of my world comes crashing down.

I wake, trying to bring the image of Mattias's face with me from the dream, but no matter how many times I've studied his smiles and his grimaces, I'm fast losing the ability to conjure his likeness from memory. Instead, I see only my oldest son, Bernhard, a near doppelgänger for his father, and young Peter grinning through a mask of blood. I shake off the memories, content to spend a few seconds of peace in the warmth of my blankets as the first orange shimmer of morning creeps into the window, but the stillness never lasts. Gretchen calls for me, screams for me, and when I rise and run to her, I find nothing but more blood.

The wolf returned last night.

One barn door has been removed with terrible violence. Herr Butter lies in the doorway, his stomach split, his entrails spilled and cold. Gretchen wails and tugs at his mane as if trying to yank the life back into him. Peter has forgotten his stoicism and weeps openly, no longer the conquering hunter but a little boy with very little left to lose.

Klara, our cow, is missing, but little investigation is required. A bloody trail leads from the barn, beyond the cedar line, and into what passes for a forest in this land. There is more blood than even I could have imagined.

The day is not improved by the appearance of Mr. Elder, knocking at my door. I'm feeding my children and trying to keep their minds from the cleanup that awaits us when he arrives. He stands framed in the doorway, the winter sun at his back, and his horse is tied to a fencepost just beyond the slaughter. He inadvertently walked through some blood and it coats his boots; this provides a welcome excuse to deny him entry into my home.

"What has occurred here, Frau?" he asks. "Have you been harmed?"

I close my children safely inside the house and join Mr. Elder on the porch. He looks as if he's swallowing back a mouth full of bile.

"A wolf killed our animals in the night."

"This is not the work of a wolf," he says. "Wolves are uncommon here."

"It was a wolf."

He shakes his head and grips his hat in his hands like he's trying to wring water from a washcloth. "It was men who did this. Maybe you've seen a wolf roaming, but this atrocity has every appearance of a Comanche raid."

Every appearance but tracks from horses or humans, I think, but I find it better to let some men run until their steam is exhausted. They will often confuse this for agreement on my part and discontinue all efforts to persuade me.

"We were on the trail of a raiding party last night, but they eluded us," he says. "A dozen red bandits if there was one, we are sure. I'm sorry we weren't able to find them before they did this to you, but you were more fortunate than you could have been. The

Emerson family lost more than animals last night. Their child was murdered."

I don't know who the Emersons are, but I feel the death of their child in my bones.

"We'll ride again tonight," he says. "We'll keep watch until they move on or they're all dead. You'll be safe tonight. I promise we'll stay close."

I bite back black laughter. If this fool knew what he was chasing, he'd know that his promise to protect me was one he could never keep.

"I want to say something and say it plain," Mr. Elder says. "You and your children are alone here, and you are not safe. I would make a good husband to you if you would have me."

"I have a husband." My laughter threatens to spill out, but the sight of Herr Butters growing rigid sobers me enough to keep it contained for now.

"Your husband is dead, Frau. A man would not leave his family in such straits if he were able to return. I believe the Comanche must have killed him. And your oldest boy with him, I'm sorry to say."

"No, they will return." It's a lie, but I use it to wall myself away from his advances.

"Maybe he will, but I think it's unlikely." He squashes his hat back on his head and takes hold of my arm. His hands are large, and the backs of them are thick with hair, like my husband's hands. His grip is tighter than necessary, but I refuse to reveal any discomfort. "Consider my offer, Frau. There are worse men to align yourself with in this world."

Sadly, he is right, but that realization is not enough to sway me. "Thank you for checking on us."

"You are in my thoughts, Frau."

Mr. Elder avoids the wide swath of blood this time as he lumbers back to his horse. The animal is as eager to leave this place as I am to have Mr. Elder gone from my porch. Only when they disappear over the horizon do I finally feel the air rush back into my lungs.

The laughter finally escapes, and when my children find me on my knees with my forehead pressed against the porch's cedar planks, shoulders shaking, they can be forgiven for thinking I've momentarily lost my mind.

The most difficult day we've spent without Mattias and Bernhard is a bleak procession of butchering and bloody cleanup, for though it would have seemed impossible to me a year ago, my family is not in a position to let any available meat go to waste. With the day drawing nearer to a merciful close, my children gaze back at me across the dinner table with expressions usually reserved for men who have survived particularly heinous wars. I am afraid that they understand the truth of things, though they won't speak that truth aloud. I was a fool for thinking my hard decisions would keep us all safe. I should have known that blood always wills out.

When the children are in their beds, I sit in a chair by the window, the rifle cold in my hands, and I watch as night erases the hills. I whisper a prayer for spring, for an end to the bloated February moon peeking through the clouds. For some kind of warmth. I'm tired of being cold, inside and out.

But we must all live with our decisions, whether they are right or wrong. I think of the Emerson child and wonder whether it would still be alive if I'd stayed in Europe. Certainly, there are others who would be. But Mattias believed our lives would improve with an ocean to separate us from that ancient forest. He made the decision to come here; he convinced me. And I'd been desperate enough to believe that our problems wouldn't follow us. Now his corpse lies alongside Bernhard's, and neither of them are here to make any more decisions.

Along the horizon, lanterns bob like boats on a black sea, likely Mr. Elder and his riding party making their rounds and alerting every man or animal within ten miles to their presence. I fall asleep in the chair in spite of myself, but a sudden hammering at my door throttles me awake and I can't stifle a yelp. Mr. Elder's voice is desperate as his fists strike wood again and again. "Open your door, Frau! I'm in mortal danger!"

My hand lingers on the crossbar, and a thin howl freezes me in place. It rides the night like a slow creeping fog and conjures my darkest memories. It's the sound Mattias made the first time he changed, and the sound of his death rattle. I have wondered for years if it might be the last sound I will ever hear. For a moment, I consider how the problem of the irksome Mr. Elder might solve itself if I simply take no action, but the howl draws closer and I haven't the heart to leave him outside.

I allow him in, and we bar the door behind us. His hat is gone, and a deep gash runs from the top of his head down one temple and across his cheek. Meat and blood reveal themselves as he speaks, and I'm not certain he understands how badly he's been injured.

"They're dead, Frau. My companions. All of them!"

"Comanche?" Even now I can't muster sympathy for him.

"No, a creature," he says. "A massive wolf."

"Wolves are not common here."

He does not recognize my mockery. His back is pressed against the door as if that will keep out the night.

Something slams against the outside of the door, and the howl transforms into a roar. Mr. Elder lurches forward as the door splinters down the middle. Peter and Gretchen emerge from the sleeping loft. Mr. Elder makes for the back window yelling for everyone to follow. It's shuttered against the cold, and he's trying to yank one shutter away in his terror instead of simply unlatching it. Peter and Gretchen eye him nervously like the wild animal he is. They understand what we are facing here, and I wish Mr. Elder had remained warm at home tonight. This man who would be my protector has led a monster to our doorstep.

The door is no match for such a creature, and the wolf is on top of Mr. Elder before he can lift a hand to defend himself. The creature is the size of a small cow, and the stench of it in the tiny cabin is as fearsome as its teeth. My gorge rises and I struggle to hold the rifle steady as it barks again and again, the lever ratcheting in my hand until the gun is empty.

Blood coats the thing's silver fur, and I can't tell whether I have wounded him or if the blood belongs to Mr. Elder. The wolf whips its head towards me, and I'm thankful I don't recognize its eyes. My children are screaming, and I swear I can hear more howls outside, growing louder, and while this lone wolf will almost certainly kill us all, I don't want to calculate our chances if he's brought a pack with him.

Now finished with Mr. Elder, the wolf lifts his ears, blood and saliva leaking from his open jaw. There are definitely howls coming from outside, and as I wrap my arms around my children and whisper a small prayer to my grandmother's god, a pair of flint-tipped arrows hiss through the open doorway and lodge themselves in the side of the wolf's neck. He yelps, then turns away from us and roars at his unseen attackers.

Two Comanche men step through the door, their faces painted black with red streaks on their foreheads and chins. Their buckskin shirts are beaded and bloody, and the first man screams and drives a feathered lance into the wolf's chest. The second launches a relentless attack with a hatchet, and the wolf wilts under the weight of every blow.

The monster is outmatched.

The first man wrenches loose his lance, and the wolf collapses atop Mr. Elder. What remains of his life spills out around us on the cabin floor. My children clutch me from behind, and I can feel their heartbeats against my back. They have heard of wolves transforming back into men, but they have never seen it happen until now.

There is a melting of the wolf's skin as it slides away and becomes liquid, and what remains is only a man, middle-aged, balding with gray at his temples, naked and still. He is no one I know. Just another unfortunate who encountered my husband in the wrong season. Someone else who can trace his doom back to a blood-ravaged cabin in the middle of an ancient German forest.

The Comanche men do not seem unnerved by what they've seen. Their chests heave with exertion, but they are otherwise still. I'm reminded of Mr. Elder's stories about Indian depredations— kidnappings, slayings, the taking of scalps—and I want to tell them that I never had any desire to leave my home. In my dreams my grandmother is alive, and my husband was never bitten by that thing in the woods, and we are all happy and warm in front of a fireplace with the comfortable smell of sauerkraut and the laughter of my three children filling the air. I don't want anything to do with this new land, and given the opportunity I would leave and never return. But I cannot speak their language and they cannot speak mine, so we stare at one another for what feels like an eternity.

Then, without a word, they leave, and I'm alone with the sound of my children's crying and Mr. Elder's moaning. We are all afraid to move, but I notice that one of the men left his hatchet lodged in the back of the dead man, and I can't stand to leave it there. I crawl over to him, pull it loose, and again I feel Mr. Elder's hand gripping my arm, not so tightly this time but just as unwelcomed.

"Frau," he says. "I require a doctor."

"No doctor," I say.

"Frau. Summon a doctor."

"You have been bitten," I say.

"Do you not understand me?" he asks.

"I understand everything."

"Please," he says.

"I'm sorry, Mr. Elder," I say, "but this is mercy."

I instruct my children to look away, then I strike him between the eyes with the hatchet, and ensure that he never again comes calling at my door during a full moon.

*

Spring finds us alive, my family and I, and that is as much as I can ask. Sunlight warms the morning as Peter and Gretchen race together through the knee-high grass, laughing and calling after one another, momentarily children again. This cannot last, but I am learning to find joy in small moments. I sweep dust away from the porch, the boards complaining beneath the weight of my steps, forever a reminder of my responsibilities.

Mattias and Bernhard are still buried together beneath those boards. There was a time when Mattias could control his rage, could recognize us in his wolf form and make the decision not to harm us, but that began to change. I will never forgive myself for what I had to do.

And yet.

The curse had to end.

But what terrifies me is this: Mattias was bitten by a wolf. Bernhard never was. When his adolescence arrived and he began to change on schedule with his father, there was only one reasonable explanation.

There is more than one way to share blood.

I killed them together so at least they are not alone.

And now I wish for childhoods that last forever. I'm terrified that Peter may have inherited more than his demeanor from his father, and that Gretchen may reach her womanhood and begin to change.

I will do what needs to be done.

But not today. Today is for sunshine.

Let them be children for just a bit longer.

RATTLESNAKE SONG

T*HE LAST PICTURE SHOW* CAME TO THE MOVIE HOUSE on the square in the fall of nineteen seventy-one. We snuck in with warm cans of Pearl and sat on the back row so we could take quick hits off our cigarettes and snub them out before anyone noticed the smoke. I fell in love with Cybill Shepherd and figured she could wind me up just like she did all the guys in Anarene. I recognized that small town that had been something once but was now engaged in a battle with time. Every sandstorm, every gust of West Texas wind stripped away another layer of paint and vitality. That dying town was our inheritance.

When the movie ended, we spilled out onto Front Street with our half-full beer cans stashed in our jackets. Dean Champion's dad had been a big hat over at the refinery in Big Spring before he hung himself, so Dean had sprung for the beer. We piled into his Chevelle and I was in the back seat, squashed tight against Stacy Bell's thigh. Once upon a time that prospect would have excited me, but that time had passed.

Dean hollered, "Pass it!" Jason or Holly or Gilbert had produced a pencil thin joint, and when it made the rounds to Stacy and she held it out to me, straining to keep the smoke in her lungs a few seconds longer, I waved her off. Things were strange enough without it. The Chevelle's tires squealed, caught the road, and we fled that nothing of a town square.

The night opened up and let us in. Half drunk, I pressed one cheek against the cold window and saw the stars collapsing down from the heavens. They looked streaky and smeared, like someone had gone at them with a washrag. I closed my eyes, felt the hum of the road, the jerk as the car found high gear. A mile or so on, Dean braked and cornered us onto a caliche road. Rocks rattled off the undercarriage. My brain latched on to the possibility of skidding off the road at this speed and flipping over into the empty cotton fields, then the rough scales on Stacy's fingers brushed mine and I found I really didn't care.

"Everyone out!" Dean again.

I hadn't realized the Chevelle had stopped moving.

The car ticked to a stop and we piled out. If there was a moon, it was afraid to shine in that place. Our feet sank into the soil as we trudged into the fields. Nothing remained of the harvest but dead, crunchy plant husks. Rattlesnakes prowled the rows. It was far too cold for snakes, but that sort of thing hardly mattered anymore.

Dean found a likely spot, dropped to his knees, and the others joined him, their hands already digging into the soil, turning it over like they were searching for arrowheads. Connecting with the blood of the place, I guess. Their forked tongues tasted the night. Hands in my pockets, I stood apart, unsteady and unsure why the rattlesnake song affected everyone else, gave them a purpose.

I stared up into the boiling sky. All around us snakes coiled and hissed and rattled, and my friends swayed in the blackness, doing their best to join the song. The wind tugged at my farm coat, iced the back of my neck. The desperate scent of Stacy's Woolworth perfume joined the smell of stale beer. I imagined too that I could smell the snakes, musty and corrupt, and the whole cocktail brought vomit to the back of my throat.

Dean grinned like a fanatic. His brother had grinned that way once, and now he was in the state hospital. His father too, and they'd found his body swinging from a beam in the garage. Some things were too hard to wrap your mind around.

I couldn't understand the attraction of staring into that terrifying sky, pondering the swirling stars and the coiling strands of colored light, not reds and greens but impossible, unimaginable colors. No human way to describe them without seeing them. But for those who could interpret the rattlesnake song it was a kind of worship. I tensed up when snakes slipped in and out of the circle, even though I knew they wouldn't hurt us. They weren't reptiles anymore; they were heralds of the gods.

After a time, Gilbert and Holly stood in unison, glassy-eyed and still swaying. Dean fished in the pockets of his letter jacket for his keys and Stacey grinned at me before jumping up and heading to the car. They called back half-hearted goodbyes as they got into the Chevelle, leaving me to trudge across the cotton field to my house.

I snuck through the front door, keeping quiet so I didn't wake my parents. Force of habit from the days when they used to care whether or not I was coming in past curfew. On the way to my room, I opened their bedroom door a crack. They were still alive. I could tell by the hissing and heaving of their snores.

We'd made it through another day without the world coming to an end.

A week later I went to see the movie again. I figured I might not have too many more chances to watch movies, so I'd better take advantage. The town was closing itself up.

The old men who liked to gather out front of the drug store with their dominoes and long-winded memories had retreated to their houses. Old women abandoned church socials, clotheslines, and ironing boards to embrace the winding down of their lives. The new reality was harder on the older people. They'd had a good long time to dig in their heels on the whole *God is Good* thing, only to be shown that the universe was terrible and unknowable.

Oh well.

The Dickensons, who owned the theater, had left the building unlocked and I knew how to run the projector from the summer I'd spent selling tickets and serving popcorn. As the film flickered to life on the screen, I dug my fingers into a bag of M&Ms and wondered if the Dickensons were still alive.

Duane was up on screen, hitting Sonny in the head with a bottle when Stacey sat down beside me. "I was looking for you."

"Here I am," I said.

"How many times have you seen this movie now?"

"A few."

"Lot of people having sex in this movie. Do you think everybody in this town is having that much fun?"

I was pretty sure nobody was having fun anymore.

"The movie's not really about sex," I said. "It's about wanting to be somewhere else than where you are and being stuck. They're all just having sex because they don't have anything better to do. They're bored."

"Doesn't sound like the worst reason why anyone ever had sex," she said.

"Why were you looking for me?" I asked.

"Wanted to see if you'd drive out to the fields with us again. It's almost dark. You want to come look at the stars? Maybe you'll hear the song?"

The last thing I wanted was another reminder of the new world order and how poorly I fit in. Stacy cupped the side of my face, gently pulled my gaze from the screen and positioned it on her. I managed not to flinch. Her scaled palm was scratchy and cool against my skin, and the change from who she'd been to whatever she was becoming had picked up speed.

"It's okay you haven't heard it yet," she said. "Don't worry, it'll happen."

I wanted to scream out how I hoped to Hell it never did happen, and how I thought maybe I'd rather die than become like Stacy and the rest of them. How I'd have preferred even to join the adults in their slow insanity and rot. But she held me in place with those blue eyes that I had daydreamed about since middle school. Her stare was heavy and uncomfortable, like she was trying to fanaticize me by force of will. I realized I was afraid of how she might react if she knew how badly I wanted to look away.

"You go ahead," I said. "Tell everybody I'll catch up with 'em later. I want to finish the movie. See if it ends the same way this time."

Stacy gave me a cold kiss on the forehead. "We'll say a prayer for you."

"Appreciate it."

I stared at the screen for another hour, but I wasn't really watching the movie anymore.

That evening, I put my ear against my parents' bedroom door. The house was quiet as a church. I remembered the tears streaking down their faces on that night when the stars changed, the way Mom had fallen to her knees like a load of laundry spilling out of the hamper, and the way the light had passed from Dad's eyes like our new gods had puckered up and blown it out. Maybe the adults were luckier than the rest of us. I thought about opening the door to make sure there was nothing I could do. Instead I loaded up everything I cared to take into the bed of Dad's pickup truck and moved myself into the lobby of the movie theater.

Within a month the rest of the adults in town were either dead or wandering the roads like children lost in a foreign country. A few of them might have left town, but I didn't know for sure. I hadn't seen anyone who wasn't local in a long time and I'd decided that the outside world knew instinctively to avoid us. The flip side of that coin was that I didn't think anyone of us was supposed to leave. I'd lived my whole life desperate to be anywhere else, but now I was stuck.

The second story of the movie house overlooked the town square: the turn of the century jailhouse that had been built to hold cattle thieves and rogue Indians, the dusty stretch of stores that hadn't been very lively even before their owners had abandoned them, and the art deco drugstore building that had developed a slight eastward lean over the years, as if it had grown tired of the constant wind and was preparing to give itself up to the world's fury. The town's lone stoplight blinked on and off forever at one corner, and the handful of old pecan trees had shed their leaves and become skeletal hands, fingers spread wide in an effort to hold up the falling sky.

A bonfire burned in the middle of Front Street, one of the only pieces of earth not swarming with rattlesnakes. My classmates strode across this sea of reptiles like Jesus on the water, assured in their new faith. The snakes themselves didn't seem to care. Dean kept gunning his Chevelle up the street and back again, 8-track blasting Black Sabbath, a couple of other kids laughing and whooping in the backseat, and the snakes would part to let him pass every time. Someone had discovered a stale keg of beer in a stalled-out delivery truck and the worshipers of our new gods had proceeded to get sloppy drunk. Gilbert and Holly both pounded on the movie theater doors and then called up to the window to invite me down, but I waved them off.

Jason and Stacy were coiled together in a kiss at the edge of the bonfire, and I felt a hot stab of jealousy in spite of myself. That could have been me for sure. But the sensation faded fast, driven off by the clamor of ten thousand rattlesnakes rising up from the blacktop like the sound of bacon frying in a skillet. That couldn't have been me. Not really. Would I have wanted it to be?

They hovered together in the crosshairs of my dad's old .208 rifle. I was pretty sure I didn't intend to shoot anyone, but having it there reminded me that the universe hadn't stolen all of my options.

Shooting them all before the world ended might be a mercy.

Problem was, I wasn't sure if they were the ones needing mercy, or if it was me.

I got in the habit of slinging that rifle over my shoulder whenever I left the theater. I had it with me one morning in the early hours, when all of my old friends had slunk back to their holes and the snakes had settled into an eerie silence. I picked out a snake that was coiled up on the step of the jailhouse and shot it in the head. The sound of the rifle rattled around the square for several seconds, but none of the snakes stirred.

The morning sun was still an hour away, and the colors in the sky still held sway. They were smeared from horizon to horizon like a kid's crayon drawing, and they felt so much closer than they'd been. Staring at those colors long enough, you could make out patterns. You could begin to see things that you didn't want to see. And yet once you stared long enough, it became hard to look away, like if you didn't keep an eye on the stars they would crash down and suffocate you.

I might have stared for two minutes or twenty, but I finally shook myself loose, lowered my head, and saw every rattlesnake in the square with its head up, staring right at me.

That was enough to put me in motion.

By the time the sun was up, I had Dad's truck loaded with my piss-poor collection of clothes and keepsakes, all the boxes of candy left in the theater, and a few dozen bottles of Dr. Pepper. The morning was cold, but the heater cranked right up when I started the truck. The rumble of the engine and the way the seat rattled beneath me reminded me of riding with Dad out to the feed store on the interstate when I was a kid. Country music on the tinny speaker. Dad smelling like sweat and soil. On Sundays I'd squash myself between my parents in the cab on our way to church, Mom with some sort of casserole dish in her lap and Dad with the window cracked to let out the cigarette smoke. Dad only ever went to church to make Mom happy, and I'd quit going with them a few years ago because basically I was an asshole and was only just figuring that out. I closed my eyes and tried to smell that casserole and the fresh, flowery scent of Mom's face powder.

Someone knocked on the truck window and I nearly pissed my pants.

I was pretty sure it was Dean. He wore his letter jacket, and a few patches of his blond hair remained. He used to wear it a little past his collar just to rile up his coaches, but now what remained of it clung in grass-like chunks to his scaled skull. The rest of him... well I couldn't have told him from any of the others. When he spoke, it was still his voice. Mostly.

"Where you going, man?"

I rolled down the window and the morning cold chased away my fortress of warm memories. Dean's tongue licked the air, but I'm pretty sure he was smiling. I resisted the urge to gun the gas pedal.

"I think I have to leave town," I said.

"Oh man, don't do that," he said.

"Dean, you know I don't belong here anymore."

"I wish you wouldn't leave." Something in his expression changed and best as I could tell, he looked genuinely sad. "I know you can't understand what the snakes are saying but it don't matter. This is your place, man. Where else would you go?"

I had no idea, but I knew I couldn't stay there any longer. It might have been my place once, but those days were long gone.

"How long before they get here?" I asked. "The new gods."

"Won't be long," he said. "Hard to say for sure but I figure a week or two. We can't change that, you know. Don't matter if you're here or out to California they're still coming. Better you stay here and we can vouch for you. You're one of us. They'll understand that."

"I don't think they will," I said.

Dean hissed. "We been friends since we were kids. Played Pony League together, you at second and me at shortstop. We worked our tails off last summer stringing that barbwire around old Jameson's cattle acreage. I vouched for you to your parents that night you got drunk at Holly's party and passed out in her back yard. Ain't we friends anymore?"

"Yes, we're friends," I said. "But I still got to go."

All that was kind and soulful suddenly leaked away from Dean's lidless eyes and I thought for a second he was going to yank open the truck door and stop me from leaving. He could have done it. He had me by at least twenty pounds. But instead he backed away and threw his hands up in mock surrender.

"Go then if you got to," he said. "But you got plenty of friends who at least deserve a goodbye."

Might be he was right. But I dreaded the prospect of reliving this same conversation with the others, and I was dead certain that Stacy would convince me to stay. I put the stuttering old truck into gear, steered it past the flower shop, and made the left turn onto the farm road that would eventually take me to the main highway.

My tires rumbled along the caliche road as I accelerated, and for the first time I gave some thought to where I was going. I'd strained against the boundaries of my hometown ever since I'd been old enough to walk. There were a whole lot of interesting places on television and in the movies, and almost all of them looked better than where I was from. But my parents weren't really vacation people. We rarely travelled farther than the next town over, and that was just because their grocery store served better cuts of meat than ours did. I'd only left Texas once. We'd driven out to the mountains in New Mexico when I was ten and I still held the cool pine-scented memories of that place with me through every miserable Texas summer. I still had a pinecone stashed somewhere at my parent's house. If our world had two weeks, give or take, before the new gods arrived, I could think of worse places to spend them than those mountains. Or maybe I could head to the border. Drink some beers on a Mexican beach or check out some of those jungle ruins I read about in one of Dad's adventure novels. It didn't really matter. The prospect of being somewhere other than the handful of dusty streets I'd walked my whole life was right there in front of me, and there was no longer any reason to stay.

When the pain came, it was sudden and bright, like getting stabbed with an icepick. My body recoiled and my knees caught the steering wheel, yanking it to the right. Before I could correct, the truck barreled off the road and into the bar ditch. One wheel caught a fence post and my head slammed against the roof of the cab as the truck rolled over twice and came to rest on its side, wedged in a nest of angry mesquite trees. Blood colored my vision and my shoulder screamed like it had gone out of joint. The rattlesnake was still latched on to my ankle, letting every drop of venom seep in. I made a halfhearted attempt to shake it loose, but I was caught tight. Frigid wind blasted in through the broken windshield and I could taste the soil in my teeth. My red vision faded to black and I could hear Dean's reptilian voice taunting me like a ghost.

This is your place, man.
Where else would you go?

I woke in an aluminum cattle trough in the middle of my parents' abandoned cotton field. The trough's brackish water had been emptied and replaced to the rim with rattlesnakes. The winter wind rushed freely across the plain, chewing away the last of the afternoon sun with icicle teeth, but I soaked in that cold reptile flesh like it was warm bathwater. The snakes kept completely still, even as I grasped the side of the trough and pushed up into a standing position. My left arm hung limp and a painful lump had settled over my ear, but I was alive.

My friends circled the trough, watching in silence with their unblinking eyes. That morning I would have screamed to wake up with them staring at me like that, but a surreal calm had taken hold and I realized what had changed. The rattlesnakes were singing, and I could hear their song.

Dean, Stacy, and the others swayed to the writhing, clattery rhythm, and when I stepped out of the trough and trudged away through the soil, one ankle swollen twice its normal size, they made no move to stop me. A couple of them started to follow but I waved them off.

"Where are you going?" asked Stacy.

"Don't worry. I'm not leaving. This is my place."

Back in my movie theater perch, I studied the town square through my riflescope. Another sundown meant another round of hell-raising, children without parents singing for the end of the world. Thing was, now I could hear the song too, and I knew none of them really understood the lyrics.

My ankle burned like someone was holding a lighter to it, but the swelling had started to go down. That bite might have killed me under normal circumstances, but it was clear the snakes had a use for me. Fever burned up the back of my neck and I fell asleep there in the chair by the theater window, wondering if I was going to have to kill all my friends sometime soon.

I dreamed of stars and snakes, coiling and cold and reaching. They lashed around the Earth, plucking it neatly from orbit and giving it a rough squeeze. Snakes beyond count, but lording over them all a giant reptilian face with supernova eyes. I realized that all those snakes were actually tentacles growing from that face. Our new gods were really just one great hungry god, and when he arrived, we wouldn't die, we'd never have existed at all. The world screamed in the thing's grip and the voices sounded like my friends, my mom and dad, like Jacy and Duane and all the other flickering black and white denizens of small-town Texas. The god squeezed harder and I could feel the breath leaving my lungs in a rush. Then it whispered its name to me, and I woke up screaming and choking on the floor of the movie theater.

Through the window I could hear the voices of all those snakes with wonderful clarity, and I understood their intentions. They didn't want the world to end any more than I did. The rattlesnake song was a plea for help. The rituals they'd taught my friends weren't meant to summon a god; they were intended to keep us hidden, to cast a shadow over the world so that those horrible burning eyes couldn't see us. Dean and Stacey and all the rest thought they were bringing on the end of the world, but their rituals were actually the only things keeping their dark god at arm's length.

They were acolytes, wearing the skins of their god. But I'd been chosen the rattlesnake's prophet, and I wasn't ready for that god to walk our Earth just yet.

I leaned my rifle in the corner, walked downstairs and joined my friends in a circle, our fingers twined together, our hands raised up, and we danced, spinning and writhing and lifting up our voices in prayer. Time began to wind more slowly around us, and the roof of creation shuddered overheard, but did not collapse. Angry colors spilled from one horizon to another like rivulets from an overturned paint can, but we continued to dance, and laugh, and celebrate what remained of our youth.

The movie never gets old.

Most nights we take our seats in the old movie house and settle in for the death of Sam the Lion for the countless time. We hate Jacy and we love her, and we root for Sonny to make better choices.

Gray threads crept into my hair long years ago and I have more in common with Sam the Lion these days than I do with all those celluloid teenagers and their desperate need to break away from their small lives. I'm okay here. It's my place. And besides, where else would I go?

The others are like my children now, and I feel their pain acutely. They are acolytes in full, with little remaining of the people they used to be, and they ache for the coming of their god. If they knew the ways I work against them, they'd kill me for sure, but I quietly resist and swallow the guilt of all the misery I'm causing them. The movie seems to be the only thing that brings them calm, so we gather together in the dark and we watch.

The movie plays every night, the refrigerators stay full of ice-cold Dr. Pepper, and the popcorn is always hot and buttery. I don't know if my rituals have frozen us in time or if the rattlesnakes have found a way to provide for us, but our tired town continues to lumber on, desperate to die but unable to rest just yet. Sometimes I wonder what's happening in the rest of the world, but it's a useless daydream. This place is our reality. These are our routines. Wanting more is just a shortcut to unhappiness.

When the movie ends, my children drift back to their warm holes and hovels, and I pull a blanket over me and sleep there in the theater seat. I dream about burning universes, about small towns full of dead teenagers, and of course the angry colors in the sky. They're always with me, asleep or awake, and they're hungry for this place.

Every morning when I wake, I look out the window to make sure the world is still there, and I give thanks. One night, I know, I'll go to sleep and never wake up.

I'm terrified of what'll happen to all of us then.

IN THE THICKET, WITH WOLVES

M AGGIE NEVER CONSIDERED HERSELF DESPERATE ENOUGH to barter with the thicket wolves. But that was before the word *complications* took on a whole new meaning in her life. Before the doctor explained that her child was going to be *different*. Maggie hadn't been out of high school that long; she remembered how *different* kids were treated. And it wouldn't stop there. Even well-meaning folks couldn't help but sneak a quick look in the supermarket or whisper something in their friend's ear about "that poor thing." She'd done it herself. And they'd tell their kids to hush, to quit pointing. He's not bad, just *different*.

"Down syndrome is a disorder that includes a combination of birth defects." The doctor's voice was without inflection, a practiced tone that made him sound like he was reading from a medical journal. "The child will experience some degree of mental retardation. Altered facial features. Heart defects. Increased chance for infections. Problems with vision and hearing. The severity of these conditions varies, but he'll most likely live well into adulthood."

The doctor continued speaking but Maggie tuned him out. It didn't matter what he was saying; it all translated into the same thing. Her baby would never have a normal life. They'd already told her it was going to be a boy, and she'd chosen a name. Bailey—her Maw Maw's maiden name. A gift to the only person in her family who hadn't disowned her. At night, Maggie would lie in bed and let Bailey's future play out in her mind. Bailey chasing a soccer

ball around a muddy field, stealing it from a bigger kid and scor-
ing the winning goal; building balsawood airplanes with a studied
expression on his face, like her brother Alan before he discovered
girls were more fun than model airplanes; graduating valedictorian;
bringing home a feisty redheaded girl that kind of reminded Maggie of herself; the first step toward engagement, marriage, children,
happiness.

And now there was a chance none of it would happen.

The doctor droned on. Maggie's heart rate quickened, and a
roaring sound filled her head like waves crashing against the inside
of her skull. Somewhere in the middle of the doctor's monologue,
the word *abortion* fell from his tongue like a rotten bit of meat that
he hadn't wanted to continue chewing. Maggie seized on the possibility.

It would be best for Bailey, wouldn't it? Why condemn him to
a life without *life*? And Maggie couldn't lie to herself; it would be
better for *her*. It's not like a twenty-year-old who works the counter
at the Dairy Queen was in a position to raise a special needs child.
She'd have to quit, probably have to live off the state. Just like everyone said would happen when she told them she was pregnant.
Her mind conjured a nightmare image of herself, drooling baby
under one arm, counting out pennies and food stamps in the supermarket line while her mother waited behind her, screaming, "Told
you what happens to little sluts who spread their legs for greasy
boys who change tires for a living? Can't believe you gave that
thing a family name."

Then she thought about those private home movies of Bailey
that played in her head and she knew that she wouldn't be able to
erase that little boy from the film. Even if it *was* for the best.

"You don't have to decide today," the doctor said, sliding the
tissue box across the surface of his desk. "But you'll need to choose
a course of action soon."

Maggie pulled a tissue from the box and dabbed her eyes. "I'm
gonna keep him."

The doctor nodded; an empty gesture that neither supported nor condemned her decision. He laced his fingers together, like her father always had before delivering one of his lectures about the kind of girl she was supposed to be. Maggie heard everything she needed to and didn't care to sit in the doctor's office for another second of his college-bought wisdom.

Maggie slid back her chair and stood. "Thanks for your help," she said, although she couldn't think of a single thing he'd done to help.

"The hospital has people you can talk to about this."

"I'm fine. Really. I'm gonna have the baby." Maggie rushed for the door, desperate to leave. She made it all the way to the parking lot before vomiting.

Maggie didn't make a conscious decision to seek out the wolves, but some part of her knew what she was doing when she drove past the Dairy Queen and kept going until Silsbee was nothing but a blinking traffic light in the rearview mirror.

Towering pine trees rose around her car like two halves of a parted ocean. It always surprised her how quickly civilization gave way to the strangling forests of East Texas. The region was called The Big Thicket, and it was the kind of place that unwary hikers could wander into and never make it out of. An endless array of pine and cypress carved up by slinky, snake-infested rivers and blackwater swampland, alive with raccoons, toads, the occasional alligator.

And, of course, wolves.

Most of the people she'd heard tell stories about the thicket wolves were backwoods sorts, unafraid to stretch the truth if their own acclaim might grow in the telling. But her Maw Maw believed in them too, and no force under Heaven could compel that woman to lie. Maggie knew that's who she was headed to see; where else did she have to go?

Seven miles out from Silsbee, Maggie slowed her old Pontiac and turned onto a rocky dirt road barely visible from the highway. She drove up to a locked cattle gate, stopped the car and drew back the rusted length of chain that held the gate closed. From there it was a short jaunt up Maw Maw's muddy driveway.

Her home was a two-bedroom cabin, nothing but whitewashed wood beneath a clapboard roof. The screen door swung open and Maw Maw stepped out onto the porch. She had the thin body of a woman raised on moderation. Her blouse was plain white cotton, and the tail hung out over a pair of faded jeans.

"Get over here, girl," she said, welcoming Maggie with a smile and wide-open arms. "Didn't expect to see you this weekend. You're working, ain't you?"

Maggie crossed to the porch and accepted her grandmother's hug. What little misery she'd managed to hold at bay came loose in a flood of tears, and she buried her head in Maw Maw's shoulder. The old woman was a rock, absorbing Maggie's pain in silence until her sobs quieted.

"C'mon, honey," she said. "Let's go inside and have a talk."

Held in the cool shadows of Maw Maw's house, Maggie could close her eyes and pretend she was a child again, back in the days when she and her parents still lived here. Daddy was gone most of the time to work the oil rigs out of Beaumont; Maggie and her mother would help Maw Maw bottle her elixirs to be sold at one of the regional flea markets or farmers' trade days. The comfortable cabin smelled of pinecones and jasmine, dandelions and honey-combs, all the earthy ingredients Maw Maw used to ply her trade. Maggie remembered the taste of fresh peaches in summer, and the sound of laughter.

Now the scents remained, but the room was clogged with an uncomfortable silence. Maggie loved her grandmother's home, but it hadn't been the same since her mother had found religion and moved the family into town. Angry voices still haunted the cabin. Maggie's mother, demanding that Maw Maw stop selling her devil potions, calling her a sinner, a witch. It was nonsense, but her mother's new way of life had no place for herbal medicines and spiritual healing. Maggie still hated her mother for moving them away.

"So what's your plan?" Maw Maw refilled Maggie's glass with steaming tea, a homemade mixture that that was slowly taking the edge off her tension. She took a seat opposite Maggie at the kitchen table and poured another cup for herself.

"I don't know. I haven't had a chance to think much about it yet."

"Well, you know you and the baby are always welcome here. Be glad to have you."

"I know. I appreciate that."

"Guess you still haven't heard from Glen?"

Maggie shook her head. And she wouldn't be hearing from Glen; she was sure of that. He'd already had one foot out the door when the home pregnancy test came back positive, and the official stamp of approval from Dr. Garza made up his mind. He'd always talked about moving to Florida to work on his uncle's orange plantation. Maggie figured that's where he went, but she wasn't about to go looking for him. Glen was a mistake she didn't intend to make twice.

"Well, the baby's condition won't make life any easier, but you're a strong young woman. Don't always make the best choices, but I've never seen one your age that did."

"I'm not sure I'm up to it."

"Well, you better *get* sure. Ain't got much choice."

"Well, I do. Sorta."

Maw Maw's face tightened. "I guess you're right. But I suggest you think on it a while. And if you decide to do it, at least come to me for one of my powders. I can't stand the thought of some doctor doing it his way. That's barbaric."

"Maw Maw! That's not what I'm talking about. I'm keeping Bailey."

Some of the well-being flowed back into Maw Maw's features. "I think that's a good decision."

"What I'm talking about is fixing what's wrong with him."

"Honey, none of my medicines will help. And you said the doctor can't do nothing."

"I'm not talking about the doctor. I'm talking about the thicket wolves."

Maw Maw sat her teacup on the table and leaned forward. Maggie wasn't sure how her grandmother would react, but she hadn't expected the woman's cold stare or the naked disappointment in her voice. "I thought you were smarter than that."

"What else am I supposed to do?"

"You're supposed to love that baby for what he is."

"I don't know if I can. Jesus God, I just want him to be normal." Maggie cried, feeling like an idiot dressed in her Dairy Queen outfit, pinning all her hopes on some ridiculous folk legend. Why did she even think calling on the wolves would work? Maw Maw took her hand, and Maggie cried harder when she realized that the most important person in her life wasn't ready to abandon her yet.

"Don't matter if that baby has two heads. When you see him with a mother's eyes, he'll be the most wonderful thing in the world."

Maggie shook her head, drying her eyes on her shirtsleeve. "You don't know that. I can't have a baby like this, Maw Maw."

"Well, you ain't going to them wolves! Damn it, girl, ain't you paid attention your whole life? You've seen what happens to folks who ask the wolves for favors."

"Yes I have. They get what they ask for. Johnny Dale Adams got a brand new bass boat one time."

"Uh huh. And Johnny Dale caught cancer and died a year later. Then Norma, then little Dodie. The whole family."

"How do you know that has anything to do with the wolves?"

"How do you know it don't?" Maw Maw squeezed Maggie's hand tighter, and tears welled in her eyes. "You think this is some silly wishing game that's gonna solve all your problems. Well, it ain't. The wolves are real, and they'll give you what you want. But there's a price. Sometimes it ain't much, but sometimes it's your whole life. Either way you ain't gonna want to pay it."

"I don't think—"

"Hush! Listen to me now. My grandma used to always have a way with the earth. Medicines. Powders. And I wanted to be just like her. Problem was, mine didn't always work that well."

"What do you mean? They work great."

"They do now. Thanks to the wolves. Some folks complained that my medicines weren't working like I promised, and I couldn't figure out what I was doing wrong with the mixtures. I swore I'd never go to them wolves, but I got desperate and I did anyway. Now I'm better at this than my grandma ever was. But them wolves had the last laugh."

"What did they do?" Maggie saw a new woman sitting across the table from her. Not the wise, self-sufficient woman who'd endured the death of her young husband and raised three children off the land, but a frightened old woman who'd made mistakes and would likely do so again. Maw Maw was human, and that scared Maggie to death.

"They gave your mama religion. A couple of weeks after I called the wolves, this preacher knocked on the door and that was the end of that. She never took to anything like she did that Bible."

"You think it was the wolves that sent that preacher."

"Yes, I do. Not even sure if he was a preacher. Might have been the devil himself, but it all washes out the same either way. I got my wish and I lost everything I loved. Your mama moved you to town and she ain't visited since."

"But how do you know that was the wolves' fault?"

"I know! You may be old enough to get knocked up, but you're not old enough to know everything that goes on in the world. You want to ruin your life, then go right ahead. But don't act like I'm some crazy old woman looking to blame something else for her problems."

Maggie yanked her hands from Maw Maw's grip and drew back from the table. Maw Maw had never been so harsh with her, and she lashed out. "I'm not the idiot you think I am, and I have enough people in this world judging me. I don't need another."

"I hope you didn't come here for my approval, 'cause you're not getting it."

"I don't want your approval," Maggie lied. "Just tell me how to call the wolves and I'll leave you alone. I'm not going to let my baby get kicked around by the world. I'm going to the wolves one way or another. You can help me, or I can figure it out myself, but it's going to happen."

Maw Maw stood and started clearing the dishes, snatching Maggie's half-full cup of tea away before she could take another drink. "Damned if you aren't as willful as I was at your age."

"I understand there's a price. But it'll be worth it for Bailey to have a normal life."

"I'm not going to try and force you to see my side of this. That's your mama's way. You do what you're going to do."

"So you'll tell me how?"

Maw Maw nodded. "If you're set on doing this, you at least need to do it the right way. You don't respect the ritual, and them wolves won't bother with granting wishes. They'll just kill you."

Maggie followed a whispering creek into the thicket. Pine needles pricked her bare feet, while underbrush and fallen maple leaves swished against her ankles. If she followed the creek far enough it would feed into the Neches River. Follow the Neches to the Gulf of Mexico and she'd come to the oil rigs she'd always hated for stealing her daddy away. But she didn't plan on going that far. Just a mile or so from Maw Maw's house and she'd be at the glade her grandmother had described.

She'd traded in her Dairy Queen outfit for one of Maw Maw's sundresses, a knee-length covering of thin green cotton with lace straps. She hadn't wanted to change clothes, and she definitely hadn't wanted to leave her shoes behind. But Maw Maw insisted that calling the wolves demanded some degree of ritual, so Maggie had complied.

Now she was thankful she had. The dress fell just below her knees and caught the scant few breaths of cool air the night exhaled. Summer nights in East Texas never really cooled off, but the sticky heat of the day became a touch more manageable. The breeze tickled her shoulders, found its way into the dress' folds and covered her in chilly kisses. The delightful touch reminded her momentarily of Glen, but she banished the thought. The good memories of that man weren't worth remembering.

Once Maggie decided to go through with it, she didn't want to wait. Maw Maw said the wolves only came out at night. Maggie figured if she didn't just get it over with, her grandmother might find a way to talk her out of it. And if that happened, Bailey would never have the life she wanted for him.

Maggie picked her way through the trees, kept company by countless croaking frogs and the ubiquitous drone of insect life. At length, the creek curled sharply to the south, and after following it a few hundred feet, Maggie stepped into the wolves' glen.

It was every bit as spooky as she'd imagined it. A boggy clearing, bound by cypress trees, many of which dropped gnarled roots into the gurgling creek. Cacti and wilted orchids grew from the forest loam, and the tight knot of trees surrounding the place swallowed every hint of breeze. A snake loosened itself from one of the cypress trees and parted the creek's surface like a scalpel. Normally, that would have sent Maggie scattering, but her fear of snakes seemed silly when weighed against what she was about to do.

Following Maw Maw's ritual, Maggie lifted the sundress and slid it over her head. She crossed her arms over her breasts. The glade might be in the middle of nowhere, but standing naked in the woods was still enough to make Maggie feel self-conscious. Civilization wasn't that far away. Maggie wasn't supermodel skinny, but she wasn't overweight either, and her stomach showed not even the humble beginnings of pregnancy. One hand dropped to her belly and she rested it there, as if drawing strength from the life inside.

This night was crazy, embarrassing, terrifying.

But none of that mattered.

Maggie found a comfortable spot and lay on the ground. Back to the earth, head to the creek, just as Maw Maw had indicated. The ground was remarkably comfortable, a natural bed of leaves and vines that felt not only cool, but sensual. She sank into the forest's embrace, momentarily forgetting the threat of alligators, water moccasins, and hikers out for a midnight stroll. Instead she reveled in the wild abandon of the place, stretching her arms and feeling the blessed breeze return for a quick trip across her body. This was a magical place; she could feel it. Like the earth's spirit, emanating from the soil and dashing her worries.

Then she heard the whispers.

At first it might have been the voice of the forest, a symphony of insect wings, crackling pinecones and the crowing of nightbirds. But these disparate sounds came together to form a single voice; the kind a shadow might have if given the ability to speak.

Sweet Maggie.

She nearly lost her nerve. Only her grandmother's warnings about what the wolves would do if she decided to run kept her from doing so. *Once they get your scent, there's no turning back. You either go through with it, or someone will find your chewed carcass floating in the Neches.* So, Maggie bit back a scream and resisted the urge to bolt. The peace she'd felt moments before fled. The trees loomed like prison bars, and the leaves beneath her back felt like tiny mouths nipping at her flesh. She remained as still as possible, praying the voice would go away.

What a glorious creature. A second voice, from somewhere to her right.

Such a wanton thing to lay naked in the forest.

Such a tasty lump of meat.

Are you with us, brother?

And a third voice answered, this one so thick with menace that tears formed in Maggie's eyes.

I am indeed. Shall we take a closer look? Maybe a small taste?

Maybe a large taste.

They crept into the glen, three massive wolves the color of midnight clouds, moving on silent paws like pieces of night detached from the sky. One ran its sandpaper tongue across her forehead while another rested its head across her torso. Maggie whimpered, as the reality of the situation hit her. The wolves weren't just folk tales, and she had no idea what they intended to do to her. The third wolf sniffed at her feet, then moved its nose up her legs until it reached her thighs. It sniffed again then raised its head, lips pulled back from its teeth in what appeared to be a terrible attempt to smile.

This one's with child.

Maggie's panicked. Would these things try and take Bailey? What the hell was she doing here? The wolf sniffed again, and she wanted to speak up, to let them know they couldn't take the baby. His life was the only reason she came here. But Maw Maw had been very clear on this point. She had to lie perfectly still without speaking until asked a question. The wolf near her head licked her neck, her ear, her face, as if trying to determine the tastiest part. The others congregated near her stomach, sniffing, prodding.

A child? Is he big enough to eat?

Not yet, but given time.

What a pity.

We could always take him now, eat him later.

Yes! When he's got some fat.

The wolf at Maggie's head growled and the others fell silent. It stood over Maggie's head, watching her with impassive eyes. *Why do you lay here in the woods?*

It was Maggie's cue to speak, and she repeated the ritual response she'd rehearsed with Maw Maw, her voice clipped with terror. "I offer myself to the gods of the glen. Your humble servant seeks a boon."

And what price will you pay for this boon?

"Anything the gods demand."

And you do so willingly?

"I do."

Very well. Name your boon.

"I'm pregnant. And the doctor says the baby has problems. I just want him to come out normal. Healthy."

Ah! Can't very well eat the child now. How she teases us.

Dangles a choice bit of meat then yanks it away.

Cruel woman.

The wolf at Maggie's head, which she assumed to be the leader, growled again. *Your boon is granted.*

Maggie wasn't sure what to expect, but there was no tingly sensation of magic at work, no sudden feeling of well-being emanating from her belly. Just the binding finality of the wolf's words, and the dark anticipation of what would come next.

Goodbye, Maggie.

Teaser.

Two of the wolves bounded from the glen, disappearing into the thicket, silent as shadows. Their leader remained. It circled Maggie several times, as if considering what sort of payment a healthy baby demanded. Surely it wouldn't kill her? If it did, she couldn't give birth to Bailey, and that would violate their agreement. Wouldn't it? But it could do other things. Cripple her. Give her a disease like Johnny Dale Adams. Gnaw out her eyes so she could never see Bailey's smile. A litany of horrors raced through her mind as the wolf continued to pace. At last it came to a stop, rested its head against her chest, listening to her speeding heart.

My brothers are shortsighted. They think only of flesh and blood. Morsels of meat. But I understand the value of subtle gifts. Less tangible to the eye, to be sure. But worth far more than muscle and bone.

Maggie felt no pain when the wolf pressed its teeth into her sternum, slowly driving them deeper. Despite that, she wanted more than ever to abandon the madness of the situation. But she feared breaking the ritual more than the wolf's price. Its teeth sank deeper, but the expected rush of blood never came. The wolf might as well have bitten into a wax likeness. When his voice came again, it was in her head, a violation of her inner thoughts.

Goodbye, Maggie. Give my love to Bailey.

Maggie tried to scream, but the world turned black when the wolf's teeth found her heart.

Maggie sat in Maw Maw's old rocking chair and allowed Bailey to feed from her breast. He was an eager eater, a healthy, happy ball of perfection that had never suffered so much as a cold in his first year on Earth.

Taking care of a child, even a normal one, turned out to be much more difficult than Maggie expected. Childcare was expensive, and when added to the cost of diapers and the suddenly unaffordable rent on her apartment, she'd had little choice but to quit her job and move in with Maw Maw. But there was no wonderful nostalgia left in the cabin. Maggie felt nothing there but a pressing sense of guilt. Maw Maw spent most days gathering plants for her medicines, or occupying herself with other outdoor activities, and Maggie was thankful. She liked to think of her Maw Maw as the laughing, loving grandmother she'd always admired, not the dour old woman who chastised her with unspoken disapproval. The one who lived in horror of what her granddaughter had become.

Bailey pulled away, giggling and satisfied, eyes brimming with life. Maggie's breast bore scars from the thicket wolf's teeth;

smooth, fleshy lumps that formed a perfect impression of its mouth around her heart. A constant reminder of what had been taken from her. Bailey kicked his legs, wanting to play, but she put him in his playpen. Maggie had no interest in the child. She realized she should be happy, overwhelmed with love and delighted at the simple miracles of childhood. But she felt nothing when Bailey attempted to say her name, smiled for the first time, popped out his first tooth.

She wanted to love him. But she had none left.

Maggie took a seat at the table. She lit a lavender-scented candle to chase away the stench of sour milk and desperation. Bailey bounced around the playpen, every laugh mocking her miserable state. Maggie sat in the growing darkness, considering the ruin her life had become, and she wondered for the first time, what kind of boon the gods of the glen would give her for such a tasty morsel of meat.

For a happy, healthy, baby boy.

CIGARETTE LIGHTER
LOVE SONG

BEFORE THIS PLACE BECOMES A BOWLING ALLEY, A ROCK AND roll dive, a karaoke bar, a Tex-Mex joint, before this place becomes the spot where the only girl I'll ever love escapes the world, this place is a roller rink, a hangout for middle school kids mostly too afraid to do more than hold hands as they take another unsteady spin together, maybe sneak a kiss in the wash of red, blue, green strobe lights. Maybe not. I'm really not sure anymore. The roller rink is where I desperately want to be. I know that much. But this place has a whirlwind nature and I often find myself sucked in by the music and the lights and taken to other whens that aren't nearly as great as this one.

No. This is the roller rink. This is 1985. I can tell because I can hear Ms. Pac Man chewing her way through another mouthful of dots and that song "Mickey" is playing on the too-loud sound system, that song I secretly love but claim to hate when all of my friends start to rag on it. Same way I claim to hate girls. Used to be I hated them for real but something in me has changed. It will change for my friends too, but they still haven't caught the bug. Lucky them. Or maybe they have caught it and want to keep their secrets just like I do.

I can't say for sure.

What I know is that on this day, in this place, I fall in love.

Her name is Melissa.

The thing is, I never had a chance. I couldn't have resisted her even if I'd known that at age twelve she was already beginning to curl up into herself. A tumbleweed in the making.

Ready to pull loose and blow away.

God damn it.

See, this is how it happens. I'm in that place I want to be, then suddenly it's twenty years later and Melissa is telling me what a son of a bitch I am and why did I have to screw the whole thing up just as she'd finally got the fucking spell right?

Maybe because I don't want her to go.

That sounds right.

This is not a roller rink anymore but a karaoke bar that only takes up half the building. The other half is a nail salon. A haircut place. Something. Doesn't matter, this is the good half, the half with the juice. The half with Melissa's escape route.

"I had it," she says. "I fucking had it!"

"It wasn't going to work," I say.

"Yes it was! It was right there. I saw it! You ruined the whole thing."

Some tone-deaf fool is trying to belt out a Nickelback song and I'm half drunk. I'm not in the mood to fight.

"It wasn't going to work," I say. "You don't know that."

"I do know! Why did you do that?"

"You can try again."

"Yeah, in ten years!"

"In ten years."

I'm pretty sure the building was a grocery store to begin with, but it's 1975 and someone's converted it into a disco. The white lines on the bar are cocaine. My two-year-old self has no clue, but my grown-up brain seems to be along for the ride and there's no mistaking the stuff. Melissa's stepdad has chopped it into nice neat rows with a business card from his car detailing business. He has one cowboy boot hitched up on the barstool. He keeps rubbing at his nose with the sleeve of his silk shirt. He's young but his hair has already left him, so he wears a cowboy hat.

Melissa's mom is beautiful. Just like her daughter will be. The daughter is straddling her mother's knee. Mother takes daughter's chin gently in her fingers and turns her gaze away from the drugs. Does that even make a difference?

Two-year-old Melissa looks right into my eyes then. She recognizes me from her future. That much I can tell.

I'm not even here. I mean to say, I *wasn't* even here. Somehow, I am now. Thank Melissa's spell, I guess. Doesn't matter. She sees me and she knows.

"What are you doing?" asks Melissa's mother. Her name is Joan.

Bradley, the soon-to-be-deceased stepdad spares her a weary look before snorting one of the lines.

"Do you want to go to jail?" asks Joan.

Melissa keeps right on staring at me.

"Fuck you," Bradley says. "No one cares."

"I care. There's a baby here. You should care about that much at least."

"She's not mine."

"You're right about that," says Joan.

The music is so loud and pulsing—I never learn to love disco, not even ironically—that I can't make out exactly what they say to one another next. Joan's wrist is draped in bracelets that slip down her forearm as she pulls Melissa tighter to her. Protective. Or what passes for protective in this time and place. What few lights that break the gloom are erratic, flashing. They splash off the obligatory disco ball in a nauseating wash of colors. I'm sitting on the floor, looking up at all this. The floor sticks to my ass, my palms. The music is so loud it's holding me in place. And Melissa won't look away. She knows where this is going. She won't break our connection because she doesn't want me to be alone with this. That's how much she loves me.

"I'm leaving," says Joan. "Tonight."

"The fuck you mean you're leaving?"

"Just what I said. I don't want to be married to you anymore and I'm going away. Tonight."

"You're not going anywhere." Bradley is grinning. All but sweating blood. "Where would you go?"

"A long way from here," says Joan.

She's holding a pistol now. Under the table so Bradley doesn't know she has it.

It's a good time maybe to press my palms to my ears, to close my eyes. But Melissa won't look away.

The noise of it all is deafening.

Not long after that, Joan takes the short cut out of there. Alone.

They passed a smoking ban earlier in the decade so there's no smoke to cover up the stench of alcohol and sweat in this crowded section of the karaoke bar. This is the first decade of the two thousands, or whatever people call them. This a few minutes before I fuck up Melissa's spell. Accidentally on purpose. This is before she gets seriously pissed at me.

She's lying to me one last time. Tellin   g me we're leaving together. I know this is bullshit. The reality is she's leaving me and she doesn't want to admit it.

"Where do you think we'll end up?" she asks.

"I think the question is, *when* do you think we'll end up." I'm playing along. I'm nothing if not a good sport.

"She always liked movies set during the war. Old black and white stuff. I think that's where we'll find her."

"Using the ten year rule, that would mean 1945. Summer. So, the war will be pretty much finished. Should be a good time to be alive."

The karaoke in this place is torture. Modern country. Classic metal. Top forty screeches. Songs an octave higher than anyone in this bar can sing. Why the hell would anyone think they could get drunk and actually sing Journey?

"You're sure we won't be . . . what? Unborn? Not in existence." I ask this like I really believe I'll be going.

"Yeah, I'm sure. I've got it worked out. The other times I screwed up, but I didn't know as much about it as I do now. It's hard because I've been picking at my memory, trying to remember things my mother said and did before she left. But I was just a baby, you know? I've talked to some friends of hers. I think maybe I have all the pieces now. You know, for a long time I was afraid she'd died, or maybe wound up somewhere worse than the place she was running from. But I don't think that's what happened. I think she just messed something up."

"And you're sure it's possible for both of us to go?"

"Yeah." She looks away, sips a cocktail through a narrow straw. "We're going this time."

I've heard this before. Every ten years a portal opens in this place. Probably been happening since before this building was even built. Before anyone lived in this country for all I know. It's about ley lines and the season and the fucking orientation of Jupiter for all I know, but it happens. With the right spell—that's what Melissa calls it, like she's a witch or something—you can step into this portal and travel forward, backward, ten years, twenty, thirty. You get the picture.

The way it's supposed to work is, you actually go there. Body and soul. But based on all the memories I have right now that I shouldn't, and the fact that these brief moments spaced ten years apart are the only times I can even remember from my life anymore, I don't think that's always how this works.

I've asked Melissa to give this more thought, to be careful, but she doesn't want to hear it. Her mother went *somewhere*, right?

"Hold my hand while I say the words." Melissa has positioned a few knickknacks on one of the rickety bar tables, just so. A candle, a bell. A paperback with the cover ripped off. This is the right spot, and this is the right time. I hold her hand and she closes her eyes. She pumps my hand twice; a covert goodbye. Then she starts to mumble. I've known Melissa in so many times, for so much of my life, but this is the perfect age for her. Early thirties with her hair still long down her back. Brown, streaked with barely perceptible strands of blond that will become falls of gray by the time we're here again in ten years. She'll still be beautiful, but right now she's perfect.

She still loves me now. In this moment.

No matter, though. She's still leaving.

The room heats up around me and she opens her eyes. Something over my shoulder and just beyond this reality reflects back at me from her widening stare. It's shimmering, beautiful, like an eruption of stardust.

That's when I pretend to slip from my chair. Too much beer maybe. That's when I accidentally on purpose manage to sweep all the elements of her spell from the table and onto the floor.

There will be another chance. In ten years.

The roller rink is the key here.

That night has none of the anger or heartbreak or sadness that our other moments have, and only a hint of the melancholy.

I hate skating. I'm only here because a couple of my friends twisted my arm and now they're off skating, playing air hockey, shooting pool. I'm not in the mood. Even the first time I lived this I must have known what was going to happen this night. I'm dressed for the occasion, I guess. Good jeans to protect my ass when I fall. Scuffed rental skates. Lime green polo with the collar down. Not quite a match for all the guys with their collars up, a couple of rolls in their short sleeves, all of them crowding around the Defender machine as if their lives depend on saving one more evacuee from the planet's surface. They're effortlessly cool and I can't compete with that.

So, I'm surprised, the first time, when Melissa finds me haunting a chair in the back corner of the arcade and asks me if I want to skate.

I can't skate worth a shit. But what am I supposed to do, tell her no?

She only makes fun of me a little when she sees how unsteady I am. Still, she doesn't leave me behind. I don't know what it is to be drunk yet but that's how I feel amid the music and lights, skating next to Melissa from history class, Melissa whom I'm pretty sure used to live down the street from my grandparents. Melissa who maybe I met when we were babies, but I don't quite remember it? I've seen her in town all my life but now suddenly we are skating. Together. In front of everyone, including all of my friends who are not quite ready to admit that girls are actually pretty wonderful.

And I don't care.

"I know this is weird," she says, skating backwards in front of me. I'm doing my best to stay on my feet. "Me asking you to skate."

"It's not weird."

"Yeah, it kind of is," she says. "But here's the thing. I'm leaving tonight. For good. And I've always kind of felt like we should be friends. So, this is my last chance, I guess. I didn't want to let it go without telling you."

"You're leaving?"

On the rink, under the disco ball stranded here from another era, together in front of everyone. That's supposed to make her my girlfriend or something, right? But she's leaving?

She grabs both of my hands, spins us around, then puts an arm around my back to catch me as I almost go skidding.

"I'm going to find my mom."

"Where's your mom? Don't you live with your dad or something?"

"Yes. That's why I'm going to find my mom."

I don't ask.

"I think I know how to find her," she says. She pulls me to the side of the rink, and in her infinite mercy, plops me down onto a chair. We sit together and I have to wait for her to speak because I'm not sure I even can.

"Can I tell you a secret?" she asks.

"Sure."

"My mom killed my stepdad right here where we're sitting."

"Yeah, I remember that," I say. But that's impossible. I can't remember something I wasn't there to witness. No way I said that the first time. Every other time, maybe.

"I'm serious," she says. "She killed him and then she left. Through a portal. To another time."

"Okay."

I remember. I think. I definitely remember how loud it was.

"You don't have to believe me," she says. "I don't even expect you to. It's just this. I'm leaving forever and I want to leave something of myself behind. My story, maybe? I don't want everyone to forget me, and I want at least one person to know that I wasn't kidnapped. In case I end up on a milk carton or something?"

"No one will forget you."

"They might."

"Why are you leaving?" I ask.

"I told you, I'm going to find my mom. I'm going through that portal when it opens up. I don't think she meant to leave me here. Something just got screwed up. And I'm not living with my real Dad anymore. He's . . . pretty bad."

"How bad?"

"Drug dealer beat you with a belt bad," she says. "There's a reason Mom left him when I was a baby. Though from what I hear, my stepdad wasn't much of a catch either."

"God, I'm sorry."

"Don't be sorry," she says. "Just skate with me."

It's hours yet until the portal opens, and those hours are the finest of my life. Pretty sad, I know, but when you're stuck in these small moments like I am, you latch on to good memories a little harder. You're reluctant to let them go. We spend those hours like we'll never have more. Like a summer camp romance in fast forward, cramming all the hand holding and laughing and secret sharing and covert kisses into that short slip of time because we know it's all we have and pretty soon the real world is going to ruin it all.

And so, it does. But not quite yet.

"Do you ever wish you'd have made it through the portal when we were kids?"

"Of course not," Melissa says. "We wouldn't have had enough time together to become *us*."

We're screaming because now the building has become a rock and roll bar and some shitty local band has finally discovered grunge a few years late and they're doing their best to chase everyone out of the room with a wall of guitar fuzz.

And that's okay because we're young and music doesn't have to be good to take hold and shake you around the room. These could be our last minutes in this place and we're making the most of them.

From what I can gather, we've been inseparable for the last ten years. I wish I could remember some of it. Melissa working overtime to figure out how to make sure she didn't screw things up this time around. Me holding on for the ride. I don't really know, but it sounds good.

The band slows down, remembers it's a bar band and dusts off a slow hair metal ballad. A cigarette lighter love song. And we know them all. About half of the forty or so people in the room lift lighters in response. Melissa and I do too. Grinning and singing along now. It's what people do.

Our hands grip—unbreakable. Afraid one of us might get sucked into the portal without the other one. In this moment we can't live without one another. In other moments things are different.

Right now, this song is about us. All of these songs are about us.

I have no idea where we're going to end up and what kind of songs they'll be singing there.

Melissa knows the words to the song. To the spell.

We see the portal explode to life near the entrance to the bathroom, exactly where we expect it to be. We are aware. No one else is hip to what's happening and so they don't perceive the change in temperature, the jarring, jagged colors stabbing into the darkness and erasing the stage lights.

After repeatedly living through this night and all the others, I've pinpointed this moment as the zenith of our relationship. The last second that Melissa loves me as much as I love her and the last night she truly plans to take me with her.

We stand together at the portal, waiting for it to let us in. A sea of cigarette lighter flames flicker as the portal exhales.

Melissa knows all the words to the spell now.

But words aren't enough.

Two thousand fifteen is the last time I see Melissa, as far as I know. I mean, apart from the numberless times I've repeated all the earlier moments.

"Why are you here?"

Melissa looks tired, and that gray hair I mentioned is in full bloom. She's not surprised to see me though we haven't spoken in years. I knew she'd be right here, right now. Our place, as I think of it now, has become a restaurant, though one in a rapid state of decline. A bad Tex-Mex joint that's one health inspector shy of turning this place into an empty building. We're picking at the chips and salsa, sipping iced tea from red plastic glasses as we wait for the portal to appear.

"I'm here to see you." The truth is, I don't know why I'm here. That's the best answer I have.

"I don't want you screwing this up for me," she says. "Not again."

I put my hands up in mock surrender. "I'm not here to get in your way. I'm just here to tell you I'm sorry for last time. And I'm sorry for . . . whatever."

"Don't tell me you're sorry!" Melissa says. "You don't even know what you're apologizing for."

She's right. I don't know what happens, what happened, outside these moments. Not anymore. But I know she's leaving for real this time.

"You're not going with me," she says as if stating it for the record.

"I know that now." Pretty sure I've always known that. "I just wanted to tell you goodbye."

Melissa shakes her head. "No, you just thought maybe you could talk me out of it or stop me somehow. And I'm not going to let you! We've spent most of our lives circling this same problem and you still don't understand it. You still don't understand *me*."

Melissa is wrong about that. I understand her completely. But I'm just starting to learn about myself.

"I've always been straight with you," she says. "I want to find my mom."

"You want to leave this world," I say.

"Yes! I want to leave this world. Is that too much to fucking ask?" A plate of onion-drenched enchiladas cools uneaten on her plate and a thirty-year-old top forty hit that we both used to love plays softly through the restaurant's sound system. The air conditioning spins a dusty piñata overhead. It hangs from the exact spot where there used to be a disco ball. Melissa is crying now and we're starting to draw attention.

"It's not too much to ask," I say in a low voice. "Let's not get kicked out of here, okay? I don't want you to miss your chance this time. Seriously."

She studies me for a few seconds, nods and wipes her eyes with a paper napkin. "I'm sorry. I've just had enough of all this."

Enough of me too.

But it's not about me and I finally realize that.

Melissa gets her wish. She knows all the right words now. She doesn't need any knickknacks to focus on. She has nothing holding her back.

I watch her pass through the portal alone.

And I think I'm ready to let her go, that I've matured to the point where I can move on and let her have this.

But I'm so fucking wrong.

There is still one more scene in my life, one more moment I'm allowed to experience. I view it by the light of a cigarette lighter for reasons of nostalgia. Memories are all I have, after all, and few enough of those. The building is nothing now. Boarded up and darkened with age. Animals scurry in the shadows. Bits of trash and broken glass shift underfoot as I cross to the exact spot where I know the portal will be.

I wait in the gloom with my flickering lighter, the near absence of everything my penance.

It seems I still won't let her go.

I've figured this whole thing out now. Melissa learned long ago, I suspect, that you can't take someone with you through the portal. You can only pass that way if you're meant too, but that didn't stop me from trying my hardest to hitch a ride. That's why I've broken loose from the natural order of things.

I can't even remember our life together.

These moments, these nights of the portal, they're all I have anymore.

I've figured something else out too. I don't think Melissa's mom wanted her along. She was running, after all. Just like her daughter would be. She had to have known. But Melissa didn't want to believe that, any more than I wanted to believe Melissa would leave me. And our fumbling attempts to hold back the ones we love somehow broke this magic.

That's what I think happened, at least. I don't know.

Somewhere Melissa and I are skating together amid a riot of kids with disco ball lights causing the room to spin. Somewhere we're singing together at the top of our lungs. But here it's just me, alone with my fleeting butane lighter and not enough memories to warm me.

When the portal opens, Melissa could be standing there, hand out to pull me in and take me with her. We had a life together, whether I remember it or not. And that's got to count for something.

Still, I don't really expect her to come. She never does. But it's possible. Every time it's possible.

And in some time, some place, I can't help but believe she still loves me.

ALL MY PRETTY CHICKENS

H AROLD WASN'T ONE OF THOSE PEOPLE WHO PRAYED TO THE chickens, but he would use them as sounding boards from time to time, and he did so on the morning his only granddaughter was scheduled to leave for Mars.

"Supposed to take six months to get there," Harold said.

They flocked around him, silent and flickering. Harold stood at the kitchen counter, waiting for his coffee to brew. He watched the chickens pass through his kitchen table legs, the corners of his cabinets, his ankles, oblivious to their surroundings. Even the hazelnut aroma of the coffee couldn't chase away the faint barnyard stench of straw and shit that always accompanied them.

"Give or take a week or two, so they say," said Harold. "Guess it depends on how many passengers and how much stuff they're carrying with them."

One of the birds, a fat red rooster with a spray of black feathers on one side, picked at non-existent bits of food and scratched one foot against the linoleum.

"What I'm thinking is, when Isabelle goes to Mars, she's not likely to come back, no matter what she says. Certainly not to live here again. Probably not even to visit."

Harold cut up some strawberries and a banana for his breakfast. When the coffee was finished, he poured a cup and took a seat at the table. The chickens paid him no mind.

"Truth be told I find the fact that you can just buy a one-way ticket to Mars a little bit hard to fathom."

He hated the fact that he was talking to the chickens. Probably a sign of some sort of looming dementia. But there were few people on Earth he cared to talk to anymore. And soon to be one fewer. After eating, he put his cup, plate and knife in the dishwasher, and plucked his car keys from the hook by the front door. Isabelle had to arrive at the launch port by noon, and Harold was her ride.

"I really don't want her to go," he said.

The chickens didn't offer any opinions.

Where were you the day the chickens came back? It was an icebreaker question that almost everyone had an answer for. What were you doing on that morning years ago when all of our world's dead chickens began appearing, one by one, in spectral form?

Harold had an answer that always kicked anyone else's answer in the ass.

"I was in a hospital lobby, waiting for my daughter to die."

Isabelle's hand was cold in his. Sticky with blood that he should have helped her clean off but there was so much of it and the day had accelerated into a blur so quickly that Harold's mind hadn't entirely caught up with events.

He couldn't remember if it was the hospital or the police who called him, or even how he got there, but Isabelle had been waiting with a nurse, amazingly unharmed by the car accident that had killed her father instantly and put her mother in emergency surgery.

Together they sat, the pale, slack ten-year-old girl and her suddenly broken grandfather. His son-in-law, Derek, a young man Harold had always liked for the way he treated his daughter, was dead. Beyond saving. Harold's daughter, whom he and his deceased wife had named Angie after their favorite Rolling Stones song, was undergoing surgery to repair damage to her brain. Harold was no doctor, but the prognosis did not sound promising.

Isabelle had not yet spoken to Harold or anyone else. She pressed her head against his shoulder, taking slow, shallow breaths. She wore her soccer uniform, but one shoe had been lost somewhere along the way.

Hours passed. Then Isabelle's chin darted up and Harold followed her gaze. Someone had let a chicken loose in the hospital and it had sauntered around the corner into the waiting room.

A few more followed, and other families in the waiting room began to notice. The chickens looked . . . insubstantial? The day had levied too high a tax on Harold's sanity, and he could almost swear they were transparent.

It was then, when orderlies began gathering to shoo the chickens away, when the sitcom that had been seeping quietly from the ceiling-mounted television had been interrupted by a news bulletin describing the appearance of chickens all over the country, when Isabelle stood, lopsided in her one shoe to reach out and pet one of the chickens, that the surgeon materialized at Harold's side, took him a few steps away from the chaos and informed him that his thirty-six year old daughter was dead.

That night, Harold had tucked Isabelle into the lower bunk bed in his spare bedroom, the one she always used when she came over for her weekend visits. The one, he supposed, that would now be her permanent bed.

His heart had not stopped racing, even with the anxiety pills the doctor had given him. He'd imagined they might dull his grief, but they had only muddied it. The grief was still there, looming and hostile, one hand gently around his throat so that he felt any second he might begin to suffocate. Certainly, others had lived through this sort of emotional trauma, but Harold saw no way of getting to the other side of it. He did his best to suppress it around

Isabelle, to pretend everything would be fine when she woke up. It was a terrible lie, but necessary.

Isabelle had eventually cried for a bit at the hospital, but had since settled back into the same state of serene shock that had greeted Harold earlier in the day. This terrified him more than if she'd been outright hysterical.

"Do you need anything?" he asked. "Some more water?"

She shook her head, covers up over her chin.

"Should I leave the nightlight on?"

"Yes, please."

He turned off the lamp, leaving only the warm glow of the Winnie the Pooh nightlight to spill across the bed. He looked back at her before leaving the room and she was smiling. The smile unsettled him, and he considered that it might be a hallucination, a product of his meds.

"Isabelle, are you okay?"

"Do you remember those chickens today?" she asked.

"Yes, sweetie."

The chickens. One of the biggest events of their lifetime, one that conjured up hundreds of questions about life, death, religion, the universe, and yet it seemed so insignificant. Harold couldn't muster up the energy to care.

"Were they dead?" she asked.

"I don't know for sure," said Harold. "I don't think anybody knows for sure yet."

"But you could see through them," said Isabelle. "Like they were ghosts. I tried to touch one and my hand went through it."

"Did it tickle?" Harold was thankful that Isabelle had something other then her dead parents to occupy her thoughts. He would open up the front door and let a barnyard full of chickens stroll in to entertain her if it helped her through this situation.

"No, Grampy. It didn't tickle. It just felt like nothing. I think they're ghost chickens. I hope that's what they are."

Harold kind of hoped they were too, and he realized that he

and his granddaughter had reached the same desperate conclusion. If God or whoever had sent back a bunch of dead chickens, then maybe the dead they were mourning might be next in line.

By the time Isabelle graduated from high school, she'd cut loose any notion of every seeing her parents again.

The chickens were so numerous by then that many people simply chose to ignore them. They were part of the scenery, like other cars passing by on the highway or songs playing quietly in the background at a restaurant. Others formed religions, became militant vegetarians, spent every waking hour probing the mystery. None of them gained much from their efforts.

Isabelle, like many, had grown to resent the chickens and everything they represented.

Harold, though, remained fascinated.

Hopeful.

As much as Harold wanted to be late, maybe to cause Isabelle to miss her launch, he was right on time. She stuffed two large duffels containing everything she was taking with her, everything worth keeping, told her roommate goodbye and then she and Harold were edging into the forever traffic of Houston, working their way around the loop toward Intercontinental Airport and the launch site extension they'd built there a few years back.

Isabelle was in high spirits for someone who was leaving her entire life behind, and Harold did his best not to spoil her mood. She had the radio tuned to a station playing a bunch of okay sounding rock and roll that he didn't recognize. At least it had guitars.

"Glad you picked me up early," said Isabelle. "It's like everyone's headed to the airport at the same time."

"You're supposed to be there two hours ahead of time for a

launch," said Harold. "That's what it says on the web site. We'll get you there on time."

"I never doubted you." Isabelle grinned at him. Twenty-three, fresh out of college, with a job for a multinational (multi-plane-tary?) technology company that did things with computers that Harold hadn't bothered to understand. Isabelle had explained it to him once, but the programming jargon had baffled him. The one thing he took away from the conversation was that she could have had a similar job in Houston, but she was taking the job on Mars. She said it would be an adventure, a good opportunity. And maybe it was. But Harold believed he understood her motives for leaving better than Isabelle did herself.

"I expect calls every day," he said. "Or at least once a week."

"Of course," she said. "But it's not technically a call. There's sort of a delay. Kind of like voice texting I guess."

"Whatever, don't forget to check in. A lot."

"It's not like I'm going forever."

But that was exactly what it was like. Harold knew it in his bones. Isabelle had been trying to pull away from her life for years, and once she got free, she'd never come back.

Harold's expression soured and Isabelle sensed his mood change before he could catch himself.

"I know what you're thinking but please don't start."

"Don't start what?" he asked. "I'm just driving."

"I'm going, Grampy. You're not going to change my mind, okay?"

Blood rose into Harold's face. He was so weary of this argu-ment. It was a lost cause and he hadn't wanted to resume it. This couldn't be the last memory of their life together. But Isabelle gave him the same headstrong look that had frustrated him when she was a child, and would forever frustrate him. The look of a kid who knows better than you do. And in the moment, he just couldn't let it go without one more volley.

"I've told you I'm happy for you," he said. "I'm not trying to stop you anymore. I'm resigned to the fact you're moving to Mars, okay? I just don't think you're going for the right reasons."

"I'm going because I've been offered a job," she said. "A good job."

"You're running away," he said.

"So what?"

"So, running away from problems isn't something you're supposed to do," said Harold. "It's not what you were raised to do."

"Yeah? Well all I know is there are no chickens on Mars. And that makes it a better place to be than here."

"Why does that matter?" asked Harold.

"God, you know why it matters."

And he did. Harold understood completely, whether he liked admitting it to himself or not.

"Nobody is ever coming back," said Isabelle. "And I'm fine with that."

"We don't really know," said Harold.

"Yes, we do."

"We can't be certain," said Harold.

Isabelle leaned her head against his shoulder, like she always had as a child. She was kind enough to cut the argument short, to make something better of their last hour together on Earth. To leave Harold his rickety hopes.

And he loved her all the more for it.

At the launch port, Harold dropped Isabelle off near the curb. They exchanged a hurried hug and more promises to stay close, despite the distance. There wasn't time for a proper goodbye, not with the line of cars behind them and the stiff security that disallowed non-travelers into the building. One second she was Harold's granddaughter, his only family, close to him in the car. And then she was a grown up, off on an adventure, no longer in need of a chaperone. It was possible that's what pained Harold most about the whole situation. Isabelle did not act like a little girl running away from her past. She was an excited young woman with her sights set on her best possible future.

Harold watched her for a second in the rearview, clutching her bags amid a crowd of travelers, all studiously ignoring the chickens passing through them, no more substantial than sunlight. He would not stay to watch the launch from the viewing lot. Couldn't stand the thought of hearing the blast of rocket engines, or watching as the launch craft blazed toward space, disappeared beyond the atmosphere. He watched Isabelle scroll her phone screen for her ticket, turn toward the bag check, and then she was gone from view.

Back on the loop, headed home, Harold was not surprised to notice a chicken in the passenger seat beside him. It sat still, barely bobbing its head, as if seated on some invisible nest. The chicken turned its eyes to Harold and blinked.

He realized he was crying, wiped the tears away with his sleeve. It seemed impossible that Isabelle was gone forever.

The chicken rode with him, all the way home, never turning its gaze from Harold. When they arrived, the chicken followed him inside and joined all the others that had flocked to his kitchen. They were as oblivious to his presence as ever, but the chicken from the car seemed aware of Harold's pain. It watched as he readied himself for bed, and slept near his feet in silence as Harold endured his first night alone on Earth.

His dreams were of Isabelle at the launch pad, coming home this time, Harold and Angie and Derek all there to greet her with tears and kisses.

And surrounding them, stretched out to the horizon in every direction, a foaming sea of silent chickens.

CAN'T BUY ME
FADED LOVE

Excerpt from The New York Times, *December 9, 1980*

L ENNON WAS RETURNING HOME FROM A RECORDING SES-
. . . sion when he was shot five times in the shoulder and
chest in front of his Central Park West apartment. Alleged gunman,
Mark David Chapman, when asked if he knew what he'd done, re-
portedly replied, "I just shot John Lennon." Chapman made no effort to avoid arrest, but instead sat on the sidewalk reading a book
until the police arrived.

Fans and admirers continue to flock to the site of yesterday's
shooting, many erecting makeshift monuments and singing "All
You Need is Love," one of the last songs Lennon recorded with
his former band, The Quarrymen, before breaking ties with long-
time collaborator Bob Wills. Janet Lumley, who was in attendance
when the Quarrymen made their now famous appearance at Shea
Stadium, flew in from Boston to pay her respects.

"This is horrible. That he could be murdered like that. How are
you supposed to deal with something like this? The world has lost
the greatest country songwriter of the past thirty years."

Excerpt from Can't Buy Me Faded Love—The Unauthorized Legend of The Quarrymen, *Ernest and Shultz, 1989*

There can be little doubt that the most important pairing of musicians in the twentieth century occurred in Austin, Texas on a hot July evening in 1961. Having traveled to America less than six months earlier from his home in Liverpool, England, a young man with "too-long" hair and a slick new Telecaster reached out and seized his destiny.

"I heard about the Playboys going on tour that summer and I had to be there," said Lennon in a 1978 interview with biographer Lon Haines. "Much of Bob's original success came before I was born, but I was a fan. More than a fan, really. That music was my life when I was a lad. My aunt used to play those 78's all the time, all the old Western Swing bands, but especially the Playboys. I never knew my father, but I remember listening to those songs and wondering if he might have gone to America to become a singer. Maybe Bob Wills was my dad, you know? I was a kid then. I reckoned Bob was the singer since the band was named after him. Later on, I understood that it was his fiddle playing that really inspired me. It made me sad. It made me long for something. A father, maybe, but something else too. I wanted to be in America, and I wanted to make that kind of music."

Lennon quit his job in the Liverpool shipyards and informed his then band mates that he was leaving for the United States as soon as he could book passage on a ship.

"Don't remember where the name came from," said Lennon, "but we called our band The Beatles. We played some swing, some skiffle, and that was popular at the time, but mostly we played rock and roll. It was the hot thing and all the lads, especially Paul and Stu, were big Elvis and Little Richard fans. I liked the music too, but I reckoned it was a fad. Swing was king, and it was primed for a comeback. Needless to say, we didn't see eye to eye. I invited them all to come along with me, but they took it as a personal slight that I would consider leaving. I was gone a week later, and I never heard from any of them again."

Bob Wills recounted that first meeting with the twenty-one year old Lennon in a 1972 interview with *Life* magazine. "He was the scrawniest thing I ever saw. Looked like he hadn't eaten in a week. He'd been following us from town to town, hanging out at the shows with his guitar, always sitting right at the edge of the dance floor. Staring like he was studying up on us or something. The only reason I noticed him was that long hair of his. That was before it caught on, of course. He was crazy as a loon for going around wearing long hair and a leather jacket in the type of bars we was playing. But he didn't know no better.

"So that night in Austin, he gets there while the boys are setting up and begs me to let him sit in on a few songs. Tells me he came all the way from England to join my band. I laughed and thanked him for being such a fan, but there wasn't no way I'd let a stranger up on stage with us. Then he pulls out that blonde Telecaster of his—and I guarantee by the look of him he must have bought that damn thing with the last pennies in his pocket—and he starts them fingers dancing on the strings. Aw, lord! You know what that sounded like. I never heard anyone play like John, before or since.

"Still, I didn't invite him on stage until near the end of the set. I'm not sure why I even did it, but I did. I still remember the look in that kid's eyes when he stepped up there in his pointy shoes and beat up jeans. Everyone loves him now, but I'll testify the people in that bar didn't know what to make of a longhair taking the stage with us. Until he plugged in that guitar and we kicked into "Take Me Back to Tulsa." He changed a lot of minds that night. Mine included."

Postcard from Bob Wills to Al Stricklin, July 13, 1962

Al,

Howdy from Austin! We still plan on being there the twenty-first. Always love coming back to Fort Worth. I'm bringing this kid with me that plays guitar like nobody you ever seen. He's a character, come all the way over from England. Wait till you hear him!

See you soon,
Bob

Excerpt from an interview with Al Stricklin, Honky Tonk Keys, *December, 1979*

"I was back running a Saturday night country broadcast then, this time for WBAP, and it suited me fine. I remembered my days touring with Bob fondly, but being on the road all the time takes it out of you. I was glad to have Bob back in the studio, though, and interested to hear this new guitar prodigy he'd been bragging on.

"First time I saw John he was wearing a new felt cowboy hat. Trying to be like Bob, I guess. But he looked out of place. The kid had more rock and roll in him than he cared to admit. He was a humble guy, helped everyone set up for the show, even helped set up the drums.

"We went live and I chatted on-air with Bob a bit, then the band kicked in with the Texas Playboy Theme. When John's solo came up, my jaw hit the ground. Bob was right, the kid could play. I was sitting in with the band for old time's sake, and I swear that kid playing like that inspired me. I pounded the keys that night like I hadn't in years. I ain't lying when I tell you right then I knew John Lennon was something special. Bob knew it too. You could see it in his eyes."

Letter from John Lennon to his Aunt Mimi, 15 August, 1962

Auntie,

I'm in Texas! Sorry it's been a while since I wrote, but I think you'll be proud of me. I know how you are about the music of Mr. Bob Wills and so it might surprise you to learn I've been playing guitar in his band! Last month we played on Mr. Al Stricklin's country radio programme and he even let me play some of my songs for him. Remember "Love Me Do?" You said you liked that one. Well, so did Mr. Stricklin, and he suggested to Mr. Wills that he record it. Mr. Wills has agreed to cut a 45. If it sells, he says maybe we can do some more. Wouldn't that be fab?

                                    With love from me to you,
                                    John

Capital Records Press Release, September 29, 1962

Straight from the Heart of Texas comes the debut LP from The Quarrymen, the hopping new band led by Western Swing legend Bob Wills. Building on the success of their hit single, "Love Me Do," the *Meet The Quarrymen* LP features the future chart topper, "Please Please Me," and a revitalized take on Bob's country classic, "Faded Love."

Excerpt from Can't Buy Me Faded Love—The Unauthorized Legend of The Quarrymen, *Ernest and Shultz, 1989*

Looking back, it doesn't seem surprising that those early records found so much success. The world was in love with rock and roll and western swing, and working the two together could only be a recipe for success. But Bob Wills, and more importantly his record company, weren't sure what type of reception these new songs would receive when they hit the record shops. In order to head off any permanent damage to the reputation of Wills' primary band, The Texas Playboys, the label suggested the album be released under a different name. Thus, The Quarrymen were born, and in this initial phase of their existence, the group was marketed as a Bob Wills side project. No mention was made of John's songwriting contributions in the album notes for the first two records, although history has corrected this oversight.

The first two albums, *Meet The Quarrymen* and *Quarrymen For Sale* were modest sellers in the United States and in England, with the single, "She Loves You," enjoying a brief stay on the Billboard Top 20 singles chart. But this moderate success wasn't yet enough to prove the concept to Capitol's record executives. By the end of 1963, a handful of new singles had been released and mostly ignored by the public, and it is unlikely The Quarrymen would have released another album if Bob hadn't pulled the strings to get them the gig that would change the face of music forever.

The Quarrymen played The Ed Sullivan show for the first time on February 9, 1964. Prior to that iconic performance, they were a band at the crossroads and John was a brilliant but unknown songwriter and collaborator, content to live in the shadow of his legendary mentor. But that night changed everything. The Quarrymen became the world's most famous musical group overnight.

And John Lennon became a superstar.

Excerpt from Lennon: Honky Tonk Hero, *Lon Haines, 1982*

It was during this rapid onset of stardom that John began to rely heavily on the experience of his better-known collaborator. Although Wills had never enjoyed this level of stardom—indeed, Quarrymania was unlike anything *anyone* had ever experienced— he had enjoyed a great deal of success earlier in his career and understood the responsibility that strolled hand in hand with fame.

Rather than wilt beneath the weight of public expectations, John took all the support and counsel Bob had to offer.

John credits Wills with "pulling me up by my bootstraps and setting me on the forward path." This perspective allowed John to devote himself to the music, and this is the time when the Quarrymen's two songwriters really began to connect. It is also the time when John began seeing Bob as a sort of surrogate parent, a replacement for and perfect embodiment of the father ideal that he had never known. Despite his subsequent protests in his declining years, it is widely corroborated by band members and personal friends that Wills shared this bond, and treated John as a son. This closeness no doubt contributed to the musical magic, but it made their subsequent sparring more difficult for both.

Letter to John Lennon from his Aunt Mimi, August 29, 1964

John,

I was pleased to learn in your recent letter that Mr. Wills has been such a positive influence in your life. Your Uncle and I had occasion to watch your movie. How odd to see your face on such a large scale! What a joy it must be for a boy your age to be besieged by the girls. I only ask that you remember your upbringing and look to Mr. Wills for guidance in matters of propriety. We are proud of you, John! Let us know when we can see you again on the telly.

All my love,
Mimi

Excerpt from an interview with Al Stricklin, Honky Tonk Keys, *December 1979*

"John started smoking pot around the time that *Hard Day's Night* was released. I'm not here to point fingers—half the band at that time was doing the same thing. In fact, I think it was Dylan, the harmonica guy, that got him into all that. There was a lot of stress in the air at that time. We put out three records in sixty-four and sixty-five: *Hard Day's Night, Help!,* and *Western Soul.* Add the never-ending tour and two movies, and it all piles up on you quick. John was the biggest music star in the world. Everyone wanted a piece of him. Nobody knows what that kind of fame will do to them until they get it. Some guys in the band hit the bottle, others turned to drugs. The number one rule was, don't tell Bob. He was a drinker, but everyone knew he wouldn't have any of that other stuff in his outfit. So, when he found out about John, I was amazed he didn't break up the Quarrymen then and there.

"But, you know, Bob felt like that kid was his son. John's dad left when he was very young, and he'd really latched onto Bob by then. Bob was his idol, his friend, and a replacement Daddy. Bob felt the same way. So, when word got out John was into drugs, he took it upon himself to fix the kid. It was going to take more than pot to put a wedge between them two. Yeah, that wedge ended up there, but it took a long while to work itself into place.

"And, you know, the drugs might have started that—Bob got a little more bent out of shape when John moved on to acid. But the whole Jesus thing is what really set the ball rolling downhill."

Excerpt from a John Lennon's interview in the London Evening Standard, *March 4, 1966*

"I don't know what will go first—rock, country or Christianity. We're more popular than Jesus now."

Excerpt from John Lennon's press conference, August 11, 1966

REPORTER: "Some teenagers have repeated your statements— 'I like the Quarrymen more than Jesus Christ.' What do you think about that?"

LENNON: ". . . I'm not saying that we're better or greater, or comparing us with Jesus Christ as a person or God as a thing or whatever it is. I just said what I said, and it was wrong. Or it was taken wrong. And now it's all this."

REPORTER: "But are you prepared to apologize?"

LENNON: "I wasn't saying whatever they're saying I was saying. I'm sorry I said it really. I never meant it to be a lousy anti-religious thing. I apologize if that will make you happy."

Excerpt from Can't Buy Me Faded Love—The Unauthorized Legend of The Quarrymen, *Ernest and Shultz, 1989*

The lion's share of books and articles written about the Quarrymen in the years since the deaths of Wills and Lennon paint Wills as an "old-fashioned" fuddy-duddy who wasn't hip enough to keep up with his partner's immersion in sixties counterculture. This was hardly the case.

Bob understood the importance of the music they were making, and although John steered the musical direction beginning with the *Colt Revolver* LP, Bob was more than willing to follow his lead. He did not agree with many of John's lifestyle choices—in particular, his experimentation with LSD—but he was quite happy to reap the benefits of those influences. Bob's subsequent love affair with the sitar can be directly attributed to John's study of eastern religions and his time spent under the tutelage of Hindustani musician, Ravi Shankar. And John's descriptions of the aural phenomena he experienced while under the influence of LSD caused Bob to experiment with his fiddle style, ultimately resulting in a new direction in his musicianship, and his still haunting psychedelic fiddle leads on the *Sheriff Emery's Honky Tonk Dive Bar Band* LP.

The fact that Bob continued to embrace these influences in his music after the Quarrymen called it quits in nineteen-seventy is evidence that his interest was genuine. Yet Bob could never reconcile the end with the means. The Quarrymen's recording sessions from sixty-six onward were fraught with strife and electric with tension between the group's two geniuses. It's widely held that this conflict is responsible for the stunning, timeless quality of the recordings produced in this period. John's cynicism about the Vietnam War and the government, amplified by his drug use and declining interest in traditional western swing stood in direct conflict with Bob's more conservative views, and his fear that the music he loved was being replaced by the new genre he'd created. Each of them viewed the Quarrymen as a tool to advance his own agenda, a signpost to direct the masses toward the future of popular music.

It was this collision of wills that created the magic.

Excerpt from an interview with Al Stricklin, Honky Tonk Keys, *December 1979*

"A lot of people have opinions on why the band broke up. But I don't have to guess. It wasn't because John started dating that woman. The drugs and John's lifestyle played a part, I suppose, but the real reason Bob and John stopped getting along was that John lost his love for western music. He started playing his guitar through Marshalls, adding all that distortion that was gaining popularity. It was like rock and roll had been living in his soul all along and now it was clawing to get out. That didn't sit too well with Bob, and it got to where they could barely be in the same room together. Bob would come in every morning and record his parts with the band, then John would lay down his tracks at night. He was into experimentation by then and Bob would come in the next morning and tape over a lot of what John had recorded the night before. So, John would up the ante the next night and the result was *The White Album*. I don't think the two of them spent more than ten minutes in the same room while that one was being recorded.

"The strange thing is, even though John was abandoning his honky tonk roots, there were a whole mess of bands trying to capture that sound he and Bob had made famous. Rock bands like The Byrds and even the Rolling Stones were scrambling to add fiddle parts and lap steel guitars to all their recordings. Bob took it as a compliment, but John resented the whole sixties counter-country movement he'd spawned. He was tired of the whole thing before it even kicked into gear. A whole lot of that resentment comes out on the last few records, especially *Let Me Be*. Bob didn't even want that one released, but John demanded it. He hired Spector to produce it on his own and it hit the stores a full six months after Bob called the Quarrymen quits.

"It says a lot that there ain't one single fiddle part on that record."

Excerpt from Lennon: Honky Tonk Hero, *Lon Haines, 1982*

Lennon recalled the dissolution of the Quarrymen and his subsequent feud with Wills with bitter regret. "I was too full of myself, wasn't I? Sometimes I wonder what we could have done with a few more years together. I listen to where guys like Gram Parsons and Clarence White took our music, and I wish now I'd kept pushing the genre. But I wasn't one for listening to criticism and it was easier to throw up my hands and be done with the whole thing.

"But the worst thing is I lost that time with Bob. I spent three years resenting him, and it was like fighting with your father, you know? Maybe some part of you knows he's right but you're too stubborn to admit it. I wish there was some way I could yank the *Imagine* album off the shelves. When I wrote 'How do you Sleep,' it was obviously a direct stab at Bob and all his lectures on how I was screwing up my life and killing the music I was supposed to love.

"I'm just thankful we reconciled to do that last record. I got to tell him goodbye in my own way."

Excerpt from Can't Buy Me Faded Love—The Unauthorized Legend of The Quarrymen, *Ernest and Shultz, 1989*

Still confined to his wheelchair, and in rapidly failing health, Bob Wills organized what would be his final recording session in December 1973. It was more of a Texas Playboys reunion than anything else, but someone invited John. He showed up in a fringed jacket with a straw cowboy hat leaning to one side of his head, and when he walked into the room, Bob's eyes lit up with tears. Everyone Bob loved and had made music with was there—John, Al Stricklin, Smoky Dacus, Leon McAuliffe—a host of friends and family. But it was John he took aside, and they spent an hour alone, whispering together in a corner, while the assembled musicians prepared to record a selection of Bob's classic songs. The recording session yielded some of the finest recordings of Bob's career, but unfortunately, he was unable to participate in the entire event. After retiring on the first evening of recording, Bob Wills suffered his second stroke in four years and lapsed into a coma. His friends, John Lennon included, finished the recording session with tears in their eyes, and what remains is a fitting tribute to a country music legend.

Much speculation has been made regarding John and Bob's final conversation. John described it in numerous interviews as "a heart to heart, between me and my father," but any hope of knowing for sure died with John Lennon's murder in New York City.

Released as *For the Last Time*, the album produced during the last hours of Bob Will's life continues to haunt listeners to this day.

His aged, raspy voice can be heard in the call and answer session of "What Makes Bob Holler," and his ever-steady fiddle decorates roughly one-third of the album's tracks. When Lennon takes the vocal lead on "Faded Love" and "A Day in the Life," his voice shakes with emotion. It's an intimate portrait of a man torn apart by human mortality, a shuddering, broken superstar. In the years following Lennon's death, these songs have taken on an added sense of gravity. We know from Lennon himself that he and Wills set aside their differences that day, and became again what they'd once been. Lennon found his father, only to lose him again.

This unlikely reconciliation did more than reunite the greatest songwriting team of the twentieth century. It returned credence to the very beliefs they espoused. For all the turbulence and strife that hounded the Quarrymen throughout their short time together, in the end, they were right about everything.

All you really need is love.

STEPHANIE SHRUGS

Stanton, TX—October, 1989

IT'S EASY TO GET GIRLS WHEN YOU PLAY GUITAR.

At least in a nothing town like mine. The kind of place people from the city drive through and wonder how anybody could live there. Nothing for a sixteen-year-old to do but get drunk and find trouble. Not that I'm complaining. Fill a Big Gulp cup half full of Coke, then top it off with a pint of Jack and life gets better in a hurry.

My friend Bobby's garage is insulated well enough that our band can usually jam for a couple of hours before the cops show up, and that's what we're doing when this woman walks in.

I'm not talking about one of the high school girls that lounge around on the stained orange sofa we keep in the corner, throwing back bottles of Strawberry Hill. Most of them think I'm a rock star.

But this is a *woman*. Early twenties probably, and gorgeous. She's got killer hair, an explosion of blonde curls falling down her back. A Whitesnake T-shirt, tiny denim skirt studded with silver. No way she's from around here. The town's small enough that you get to know everyone, for better or worse. And besides, she's made for MTV. Last I checked, they aren't shooting any rock videos in the Dairy Queen parking lot.

I'm choking out the lyrics to "Youth Gone Wild"—not that I'm much of a singer, but I'm doing my best—when I feel the vibe change in the room. All eyes, mine included, lock on the woman as she takes a few steps into the garage and lights up a cigarette. You can tell straight off all the girls hate her. Foreheads pressed together, lips hidden behind their hands, nervous laughter. Probably talking about what a slut she is.

Our jam sessions attract guys too. A few friends, always ready for a party, and a bunch of guys who aren't part of our crowd but would like to be. They look all serious and nod their heads, like they're really into the music and too cool to bother with the girls. Meanwhile they're wondering if they have a shot at getting laid and telling themselves they're finally gonna buy a guitar and learn to play. Can't be that hard, right? But none of them ever will.

That's the difference between us.

Now they're staring at the woman, trying not to look like their minds are totally blown, trying harder than ever to seem cool. And I realize I'm doing the same damn thing.

We finish the song and there's some restrained clapping from the guys, a few hoots and whistles from the Strawberry Hill section.

"I need a beer." I slip the guitar over my head, place it gently on its stand. My fingertips ache and I love it. My heart's thumping like a Metallica riff, and I'm not sure if it's the adrenaline or the fact that a woman who should be hanging on my bedroom wall is standing in Bobby's garage, staring at me. But she might as well be the plague. The girls won't have anything to do with her, and the guys know she's way out of their league. Mine too, but I guess she hasn't figured that out. While I'm digging a beer out of the cooler, trying not to stare, she makes her move.

"Got something for you," she says.

I stand up, pop the tab off the beer and offer it to her. I hope my hand isn't shaking too much.

She shakes her head and reaches into her bag. "No thanks. Just came to give you something."

She smells like some kind of berry, one of those perfumy soaps girls use, and it starts to drive me a little crazy. Then she places a record album in my hand.

"What's this?" My best "too cool to care" tone.

"Look at it."

I do, and it's just a normal record. The cover is a black and white photo, a reverse negative of some long-haired dudes rocking out. Looks a hell of a lot like every other garage band on the planet. The album's called *Bleach* and the band's named Nirvana.

"Yeah? Who're these guys?"

"Nirvana."

"I can read. But what's this for? Why're you giving it to me?"

She leans in so close I can feel her earrings against my cheek. Her whisper is warm in my ear. "Because it's going to change your life."

She pulls back, kisses me right on the corner of my mouth. Before I can recover from my mini heart attack and figure out how to respond, she's ducking beneath the half-open garage door.

A second later, she's gone.

Realizing everyone's staring at me, I chug the entire can of beer and strap on my guitar like it was no big deal.

Later that night, I drop the needle on the record.

And my whole fucking life changes.

Seattle, WA—October, 1993

It's easy to get coffee when you live in Seattle.

French roast, espresso, latte, some frothed something or other topped with whipped cream. Might as well be a milkshake. Me, I'm drinking plain old American Joe—black—watching rain streak down the window.

The place is called Bean There, Done That and it's homey. One of those little hole-in-the-wall dives that makes you feel like a local just because you know it exists. I guess that's what I am now, a local. Been here a couple of years and people have mostly stopped commenting on my Texas accent. My coffee cup's empty and I'm trying to decide if I have time for another before rehearsal. I've been stalling, hoping the rain would stop. I should know better.

The brass bell over the door rings. I look up, and there *she* is. I haven't seen my mystery woman since the night she turned me on to Nirvana, set me on the path that ultimately led here. Different hair, different clothes, but nothing else has changed. She's still a knockout, like she hasn't aged a day. Obviously, the woman's a few years older than me, but she doesn't look it. She doesn't have to scan the room; she already knows where I'm sitting. I'm not surprised when she takes a seat at my table.

Her jacket's denim, her tights are some sheer black fabric, her skirt's tie-dyed cotton. The blonde curly hair doesn't have nearly as much hairspray, but it's just as beautiful. So's her voice. "I knew you'd be here."

I laugh, wondering whether she means Bean There, Done That or the state of Washington. Wondering whether that even matters.

"Was I right? Did the record change your life?"

I nod. She already knows it did. "What's your name?"

"Stephanie."

Her name yanks me from the overcast world of today and drops me smack dab in the middle of memory. A weedy, elementary school playground, sitting with Stephanie Warner on a bench built to look like a caterpillar. Green paint chips flake away as she scoots closer to me, then plants a kiss on my cheek. Her lips rest there for two wonderful seconds and a whole new world of possibilities is born in my mind. Then she takes her lips back and runs away. I realize how much Stephanie Warner reminds me of the Stephanie sitting across from me. She smiles, and I get the uneasy feeling she's sharing my memories.

"I like that name." A day hasn't passed in three years that I haven't thought about this woman, and that's the best I can muster. I'm so overloaded with questions, I don't even know where to start. Just like last time, Stephanie leads the way.

"You're wondering who I am."

"For starters."

"And whether or not I'm an escaped mental patient."

I laugh. "The thought had crossed my mind."

"You tired of Garageland yet?" Her question comes straight out of left field and I'm not sure exactly what she means.

"The song? Shit no. The Clash never gets old."

"Not the song, the lifestyle. Wake up, go to your suck day job, then jam in somebody's garage, or somebody's cousin's rented rehearsal space. Then on weekends you scramble for third bill at a bar you've never heard of, just so you can make no money and do it all over again. That's Garageland. You tired of it?"

"At least I'm doing something I love."

"So, you wouldn't rather do something you love *and* get paid for it? Your band is good enough. All that's holding you back is contacts. You don't know the right people."

"I know the guys in Nirvana." I'd moved to Seattle right after graduation and met Kurt Cobain just a few months before everybody on the planet figured out who he was. Good guy, pretty shy actually. Now he's been harnessed with a level of fame I can only imagine. I haven't seen him in over a year.

"Good for you. How many gigs has that gotten you lately?"

"Not many."

"You want to headline?"

"Of course.

"Then call this guy." She hands me a business card with a booking agent's name and phone number on it. Before I can tell her I've hounded every booking agency in the Northwest, she starts talking again. "Invite him to your next gig. He'll pay you lip service, then hang up on you. But he'll be at the gig. Play your ass off. If you do, it'll change your life."

She pushes her chair back and stands.

"Hang on," I say, not comfortable enough to grab her arm, but desperate to keep her from walking away again. "Where are you going? Do you live around here?"

She shrugs her shoulders and smiles. "Chill out. You'll see me again. Probably." She gives me another kiss, and this one lingers on my lips even after she pulls away. I can't do anything but watch as she walks out of the coffee house. I want to follow her, but I'm afraid of what might happen if I do.

The business card is like an unfulfilled promise in the palm of my hand.

She was right last time.

"That a public phone?" I ask the waitress cleaning off the table next to me.

"Sure, if it's a local call."

It's hanging by the door. I have to pass it before I brave the rain.

"Fuck it," I say, and dial the number.

Seattle, WA—April, 1994

It's easy to kill yourself with a shotgun.

Just ask Kurt.

Stick it in your mouth and pull the trigger. Nothing left but an ugly stain to clean up, a generation of people blindsided by reality, and one bona fide rock and roll legend.

Too fucking easy.

Rain pours from the sky like it always does, but nobody gathered at the makeshift memorial gives a shit. They're all too stunned. Plenty of tears and mumbled prayers. Ink smearing on condolence cards, wilting flowers, crushed cigarette packs, beer cans. Disillusioned, muddy mourners. Some guy with an acoustic guitar keeps playing "All Apologies" over and over again, like it's going to change anything. He'd better stop soon or I'm gonna knock the shit out of him.

My anger surprises me. Something like this, you figure I'd be sad. But instead, I'm pissed. What was the guy thinking? I knew about his drug problems and his screwed-up personal life. But I can't imagine it getting to the point where somebody decides to end it with a shotgun blast. Kurt was the biggest rock star in the world. The guy had a kid, for God's sake.

A few of the guys in my band were here earlier, but the rain chased them away. Me, I'm here for the long haul. I'm looking for some kind of understanding.

Stephanie appears next to me, and I realize I've been expecting her to come.

She looks no different than she did that day in Bean There, Done That, except now she's wearing a bright yellow rain slicker. Her hair is pasted to her skull, just like the rest of us. She laces her fingers through mine and leans her head on my shoulder.

"Why'd he do it?" There are so many other things I'd like to ask her, but none of them seem important right now.

Stephanie shrugs. I don't expect anything more. I gave up trying to understand her a long time ago. Stephanie is Stephanie. She just *is*.

"You heard my song on the radio?"

"Of course," she says.

Stephanie's advice had been dead on. The booking agent was an asshole, but he loved us. Got us gigs at all the cool clubs and we wound up signing with Sub Pop. We've been getting some pretty good local airplay. Nothing major, but we're famous enough around town that quite a few of the mourners recognize me.

"What are you here for this time?"

She looks into my eyes and her usual amusement has been replaced with sadness. "You sure you want this?"

I'm used to her answering my questions with questions, but I don't know what she means by *this*. "The fame or the suicide?"

She doesn't answer, she just keeps staring.

"Look, I love Kurt, but the guy obviously had problems. If you're asking whether I want to give up my dream of being a rock star, the answer is no. It's all I ever wanted. My head's on straight."

"I'm not saying you'll kill yourself. Just that not every dream is worth falling asleep for."

"I'll take my chances."

"Then think of me, next time you write a song."

"Let me guess. It'll change my life."

"Hopefully not too much." Stephanie kisses my nose, then disappears. I don't mean she gets lost in the crowd. She just fades away, and so does any pretense that she's a normal person. Not that I hadn't already figured that out.

A melody pops into my head. Something radio-friendly but not so much it makes me feel like a sell-out. I think about the sadness in Stephanie's eyes, and the coy way she shrugs her shoulders. I think about how beautiful and strange she is.

And the lyrics come in a torrent of inspiration.

New York, NY—March, 1999

It's easy to lose perspective when you're the biggest rock star in the world.

It's also easy to lose hope.

I stare out the window of my New York penthouse, past the jagged landscape of skyscrapers, to the far horizon. Somewhere out there is Bobby's parents' garage, and I wonder if it's changed. Could be they've converted it into a workshop or filled it with all the junk they don't have room for in the house anymore. Maybe just parking their cars there like normal people. But I like to think it's still the same. Amps humming, a skinny kid smacking the snare drum, impatient for the song to start. Another one tuning a hand-me-down guitar. The place clogged with cigarette smoke and laughter.

That's what it's about, right?

Rock and roll. Not rock stars.

I'm alone, thank God. Finally ushered out all the people with their hands in my life, the ones pulling the strings and the ones just content to push me closer to the edge. People who only want to be near me because I'm famous. They don't care about me, and the feeling's mutual.

I don't even turn around when I see Stephanie's reflection in the glass. But I smile. I used to think my unhappiness was Stephanie's fault. But she's never done more than give me what I wanted most in the world.

"How's the dream?" She comes into focus and she's standing beside me. She still smells like berries, and she's still painfully beautiful.

"Not bad. It has its rough edges, but it beats living in obscurity." I only half believe my own words.

"Glad to hear it. 'Stephanie Shrugs,' huh?"

"Not a bad name for a song." Not a bad name for a cultural revolution either. "Stephanie Shrugs" launched us from nightclubs to stadiums. It was the kind of song you can't escape. Airport lobbies, restaurants, elevators. Every fucking station on the radio dial. The album hugged the top of the Billboard charts for two years. Even my grandma bought a copy.

"Just before your CD hit the charts, I gave a copy of it to this kid living in Garageland. Changed his life."

My smile fades. "You did, huh? Didn't know you got around that much."

The realization that I share this vision with someone else causes me to feel betrayed. Jealous even. Ridiculous, but I can't help it. I've seen this woman a handful of times in my life, but I'd convinced myself she existed *for me*. I'd even entertained thoughts that one day she'd stay. How can someone who's so fleeting be the most important person in your life?

Stephanie shrugs, and I've never been so hurt in my life.

"Why are you here? Do I need you anymore?"

The pain in her eyes immediately makes me regret my words. A face like that isn't supposed to hurt.

"I came to see if you were tired of this yet."

"How could I be?"

I can tell she wants to shrug, but she thinks better of it. "It can be a little much."

"I'm fine. You can stop worrying. Anything else?"

Stephanie shakes her head. She's stopped looking me in the eye.

"Then have fun with your new pet project."

Stephanie steps through the glass and vanishes into the New York night.

She doesn't bother to kiss me this time.

Dallas, TX—April, 2004

It's easy to contemplate suicide when you're this fucking lonely.

Bottle of sleeping pills, straight razor to the wrist—lengthwise, not across—a noose dangling from that gigantic oak in the back-yard, Drano cocktail, stepping in front of a bus. Doesn't matter. It all ends the same way.

Christ, how did I get here?

My North Dallas home is cluttered with junk. Unwashed dish-es; stacks of CDs removed from the rack and left on the coffee table, couch, kitchen table, bookshelves, floor; way more guitars than any human needs, a drum set, a whole wall of amps; half-empty beer bottles by the score; a half-smoked bag of weed; me. Barefoot, torn jeans, shirtless.

In the middle of it all, I see the latest issue of *Spin*. A com-memoration—ten years since Kurt's death. All that time, but he's still staring at me, and those eyes don't offer any answers. But the journalists think they have him figured out. He wasn't built for fame. The drugs, the upheaval, the way every person you meet wants to be *right fucking next to you*. Wants to touch you, wants you to say something cool they can tell their buddies about, wants you to *see* them, with *those* eyes. So, all the pressure drove him to heroin, misery, depression. Death.

I'm not mad at Kurt anymore. I think I understand why he did what he did.

The thing is, Kurt never got to find out what life's like on the other side of the rollercoaster. When the sales begin to slump and the record label drops you. When all your friends find new friends, and all the skinny tan twenty-somethings in their hip hugger jeans and belly shirts find a new God to worship. When nobody gives a fuck about any of your new music because it's not "Stephanie Shrugs." When you realize they're right and your muse has abandoned you.

When you're so in love with a mystery you can't even function.

The place smells like an ashtray and so do I. I've cleared just enough space on the carpet for me and the shotgun. It's an old Remington my granddad used to hunt quail with, and I figure if it's good enough for Kurt, it's good enough for me.

I take a drag off my cigarette and think about the way Stephanie looked the first time I saw her. The way she'd look now if I hadn't chased her away. Would I have really been better off working in my dad's video store for the rest of my life, marrying the best woman I could find in a town that small, letting a couple of kids put my dreams on hold? Maybe. Probably not. But it doesn't make today any easier to live with.

My face is wet, and I realize I'm crying. No one to be cool for, so I let them come. The tears, the heaving sobs, all building toward the resignation I'll need to pull the trigger.

Somewhere, "Stephanie Shrugs" is playing on the radio.

Then I feel her arms wrap around my bare shoulders, her kiss on the back of my neck. I smell berries and second chances. No way I can hold back the tears now. My whole body shakes, and I can't even face her.

We sit there for an hour, silent. Contemplating one another. Then Stephanie stands and I look up at her for the first time. I'm older than she is now. She's wearing jeans and a loose-fitting Get Up Kids T-shirt, tucked in. I can't help but smile.

She doesn't speak, but she offers me her hand.

I take it without hesitating, and pray to God she's going to change my life one last time.

Garageland—November, 2006

It's easy to find Garageland again, when your muse leads the way.

Different garage, same concept. I even have an ugly old couch. Of course, I'm a little more high-tech now. This garage isn't just a place to jam, it's my recording studio, soundproofed to the max and the only place in the world I want to be.

I made a deal with this indie record label out of California. Nothing major; I'm through with all that success bullshit. Just someone to get my music into the hands of whoever wants to listen. I might sell one copy, I might sell 100,000. Either way I'll be happy. The pay's shit, but who needs money when you've got cult status? Besides, residuals keep me in CDs and cigarettes.

I'm remixing this bluesy track I've been working on for weeks when I see Stephanie sitting on my couch.

"You look better than you did last time I saw you," she says, and I can tell by the look in her eyes that she's not just blowing smoke up my ass.

"Thanks. You look pretty much the same."

"The curse of long life," she says, smiling, and I realize she's revealed more about her true nature in that sentence than in every other conversation we've ever had.

She pats the couch next to her and I take a seat.

"Thanks," I say.

"For what?"

"Bringing me here."

"It's not something you need to thank me for. It's what I do. Why I was sent here in the first place."

I get the sense that Stephanie is on the brink of spilling all the answers I've been waiting for since I was a kid. Just a little urging and I'll understand Stephanie's reason for being; why she delivers her mixed blessings. Why she chose me. But I understand myself well enough now to know the mystery is what I'm really in love with.

"You just here to check on me, or do you have some nugget of wisdom you've been saving? Maybe a stock tip?"

She laughs. "You're in a good place now."

"The best place. Guess you won't be staying long?"

"I can hang around for a while if you need me to."

I shake my head. "Go change somebody's life."

I realize it's very possible I'm seeing Stephanie for the last time. Before she can disappear, I kiss her, then I ask the one question I can't stand to leave unanswered.

"Do you love me?"

Stephanie shrugs, and that's good enough for me.

THE BEAUTIFUL PEOPLE

THE ACADEMY AWARDS CEREMONY WAS HELD AT THE OLD Pantages theater in April of 1960 and that venerable venue never hosted anything again for obvious reasons. These were the awards given for achievements in 1959. Afterward, we pillaged the debris to uncover the envelopes containing the names of the would-be winners. *Ben Hur* would have won Best Picture, had the evening been allowed to proceed to its conclusion. Why were so many of us inclined to search for those envelopes? The simple answer is we were curious. In spite of everything, most of us still loved the movies.

What do I remember from that night?

Everything.

First was the scent of Audrey Hepburn's Chanel N°5 as she passed within just a few feet of me on the red carpet. My sight was fading by then, so she passed by in a chiffon blur. But the smell of her was unmistakable. I would have called the whole thing off for a chance to follow that scent past the marquis and into the red satin confines of the theater; I might have given up everything for one chance to float in that sea of beauty and grace.

The snap-flash of cameras stirred those assembled into a frenzy. Stars advanced through that gauntlet of light, drawing all of us in with the gravity of their smiles. We weren't supposed to be there, of course, but our disguises granted us access. Hats were in fashion and the cool night gave no one reason to question our bulky overcoats. The NBC television cameras captured it all, and some of us can be seen in that old video, haunting the sharp edges of a dream world.

The cameramen shouldered closer to the fray, shouting to be heard over the brass band pounding out another refrain of "Hooray for Hollywood."

"Mr. Wilder! Say, do you think you'll win for *Some Like it Hot*, or is Wyler gonna take it this year?"

"George! George! Is *Anatomy of a Murder* gonna run the table?"

"Doris! Hey, why don't you look this way?"

And when one of those forever faces turned and smiled, the effect was every bit as mesmerizing as you'd hope it to be. I was in love with every one of them.

They were the soaring angels of an age, but they wanted more. They all craved eternity.

And we gave it to them.

Have you seen the 1951 classic, *Strangers on a Train*? It's one of my favorites. One of Hitchcock's best, and that's saying something. Farley Granger was memorable as Guy Haines, but the standout in that film was the doomed Robert Walker, on loan from MGM to Warner, in the role of Bruno Antony. Walker reached deep inside and summoned up a perfectly charming psychopath, and in a better world that role would have granted him immortality.

But Walker was already a broken man by the time that picture was filmed. His movie star wife, Jennifer Jones, had left him for director David O. Selznick, and he didn't recover. He started drinking. Living like a man with nothing to lose. No matter their circumstances, some people just can't bear the weight of their humanity.

Robert Walker was dead before *Strangers on a Train* ever made it to the big screen.

One of my kith mates was, of course, intimately linked to Walker, and he spent considerable effort absorbing the poor man's misery. Giving the troubled actor, in return, that elusive *something* that made people special. My kith mate did his best.

But not everyone gets the Hollywood ending.

Ushers drew velvet ropes across the entrance to the Pantages, sealing the Hollywood elite inside the building. They left behind them a void in the Los Angeles night, a hollow space that could not be filled.

Tired reporters lodged freshly lit cigarettes in their lips and gathered around a bank of payphones. Automobiles idled up and down the boulevard, and those few fans who'd been allowed to watch the proceedings from hastily constructed bleachers engaged in an orderly exit, autograph books clutched in their hands, already feeling the memory of those beautiful faces beginning to soften and distort in their memories. A few of them lingered, taking a seat on the curb and casting occasional looks at the closed theater doors, but most crept off to nurse their sudden longing alone.

My kith mates and I gathered in the glow of the marquis, forming a loose semicircle as we linked hands, facing the theater. We could feel our charges inside, pulling at us, alive with laughter. In our minds they were creatures of brilliant white light. They would never darken, never burn out.

A few police officers encouraged us to scatter, but it was easy enough to change their minds, elevate their night with pleasant thoughts and the desire to be somewhere else.

Even in those final moments, we poured what remained of ourselves into our charges. We clung to one another, our spines coiled, our faces grown flat and fissured. Those of us who had not entirely lost our sight felt darkness closing around us. Bones crackled and tendons groaned. Those of us who still had teeth felt them blacken and break.

Our beauty and our souls are our treasures.

But we have always given them away willingly.

There had been a film script making the rounds for a while in the forties. A grand tapestry of Los Angeles glamour and human ambition threaded with secret societies and dark bargains that had been the fabric of this place since Hollywood and Vine were still known as Prospect and Weyse.

The script was called *The Beautiful People* and it would have been a blockbuster if it had ever been made. Might even have given *Ben Hur* a run for its money.

Here's the pitch: A producer with a struggling film studio finds an ancient book—because there is *always* an ancient book in those kinds of films—and he summons a race of immortal beings from the belly of the Earth to feed his actors and actresses their grace and beauty. The stars call these beings Brutes, and the Brutes do not mind this service. It's their reason for being. And every star simply must have at least one. But you can't help but feel bad for the Brutes. They don't just give away their grace like the fallen angels they are. They absorb the misery and the human failings of their charges, and the weight of it twists them into monsters.

There was even a romantic subplot where an actor falls in love with one of the hideous Brutes; this is a ridiculous notion, but Carey Grant was supposedly attached to the project and I'm sure he could have sold it.

Like a lot of scripts, this one never made it to production. Hollywood keeps some stories for itself.

I read a draft of that script at some point and it came to mind as we stood there before the Pantages whispering prayers to the Beating Heart who bled every one of us into existence. The scriptwriter took a lot of license with the details but he got most of the important parts right.

The ending though? He got that all wrong.

*

Another of my favorites is *The Thin Man* from 1934. William Powell and Myrna Loy are pure perfection as Nick and Nora Charles. That sounds like I'm reading from a studio ad, but you just can't oversell this movie. It's whip-smart and joyous, and it's all due to the sheer *presence* of those two on screen together. They're so alive and invested in their roles that even as I laugh at their antics, I can't help but feel a touch of melancholy. Humans can never really be that perfect, can they?

My two kith mates who'd attached to Powell and Loy were practically dust at the end. They gave all of themselves to lift their charges to such heights, but neither of them had regrets. This is our reason for being. We weather the crippling empathy, but we're repaid with flashes of euphoria. Powell and Loy were brilliant without us. But with our help they were able to connect with that spark of the divine that lives in all humans. And through our charges, we caught a brief glimpse of that which we've been forever denied.

We love our charges, but we are not entirely selfless.

William Powell and Myna Loy were two of our greatest success stories, but even they have been forgotten by so many.

We give our charges everything. We love them unreservedly.

But it never seems to be enough.

The Beating Heart heard our whispers.

The belly of the world groaned and shifted, reminding us of our own bloody, rebellious births. Every one of us felt the acute homesickness of the runaway, even though most of us had decided long years before that we never wanted to go home again.

Beneath our feet, the earth yawned so suddenly that the reporters at their payphones had no time to scatter. The Beating Heart raised up his hands, grasped at the folds of the world and pulled them apart.

Hollywood shattered.

Fires erupted from the sudden starburst of fissures; I cannot say whether this was from broken gas lines or a manifestation of our father's anger at being summoned. The earth was hungry, swallowing police cars and stoplights and tourists with the cameras still strapped around their necks. The fire found the Pantages with supernatural alacrity, and the building became a bonfire.

Screams and howls rode the smoke, and The Beating Heart silenced them with a sudden *clenching* of his fist. The walls of the Pantages caved inward with terrible speed, and the building tumbled into the opening earth.

My kith mates and I hovered over the void, nearly faltering beneath the weight of all that pain. We had cast those souls into a charnel pit, confident that the fire would render them truly timeless. Forever young. Forever beautiful.

Modern day myths.

We joined in the intimacy of their death throes. We watched through their eyes as they gazed on the divine.

And for the briefest second, the divine gazed back.

Next time you watch *Casablanca*, look for me in the background. During the scene in Rick's Café Américain, when Victor Laszlo leads the defiant chorus of La Marseillaise, you can see me hunched over one of the tables, raising my drink and my voice with the other extras. I had given away very little of myself at that point and could easily pass for a weathered but still able-bodied human.

It was the love of film that compelled me to sneak onto Michael Curtiz's set and claim that tiny portion of history, but it was vanity too. Is there not a part inside all of us that craves to be in the picture? A part that desperately wants to be noticed?

I've served my purpose. I'm bent and blind and monstrous. There lives inside me a constant ache to give away what little grace I have left, but it's hard to find any takers these days. I've become what the movies would make of me, a nightmare demon, summoned from the pit to exchange souls for earthly glory.

And I miss my charges so very much.

There's no home for me in the belly of the world any longer. My kith mates have all been consumed and bled back into a new existence, but I can't seem to let go of this place even though it no longer wants me. I can't shake the black and white lure of Hollywood dreams or the Technicolor memory of that day in 1960 when we turned women and men into legends and our actions caught the eye of God.

I want that eye to notice me again.

ESCAPING SALVATION

Co-Written with Samantha Henderson

Fifty miles outside Fort Stockton, on the hunt for dirt angels, I saw the red empty light glowing from the dashboard. It might as well have been a death sentence.

"Damn it, Roe! You were supposed to fill this tank."

"Thought you said you was gonna do it," said Roe.

"*You* fill the tank," I said. "You always fill the tank. It's your job."

"Well, hell then, I forgot," he said, eyeing the empty light like he might be able to will it back to full. Roe never had much sense, but he was always flush with excuses. I'd have found another hunting partner years ago but people crazy enough are damn hard to find. Roe ran his hands through his hair. Driest patch of land on Earth and that man still looked like he combed it with motor oil. People always figure since he's a man and I'm a woman that we must have a thing going. But I say one look at Roe should erase that notion from any sane mind.

A flat blue sky glared blindly down at the hard-packed West Texas earth, and despite the heat it gave me the chills. If God's still here, he must see every little thing we do, know every stray thought, every tiny gesture. It wasn't a comforting thought.

"Is there anything ahead?" I leaned forward in my seat, peered up through the sand-scored windshield. Nothing but sky and sky and sky.

"Maybe a tent town. Nothing fortified." Roe's mouth hung open as he gaped at the flat expanse in every direction. Half the teeth were missing from his upper right jaw. He had a dirt angel's foot to blame for that. Just because they're made of dirt or sand or whatever else the wind will whip up doesn't mean they're not hard as nails.

"I know there's no fort towns nearby," I said. "I'm not an idiot. What I'm saying is we won't make it anywhere close to Fort Stockton before we're out of gas. We're going to have to walk."

"Sandstorm's coming," he said, pointing out to the west.

Crap. A towering brown wall spanned the horizon and wind buffeted the car. I sped up, as if there was any way to outrun it. The sand was maybe a mile off—wouldn't take long to get here. If we were lucky, we might be able to walk our way to civilization without being killed. We knew the creatures that lived out here better than anyone else; killing dirt angels and parting out the bits is how we earned a living. But a wall like that could be hiding an army of them, and Lord knows what else. Sniping the bastards as they formed in a swirl of sand and scrub and mesquite branches was one thing. Trying to survive a horde of the things in the open was laughable.

"Shit, Lizzy," said Roe, stabbing the windshield with a dirty fingernail. "There's a town!"

"No towns out here," I said, but I looked anyway, squinting against the sun.

"Right there!" he said.

And then I saw it: a tent town. Some band of nomads without the sense to live in a fortified city. Crazies that thought canvas walls and dumb luck were enough to keep them safe.

I hit the accelerator, headed for the village. I doubted we'd be any safer there than in the car, but the dirt angels were coming regardless, and maybe there'd be strength in numbers.

Ochre-colored sand pattered against the car, and although we'd rolled up the windows tight as we could, a few grains whirled around the interior. They had that heavy sweet smell, like hot blood, that meant angels were forming in the dark cloud behind us.

The tires chewed through the scrubby thistle that choked the landscape for miles around; they'd held up pretty good. But it was the gas I was worried about now, and suddenly the pedal beneath my foot felt lax, like I was pushing against thin air. A sick feeling hit my gut.

"Aw, hell," said Roe, as the engine sputtered over the howl of the approaching storm.

"You don't need to worry about it, Roe," I said between my teeth. "Angels won't get you."

"How you figure?" He turned to peer through the back window, rubbing a string of drool away from the ruined side of his face with the back of his hand.

"Because I'm gonna kill you first."

He grunted and faced forward, probably willing the tent town closer same as I was. The khaki structures had a squashed look, and no one was in sight. The inhabitants were likely crouched under the shelters, pulling down the tops of the tents to minimize their profile to the storm. If so, that was a good sign. It meant that they might know what they were doing. When dirt angels are forming, they grab at any high point in the landscape as a nexus to coalesce and take shape. If you stayed flat, they might pass right over you, like a wildfire moving too fast to outrun.

The soil and scrub sloped gently down towards the flattened tents. With a last sputter of the engine I pulled the wheel sharply to the right, skidding us sideways through a small dune that banked the edge of the settlement. The brown boiling wall was almost upon us.

I kicked open the driver's door and turned to yell at Roe to grab the gear. For once he'd thought on his feet and had the dull green duffle tossed across his shoulder. We both dashed from the car and headed for the largest tent, collapsed like a big fabric pancake on the ground. The air was gritty, and the roar of the storm closed in on all sides.

As we got to the tent the edge heaved up and I got a glimpse of a figure, shrouded around the head with coarse fabric, a pair of eyes shadowed inside. A slight pause, as the person no doubt reckoned the risk of letting us in versus the damage we'd do in desperation to find shelter, then the heavy material was lifted enough for us to dive under. I landed belly-down on cords, groundcloth, and various hard objects while the roof was lowered, closing us in with the muffled sound of the storm, and the smell of dust, old canvas and live bodies.

"Who the hell are you?" someone growled.

I made to answer, but then the storm was on us and the only sounds left in the world were the rush of wind overhead, the shudder of the cloth as it struggled against the grips of all those holding it down, and the plaintive whines of potential dirt angels, spectral voices in search of bodies. I'd heard those voices plenty of times, but mostly from a distance. Hunting dirt angels, it was best to stay back while they formed, to make sure there were only one or two. You do that, you got a chance of taking them. But hearing those voices while in the teeth of the storm ran my blood cold.

One voice rose above the others, then a second one joined it. The clattering sound of sticks and stones and debris colliding in the air and the solid stench of decay, like ancient earth upturned. The muffled *pop* of car tires exploding one by one and the brittle crash of windshield and windows as they flew into shards. The hissing intake of air into a pair of new living vortexes as glass, rubber, earth, weeds, and rocks rushed together in a horrible act of creation.

I couldn't see much beyond the whipping flaps of the covering canvas, but I could reckon what was happening. There were at least two of them. Wraiths cobbled together with earth and debris. They'd be wandering eyeless and enraged, looking to complete themselves before the storm blew through and took with it their hopes of achieving a perfect body.

A sandy foot planted a few feet from our shelter. I could see talons flex, and I sensed the thing sniffing for us. The only reason they hadn't found us yet was because their eyes formed last. Thank God their eyes formed last.

The sandstorm was mercifully fast, and it blew through in less than fifteen minutes, leaving only a gentle wind in its wake to rustle our covering. No one moved under the canvas. I listened, trying to determine if the angels had moved on or were lingering, waiting to spring on the first one that moved.

I lifted the edge just enough to get a good peek of the surroundings. One angel, kneeling beside my now ruined car. Hands digging in the soil. Jamming clumps of the stuff into its empty eye sockets. Any others had moved on. Either that, or they were lying in wait beyond the range of my vision. No matter, it was time to act.

"Bring the bag," I whispered, then shimmied forward on my belly, crawling out from under the canvas. A few excited whispers and a quick grab at my ankles gave me the temperature of the locals. I kicked free, stood, and was relieved to see Roe slip in place beside me. Already he'd opened the bag, and he handed me my tomahawk. Next he pulled out his tiny bow. Damn thing looked like it was made for a kid, but I knew it had enough punch to send an arrow through an angel.

The angel got our smell, stood, and turned.

Roe already had an arrow notched and he sent it razoring through the thing's chest. The angel shook, clods of dirt flying from its newborn body. The vaguely humanoid thing spread wide its wings and shrieked. A few sticks and stones clattered around it, and it began to fall apart from the point where Roe's arrow had struck. Then it was in motion, lifting into the air with one brutal lash of its wings. It crossed the distance between us in less than a second, and if I hadn't had my tomahawk ready it would have taken off my head.

The angel shrieked when my blade sliced clean through its

wrist, and it slammed into the ground in shock, unable to control its momentum. I rounded on the monster just as Roe got it with another arrow, and when the thing turned to face me, I let fly with my tomahawk and the weapon planted itself diagonally across the angel's face.

The angel stilled. I pulled my tomahawk loose, satisfied the creature was dead.

Some angel hunters preferred guns with bullets notched and furrowed so they'd punch holes in the angels the same way Roe's arrows did. But gun are expensive and keeping them in good repair is difficult in the desert. I preferred a weapon I could trust absolutely. More than a few angel hunters had charged in, guns at the ready, only to have the damn things jam with an angel bearing down. The results weren't pretty. Killing an angel wasn't pretty either, but a lot less red and wet.

Roe hit the thing a couple more times for good measure, but the angel was plainly dead. We'd killed enough of them to know.

"It's killed," said Roe, lowering the bow.

"Hell, I know that," I snapped, less annoyed than relieved.

We both reached into the bag and pulled out the long-bladed, serrated knives we used for separating the angels up into their valuable parts. We went to work on the carcass, hurried by long experience. If you don't piece them out quick, they'll turn right back into the earth they came from and then the whole hunt's been for naught.

I worked on the neck, glancing at the thing's angry face, its empty eye sockets. I'd only seen a couple of them with eyes before. I wasn't in a hurry to see more.

"That's *our* angel," said a voice.

Roe and I turned, saw a tribe of rag-tags dressed in rough homemade clothes. Most didn't even have shoes, but they all held weapons of some sort. I'd been so caught up in the kill that I'd forgotten the nomads. One of them stepped forward, a tomahawk similar to mine hanging loosely in her grip. She was a wiry woman, young and sun scorched like the rest. She eyed the angel hungrily, and spoke again. "We let you shelter with us. So that angel is ours."

"We killed it," I said, standing. "So, back off." You had to stand your ground out here or else you'd end up dead.

Roe separated the angel's forearm from its elbow and tossed it at the woman's feet. "You want a piece? There you go. Arm's the best part, ain't it? Plenty of good meat." He laughed and the ruined side of his face looked all the more ghastly. Not for the first time I wished Roe would just shut up and let me take care of things.

"I don't want the arm," the woman said, hefting her tomahawk. "I want the eyes."

Roe laughed some more, earning a dirty look from the girl, and I just grinned.

"Eyes are the last to form," I said. "And that's a good thing, or it would be hard to get a jump on the bastards. What would you want with the eyes, anyway?"

Arms and legs, that's how we made our living. That's what folks wanted out here in the remains of Texas, other places too, for all I knew.

The girl glared at me and walked to where Roe was dissecting the creature. She stared a long time into its hollow sockets, as if by willing it hard enough she could create what didn't exist. With a snort of disgust, she turned her head and spat. The dry sand soaked up the spot of moisture fast.

Not letting my nerves show, I stood cross-armed and casual by Roe as he went about his work. He wasn't brilliant, but he had a kind of genius to him when he parsed out one of these things, a delicacy that belied the violence of the work. He'd managed to separate a massive leg just above the thickest part of the thigh, and there was no sign of disintegration as yet. Most hunters thought they did well to get one, maybe two limbs out of a kill—I'd never seen Roe bag less than two, and most often it was three and even four. I'd cut off one of the thing's hands and the rest of that arm was useless, so he wouldn't get a four-out here. But it looked like we'd have three to trade, at least. Two if they decided to keep the one Roe had tossed their way.

Eyes, the girl had said. Never heard of collecting the eyes. Must be nigh-on impossible.

I looked past the girl at the other ferals. They were a well-organized lot, tugging and shifting canvases back in place. Faster than I expected, the tent city was back, a sturdy silhouette against sky tinged brown by the dying dust storm. Banners snapped from the apexes, yellow and dull red, giving the place an almost festive air.

The girl still stood beside me, and I saw that she wasn't just watching as the others worked—her gray eyes snapped back and forth across the campsite, missing nothing. The corner of a large tent sagged and she frowned. As if in response, there was a mighty tug and shuffle and the cloth wall steadied and straightened. At her nod two women, girls also, really, but a little older than her, emerged from the same big tent and approached us cautiously. The dead angel's massive forearm still lay at the girl's feet. Wordlessly and competently the women produced a length of fabric and wrapped it up.

All right then. They did shelter us; I wouldn't argue about one arm.

The women walked back to the tent, one carrying the bundled arm like an improbable baby. The girl hadn't said a thing. Either her folk had great confidence in her, or great fear. Probably both.

"Your car's shot," she observed, shifting her gaze to me.

"True," I conceded.

"You plan on hiking back to Fort Stockton to get another?"

I shrugged. "Wouldn't be my first choice."

"So," she said, and squatted on the ground, hitting the compacted dirt lightly with the heel of her hand. I followed suit. Formalities must be observed when striking a bargain. Roe gave me a quick sideways glance and turned back to work. The business side of our operation was my responsibility.

"So, we saved you from that angel," I said. "Guess you owe us something."

The girl laughed. "You didn't save shit. That angel wouldn't have known we were there if you hadn't jumped up like a fool and attacked it. Besides that, you attacked too soon."

"I don't need your advice on killing angels," I said.

"Maybe not," she conceded. "But you do need a way to get back home without hoofing it through angel country. You're liable to hit eight or ten sandstorms between here and there. You might know about killing angels, but you'll have a horde of them on your ass. You and your man won't beat those odds."

"He's not my man."

"Don't matter; you'd best wait for the caravan. Strength in numbers and all that."

"Billy's caravan?"

The girl nodded. "That's the one."

Everyone knew Billy Black. One of the old school angel killers from the days before people figured out parts of them could be salvaged. Now he ran a trading business, moving from town to town with loads of canned goods, gasoline, toilet paper, angel parts, all kinds of salvage. His band travelled in numbers and was heavily armed, more or less a match for a roving band of angels. If he was coming through here, me and Roe could catch a ride to Fort Stockton. Might be the only way to make it back alive now that the car was trashed.

"When's he due back through here?" I asked.

"Hard to say," said the girl. "Billy keeps his own schedule. But he'll be through eventually."

"So, what are you proposing?"

"Shelter, for you and your man."

"I told you, he ain't my man."

"Whatever he is. You can both shelter here. We have food, tarps and water."

"In exchange for what?" I asked.

"A pair of angel eyes. And a tongue."

I snorted. "I've hunted over seven years now and never met

anyone that's harvested the eyes. And a tongue? What do you need one of them for?"

"That's the deal. Take it or leave it."

I could hear Roe's heavy open-mouthed breathing behind me, and the townspeople formed a suffocating ring around us. I didn't relish the thought of living out in the open with these people until Billy Black came this way again, but they had sheltered us, and the alternative was even less appealing. I held out my hand and the girl took hold.

"What's your name?" I asked.

"Genj."

"Well, Genj, I'm Lizzy. I guess we have a deal."

Genj smiled, and I couldn't help but feel like I'd been maneuvered into some kind of trap. Like maybe Roe forgetting the gas had all been part of this wild woman's plans.

"Nice to meet you, Lizzy," she said. "Welcome to Salvation."

Salvation was a shithole, but a well-designed shithole.

The tarps had all become tents again, and they formed a crude circle around a stone cook pit. Shallow trenches had been dug around the town limits, an old ploy for warding off angels, or at least turning them another direction as they formed. I'd never taken much stock in that defense, and they certainly hadn't done much to help out that morning, but the trenches made me feel a little safer anyway. Genj and her bunch had salvaged a couple of old port-a-potties from God knows where, and had scrawled BOYS and GIRLS across their respective front doors. For some reason I found that hilarious.

Dried food stores were kept in a series of mesquite covered holes to keep them reasonably cool, and what precious canned goods they had were locked in a rusted, military footlocker. Genj had the only key. Despite this, the people of Salvation were surprisingly free with their water. Everyone seemed to have a full canteen, and more than once I'd been offered a drink. I even saw one man washing dishes. I intended to ask Genj just where the hell they'd found so much clean water. Even in Fort Stockton, people weren't that lax with the stuff.

Me and Roe squatted by the fire as an old man stirred up a mash of corn and beans in a cast iron skillet. He introduced himself as Shooter, and his hands shook constantly. He was sun worn like the rest of them, and what remained of his white hair was long and thin. He squinted so hard his eyes were barely visible, just slivers of dull gray glass like some old cowboy from one of the film photos they had on display at the museum in Fort Stockton. The ones that would make a story if you looked at them one after another.

Someone had shot a coyote, and a couple of skinny girls were working that up for dinner too.

Genj had disappeared on some errand or other, then came back just as the sun began to dip over the flatland to the west. When she emerged from the long shadows, she had a teenaged girl with her, pale and pretty except for the fact that she didn't have any eyes. The flesh had knit fairly well around her sockets, but two black cavities were still mostly visible, and it was an unsettling sight. Most folks lost eyes, they'd put a patch on or something. Genj tugged at the girl's overlong shirtsleeves and helped maneuver her into a sitting position next to Roe. He leaned closer to me and didn't have the decency to hide his spooked expression.

"We got guests, Bea," said Genj. The girl nodded, but thankfully kept her sightless gaze trained on the fire. "They say they're angel hunters." Genj looked at me. "This is Bea. She's my little sister."

"I'm Lizzy and this is Roe," I said, extending my hand and feeling stupid. The girl just nodded, but of course she didn't see my gesture. I wasn't sure if I should reach out and grab her hand to shake—then I noticed she still hadn't produced any hands from those long sleeves, and I yanked my arm back like I'd seen a snake.

Genj laughed. "Don't bother being delicate with Bea. She knows she's all fucked up."

"Damn sure is," said Roe, pressing so hard against me now that I thought he'd shove me right into the fire.

"Shut the hell up," I said.

Bea nodded vigorously, and I wasn't sure if she was thanking me or just agreeing with Genj.

Genj shoved Shooter out of the way and started stirring the bean and corn mix herself. "We got this little fresh spring nearby. I figure there's no use hiding it because you'll find out if you're here long enough. Don't tell nobody from the city or I'll gut you and that ain't no idle threat."

I believed her. "I noticed you weren't hurting for water."

Genj nodded. "So then, Bea here likes to hang out by that spring more than damn near anything else. Don't you, honey? One minute she's here the next she's gone and you don't need to look nowhere else for her but that spring. One day, she's off there by herself and she knows better than to do it but she can't help it I guess. So we got a couple boys here, brothers, decide they'd have some fun. Caught her all by her lonesome, dug out her eyes, took her hands. Took her goddamned tongue too. Guess they thought they were safe if she couldn't talk, or write, or point them out. They were wrong."

Roe looked ready to crawl on his knees alone to Fort Stockton if it got him away from Bea, but I saw her for what she was, just another victim of the broken world we'd all inherited from our god damned grandparents. Genj noticed him cringe and grinned.

"I staked them out in the badlands for what they did to Bea. Tentpoles through their hands and feet, and cut them just enough so the coyotes came the faster." She glanced at me sideways, maybe to see if I had a problem with that.

I shrugged. Out here justice was fast and rough. It had to be.

"Wasn't the Adams boys done it," said Shooter. He looked irritated that Genj had relieved him of his cooking duties, and at the same time scared, like speaking up around Genj might be a bad thing. "Was an Injun. Comanche dead, mad at being dead, picking off the living one by one for what we done to them two hundred years ago."

"The hell it was." Genj rolled her eyes and stirred the food with new vigor. "I swear I hear about one more dead Indian and I'm gonna shove this spoon down someone's throat."

"It's as good an idea as any," said Shooter.

Genj glared at him. "It's fucking stupid is what it is."

"You got Comanche, Kiowa to blame for all of this." Shooter waved his arms around and a collective groan rose up from the Salvationers near the fire, as if they'd heard all Shooter's theories before and had long since grown tired of them. He knelt beside me and pinned me with a half mad, all earnest look, like a preacher trying to force feed me religion.

"Injuns never wanted us here. That's a fact and can't be disputed. They fought tooth and claw to keep all them wagons and men and such from moving this way and setting up cities. You go to the city and you find yourself a book and you'll know that's the way it was. Well, then, them Comanche was licked but they bided their time and then when we was all high and mighty, they knew it was time to strike."

"I don't see how Indians could have caused the Walking Cough." I was hungry and tired and in no mood to humor the old man. "Two hundred years ago? They're dead and forgotten. You're just being foolish."

"Indians got long memories," he said, undeterred. "They pass them stories down from generation to generation. Don't even write things down like civil folk but just talk and talk and talk and if there's even one left, I figure he's out there planning on what to do next to ruin us even more. This land is cursed and it's all because of the medicine the Indians put on it. We should have just left it alone. Now we got angels and devils and dead Indians cutting off little girl's hands. Makes a man eager to find a grave and be shut of it."

"Wish I had a cure-all for crazy," said Roe, and Genj burst out laughing. Shooter sniffed and shuffled away from the fire. Roe was coarse, but I was thankful he'd chased the old man away.

"He's a fair hand with a skillet or I'd boot him to the desert." Genj began ladling the hot muck onto plates and handed them around the fire. She tossed me her canteen and I drank greedily before handing it to Roe.

"I'd like to see this spring of yours," I said.

Genj gave me an appraising stare before smiling. "Well, I guess you ain't much use around here until another sandstorm heads this way. You can help me refill the water jugs and carry them back in the morning. Besides, I figure you could use a bath."

The dawn light colored the sand and scattered rocks pink as I followed Genj and Bea towards a distant curving line of giant derelict windmills frozen by the passage of time. They stretched away along the top of the mesa, and their like could be seen on other small rises in the distance. I didn't see any trace of a spring and was beginning to wonder if it really existed when we followed the hardscrabble path around a fall of boulders and I saw where the mesa split into a shallow valley, floored in green.

I'd assumed Genj's comment about the bath was a wise crack, but she was dead serious. No sooner had we reached the place where the spring pooled deep and blue, she stripped and waded in. I flinched, thinking about the scarcity of water and how casually she'd polluted the place, but she'd obviously done this before.

"Come on in," she said, but I just shook my head. The sight of that much water in one place, not in the precious, rusting tanks of Fort Stockton but out here under the hard blue sky, spooked me. I knelt beside the water, the lip of it dampening my pants at the knee, and stretched my hand over the surface, scarcely daring to touch the stuff.

Bea walked into the pool up to her ankles, then plopped down on her ass and stared sightlessly at her sister. There was some rabbit and coyote scat littered around, but now we had the spring all to ourselves.

I started filling the jugs and canteens, and presently Genj had returned to shore and dressed. She sat on a rock, close to Bea, and eyed the windmills over the lip of the shallow mesa.

"See them windmills?"

"Of course," I said.

"You're looking at the key to civilization."

"How do you figure?" I asked, rising, the weight of the jugs biting into my shoulder. Truth be told, I didn't have much interest in the windmills. I had a hard time pulling my gaze away from all that water.

"You know what they were for?" asked Genj.

"Nope."

"They made electricity."

"Bullshit." It was a foolish notion. Everyone knew electricity came in batteries, and those suckers were scarce as hens' teeth.

"You ain't as smart as you think," said Genj, grinning. "They're all rusted up now, but used to be the wind would catch them and they'd turn."

"I know what a windmill does," I said. "I reckon these were used to pump all this water."

"No they weren't. They'd turn and turn and turn and that would make the electricity. I read a whole book about it when I was a kid."

I didn't say anything. It was obvious she wouldn't hear any arguments. Bea turned toward us, nodding. I wished she'd stop doing that.

"We get those windmills turning again," said Genj, "then maybe we get this place back on track. That's why I'm out here. I ain't stupid. I know it's crazy to live outside the fortified towns. We all do. But someone's got to do it. I'll admit I'm god damned obsessed with them windmills. Figuring out how to get them going again. Used to be, people had more electricity than they could stand. What do you think will happen if we can get back there again? No more scrapping for batteries. Use cars and radio transmitters all you want. Maybe we could even build an airplane."

I'd heard enough. I stood, wiped the sand off my pants and hefted two of the water jugs. "Sun is burning your mind. There ain't no such thing as airplanes."

"The hell there is," said Genj. "I seen a skeleton of one once. Up near Pecos."

"Well damn, I've seen 'em too. And maybe they did fly once. But those days are over for good, Genj. I'm going back to town before a storm blows in. You can sit here all you want figuring out how to bring a dead world back to life. You're so keen on fixing those windmills, why don't you climb your ass up there and do it."

She grinned that grin I was beginning to hate. "I would," she said. "But they'll kill me for it."

"Who'll kill you?"

"Angels."

Girl was even crazier than I thought.

I got an earful on the walk back to camp. Genj used to live in a fortified town with its own crop of windmills rusted and useless on the outskirts. Seems that she'd convinced herself she could fix one and snuck out one night to try but got chased off by a dirt angel that manifested itself between the poles. Not taking the hint, she tried again, and all Hell broke loose. Apparently, angels don't like the windmills, and Genj's efforts had brought them down in force on the town.

Town almost killed her for it, but some, especially kids, bought into her talk about windmills and electricity and airplanes, so they told her to hit the road with anyone that would follow her. So out she goes with her sister and a few other crazies to live in the desert. Knows about the spring because her mom told her about it: before the Walking Cough her family owned a store in the tiny town, crumbled to nothing now, that lived alongside the mesa. She takes her best guess at the direction and gets lucky.

There was a good chance she was full of shit. I've never known dirt angels to organize, and certainly not to gang together and attack a town. They were usually doing good just to keep themselves in one piece. And I couldn't imagine them caring one way or another about rusty windmills. Still, I'd seen enough crazy things in the desert that I was willing to consider the possibility.

But then Genj mentioned water angels.

"I don't take much stock in tall tales," I said. "You're more likely to sell me on airplanes than water angels."

"I'm telling you, Bea saw one. She told me and she don't lie," said Genj.

I glanced back at Bea, and she seemed to be watching me with her empty eye sockets. She smiled vaguely and I shuddered.

"It was before she lost her eyes. She went to the water alone. Said she felt the wind blow in cold around that spring and then they just rose up like glass sculptures from the water. Didn't attack, didn't do nothing but stare at her and scare the hell out of her. She froze in place she don't know how long, scared to move, then all of a sudden the water angels evaporated. Bea says the wind whipped up again and blew all that mist her way. Said right then she lost all her fear because that mist felt like them water angels were giving her a whole bunch of goodbye kisses. You believe that? Sorry to say, but my sister was a little touched even before she lost half her parts."

"She was a *lot* touched if she's seeing water angels." I said.

Genj threw me a sullen look and shifted the weight of her cluster of canteens. I think she was starting to resent me. She was accustomed to being taken at face value, but I had a lot more sense than the loonies that populated Salvation. I could be sold a load of bullshit, but it had to be offered at a hell of a bargain. This time, I wasn't buying.

"You believe what you want," she said. "But I promise you, that girl don't lie."

*

Me and Roe passed a few weeks in Salvation with no sign of Billy Black's caravan. We fell into the day to day chores, toting water, hunting for food and all that, but we also resumed our angel hunts, and already we'd bagged a couple of arms and half a wing. The arms were intact up to the shoulder and would fetch a mint when we got back to town. Arms like that could replace withered stumps and make the wearer stronger than sin. Hell, I'd known more than a few people who'd had a doctor take a perfectly good arm so they could attach the angel flesh. People were fucking crazy sometimes. The bit of wing we had could be pounded down and used to make healing tonics, psychedelic drugs and all manner of things a sane person would never ingest.

We bagged a pair of hands one day and brought them back for Bea. I asked Genj if Bea'd want them and she considered a while and said yes. I wish I'd never done it. Truth was, the girl's blank stares and blind nods were getting to me. Maybe with hands she'd let up.

I let Roe handle the burning. Call me gutless, but I couldn't hold that hot brand to Bea's smooth scarred stump. I stayed outside the tent, even. If I'm cursed to live a thousand years, I'll never get over the smell angel flesh makes when it knits itself to its human host, or the way human and angel seem to slither together like a nest of snakes beneath the flames. I've never worn any angel parts myself because it creeps me out so much.

And I'm not entirely convinced the angel flesh doesn't call to itself. I've seen too many folks with angel parts hunted down and killed by dirt angels. I hunt the things; I damn sure don't need them coming for me first.

As soon as Bea's new hands knit together, she started using them, but I couldn't tell as they did her a lot of good. She'd draw things in the dirt, and scribble symbols that might have been an attempt to write, but I couldn't make any sense of it. Genj would sit with her for hours, watching what she wrote, but eventually she'd huff away in frustration and I figured she was more put out than ever that her sister couldn't get across what had happened to her. Every time I saw Genj she'd jump on me about that tongue and them eyes. Got to where I tried to avoid her just so I could keep from hearing about it.

One day I dragged Roe along with me to the pool to get water. Roe never was much for company, but taking him along was a sight better than listening to more of Genj's nonsense. While I filled the jugs, he stood and stared up at the windmills, eyes squinting away the yellow sun.

"So Genj says they make electricity?" he asked.

"Genj says a lot of things," I said. "I wouldn't believe too many of them."

"Had to be some reason they were built," he said. "They're damn large to be used just to pump water. Ain't no pipes anywhere neither." Roe climbed up onto one of the scattered boulders and began picking his way up the side of the mesa. There was work to be done, so I wasn't surprised he'd found something else to occupy his attention. I shook my head, finished filling the jugs, and put my bare feet in the pool. It was sinful, but Lord it was nice.

A few minutes later, Roe topped the mesa and stood at the foot of one of the windmills, rapped at it with his knuckles. He put his arms around the massive thing, like maybe he figured he'd climb it, but then withdrew them and put his hands on his hips. What the hell did he hope to accomplish, messing around with those things? I remembered then what Genj had said about the dirt angels getting pissed off when people fiddled with the windmills, and it sent a quick chill down my arms. But that wasn't the real thing to fear. The real fear was being away from the camp any longer than necessary. The real fear would come if dumb ass Roe was still on top of that mesa when the winds kicked up.

Even tall tales sometimes have a kernel of truth, so I'd turned the whole thing over in my head a time or two. Never was able to come up with a reason why dirt angles would want to keep the windmills still. Way I saw it, the more wind the better for them. I had my way, the wind would never blow a lick. The thought of water angels was even more vexing. I supposed such a thing was possible, and water was scarce so there was a slim chance they could have kept themselves hidden, particularly if they weren't attacking everyone in sight like the dirt angels. But if I started believing all the stories people told about what lived on the plains, I'd never have the nerve to leave town again.

No one knew where the dirt angels came from; just that they'd come in the wake of the Walking Cough. Me, I wasn't too interested in where they came from. I just wanted to kill them.

"No way up there," said Roe. I looked up at him and he really was trying to shimmy up the windmill shaft, a sheer pole far too big around to get a grip on. Dumb ass.

A hot wind kicked up and lifted my hair. I stiffened, looked around for signs of a storm. "Get down here and help out," I said. "And leave that windmill alone!" The wind hit me again, and tiny swirls of sand blew through the brush like rattlesnakes.

"Roe! Let's go."

Roe released the windmill, scampered back down the mesa, and helped me with the water jugs. The wind intensified, snatched at our clothes and crackled through brittle mesquite branches. Dust lifted around us, but it was just dust for now. We walked quickly, the sudden fear unspoken between us, and when the western sky turned brown, we dropped the jugs and broke into a sprint.

The sandstorm beat us to Salvation, and by the time we got there, everything had already gone to Hell. The world had turned utterly brown and we could hear the canvas tents flapping before we saw them. We hurried toward the town, and when we got close enough to make out details, we realized the angels had descended on Salvation in force. I thought about Roe fucking around with that windmill and guilt welled up inside me like bile.

Genj and her gang had done a fair job of fending them off, though not without cost. The broken bodies of a least a dozen Salvation kids were strewn around the camp. Five dirt angels lay decomposing back into the earth. Even with the danger at hand, part of me lamented the loss of those bodies.

One angel remained, and it was a hell of a specimen. Eight feet tall at least, biggest one I'd ever seen, and its wings were unfurled and driving up a storm, pulling more substance to itself, continuing to grow right before my eyes. Three of the Salvation kids had pierced the thing with arrows tied to thin ropes, like crude harpoons, and they tugged in opposite directions, trying to manipulate the angel and keep it still while others darted in with spears and axes. A man tried to sneak up from behind with his blade, but one of the angel's thrashing wings clipped him in the jaw and drove him to the ground. He rolled away, one hand holding the flesh to his ruined face, and the angel whipped its head around to scream at him as he fled.

That's when I got a real good look at the monster's face. It was an abomination of weeds, rocks and what looked to be bits of glass.

And the fucker had eyes.

"Jesus lord."

"Look out!" yelled Genj, ducking and weaving around the perimeter. The angel whirled and struck at a young woman who was about to spear it in the back of the leg. The spear snapped in half and so did the girl, bending back at an obscene angle, suspended for a second before she crumpled, broken, to the ground.

I moaned involuntarily. I'd fought near to a hundred of these things, but never one so powerful. My hand fell to the tomahawk strapped at my side. I took a tentative step forward, then the angel turned, saw me, *looked* at me with those eyes. I've only seen a couple of angels with eyes before, and I'd never seen any eyes like these. I stared into them, and I just froze, my weapon dangling useless at my side. My knees felt weak.

The angel didn't relent. It battered back its attackers, but it kept its gaze locked on me.

Oh, God. Those eyes.

I heard Roe whoop, then he ran past me, an arrow ready. He let fly and it struck the angel right in the throat, passed clean through. Bits of the angel blew out the back of its neck and its horrible, birdlike scream stopped. The angel lurched then, pulled two of the harpooners off their balance and yanked free from their arrows. The monster pulled its gaze away from me and keyed on Roe. One second Roe was notching up another arrow, the next he was cold and still as a statue, eyes locked with the angel, jaw slackening.

I shook off my paralysis. God, those eyes. What the hell was it with those eyes? The tomahawk was in my hand, the handle smooth and warm and good in my grip. I hefted it and ran toward the angel.

It stared expressionlessly at Roe, close now. Before I could reach it, the angel had one talon on Roe's head, stroking it like you would a puppy you were about to have put down. Roe didn't move; he just stared. Then the angel began to *press.*

Howling, I slammed my tomahawk into the creature's side, shattering a huge pane of glass it had incorporated into itself. Bit of windshield from our car, like enough. It deflected my blow and the angel swatted me aside. I slammed into one of the big water barrels and the wood shattered beneath me, spilling warm water over me like a summer monsoon.

The thing turned its attention back to Roe, pushed him down and pinned him through like a lab specimen with one long talon. Roe didn't even shriek; he was still under thrall.

The angel seized the thin flannel shirt over Roe's belly and the skin beneath it, tore both away like wet paper. Finally, Roe began to scream.

The angel poked casually at the raw red slab of exposed muscle before splitting it down the middle. Loops of intestine spilled out on the yellow sand.

Roe began chanting. "Oh help me help me oh my lord help

me." The monster continued to poke and prod like a scientist examining the biology of some alien creature, even as Genj and her gang circled it for a renewed assault.

I screamed, took aim, and let fly with my tomahawk. It struck home with a solid, meaty thunk, dead in the center of Roe's skull. He stilled, and the angel looked up at me again. Its face reformed into an angry, wailing hole and it spun toward me in a rage, those eyes locked on me again.

Told you I'd kill you before them angels could, Roe.

Then I fell again beneath the weight of the monster's stare and cold darkness closed in around me.

I woke to Genj wiping my forehead with a wet cloth. I was in the tent Roe and I shared, and only a thin sliver of sunlight crept in through the narrow door flap. My head ached like I'd got some bad liquor.

The angel. Roe. Those eyes. I flinched as I remembered, and Genj held me down when I tried to jump up from my pallet.

"Hang on," she said. "You need to keep still. Not sure what that angel did to you, but it messed you up. You're lucky as hell we killed that bastard before it did the same thing to you it did to your man."

"He's not . . . he wasn't . . ." I gave up. "Those . . . those eyes." My throat burned when I spoke, and I couldn't manage more than a faint whisper. I tried to sit up again, but Genj held me down without much effort. I felt clammy and cold, and I couldn't shake whatever that monster's gaze had done to me. Each time I blinked I saw things, red bloody things, Roe's guts, shattered bones, strips of skin. If I could've screamed I would've.

"I know," she said. "It had eyes. I only half believed it was possible until I saw them. You and your man messed with the windmills, didn't you?"

"They're . . . you've got to . . ." My voice was a whisper.

"Don't worry," she said. "I ain't mad. I should be, you getting folks killed and all. But we were rewarded. You didn't piss them off, they'd have never come in such force. We'd have never had them eyes and that tongue. It was meant to be. Bea says so."

Genj laughed as she poured some more water on cloth. She put it back on my forehead and squeezed. Streamers of warm water coursed down the side of my face.

"The . . . eyes."

"Hush. They're safe. They're in a good place now."

"Hurts . . . fuck, it hurts."

Genj looked down at me with an understanding smile, and she spoke in a quiet, peaceful voice as if she were trying to reassure a child who's scared of the dark. "Don't worry, Lizzy. I know all about those eyes. I'm sorry they hurt you. But you're going to be rewarded. Bea says you're part of this now. You can be one of us."

"No. Crazy bitch."

Genj laughed good-naturedly. "Hell, you're already starting to get some of your old spark back. Bea said you would."

"Crush those . . . eyes. Powder."

I looked into Genj's eyes and they were nearly as bad as the angel's. Something that lay inside her, barely restrained, had broken loose. She looked to me like a sinner who'd laid eyes on the Christ.

"I've already put them eyes to use. The tongue too. Water angels say that's the most important part. I can't hardly think of her as my sister anymore. She's beautiful . . . better? I guess that's it. She's better. We're all better for it. Those windmills—I thought I'd be a hero if I got them up and running. Feels like a waste. Way Bea tells it none of that matters now that the water angels are coming back. Gonna be a hell of a world. We have a future, and Bea can see it."

I blinked tears away. The angel's stare still burned in my skull, shattered like a kaleidoscope with a hundred unwelcome images. Roe's eyes bulging as the angel tore him open. Bea opening the dark chamber of her empty mouth wide. The pool in the split mesa, boiling and red as blood.

I shook my head, trying to dislodge the pictures. Something bad was going down. I had to focus.

Genj must've killed the angel after I passed out, else I wouldn't be in one piece. She must have salvaged the eyes and tongue and joined them with her sister. Of course she had. She had no idea what she'd done to her sister. Those eyes.

And water angels, still going on about water angels. It was all I could stand. I pushed myself up, managed to get into a sitting position without Genj holding me back. She took a step back and put her hands on her hips, seemingly satisfied that I was on the road to recovery.

"Damn, you're stubborn," she said.

"You need to get . . . eyes out of her," I whispered.

She frowned. "Those eyes ain't yours. I killed it."

"Don't care . . . whose eyes. Get them out."

She shook her head. "It's just never gonna make sense to you, is it? This is the way things are supposed to be. This is the fucking plan, Lizzy. You think some fool just come along and cut Bea up like that? Hell no. It wasn't the Adams boys and it wasn't no dead Comanche spook, neither. I done that to her. I love her and you wouldn't understand a god damn thing about that, would you?"

I stared. "How could you? She's your sister." Another image floated by, frozen like an old picture in a book—a boy's hand pinned to the ground, a coyote's eyes gleaming as it crept near.

Her eyes were glazed as glass. "I'm sorry as hell if that upsets your sensibilities, but we don't have to hide nothing anymore. She's whole, just like the water angels promised. She was simple as a baby and now she's whole and who the hell are you to deny her something like that. Them water angels promised her they'd send pieces to make her better and they did. Sent their servants, didn't they? You think you're better than us but you're wrong. We're better. Bea's got a destiny, and so do I. And that's a hell of a lot more than you got to hang your hat on."

"God . . . crazy."

"Tell you what, angel hunter," said Genj, wiping her hands on her jeans. "It's about dark and you done worn out your welcome. Get on your feet and start hiking. You can take your chances with the desert. We don't want you here no more."

She slipped out of the tent and left me shaky and weak, tears and dirty water drying on my face. She'd taken those eyes and given them to Bea. Roe was dead, I wasn't sure if I could walk, and I was stuck fifty miles from civilization with a band of lunatics.

I tried my legs and they worked. My head swam with horrors, and I was still a little dizzy, but I wasn't staying here where that crazy bitch-girl was queen.

I found my tomahawk by the makeshift bed and strapped it on. Still had a little of Roe's blood on it. I felt better with it at my hip.

I pushed back the tent flap and stepped into dusk's lengthening shadows. The people of Salvation were about their duties, though a few stopped to look at me with uncertain expressions. I wondered how many of those people still thought they were on a mission to restore civilization, and how many realized they were following a lunatic. I nodded to a couple and headed for the edge of town, hoping to slip away without running into Bea or Genj.

Just my luck, as I left Salvation behind, I spotted the two of them, barely more than spots on the horizon, headed in the direction of the pool.

"Fuck me."

They were up to something. Every ounce of common sense told me to run like hell the other way, but I thought about Roe and I thought about those eyes and I knew I couldn't just leave those psychos to their business.

I turned to follow them, every step an effort.

They reached the pool ahead of me, and by the time I got there Bea was thigh deep in the water, her skirts lifting up so they floated on the surface like foam. Her back was to me, but her new angel hands were at her sides, spinning circles on the surface of the water, faster and faster as if she was writing on a sand table. Genj knelt at the edge of the water, watching her sister intently.

I crept closer, terrified that Bea would turn around and look at me. But it was no sense keeping quiet. What had I come to do, kill them? I'd killed plenty of angels, but never a person.

"Hi, Lizzy," said a musical voice, a beautiful, heartbreaking, glorious singsong voice that made my knees buckle. I knelt rag-legged on the ground.

Genj whipped her head around, saw me and smiled. "That tongue of hers is something special ain't it?"

I nodded, not sure what else to do. How had Bea even known I was there? She had so many angel parts now; maybe she was infected with whatever magic made them. I tried to stand, but Bea dropped me with her words again. "Just sit tight, Lizzy. Nothing bad's gonna happen to you. I promise."

Her hands moved quicker, and the surface of the pool began to roll like the ocean. Genj stood and backed away as if to give the water room to grow.

Bea began to sing, not in words I could understand, but in a lilting language that tore at the heart.

The boiling intensified, peaked, and two figures rose from the water. A third joined them, towering over us.

Water angels. They were not crudely formed monsters like the dirt angels; they looked delicate as the blown glass goblets I'd seen in a church at Fort Stockton, a lifetime ago. As they rose, they caught the moonlight and held it in their transparent bodies. They wore waterfalls like skirts, and the waters that made them were constantly in motion, like lifeblood pumping through their bodies. I stayed on my knees, jaw hung open in an unwitting imitation of Roe. I was stunned by the creatures. They looked like nothing short of gods.

Genj was similarly impressed, but she was afraid too. I could see it in the way her smile faltered, in the way she began to back away from them. Bea stayed in the water.

She didn't even flinch when the water angels began screaming.

I covered my ears and screamed along with them. Their voices sounded like saws cutting through concrete, and the noise threatened to shatter my bones. Genj had her ears covered too, and beneath her tan and the dirt on her face she was white as chalk.

You didn't expect this, I thought.

Dirt rose from the valley floor, spinning around the mesa walls like a small whirlpool. Abruptly the angels stopped screaming, and in the ensuing silence I saw a good dozen fully formed dirt angels surrounding us.

"That one," said Bea, pointing to her sister.

Genj was frozen in place, then tried to run. Too late. One dirt angel blocked her easily, while the other casually took her left arm, considered it for a second, then tore it from her body.

I tried to stand, thought about sending my tomahawk through Genj's brain like I'd done Roe, but Bea simply said, "Stay put," and that was that, I was stuck in place. It took about ten seconds for the angels to reduce Genj to pieces, then they all turned their eyes to me, waiting for Bea to speak again.

"She's nice," said Bea. "Don't hurt her, okay?"

The dirt angels backed away and formed a loose perimeter around the pool. I was on my hands and knees, breathing hard, trying not to vomit, when Bea turned, waded out of the water, and knelt down in front of me in her muddy skirts.

"Do you have a sister?" she asked.

I shook my head, kept my gaze aimed at the dirt.

"Mine was mean. She loved me, I know that. But there was always something in her that wanted to hurt me."

She looked up at the nearest angel and I flinched away from the sight of her eyes. "When I was five, six, we were fetching water from the cistern. There was no one else around and when I was reaching down to scoop up the water she pushed me in. And then she held my head under. To see how long I could hold my breath, she said."

She smiled sadly. "Someone came along and got me out, although I wasn't right in the head for a long time. Genj got beat, real bad. More for fouling the water than for hurting me."

I understood. It seems harsh, but I understood. Water was everything.

"Genj was nicer to me then. Almost too nice. She looked after me, protected me from anyone who would tease me. Thing is, Lizzy, since she stuck my head under? I've heard voices, beautiful voices singing to me. And I think she knew that, and was jealous."

It was all the more horrible for being said in that beautiful voice.

"I forgave her, you know. Came with her to this place with the rest of them. I had faith in Genj. She was going to change everything. Back to how it was before. But out here, out by the water, I learned it can't ever be the way it was before. The voices in my head, they spoke louder to me here. The time of mankind is passing, and now comes the time of all that men are made of. I tried to tell Genj that. I tried to tell her that if I could see them, talk to them, touch them, I might know what was happening.

"And so she cut out my eyes and my tongue and my hands, and told herself that was what I wanted."

Her voice was the chiming of a silver bell, the warble of a bird at morning. I couldn't bear it. "She should have been nicer to me, Lizzy. You think?"

"Maybe so."

"Maybe so. Right. Well, too late now."

"Yep."

"I kind of like you, Lizzy. You want to go home?"

Still looking down, I nodded.

"You can go," she said. She stood and helped me to my feet. My legs were unsteady. I was about to keel over again when she caught me, and then without thought I looked up, our eyes met, and the universe fell open and exposed itself in one violent motion. My spirit shuddered with me, and suddenly I was completely underwater, in the ancient oceans that used to cover this place, and the water angels, the water *people,* were there in all their glory. They lived in cities with silver towers and no walls, strolled through gently swaying fields of flowers, laughed and fell in love and never dreamed of the day the ground beneath them would rumble and the water would dry away and a huge blast of wind would lift their ancient buried servants from the earth in a rebellion that would send them screaming to their dry deaths and hiding out in raindrops.

And I saw the dirt people, ruling this place until men came with their spears. The dirt people weren't afraid of them at first, but the men continued to multiply until at last they began to drive the dirt people back into the earth. I saw the Indians, finally driving the last of them to their graves with tomahawks just like mine, and they ruled this land until the white men came. That was the end for them too. Guns and liquor and diseases and railroads and oil and death. These new men seized the land and held it for a while, a very little while. But most of them believed it was their land. Land they owned. Land they'd always owned and always would.

The world shifted around me again and people started hacking up blood. The new men had their day, but they couldn't fight their own crumbling civilization. They couldn't fight the Walking Cough. The disease struck like lighting, blackening the world with sudden death. The few that remained scrambled to put some semblance of society together again, but things were not the same. They held no power over the land now. Quietly at first, and then with wild abandon, the dirt people rose up. There weren't enough men to stop them anymore.

All the while, the water people watched and waited, spies living in the lakes and springs and storm clouds.

A girl was born, and died and was born again in a border town cistern, and she could hear them whispering to her, telling her that she could see them and bring them back into being if she would take the flesh of the dirt people and make it her own, feel with their hands and speak with their tongue and see with their eyes and use the ancient knowledge deep and residual within them to call the water people back. The one who would sing the song that would bring a fallen nation out of hiding.

The rains would fall again, and this time they would never, ever stop.

I felt Bea's pain then, hands hacked away from tender wrists, eyes scooped away, and worse, the agony of joining with the dirt angel's flesh, and I was screaming, me, Lizzy, with my own mouth and soul. The pain was really mine now, and I thrashed and shoved away and felt myself go backwards over a rock and onto my ass.

I stumbled to my feet, my throat raw with screaming, and turned away from Bea. What the fuck had that psycho done to me? I kept my eyes down, terrified she'd pull me back into the nightmares of her eyes.

"You understand, don't you?" said Bea, and God help me, that beautiful voice made me want to look at her again. I resisted. "It was always me that was going to change things, not Genj."

"You're both god damn crazy!"

"Don't be mean, Lizzy. Okay? Don't be like Genj."

I turned away from her and walked slowly between the two nearest dirt angels. They let me pass. Once I was sure they weren't coming after me, I started to run.

Bea began singing again, and for a dreadful moment the music of her voice almost drew me back, but I shook it off and stumbled forward. Black storm clouds crept slowly in from the west, rumbling and roaring and crackling with lighting. One by one, drops of rain began slapping the ground, wetting my shirt, the back of my neck. When I blinked, I saw images, fast and jagged as a flash of lightning: Bea's face, uplifted to the rain, the water pooling in her dirt-filled eye sockets, mud trickling down her cheeks.

The rain pattered the ground, dampened down the dust. I had to get to Fort Stockton and warn them. Maybe if we could live in a world of dirt we could live in a world of water.

Didn't seem likely.

Mud under my feet, I ran as fast as I could away from Salvation.

POSSIBLY GRIEF

A NY CHILD LIVING BETWEEN THE ANGEL MOUNTAIN HIGH-way and the mossy south bend of the Red Devil River can tell you about the War Witch. She is in turns ancient and gray, haunting and haunted, blessed and cursed. She is a soulless hag, a bony night-kissed children's nightmare. She is a grieving, pitiable thing wrapped in sixty-year-old rags who lifts her ear to moon-lit skies and listens for the echoes of long-dead joy. She feasts on baby fingers and dances naked before pagan gods. She whispers the words to church hymns and kisses her Bible with desiccated lips.

The stories are many and diverse, but they all follow variations of the same twisting path. And at the beginning of that path where the feet of truth meet the cobbles of exaggeration, you will find a dead man named Charlie.

Charlie was the War Witch's son, although she had not yet earned that name in those days. If you believe old people, and when I first heard this story I had not yet learned to do otherwise, you will imagine Charlie as a generous, though not terribly brilliant boy who turned eighteen as the world teetered on the edge of destruc-tion. He might have been a brutal killer, a grinning idiot, a loving son. He might not have lived at all.

His uniform fit him well, and the only woman in town who dis-agreed was his mother. Charlie's father had succumbed to the lure of train songs and liquor while Charlie still wailed for the breast, or he'd been killed by a monster in the woods, a wolf or something worse. Either way, the War Witch had no intentions of losing another of her men. She forbid her son's enlistment, noble cause be damned. But Charlie defied her. He enlisted, or was drafted, or caught a steamer to China, and launched his own offensive against the Japanese.

Now, we've reached the point where you'll notice our paths beginning to divide, and you may follow whichever fork you choose. If we get separated, be assured we'll meet again. It's the nature of story.

Charlie fought the ground war in Europe, and he was among the soldiers that assaulted the beaches of France. He piloted bombing raids over Dresden and Hamburg. He battled Zeroes in the Pacific, gunning them down with antiaircraft fire from the deck of his battleship. Bloodied but unbreakable, he carried men on his back from killing fields in Salerno and Guadalcanal, flew supply routes over Burma, led sniper missions deep into Germany's Black Forest. Yet heroism is not enough to save young men in times of war— would that it were. Luftwaffe bullets downed Charlie's bomber, a kamikaze drove its nose into his ship, Nazis tortured him to death in a POW camp, and Rommel's tanks ground him into the North African sand. In all cases he died heroically, as befitting a man of such legend.

And what of the War Witch? She received a telegram that she still keeps shoved beneath her bedbug infested mattress or tucked in a picture frame behind a photo of Charlie at the train station on the day he left to die for us all.

Are you keeping up? You haven't wandered from the path yet, have you? This is where it enters deeper woods.

Before Charlie left, the War Witch bound him with a spell. No one knew she was a witch then, but the magic was in her blood, a product of her voodoo heritage, a gift from the devil in exchange for her soul, a heavenly blessing for her unshakable faith. She buried a lock of his golden hair beneath a harvest moon, said twenty Hail Marys, offered virgin entrails to Baal, cut off six of her own fingers and kept them in six mason jars full of demon spit. She prayed with her knobby knees against the hardwood floor, gave her body to the Lord of Chaos, feasted with the goblins of the forest, eating their offered flesh and drinking their blood.

All of this, some of it, none of it, so that Charlie would survive the war.

But you've already walked that path. You know she failed. Charlie died. Didn't he?

Now we find ourselves together once again where the myriad paths converge in a clearing of reality, where before us stands an uncared for shack built of wood and scrap metal, besieged by mosquitoes and hissing cedars, awash in a sea of yellow weeds, leaping grasshoppers and fallen pine cones. Maybe that's a cottonmouth causing the dandelions to sway, or an approaching cold front, or a labored, graveyard exhalation.

When Charlie died, his mother moved from their home near the elementary school he'd attended to this place just outside the city limits. Here she could perform her dark rituals without being seen and escape the well-wishers and hand-wringers that reminded her every second of every day that her son was dead. Or hideously injured. Or miraculously healed. Depending on which path you choose to walk, the War Witch's magic failed, brought a limping Charlie home to a hero's welcome, brought him back in a wooden box which she filled with cursed herbs and jewels from the teeth of a barbarian king in order to bring him back from the dead. She crawled into the coffin with her dead son and still sleeps there every night like a vampire. She buried him behind the shack and when she comes home from church every Sunday, she lays down in her garden, listening for any sounds of her son's resurrection. She prays for it to happen and prays that it won't.

There are so many possibilities, and the county's children know them all. They are all true. They are all fabulous lies. Teenagers gather near the river, not far from the War Witch's shack, and they scare themselves with stories about Charlie Hook and his hatchet-wielding mother while they toss back bottles of strawberry wine and smoke homemade cigarettes. Their younger siblings wouldn't be caught dead in the woods, so near the serial killer who keeps his rotting mother tied to a bed in the basement, or the grieving ghost who walks the river, searching for her murdered child, or the family of cannibals who set traps in the undergrowth for unwary children. Every kid has an older brother with a friend whose cousin fell prey to something in the woods, right here where our paths come to an end at the War Witch's doorstep.

There is someone else with us. Have you noticed? A boy of ten who looks very much like I did at his age—perhaps it's me; perhaps it's a cousin of a friend. Some children don't fear the legends, they thrive on them. They simply can't resist the lure of some place as horrible as this chamber of death.

I've been inside before, or at least this boy has, and we remember the smell of dirt and rot, fresh cut flowers and gingerbread. We remember the lace coverlets on the arms of her furniture, just like our grandmother's house, and we remember the bloodstains on the walls, the broken cross, the breathing shadows. Let's follow the child inside. Turn right into the living area and you'll see where the child—still not sure if it's me or not; maybe it's you—saw the War Witch kneeling before her son's coffin on an autumn day not so many years ago.

She looked like those old people who tell stories, and yes, even though I like to tease them, I'm one of them now, not so young, not so inquisitive or willing to believe what people tell me. You'll be here someday.

The child approaches the old woman. This is happening a long time ago, or today, or never. What does it really matter? Hollow moans rise from the coffin, or the air conditioning unit lodged in the window hums a sad tune, or the War Witch is speaking in tongues to her heathen master, bringing her son back to life for another day of killing children, carrying food to shut-ins, wading beneath the murky river water to catch skinny-dippers' ankles. The gauze of memory or the bright sunlight streaming in through the broken windows makes it hard to tell if it's really a coffin. Maybe it's a coffee table, a sacrificial altar, a pulpit with a Bible open to passages of hope.

Closer, now, and the child decides it's a steamer trunk, covered in human skin, draped with an American flag. Shadows leak from inside like living ink. The trunk smells of moth balls and sour cologne. The War Witch is crying, fumbling with the body parts inside, her son's powdered bones, his wickedly preserved corpse, his Medal of Honor, his letters from the front, his still-beating heart. The boy is almost close enough to see what she's *really* doing when her head spins around and she sees him. Her ancient face is caked with grave dirt, she cries bloody tears, her teeth gnash together like she's trying to bite off her own tongue. She looks like your grandmother, more frightened than frightful. She wears a wide-brimmed laced hat and a mask of porcine flesh. Her stubby snout sniffs the air. She screams obscenities at the child and begs him not to hurt her. He turns and runs, leaving behind the hint of cinnamon and death, and he doesn't stop until he's beyond the river and away from the place where Charles the Butcher slaughtered all those kids back when his uncle was in school. He doesn't follow the paths we walked; he makes a new one.

Calm down. That was then, this is now. Can't you tell? We're all alone in this place, with the droning refrigerator, the ticking clock and the scraping of finger bones against the underside of the floorboards. All those paths led here, but you're still alive. The Witch has been dead for thirty years. She's catering a luncheon at the church over in Bradbury. The one where they worship snakes. She's digging a hole to Hell with her claws. Whatever. She's not here. This is my chance, your chance, that kid's chance to find out what's really going on.

Unless you think we should leave the poor woman to her misery and her spells. Make up your mind before Charlie drags home a slaughtered goat for their dinner, before God burns this place to the ground with His fiery vengeance, before the War Witch gets home from her garden club meeting and calls the cops on us for being here. Just climb up on the coffee table, listen for the wind to whisper instructions, dig around in that coffin, feel the bloody soil between your fingers, lift the lid on that trunk and find out what medals Charlie won, how many men he saved, how many children he's eaten, what really happened to that young man our country called overseas.

Hurry up, before the sun goes down. This is the end of the path, kid.

Time to open your eyes.

IN THE TEETH

THE SMILING WOMAN ARRIVED THREE DAYS AFTER LYDIA'S funeral. Kevin discovered her on his way to retrieve Lydia's sunglasses from the car. There was no reason he needed them, just a compulsion to clutch everything of Lydia's close to himself. Kevin had shoveled through dresser drawers and the master bedroom closet all day until he realized the sunglasses were probably in the car. They were plastic tortoise shell shades that had spent more time pushed back over Lydia's red hair than they had covering her eyes, but Kevin's need to find them had risen to the level of panic. When he pulled open the door, the smiling woman blocked his exit and startled him so much that his only response was, "Hello?"

She was older, gray hair cut close to the scalp, and she continued smiling at Kevin without offering a response. Not a pleasant smile, but the pained mourning smile shared by everyone in Kevin's orbit since his wife's suicide. An upturned grimace with eyebrows collapsing down over her eyes, a face searching for the perfect mixture of *Everything will be okay* and *I can't imagine the kind of pain you're going through.* Kevin didn't recognize her. Maybe she was someone who'd worked with Lydia?

The woman didn't offer up a name or respond to his greeting. She smiled right through him like her misery was meant for some distant horizon.

"Can I help you with something?" Kevin asked. "Did you know Lydia?"

She remained silent, held in place by the weight of that an-
guished smile. Summer heat rose up behind her like a conquering
force. The hiss and sizzle of afternoon pressed through the doorway, an assault of cut grass and flitting insects engaged in their own
desperate industry, a reminder that the world continued just beyond
the periphery of Kevin's pain. A line of sweat cut across his cheek
and it put him in mind of the funeral. He could still smell the sour
stench of his own grief. Black suit and gray tie, wrinkled dress
shirt wet against his back, and his fingers grasping at the sleeve of
Amy's dress as if afraid the urgent, hungry hole waiting for Lydia's
coffin might decide to swallow his daughter too. Bludgeoned by
heat and memory, Kevin retreated into the cool hum of the air-conditioned foyer and closed the door. The smiling woman stood vigil
on the porch, absorbing the afternoon's assault without complaint.

"Dad?" Amy said. "Can you come here?"

Amy was in the kitchen, pulling back the tin foil from a plate
of cold fried chicken. Casserole dishes fought for space on the
countertops, their contents aging into hard slabs of cheese and fatty
meat. Amy surveyed this landscape of pity food without hunger.
She wore her mother's oversized Texas Tech sweatshirt and a pair
of floral print pajama pants, and Kevin was pretty sure she hadn't
changed her clothing in the last couple of days.

"What's up, honey?" Kevin asked.

"There's a man outside." Amy sounded half asleep.

A face pressed against the window over the sink. Kevin was
pretty sure it was the guy a few houses down who appeared at their
door once a year, dragging a wagon full of his daughter's Girl Scout
cookies to sell. His face was twisted into the same expression as the
woman on the front porch, and he rested a sweaty palm against
the window, the dreary patina of his wedding ring hot against the
glass. Kevin didn't really know the man, but presumably his wife
was still alive, and his daughter was able to sleep through the night
without screaming herself awake every few hours.

Kevin rapped his knuckles against the glass.

"Hey, go away!" he said. "What are you doing?"

His neighbor didn't flinch. A teenage boy in a black T-shirt and cutoff shorts wandered up and stood beside the first man. Kevin had never seen the kid before.

He tapped on the glass harder this time. "Get out of here!"

The teenager radiated condolences with his smile, but his eyes never quite met Kevin's. He stared past the sink full of half empty coffee cups and food crusted utensils, eyes squinting to see through the glass. Kevin snapped closed the louvered wooden shutters that Lydia had installed over the window. She'd always been the handy one.

She'd also been better at making quick decisions than he was. Kevin picked up his cell phone to call the police but decided against it. What exactly would he tell them? Some guys are peeking through my window? There's an old lady hanging out by my front door? They weren't even trying to get in. The memory of police officers tracking through his home was a fresh bloody wound and inviting them back was no way to heal.

Kevin put a hand on Amy's shoulder. "Let's go in the living room for a while."

Amy nodded and Kevin led her away from the kitchen and the gray funk of sour food that had claimed it. Kevin knew they should put the food away, maybe wash some dishes. But what did it really matter? They were both motivated by other needs now.

Kevin led Amy to the living room recliner. She sank into it, tucked her feet underneath her, and Kevin covered his teenage daughter with a blanket like a newborn. A couple of days before, when the house had been overwhelmed with mourners, someone had turned the television to a home improvement channel, and it remained there. Families engaged in good-natured arguments about stretching the budget, the desirability of ranch style versus colonial, and the absolute necessity of an open concept floor plan. Lydia and Amy had loved these types of programs. Now Amy stared at the screen, her mind pursued by darker thoughts.

The television was a necessary distraction. Kevin had discovered that he couldn't endure long periods of silence. Guilt and horror boiled inside him, overflowed and scalded him. The background noise kept some of the heat at bay, some of the second-guessing. He had a notion that he might never spend another night without the low drone of a television for company.

"Is it terrible that I'm glad everyone has gone?" Amy didn't look at him when she spoke. Her eyes lingered on a young married couple. They were desperate to find an ocean view with a quick commute to work.

"It's not terrible," said Kevin. "At least I hope not. I feel the same way."

"I know everyone just wants to help," said Amy, "but having them here is . . . too much. I don't like the way they look at me. Like I'm broken, and they don't think I can be fixed."

"You're not broken."

Two women and a young girl approached the sliding glass door that led into Kevin's backyard. All three wore swimsuits and the now familiar smiles, and their hands linked them together like children playing Red Rover. Water puddled around the little girl as if she'd just emerged from a swimming pool and bits of clipped grass clung to her feet. They peered with sympathetic eyes into the living room gloom but made no move to enter.

"Dad, I don't want them here," said Amy.

"Who are they?"

"It doesn't matter," said Amy.

"Go away." Kevin raised his voice so they could hear him through the glass.

"I don't like them looking at me."

"I said go away!"

"Dad, do something."

Kevin latched the sliding glass door and drew the heavy blue curtain across it, eclipsing their view of the backyard and blackening the afternoon sun. Gloom settled over Amy like a second blanket and the light from the television washed her face in ghost paint.

"I should call the cops." Kevin assumed the women and the child had either hopped the fence or busted the padlock on the gate. What the hell did they want?

Amy shook her head. "Please don't. I want to go to sleep. I don't want any more people here."

"Okay, honey."

Amy closed her eyes and was asleep in a few minutes. Kevin held her hand and fought back the terror that something might happen to her too. His friend Angelo had lost his wife to cancer a year back and had given Kevin some uncomfortable advice at Lydia's funeral. *You're in the teeth of this thing right now, brother. There's no way out but through it. It's never gonna get much better, but it will at least become something you can live with. Mostly because you don't have much choice.* Amy's breathing hitched like a car slipping out of gear, and as Kevin waited for her screaming to start, he thought maybe Angelo was full of shit. There was no getting better. No pushing through to some new normal.

When Amy finally started screaming, Kevin hugged his daughter and let her rage against him until she wore herself out and was asleep again. Tears burned his eyes and panic fueled his heartbeat.

They were in survival mode.

No way out but through it.

Kevin fell asleep. When he woke, Amy was staring at the television. Maybe it was deep in the nighttime or maybe he'd slept through to the next afternoon. It was impossible to tell in the comfortable nest of darkness they'd assembled. People had quarterly business reviews and second period geometry exams and dinner reservations somewhere beyond the walls of Kevin's two-story craftsman, but if he and Amy were allowed to shun the world and remain there forever, Kevin was certain they would do so. His phone glowed with texts and phone messages from his parents, his friends, all checking to make sure he and Amy were doing okay. But they weren't doing okay, and nobody wanted to hear that, so he tossed his phone on the coffee table and stood up to stretch.

"Amy, can I get you anything? Glass of water?"

She shook her head, attention locked in on a middle-aged couple who were really hoping that five million was enough for the island of their dreams.

"Let me know if you change your mind."

Kevin pulled back a corner of the drape and peered outside. The sun was a razor cut along the horizon, and orange light bled onto the hundred or so people who'd gathered in Kevin's backyard. The women and the little girl in swimming suits were still there, but now the weight of so many new additions pushed against them. Their cheeks pressed flat against the sliding door, forming sticky swirls of sweat on the glass. The assembled mass of mourners stood rigid, faces tight with concern. Still, they made no move to enter. They were a single organism, breathing in unison, eyes wet and searching for some way to make everything okay again.

Kevin let the curtain fall back in place. Amy nestled in her cocoon, heavy eyes still locked on the television. A peek through several other curtains revealed that the crowd had encircled the house, and Kevin felt suddenly hemmed in by their grief.

"Hey, Amy, I'm going to go upstairs for a bit."

This was enough to pull Amy from her television trance. "What for?"

"I just need to go up for a couple of minutes," said Kevin. "I'll come right back."

"Don't stay up there long," said Amy.

"Two minutes, tops. I promise."

They hadn't gone upstairs for anything but a bath or a change of clothes since the afternoon Kevin had found Lydia dead in their bedroom. The memory of her lying there still and cold as the surface of a winter lake with her mouth slightly ajar had banished him to the living room for the foreseeable future. It hadn't been like in the movies. One slender arm falling artfully over the edge of the bed. A constellation of pills fanned out from a toppled bottle. There hadn't been any pills left because Lydia had swallowed them all, and she'd taken the time to put the cap back on the bottle before falling asleep. A half empty glass of ice water had warmed on the bedside table, the coaster beneath it drinking in the condensation. She'd pulled the duvet up to her neck before surrendering herself to oblivion; no matter the weather, Lydia was always cold.

Kevin reached the upstairs landing and couldn't help but glance into the bedroom as he passed. Someone had stripped away the death bed linens but hadn't bothered to replace them. A protective plastic cover hugged the mattress like a body bag.

Kevin hurried to the bathroom, looked out the window, and saw that the crowd was larger than he'd thought. Ten, maybe twenty people deep in places. Every face wore the same pained smiles, but their bodies stood still as stone figures.

"Daddy, please come back down."

"On my way," he said.

Kevin retreated downstairs.

Amy's face was swollen from crying. "I just want this to be over."

"Everyone's gone now, honey."

"I mean I don't want to feel this way anymore. It's selfish, but I just want to be past it. At some point it's going to stop hurting, right? Life will be sort of normal again. I just want to fast forward and make that happen now. I don't want to forget her; I just want to be *finished*. Isn't that terrible? That's all I could think of at the funeral too. Can't this just be finished? What kind of person doesn't want to grieve for her mother?"

Kevin understood. Grief was exhausting. Ultimately, he'd come to believe a little selfishness was necessary to survive it.

Every second was aflame with questions, burning him slowly down to nothing. It was the main reason he'd been relieved when everyone who'd come to the funeral had eventually gone home. For every *You couldn't have done anything to change it* there was a

Weren't there any signs? And yes, of course there were signs when you dared to glance back at the wreckage through the rear-view mirror. And maybe he could have done something to change it. Maybe if he hadn't taken that last phone call at work, he'd have made it home thirty minutes earlier and would have been able to discover Lydia before she was cold and gone. Maybe it wouldn't have mattered. But it was something he'd chew on for the rest of his life.

"It's okay for you to feel that way," said Kevin. "Feel whatever way you need to. Your mom would understand."

Amy grunted. "How do you know what Mom would think? Mom was apparently full of surprises."

"That's not fair."

"Thought you said I could feel however I want."

Kevin dropped into the recliner, saw a true crime paperback that Lydia had been reading on the side table. It was situated face down and fanned open in the way that drove Kevin crazy. He thought about closing it but decided he might just leave it there forever.

"You're right," he said.

Amy pulled the blanket up to her neck and closed her eyes. Kevin watched her until she was asleep again and wondered if they'd ever be able to dig themselves out from the emotional cave-in that had trapped them in their living room. They would have to leave the house again at some point, but they'd carry this darkness with them when they did. Kevin shuddered as he considered the slow, painful slog that would be required to travel from this day to the last day of his life.

He couldn't see the mourners outside his house, but he could feel the weight of them pressed against the windows and the walls. Wood stretched and groaned, like the house itself was asleep and breathing. Kevin hated to admit that he took comfort in the presence of so many strangers. He could not divine what power or purpose had summoned them, but he was coming to realize that he and Amy needed them.

These mourners asked no questions; they just listened.

*

A day later, or a week. Maybe longer.

Amy sat on the couch, her knees pulled up to her chin, dipping a piece of burnt toast into a cup of black coffee. Anytime Lydia's grandmother had accidentally burned the toast, she'd served it this way, and Lydia had picked up a taste for it that she'd passed down to her daughter. Kevin had always thought it was mildly disgusting, but he was happy to see Amy eating something. The television still soldiered on in the corner, but Amy's eyes were on Kevin now and he could tell she was working up to something.

"They're still out there," she said between bites of soggy toast. "I can feel them breathing."

"Who, honey?"

"Dad, I don't need you to lie to me, okay?"

Amy was right. Kevin hadn't looked outside in a while, but the number of mourners had to be growing. The walls shuddered with every coordinated exhalation.

"You're right," he said. "They're still out there."

"Why do you think they came?" asked Amy.

"I don't know. Maybe we need them here?"

Amy nodded. Kevin wasn't sure if she believed that or had come to some separate resolution. She took the last bite of toast, wiped the stray crumbs on the edge of her blanket, and stood. "I want to see them."

"That might not be a good idea." Kevin made to stand up and Amy put him back in his chair with a gentle push against his shoulder.

"It's okay," she said. "If they meant us any harm, they'd have figured out how to do it before now."

Without hesitation, Amy crossed to the sliding glass door and pulled open the curtains.

It was dark outside, and impossible to tell how much the crowd had grown, but those who had stood vigil from the start remained. One of the swimmers still had her face pressed against the glass, and Amy put her hand up like she meant to caress it. The woman's sad expression drew tighter, like she'd found a way to increase her capacity for sorrow. The crowd groaned in unison and the glass vibrated. Amy put her other hand against the door and though she was facing away, Kevin could see her tears reflecting back at him.

"It's not fair," said Amy.

"Amy, close the curtains. Okay?"

"It's not fair!"

Voices rose up in horror. Bodies rattled against the house in pain. Mouths gaped to swallow in the grief.

"Get back from the glass," said Kevin.

Amy began screaming. She pounded the glass with both palms, her grief a feral howl that conjured instant tears in Kevin's eyes. His hands gripped the armrest of his chair and he tried to stand again, but he couldn't compel himself to stop her anymore. Amy kicked out at the sliding door and screamed until she was gasping for breath. One minute, two, and Amy dropped to her knees, coughing and shaking and bent over in front of the tiny girl in her swimsuit. The girl tried to reach out, but her hand touched only glass and she began to cry. Kevin found his footing, pulled the curtain closed, and helped his daughter back to the couch.

Overfull with grief, the mourners began to cry.

Kevin woke in a dream.

Daylight had broken through their defenses and penetrated their vault. Curtains yawned wide, surrendering to the inevitability of morning. Sashes held them in place, unwilling to let the darkness gain hold again. Kevin pushed up from his recliner and stared out the sliding door and across the empty expanse of his backyard. August continued to victimize his lawn and a few islands of brown bobbed in the green sea of Johnson grass. A couple of posts needed shoring up along the fence line. Whenever he had the strength, he'd need to go to the hardware store for some nails.

"Dad? Are you hungry?"

Yes, he was. And rediscovering something as mundane as hunger was like finding a lost friend.

Amy's voice and the smell of breakfast drew Kevin into the kitchen. Steam rose from a plate of scrambled eggs. A stack of toast towered beside it, not burned but perfectly browned. All the leftovers had been relegated to the trash and the coffee pot gurgled and spat as the decanter slowly filled. The wooden shutters above the sink framed a wide-open window, and sunlight rushed in, flowing over the proceedings like a runaway river.

Amy stood with her back to Kevin, pulling a couple of coffee cups from the cabinet. She wore a pale blue dress from her mother's closet, and for a fraction of a second, he thought Lydia had returned. The illusion was strong enough that Kevin's breath caught in his throat.

"About time you woke up," Amy said.

"You didn't have to cook," he said.

"I'm hungry."

"Yeah, me too."

Amy filled the coffee cups, then sat down across from him at the table. Kevin grabbed the darkest piece of toast from the stack and dunked a corner into his coffee.

"Your mom always said it was an acquired taste."

A thin curl of a smile appeared on Amy's face, like a stray brushstroke on a new canvas.

By the time Kevin's dream was over, the smile had reached Amy's eyes.

FURY'S HOUR

THERE'S NO RELIGION WORTH FOLLOWING EXCEPT FOR PUNK. No god worth praying to other than Joe Strummer. Some people think he's coming back to save us, and I'm starting to believe them.

I hate the way the city feels now. Every door was open when I used to be part of the Corp, but now hidden eyes stare through windows and trace any potential misstep, eager to reduce your status and give their own a boost. I used to be so high on that ladder that I couldn't even see the people who haunt the warehouses and squats and backsides of buildings. Now they belong to me and I belong to them. We're one people. We all taste the same flavor of grit.

The alley is silver with old rainwater, wet with light reflecting from the van's headlights. The engine grumbles and smokes as we rush to unload the gear and get everything inside. Vinnie knows the guy working the backstage door and he sneaks us in. Poor guy will be hunting for a new job tomorrow. Maybe doing his best to avoid getting killed. But it's for the cause and he knows it's worth the cost. I think about news videos I've watched about suicide bombings. Sneaking in like this with what we're planning draws an unsettling comparison. But that's not the sort of bomb I'm planning to drop.

*

I was already coughing up blood when I discovered Vinnie and his church. Six months removed from my Corp job and all the benefits, and I was hungry enough that I was considering stabbing a suit for his FroYo. Thankfully some kids living in an abandoned middle school told me about this guy in the warehouse district who was free with his food. I was expecting at best a soup kitchen, at worst a gang of Corp sweepers who'd tag me for forced factory labor or stick me in one of their camps for troublemakers. What I got was Vinnie, every inch of six-five with a face like a cherub who hadn't shaved in a decade or two. He dropped an arm around my shoulder and put a turkey sandwich in my hand without even asking my name.

"How long you been sick?" Vinnie watched me chew through the sandwich, pausing occasionally to choke up a piece of lung. He lived in a warehouse he'd converted into a makeshift homeless barracks, and about two dozen people laughed and snored and traded war stories around us as we spoke.

"Ever since I went off the pharm," I said.

"I figured you were ex-Corp," he said. "No offense, but you got the look."

"I appreciate the food."

"You look like you need it more than us. Did you leave the Corp or did they kick you out?"

"I don't know you well enough to share my life story."

"Yeah? You know me well enough to eat my food."

I grinned in spite of myself. "Okay, you're not wrong. So you heard about that space elevator the Corp was building. The one that got sabotaged?"

"Pretty hard story to miss," Vinnie said. "There's more underground anti-Corp factions popping up all the time, but not many with the guts to do that. Somebody blows up a multi-trillion dollar piece of tech and even the state news service can't keep that totally under wraps."

"I was closely associated with that project." The coughing took hold and shook me for a full minute before I could continue. "Insurgents take down a major company project and the Corp has to chop some heads off. Honestly, I'm glad that getting fired was the worst that happened. The Blessed President doesn't know my name. But he had specific instructions on how to deal with my supervisors."

"Man, I know it's a hard adjustment," Vinnie said, "but at least you got out."

Got out? Vinnie made it sound like a positive. The Corp provided everything—a decent apartment in a prestige zone, plenty of disposable income, and pharmaceutical mixes that blocked diseases and kept you in a constant state of relaxed efficiency. The Corp gave you purpose. Even religion if you wanted it. Every friend I had was in the Corp and every one of them had forgotten my name the second I'd been cut. And Vinnie thinks all of this was worth trading in for a slow death in the sewers?

But there had been days when it all seemed wrong. That much power doesn't come from nowhere. Someone is paying for it. Life in the Corp was great, but even with the pharm cooking your brain, dark thoughts could creep in. You might pretend the news you watched was truth, but some primal part of you knew you were buying a lie.

"The best years of your life and they want to steal them," I said.

Vinnie sat up sharply. "Huh? Where'd you hear that?"

"Hear what?"

"You practically quoted from our gospel," he said.

"I didn't quote anything." I stood, thinking maybe it was time to leave. A wild intensity had settled in Vinnie's eyes and I was afraid he might be more dangerous than I'd imagined. "That's just some words that have been running through my head. I'm mad at the Corp, okay? Maybe I don't like the person I was, but I still wish

I could be him again. What kind of guy does that make me?"

"You never told me your name," Vinnie said.

"Joe."

Vinnie put one big hand on my shoulder. "Joe, if you don't mind, I'd like to show you something before you leave."

The music is nothing but a steady bass thump washed over with droning, atonal synth and string bits, and it crawls up my back and squeezes my skull. From backstage, we can see the pulse of life on the dance floor. It's a private Corp club, an afterhours hangout for rank and file suits who want to max out on the booze and pharm, and with any luck find someone to take home for the night and forget about in the morning. The music is a concussive force, but they try gamely to yell over the top of it. They're dancing, sizing one another up through glowing oculars, but no one is hearing the song. The air is clogged with synthetic smoke, and the hellishly hot room smells like stale beer and too much oxygen.

"You ready?" Vinnie asks.

"As ready as I can be," I say.

"And you're sure you want to do this?" he asks. "No one is going to think less of you for backing out now."

"Yes, let's just do it."

Vinnie nods at his guy, and he turns the volume on the house sound down to zero. The suits in the crowd continue yelling for a few seconds before they realize the music has stopped. While they shoot expectant looks at the bartender and the doorman, I drag the old 100-watt combo amp through the curtain and onto the stage. I plug in the amp, then my guitar, and turn the volume all the way up, per Vinnie's instructions

A microphone hangs from the ceiling like something out of an old wrestling video. Vinnie's guy turns up the level on the mic and I cough into it for a full thirty seconds, eliciting unmasked disgust from a large percentage of the audience.

"Try not to lose your jobs, kids," I say. "Coming down off the pharm is a bitch."

What Vinnie wanted to show me was his church.

"I'm not interested in religion," I said.

"Just listen to what I have to say, would you?" he asked. "You decide if this is religion or something better."

The church was nothing but another walled off space in the warehouse. This one had two rows of rickety metal pews and a scattering of bent folding chairs, all arranged to face the front of the room. Someone had salvaged a huge roll of pink shag carpet and it covered a majority of the concrete floor. The back wall of the room was built with cinder blocks, and someone had spray painted THE FUTURE IS UNWRITTEN: KNOW YOUR RIGHTS in giant, blocky red letters. An ancient component stereo system loomed at the front of the room like an altar, and above this, where a cross might often be found, was a guitar. A really, really old Telecaster. Black and battle scarred with a white pick guard and a rosewood fretboard, the hardware pockmarked with rust. It was beautiful.

Vinnie saw that it had drawn my eye. "You know guitars."

"Yeah, I play a little. It's a hobby. Never played one like that before, though."

"No you haven't," he said. "That's Joe Strummer's guitar."

"Who's that?"

Vinnie walked me closer to the front of the chapel and I was afraid he was going to try and baptize me. But all he did was take the guitar off the wall and put it in my hands.

"He was a member of a rock and roll band called The Clash. They were part of the punk rock scene in the late twentieth century. No real shock that you haven't heard of them. That kind of music is so forbidden you can't even find it on the undernet. You want to hear their music, you've got to track down the physical media. You want to read about them, better find someone willing to part with honest-to-god paper magazines."

I played a few notes, loving the feel of the neck in my hand. They didn't make guitars like that anymore. Real wood, no synthetics. "So other than the fact that this is a really great guitar, why should I care that it belonged to a rock star who's been dead for a hundred years?"

"Joe Strummer wasn't a rock star. He was a teacher. And those words you said about the best years of your life? That's a lyric from one of his songs."

"The hell it is," I said.

"If you're telling me you haven't heard it before, then it's quite a coincidence," Vinnie said.

"So you worship this guy?" I ask.

"He would hate that," he said. "What we do is we come here together, we listen to his music, and we talk about how we can make the world a better place. Then we act on it. It's all there in his lyrics. The way the world is now, it's everything he warned us against, but I guess when he was singing about it nobody was paying attention. Some of the people here . . . they like to tell stories about how Joe Strummer is going to be reborn as our savior. I'm only telling you this because you being named Joe and quoting the man's words... some people around here may start thinking it's you."

I handed the guitar back to Vinnie. "I just came for some food, not to join a cult."

"This isn't a cult." Vinnie hadn't appreciated my comment. He gripped the guitar like he was thinking about putting it upside my head, and I was trying to remember my Corp self-defense training when the doors banged opened and Vinnie's tattered followers began filing in and taking seats in the pews.

Vinnie pulled away, hung the guitar back on the wall. "No one is keeping you here against your will. All I'm saying is I fed your ass so maybe you could do me the favor of just sitting here for a few minutes and listening to some music. You don't like what you hear, then you can leave anytime, and I'll pack a lunch to send with you."

If I'd had anywhere else to go or anyone else offering to feed me, I'd have bolted. But instead I sat down in the back row next to a woman with a shaved head and jacket that looked like it was actually made of real leather.

Vinnie didn't address the room. He just removed an old record album from its sleeve, placed it on the turntable, and dropped the needle.

The hostility in the room has me by the throat.

The entire back wall of the club is a mural of the Blessed President, fourth of his name, heir to his great-grandfather's corporate overthrow of the old government, a more beastly and vacuous creature than even his forefathers if that can be believed. He's the god of the Corp and his worshipers stand before me with their oculars flashing, pulling in instant information about the ragged man with the guitar on stage in front of them. They're streaming everything they see to the overwebs and more than a few of them have already summoned security patrols because they can tell even without their tech that I'm not someone who's supposed to be there.

Hands lower instinctively to the Corp-mandated side arms at their hips, and they're so in sync with one another that the motion appears choreographed. They are the elite, and not that long ago I was one of them, and that scares the hell out of me. I don't know if anyone will shoot me, but they obviously want to.

Whether it's the pharm inducing them to action or whether it's simply their conditioned disdain for anyone without the gray Corp business uniform, I don't know. The sicker I get, the farther away I get from those memories. I'm dying; that much I know for sure. One last gift from the Corp. But that doesn't mean I want to die here and now.

Time to get moving.

No bass, no drums. Just me, this old guitar, and a dead man's words.

I crash into the first chord and launch into the sermon.

It was partly Vinnie's words that made me a believer, and partly the stories from his congregation. But mostly it was the music. I wasn't sure I'd make it through one song, but hours passed, and I was still listening, trying to pull meaning from the teeth of a storm. Lifting the needle, dropping it again, over and over after most of the others had left. That music was a revelation. And what terrified me was that I already knew a lot of the songs. They were like dream memories. Some of them were so familiar I found myself singing along on the first pass, like they'd always been inside me, fighting to be shouted to the rafters.

As Vinnie predicted, this freaked some people out, and though they took me in and gave me a home, it took months for some of them to fully trust me. Those who were more desperate for salvation were convinced that I was the second coming of St. Strummer, and no amount of arguing would dissuade them. But they were wrong. This wasn't about me; it was about the message being directed through me.

It was about the songs.

"London Calling" with its apocalyptic images of rising seas, dying crops, and nuclear war was a dead-on prediction of a world Joe never lived to see. "Lost in the Supermarket" warned of runaway consumerism. And "Know Your Rights," a condemnation of the police state and statement of basic human rights in one glorious, jagged tune. These songs were big red warning signs that humanity had already blasted past at a hundred miles an hour, tossing cigarette butts out the window in their wake. But they were also roadmaps so that we might find our way back.

*

That first chord knocks the suits back a step, but they regroup, blowing angry blue vapor from their lip implants. One of them tries to grab at my ankle but I shake him loose, give him a kick. A feverish group of men wearing the insignia of mid-level management push to the front, howling at me, but the amplifier roars back. Every chord that originates at my fingertips punches them in the chin. The song I've chosen, maybe the only one I'll make it through, is called "Clampdown," and it's the greatest song The Clash ever recorded.

Right this second, it's the greatest song ever written. And it's perfect for this crowd. Oculars bounce in the semi-darkness, pulling in every bit of information they can, all of them aimed right at me. They're active devices, data conduits meant to provide the wearer whatever information they're allowed to know from second to second, but now they're all pulling data back from me and the permission filters are working overtime.

"Clampdown" shatters ugly nationalism. It practically begs you to take control of your life, to use every fleeting second you have to make a difference. It demands that you take hold of the world and give it a fucking shake.

A few of the oculars flicker and the lenses fade from gray to clear, and I can see flashes of who's really wearing them. The real people underneath the tech, not the characters they play to stay in Corp's good graces. I look right into their eyes and see them looking back at me. They've never heard anything like this. They've never *experienced* anything like this. I'm not saying Joe Strummer is coming back to save us, and I'm sure not saying that one song can suddenly cause everyone to question their existence. But if even one or two take the bait, it's a start.

With so many oculars streaming, I know for sure the content aggregators have me featured on half the video screens in the prestige zones, and they will until Corp notices and kills the feed. I give them a show.

Screaming, spitting, raging.

Right before we left the warehouse, I carved RESIST in deep

jagged letters into the face of Joe's guitar, and I lunge out to the front of the stage with that guitar front and center. As I sing, the oculars pull my words and drop them in a steady fall of text across their view screens, and the image of that wonderful guitar is seared into the memory of everyone who sees it, whether my performance changes their mind or not.

"Clampdown" rumbles toward the last note, and if I can just get to the end of that one perfect song, I might be able to slip out the same way I came in. The crowd still isn't sure if they should be dancing or dragging me off the stage, and the security team hasn't arrived to arrest me yet. I'm seconds from finishing the song, from escaping out the back door in one piece. With any luck this is just the first of many guerilla concerts, each one designed to chip away one more piece of the establishment. Maybe I'm the second coming of Joe Strummer after all.

Then a gun comes up and its targeting laser locks on to the guitar. One stoic gray suit—I can't make out the face behind the ocular mask—pulls the trigger and sends a bullet through the guitar, through my gut, and through the curtain behind me.

I'm on the floor before the chord ends, but the feedback holds me tight as I bleed out on stage. Everyone rushes for the exits except for Vinnie who's on his knees, gently unstrapping the guitar and lifting it off me.

Security sirens are all I can hear, and I know that if Vinnie doesn't leave, the Corp is going to bury him for this. I try whispering that he needs to go but there's no more air to drive my voice. No more air even to cough. Vinnie stands, slings the guitar over his shoulder and heads for the back exit. Even the sirens fade and it's just the sound of my own death in my ears. I'm dying, but I already knew that coming in.

And here's the thing.

Vinnie is never going to hang that guitar back up on the church wall. Not after tonight. He's going to learn how to play it. He's going to teach someone else how to play it. Every believer who shows up on Vinnie's doorstep wanting to change the world is going to put their hands on that guitar and make some noise.

Vinnie might not be as religious as the others, but he's going to tell them that Joe Strummer died for them. Joe Strummer tore this motherfucking place down.

But he's not coming back to build it up again.

That part's up to you.

BEST ENERGIES

THE KING

THE DAY AFTER THE WAR ENDED, KING GEORGE TOOK BREAK-
fast in his office. Black cherries, toast, and Coca-Cola. He
relished the simple act of eating. No matter how many years he
lived, he'd never shake the memory of those wooden teeth, and he
thanked Providence that his immortality had carried him to such an
advanced age. What the young took for granted, George appreciated for the miracles that they were. Reliable false teeth, automobiles, modern medicine . . .

. . . and, of course, the atomic bomb.

The morning edition of the *Times* announced the Japanese surrender, but it had been a foregone conclusion for the last week.
What else would the enemy do in the face of such suddenly over-
whelming odds?

The phone calls began while he was reading the comics section. George was scanning the page for the Dick Tracy strip when
his secretary's voice announced that the President of California
was on the line. George took his congratulations with the proper
mixture of false modesty and unquestioned power. That call was
followed by countless others—friendly nations eager to claim their
places in the new world order created by Hiroshima, as well as old
enemies making transparent attempts to claw themselves back into
George's good graces.

He took pleasure in every call, but his delight doubled when his secretary announced that the President of Texas was holding on the line. George waited a full minute before lifting the handset.

"Sam!"

Sam Houston released a weary sigh and spoke in an irritable drawl. "Morning, George. I suppose you're in a fine mood today."

"I will admit, the air smells a bit more like freedom this morning."

"To some, I suppose."

"Not to worry," said George. He slipped a Camel between his lips, struck a match, and lit it. "You still enjoy the protection of the United States of America." George inhaled deeply, enjoying the burn of smoke in his disease-proof lungs.

"The Republic of Texas does not need outside help in guarding our own interests," said Houston.

"Sam, I don't like to touch on unpleasant matters, but it pains me that you haven't shown me any inkling of respect in the last hundred years or so. I'd think you would feel some kind of debt to the man who shared immortality with you."

"Most days, I wish to Hell you hadn't."

"Yet you'd have me open the gates and let anyone drink who cares to. That's why you've called, is it not?"

"I certainly didn't call to help you plan the victory parade."

"So you'd have me hand that kind of power over to the savages?"

"It was theirs to begin with, wasn't it?"

"That's a matter of some debate," said George.

"Well, I disagree with your take on things."

"So, because the savages were here first, the United States must cede everything we've built to them and call it a day? I suppose, then, you'll be handing over that city they named after you to the Mexicans? Or the Spanish?"

"This is different. That kind of power shouldn't be confined to one nation."

"Damn you, Houston. Here I am, celebrating the liberation of half the free world, and you can't even choke back your pride long enough to admit that I've done you a favor. Instead, you choose this day to call and pursue the same tired matter that you've been carping about for more years than I care to remember. The Immortality Pool is on U.S. soil, and that makes it mine to use as I see fit. Now that we've figured out how to harness it for other uses, I'm even less willing to share it with those who are disinclined to support American interests."

"That's the main point of my call. What the hell did you do? Those bombs you made—you can't tell me that's not a product of the Pool's magic. I knew you'd managed to do some heinous things with that water. I've heard of the Special Forces you sent against the Germans. But now you've passed well beyond the borders of national interest."

"Yes, I have. We are a magnanimous nation. We're protecting the world. You Texans, and all the savage nations, should be thankful. The whole continent is better for my actions. The Nazis ripped a hole straight through Europe. Do you think they'd stop there? Certainly not. So, while you were unwilling to pick a side, we knocked the fascists and their Japanese whipping boys down so many pegs that they won't be capable of starting new trouble any time soon."

"I'm not arguing that the Nazis weren't a threat. We would certainly have responded in kind, had our interests been threatened as yours were. But you cannot tell me you wouldn't have steered clear of that war if you'd had a choice. Any sane country would have."

"Or any cowardly one."

Houston remained silent for a few seconds before speaking. "George, I've called to ask you, one more time, to allow others access to that pool. That power should be shared. This is something you need to do."

"Do I sense an ultimatum in your tone?"

"What you sense is a demand."

"Goodbye, Sam." King George dropped the phone in its cradle and fumed.

What a mistake it had been to let Houston drink from the Pool those many years ago. Sam had been a good man once. He'd served under General Jackson and killed his fair share of savages, and the General himself had recommended the young man for immortality. Yet not a month after Houston tasted that glorious, wondrous Water, he'd been convicted of nearly killing a man and fled to the wastelands they called Texas. The deserter had been nothing but a thorn in his former nation's haunches ever since.

Simply organizing dirt farmers and rabble-rousers into stealing land from Mexico did not make a man presidential, yet Houston had taken that title with little protest. A few years later, he'd been succeeded by one of his staunchest detractors. That was the limitation of Houston's form of government. The man wasn't old enough to remember when the United States had toyed with the idea of limited-term presidencies and, thus, never knew the folly of turning one's best laid plans over to someone who does not share the same dreams. George had learned quickly what a mistake that was.

Of course, being long-lived, Houston found himself elected again and again to the Texas Presidency, and each time he regained the title, he bucked against the United States rightful place as their continental superior.

A painting of the Immortality Pool hung opposite the King's desk in the Oval Office. It showed the Pool as it had been when Captain Smith and his men had claimed it for England. That Spanish fool, de León, had wandered half of Florida, following trails conjured by lies and false legends. Had he turned his eyes to the north, past those miserable swamps and tangled nests of cypress, he might have found what he sought in Virginia. But to the great detriment of Spain, he never had.

George pushed back his chair and crossed the room, towards the painting. He was often drawn to it, and he ran his fingertips over the familiar bumps and swirls of oil on canvas. The artist had captured the Water's elusive shade of silvery-pink, and George could almost feel the cool kiss of dogwood flowers on his cheeks and the soft wind that blew from the Pool like holy exhalations. Now, the Pool was surrounded by metal fences, barracks, and processing plants. But George still remembered it as a peaceful place.

And although he'd only had one drink of the Water, he'd never forgotten the taste. Earthy, sweet, and utterly pure. Drinking it was like embracing the divine.

George hated men like Sam Houston, who would see the place overrun by fascists and savages and communists who'd sooner piss in the Water than worship it with the reverence it deserved. George had no idea how the Pool had formed, but he knew God's hand had played a part. One tiny sip and you'd live forever. After all these years, that miracle had never paled. But it was so much more than that. The Water had other uses, uses beyond count. And though they'd graduated a succession of alchemists from government sponsored programs, none had ever managed to harness the Pool's full potential until they'd enlisted the foreigner.

Einstein was an alchemist without peer. Spinning the Water into gold was an old trick. This man could spin all of that magic into power.

The phone rang again, and George returned to his desk, eager to put Houston and his petty concerns behind him for the morning. According to his secretary, the new interim Chancellor of Germany was on the phone, and that was not a call he intended to miss.

THE STATESMAN

President Sam Houston felt every one of his one hundred fifty-two years. He stepped into the war room, still fuming from his conversation with Washington. The assembled Secretaries of *This*-and-*That*, Joint Chiefs, Vice President Ferguson, and various other advisors stood as one. Sam closed the door behind him and took a seat in the empty leather chair at the head of the table.

"Sit down, all of you," he said. "Still never figured out how standing up, just to sit down again, is necessary every time I walk into a room."

Sam hated ceremony, absolutely loathed it. He'd been president far too many times to have people bowing and scraping just because his name was on the door to the big office and his face was on the dollar bill. He had to constantly remind himself that, although these men and women seemed of an age with him, they were comparatively young and regarded him with an inordinate amount of respect and awe. It was just another of the countless things that irritated him about being immortal. He wasn't just President Houston, he was *the* Sam Houston—the last living Father of Texas, hero of the Battle of San Jacinto, and all those other titles he didn't care to remember. Texas was a country that took a great deal of pride in its own mythology. Being a living architect of that mythology was a unique and uncomfortable burden.

"Can we assume, by that sour milk expression on your face, that King George hasn't yet built a public diving board at the Immortality Pool," said Vice President Ma Ferguson with the trace of a smile.

"He's as stubborn as ever," said Sam.

Ma nodded. Sam knew that she was intimately aware of King George and his fanaticism. She'd served as president some years back and done a fine job of it, but she'd had no more success in her attempts to wring common sense and decency from the immortal monarch than any of her predecessors had.

"So we move forward with Operation Floodgates?" asked General Eaker, Commander of the Texas Ground and Air Corps. His face was solemn, but Sam could see the excitement in his eyes. War wasn't something to be wished for, but Sam understood how the General felt. He wasn't the only person in the room that wanted to take George Washington down a few pegs.

"I will go on record, again, to urge caution in this matter," said General Nimitz, Supreme Commander of the Texas Navy. "We can't win a war against America, Sam. Mr. President. Even a war of conventional weaponry, which we know this will not be."

"This will only be a war if Operation Floodgates fails," said Sam. "And I'll admit, we stand little chance in that case. But if we succeed?"

"If we succeed, we don't know *what* will happen," said Nimitz. "We have only the theories of a mad scientist to go on."

"Mad *alchemist*," said Eaker, humorlessly.

Nimitz scowled. "Whatever you call him, we have no proof that the man is capable of doing what he says he can do."

"I'd say the Japanese would vouch for the man's capabilities," said Ma. The room grew silent. Even Nimitz could not argue that point. What had once been the miracle of everlasting life had been changed. It was now altering men into mindless killers, heedless of pain and injury, who powered silent flying machines that were faster than airplanes and capable of launching payloads of unquenchable fire and infectious madness. Some reports stated that the aircraft could fly backwards through time. If the US Army Air Corp lost a battle, they'd simply rewind and start again and then again, if necessary, until it turned out in their favor. There was no tangible proof of this, but a few spies had reported it to be true, and even Einstein confirmed it for them in his cryptic way. The man's reports were maddeningly vague, but he'd smuggled out what knowledge would be necessary to their plan.

A few encoded transmissions, engineering plans received in stages, everything needed to build Bluebonnet Betty. It was an obscenely innocuous name for a bomb, but Sam took some small comfort in the fact that their bomb would be nothing like the one George had unleashed on Japan. Although they were both created by the same man, Bluebonnet Betty was not technically even a bomb. If a description must be applied, Sam preferred to think of it as an *agent of change*.

"The device is finished?" Sam asked.

"Betty's fully constructed," Ma said. "Along with a backup shell, just in case we need it. All we lack now is the ignition element."

"I just can't see how this plan is in the best interest of the Republic," said General Nimitz.

"The Ground and Air Corps is prepared to follow the orders of the President," said Eaker. "Chester, are you sure you're not just bucking on this plan because the Navy isn't involved? We'll get you in the history books somehow. Don't worry."

Nervous laughter filled the room. Sam knew that they were old friends and that Eaker enjoyed pushing his colleague's buttons even more than he loved tweaking King George. But it was a bad time for humor and the President cut off any potential retort with a pronounced cough.

"I have no doubt that Chester holds the fate of Texas above all other considerations, particularly personal gain," said Sam. "His dissent is noted and welcomed. None of us are certain we're following the right path, but our options are few. Washington is flush with pride right now, and he's only going to get stronger. We can wait around for him to turn his eyes our way and decide it's time to annex us, or just to blow us off the map and start fresh, or we can take a proactive stand. In light of the destructive power unleashed on the latest of George's enemies, I think we know what the outcome would be if our nations ever came to blows. Even with all the Native Nations, The Republic of California, and Mexico behind us, we couldn't fight back against magic. We would die, and our country would die."

"But if we had magic," said Ma, "the shoe would be on the other foot."

"But we don't know for sure we'll have magic," huffed Nimitz. "That's the whole point of my argument, Madame Vice President. You may be in charge of all these spies of ours, but can you really vouch for the motives of the man who enabled the United States to build the Atomic Bomb?"

"Tread carefully," said Ma with a feral smile. "I might take issue with a man who questions my capabilities."

Nimitz blanched. Ma was a formidable ally, but she was an

even more capable enemy. Not even a man in Nimitz's position could afford to rub her the wrong way.

"I'm not questioning your capabilities," he said in a lowered tone. "I'm questioning this alchemist. He claims to serve our interests, but he ends up building the most horrible weapon the world has ever seen. You've said in the past that he must continue to advance the goal of the Unites States in small ways, in order to keep his position and appear loyal to their cause. This is necessary in order to advance our own goals, and I understand the need fully. But he's created an unstoppable force. He's forged the key to world domination and placed it right in George's palm."

"I do regret that," said Ma. "But the man didn't know how powerful that weapon would be. Even for skilled alchemists, magic is a tricky thing to manipulate."

"Exactly!" said Nimitz, slapping the table. Those assembled around him jumped. "He didn't have a full understanding of what would happen when that bomb exploded. How can we know that Betty will perform as he says she will?"

"We can't," said Sam, cutting off any further argument. He'd listened to the exhaustive opinions of every man and woman in the room on numerous occasions, and truthfully, he'd made his decision the second he'd finished his call to Washington. Once Einstein arrived with the last piece of the puzzle, Betty was going to fly.

Sam shared Nimitz's doubts, but they had little choice. If Betty performed according to spec, she'd be dropped into the Immortality Pool by a shiny new Boeing B-29 and would create what Einstein described as magical fission. Whatever force was binding the magic to the water, to that place, would come apart, and it would flow into the world. Sam had spent time with some Cherokees in his younger days, and they had sworn that the magic in that pool had been trapped there by an ancient warlock and screamed for release. If that was the case, Sam intended to be its liberator.

What would happen when all of that magic returned to the universe was something that no one could guess. Whatever the result,

Sam had a strong suspicion that it would be something preferable to being bullied and beaten by an increasingly mad, two hundred-year-old, petty tyrant.

"This is a matter of faith," said Sam. "And I will take responsibility for the outcome."

"Then Operation Floodgates is a go?" asked Eaker.

"On the President's order, I'll send word through the channels," said Ma. "It's time to retrieve the alchemist."

THE ALCHEMIST

Defecting from the Unites States wasn't the easiest of tasks, especially for a man as recognizable as Albert. He'd shaved his mustache and cut his wild hair into a short and messy patch with his pocketknife. He'd done so in a gas station restroom, somewhere west of Memphis, after being recognized by a poultry truck driver who'd given him a ride from Nashville. The man had let him off at the station with few questions and little trouble, so either he hadn't been listening to the radio or had somehow missed the alerts airing constantly for Albert's capture.

Albert trudged along the side of the road, cursing the damned Ford that he'd left smoking alongside the highway a few hundred miles behind. He had finally received the call to put the plan in motion, and the car picked that day to die. As far as signs went, it wasn't the most promising.

He'd left the Pool Compound in the middle of the afternoon the previous day. Better to make it look like he was leaving for some quick errands than sneaking out in the middle of the night. By suppertime, the reports of his flight had already reached the press, and King George's propaganda experts were earning their money. Albert had woken a national hero, and by the time he went back to sleep, half the country thought he was a murderer. Killed two men and stole state secrets. Tried to pollute the Immortality Pool. It was nothing but lies, but that wouldn't matter if he got caught.

Albert had expected this sort of thing, but not so quickly. Technically, he wasn't even a citizen of the United States and could come and go as he pleased. But he had no more personal freedom than a prisoner. Albert knew far too much about the internal operations of the Compound, and about the Water itself, and he knew how the King would react if he simply disappeared. Better to cut his losses with his pet genius than let that sort of knowledge fall into foreign hands.

The King had never trusted him; Albert doubted there was a man on Earth he trusted.

Albert heard the gray pickup rattling before he saw it appear over the rise. He stuck out his thumb, and pulled his hat down a bit, hoping the lack of mustache would be enough to disguise his true identity. The locked, steel briefcase he was carrying wouldn't make him any less conspicuous.

The truck stopped and the driver pushed the passenger door open. "Get on in."

Albert climbed into the truck and put the briefcase between his feet on the floorboard. The cab smelled like liquor, and the driver looked as if he was quite familiar with the stuff. He was handsome, and had a better shave than Albert, but he was rail thin and wore only a stained undershirt with his worn pants and boots. He had a crooked sort of smile that made Albert a little nervous, and his eyes seemed to be staring at some point just beyond the horizon. His hand jumped slightly when he offered it to shake, and Albert wondered if he might be affected by something more than just alcohol.

"Name's Hiram," he said. "Where are you headed?"

"Austin, Texas," said Albert. "I have family there I plan to visit."

"You don't sound like a Texan. Don't really sound like an American, either. Where are you from?"

"Switzerland," he said. He doubted the driver would know the difference in the accents, and choosing Switzerland was a safer bet.

"What are you doing all the way over here? The Nazis didn't run you out, did they?"

"No, the Nazis never marched on Switzerland, thank goodness. My family left before the war and has been living in Texas since. You can imagine, I'm eager to see them again."

Hiram dug a flask out of his pants pocket and held it out to Albert. "You thirsty?"

Albert shook his head, pleased that the man hadn't pressed him on his invented family, but leery of riding too far if he insisted on drinking more.

"I just need a nip," said Hiram. "Hope you don't mind. My back hurts like the devil. Does most days."

"You're a young man," said Albert. "Have you injured yourself?"

"No, I was born with pain. Haven't figured out how to chase it the hell away yet, but I'm working on it." Hiram drank from the flask for several seconds, then left it in the seat between them. "Tell you what, I'm heading to Texas too, though I'm going to Dallas. I've got a show there in a couple of days on the radio. I'll drive you as far as I can."

"Radio?" said Albert. "Are you an actor?"

"No, I'm a singer. I've sung on enough radio stations in the south that I've lost track of how many, but I ain't never sung for foreigners before. This should be something, shouldn't it? I figure them Texans are pretty much like southerners. I mean, they speak English and all. And they ain't got no love for Washington. We'll get along just fine."

"You don't agree with your president's politics?" asked Albert. It was a subject far too close to the truth of things, and he was a fool for pressing the point, but he'd so rarely met someone who'd speak out against the government in front of strangers. He was fascinated.

"I don't agree with a man who hoards power. And what else is that damn Pool he's got but power? He makes all his buddies immortal and lets everyone else just go to Hell. You think, if I knocked on his door, he'd give me a sip of that Water? Hell, no. He'd run me off and then go make a speech about responsibility and how he's single-handedly taking care of us all. Like he knows better than we do what's good for us. No, sir. I do not care for that man. I'm sorry if you're offended."

"No apology necessary."

"So what do you do for a living back there in Switzerland?"

"I'm a scientist." It was the truth, for what little that was worth, though he'd let ambition twist it into something less noble. He'd gained worldwide fame for his theories of mass-energy equivalence and the particulate nature of light. He'd even won the Nobel Prize. Albert had a way of looking at the world from angles that others hadn't discovered, and when King George had offered him a chance to apply his mind to the mysteries of magic—the very antithesis of everything he'd ever known—he could not turn it down. He'd secretly come to believe that he'd reached the limits of what he could achieve without violating the fundamental laws of the universe. But the Pool was without limits, a grand mystery that defied physics and called into question even the most ironclad beliefs of the scientific community.

Upon his arrival at the compound, Albert had been astonished at all of the things Washington's alchemists had managed to do with the Water: simple mind reading, pain relief, and brief moments of enhanced speed and agility, all from ingesting drops of the Water mixed with various compounds. Albert immediately set his heart to the task of finding new uses for what proved to be nothing more than a previously unknown element, bound in an unchangeable liquid shape, sizzling with electromagnetic force. Within weeks, he'd learned more about the Water than the Americans had in several hundred years, and within a few more years, he could do absolutely anything with the Water. Anything.

Not that he had free reign. All of his research had to benefit the American good, and he was thankful to King George for allowing him access to what was sure to be his life's work. So much so that he even shared his suspicions that the Nazis were working on a nuclear fission weapon, a monstrous bomb capable of untold destruction. George had laughed and told him he'd better get to work on magical fission. And so, of course, he had.

By the time he realized what kind of fury he was set to unleash on the world, it was too late to reverse his research.

It was his own guilt that had driven him to spy for the Texans; even before the bomb was finished, he knew that he would have to seek redemption somehow. The Texans offered it to him, and he seized it. They had sought to stop the manufacture of the bomb, but by that time, it was out of Albert's hands. So they settled for making a weapon of their own, and Albert gave them the intelligence they needed. The fools wanted to release the magic into the world so that everyone could gain access to it. Hadn't they seen what that Water could do? It was madness, and when Albert had heard of their intentions, he'd almost laughed.

No, the Texans would have their weapon. They had great faith in him. But it would not function in exactly the way they expected.

"A scientist?" said Hiram. "You know, you look like a scientist."

Albert laughed nervously. "I think I always have. Even as a child, I knew this would be my profession."

"We're alike in that," said Hiram. "I've never been good at much but singing, but that suits me fine. Say, you think we're close enough to pick up any Texas radio broadcasts? I'd like to know if they got any singers there can give me a run for my money."

Hiram switched on the truck's radio, and Albert suppressed a gasp. A preacher was shouting through the tinny speakers, urging them off the lost highway to sin, when the news cut in with an announcement that the famous alchemist and Nobel Prize winning scientist, Albert Einstein, was still at large after magically murdering half the Immortality Compound and trying to destroy the world's supply of Water. Albert reached instinctively for his briefcase and put his other hand on the passenger door handle.

Hiram grinned. "Settle down, Doc. I'm not an idiot, and I read the papers. I knew who you were the second you jumped in the truck. I just didn't want to run you off. I have a notion that you ain't done none of that stuff they said you did. More of the King's bullshit, I'll wager. I'm just going to keep on driving, and you don't have nothing to worry about from me. Okay?"

Albert nodded thankfully, still clutching his precious cargo. "You are a good man, Hiram."

"No, I'm a sight worse than most. But if you took off, you probably got a good reason. And I can't imagine it makes old splinter teeth too happy. Any man willing to spit in his eye is a friend of mine."

Hiram stuck his hand out again; Albert released his grip on the case and shook it.

The Hell-Raiser

Hiram's world was a dark blur of asphalt and pine trees awash in threatening yellow headlights. Fresh pain, born of hours on the road, lanced through his back, and he resisted the urge to sip some more whiskey. He was drunk enough as it was, and he didn't intend to kill such an important man as Albert Einstein.

Besides, they didn't have much farther to go. The Republic of Texas was coming up fast.

"I appreciate your help," said Einstein. "But please, don't feel compelled to risk your life for mine. You can stop and hand me over, and they'll make you a hero."

"The hell I will. We're twenty miles from the border, and getting into Texas is easier than getting into Mexico. Those old boys behind us may be bold over here, but they won't follow you into another sovereign country. Washington just finished up with one war. I reckon he ain't looking to start another."

Hiram hoped that he sounded more confident than he was. Two identical black Packards had caught up with them about an hour back, and they'd been pressed up nearly to his bumper ever since.

They'd fired a few shots in the air, but it hadn't taken a scientist to figure out they weren't shooting at Hiram's truck. If they had been, they'd have hit it. And besides, they wouldn't want to kill the greatest alchemist that the world had ever known. They needed that man.

"You have Water in that briefcase?" he asked, fear and adrenaline finally stripping away his manners. He'd been waiting for the man to volunteer the information, but he wasn't much for conversation unless you prodded him a bit.

"Yes, but it won't grant you immortality. It's been converted into a Water Uranium suspension with a—"

"I don't care to be immortal," said Hiram, guiding the groaning old truck around a corner. "I just thought maybe you could use it against them." He motioned behind him with his thumb, and the Packards seemed to sense it. They revved their engines and pulled close again.

"The suspension in this case has only one possible use."

"Well, it was worth a shot. They're supposed to have them airplanes can fly back in time. Wish they'd fly back to when these yay-hoos didn't know where we were."

"You may get your wish."

"What's that?"

"If we get to Texas alive, I'm going to turn all of this back. The whole war. Everything. What do you think of that?"

Hiram would have thought that any other man in the world was crazy, but he knew Albert was serious. Reading about the Eighth Air Force's Rewind Missions in the magazines was one thing; best as he could understand, those time reversals were localized occurrences. They wouldn't affect anything more than a mile or so from the aircraft. But it sounded like Einstein was talking about something more dramatic, and that scared the hell out of him.

"How do you intend to do that?"

Einstein studied him with that famous face, the one he'd recognized immediately, even without the wild hair and mustache. His eyes were wet with sadness or fear, and he held onto his briefcase with both hands like a child with his blanket.

"Hiram, you're risking your life to get me to Texas, so perhaps you should know what you're risking it for. The Texans are going to build a bomb."

Hiram nearly swerved off the road. "What kind of bomb? If you mean to build another of them atomic bombs, then maybe I *will* just pull over and let you walk."

Einstein shook his head. "No, not one of those. Never one of those. It's more of a time bomb, though that's not exactly what the Texans are expecting. I've been sending them the plans, sneaking out bits of information at a time. I simply want to make amends for my part in the atrocity that is Hiroshima. The Texans, they want to free the magic so that everyone in the world has an equal share, but that would only exacerbate the problem. We don't need more people making weapons, we need fewer."

"So why are you helping them if you don't see eye to eye?"

"They are manufacturing the bomb to my specifications. I could never have built such a thing under the King's thumb." Einstein patted the briefcase. "Once I put this inside it, the device will be functional. But that's where our paths diverge, hmm? These Texans, they chase one goal, and I chase another. Let them believe that this Bluebonnet Betty of theirs will free the magic. I know what it will really do. It will turn back this world, all of it. Not too far, mind you. Violating history is not something to be taken lightly. But if time were to reverse to a point before I joined my efforts to the Americans, I am confident they could not discover magical fission without my assistance."

"That's all well and good," said Hiram, "but who's to say you don't just join up with old Georgie again? If time goes backwards, you ain't gonna remember none of this."

"That is where science and alchemy must bow to faith. When time reverses, I believe nothing will be exactly the same. I must hope this new version of me will be less prideful. Perhaps he will see the dangers inherent in such unchecked power. And if he does not, then I hope he has the opportunity to do all of this over again."

Hiram's head was hurting as badly as his back, and he wished to hell those boys chasing them would give them some room to breathe. His mind reeled at the thought of years of history being wiped away. When had Einstein come to America? He couldn't remember exactly, but it had been when he was a kid. Life hadn't been wonderful, and he wasn't entirely sure he wanted to live it all again. But putting the alchemist out now would be the same as sentencing him to life in prison. And though Einstein's plans weren't comforting, they were far less worrisome than what business the King would put him to if they drug him back to the Compound.

"My life hasn't been much to write home about," said Hiram. "I don't think I'd care to go through it all again. Besides, I'm starting to get a little success. A little money. There's a feller out in Nashville told me I got a million dollar voice. I might be somebody famous one day, like you. I hate to turn back now."

"You are right. Things will not necessarily follow the same path. But perhaps you could have a better childhood this time. And if you are the musician you claim, then I expect you will be so again. Admittedly our experimentation has been limited, but certain aspects of people's nature do not change. If there is music in your soul, it will remain there."

Hiram drank the last of the whiskey in his flask and fished in his pockets, once again, for pills he knew weren't there. They'd been gone before he left Alabama. He clenched his jaws together, waiting for the worst of the pain to pass, and he wondered what he'd done to be born with a bent-to-hell spine.

"How far are you planning to turn back time?"

"As little as possible," said Einstein. "I came here in the thirties, so some time before that."

"How about nineteen twenty-three?"

"Why would you suggest that year?"

"It's the year I was born. In September. I ain't in the best of shape, in case you ain't noticed. There's plenty of reasons for that, but mostly it's cause of my back. I was born with something wrong. It's all bent up and causes hellacious pain more often than not. I throw back some whiskey and pills, and it don't make everything better, but it helps a little. If you were to go back before I was born, is there a chance I might come out right? I mean, be born without this problem?"

"There is certainly a chance, though there is an equal chance you will retain your affliction."

Hiram nodded. "I don't care for the idea of messing with time. But if you got to do it, you go back that far at least, would you?"

"I think nineteen twenty three would be an ideal year," said Einstein. "Life was fine then."

Lights flooded the highway ahead, and for a second, Hiram thought the sun had risen early. Then he realized he'd reached the border, and the Texans were bathing them in floodlights. Armed soldiers stood atop several guard towers, and three tanks, emblazoned with the Lone Star insignia, idled alongside the highway ahead with their guns directed straight towards them. A contingent of U.S. border guards manned their own towers, rifles pointed at the sky. The way west was unobstructed, but the road back in from Texas was gated and heavily guarded. The men on the towers watched the cars approach with casual interest. They apparently hadn't gotten word that the great fugitive Einstein was headed their way. Another man, wearing the same stiff blue uniform, peeked out of a booth and waved at Hiram so he might slow his approach.

No doubt sensing time had run out to capture their escaped alchemist, one of the Packards rammed into Hiram's back bumper. Metal screamed and the truck shuddered, but he kept it riding the center stripe. They slammed into him again, and then fell behind as Hiram pulled within firing distance of the soldiers. The Packards braked, and Hiram shot across the Texas border with a whoop of triumph, the loose bumper clattering against his back tire and the engine whining from the strain of the chase. Once he'd passed, the tanks pulled into the road, and the soldiers hurried to drop a striped crossbar over the highway, shutting off entry through the Texas half of the emigration station. The U.S. border control agents had finally realized that something was amiss, but they had no intention of testing their rifles against the Texas tanks.

Whoever was in charge over here had known they were coming, and Hiram was damn thankful. He doubted his old truck would have held out much longer.

He eased it to a stop, removed his shaky hands from the wheel, and wiped them on his pants. Blood thundered in his head, and he wore a wild grin. He hadn't realized how worked up he'd become. The engine ticked, and Einstein breathed heavily. Hiram started to laugh.

"Welcome to Texas, Mr. Einstein."

The Vice President

Vice President Ferguson stood in the far corner of the hanger as she watched Einstein and the crew of engineers he'd been assigned put the finishing touches on Bluebonnet Betty. Men pulled and tugged at a proliferation of levers and dials that sprouted from the bomb's surface, a process that was, according to the alchemist, just as vital to the bomb's proper function as the Water they'd already inserted into the fission chamber. Unable to contain her excitement, Ma crossed the hanger, her footsteps echoing off concrete and steel, and she took up a supervisory position just off Einstein's left shoulder.

"You're sure everything is in order?"

Einstein sighed. "Your engineers have done a fine job. I've told you, this bomb will function as planned. What more do you want from me?"

"The United States won't sit around waiting for us to move. I'd be shocked if they haven't already sent a squad of their Special Forces freaks across the border to track you down and bring you back."

She thought she saw Einstein shudder at the prospect and suppressed a smile. She didn't care for the man, but he was a necessary evil. Wasn't he responsible for elevating King George to an even greater threat than he already was? It had been a coup to win the traitor to their side, but that didn't mean she trusted him.

"They will come, or they won't," said Einstein. "Either way, this device must be properly calibrated. Else this entire endeavor has been a waste of effort."

"Then please finish."

"Another few minutes should suffice. Just have your men ready to leave."

She'd already seen to that. The B-29 waited outside the hanger, belly open to receive its payload. A squadron of P-51 Mustangs, ironically purchased from an American defense contractor, were ready for escort duty. Their pilots smoked cigarettes and traded nervous jokes. The Pool was in Virginia, and there was a lot of airspace between there and Texas. But the United States would never expect such a sudden attack, even in the wake of Einstein's defection. It was entirely out of the Republic's character, and that would be their chief advantage.

Flying low to the ground would hopefully allow them to avoid radar, and if civilians spotted them, they'd likely be mistaken for American aircraft. If the military got wind of them, then their only shot was for the Mustangs to keep the enemy at bay long enough for the bomber to release its payload over the Immortality Compound. When Betty blew, all bets would be off. Einstein said it would release whatever power was binding the magic in place, and nobody knew what would happen then.

Whatever it was, it would be preferable to that miserable man in Washington holding all the cards. Ma only wished that she could see his sallow face when he learned that somebody had pissed in his sandbox.

"When this is done, I'd like to keep you in our employ," she said.

Einstein pushed a confused looking young engineer out of the way and turned three of the knobs a fraction of a turn. "We'll need you to help us harness all of that free magic roaming the countryside."

Einstein turned a tired scowl her way. His frustration and impatience was etched into every wrinkle on his face. The man didn't even have the decency to hide his dislike of her.

"I thought you Texans wanted to liberate the magic, not usher it into another prison cell."

"We do want to liberate it, but only to make it available for everyone. Do you expect us to gain access to the magic and then turn our noses up when it comes our way? Oh, Houston's a little idealistic, I'll grant you. He likes to think sending all of this magic into the world will empower mankind and help it all come together. But I don't think he has a real understanding of human nature.

"It puts everyone on equal footing, that's for sure. That's the goal. Take away America's advantage. But once it's a free-for-all, you can damn well bet I'm going to put Texas in a position to succeed. If I did any less, I wouldn't be worthy of office."

Einstein studied her for several uncomfortable seconds. He scratched his stubbly head and leaned against Betty's side, as if the air around him was too heavy for a man of his age. He licked at parched lips, then turned away from her and tapped a fingernail against one of the device's gauges. "This isn't exactly right. Look, you need to dial it in to thirty. No, move please, and I'll show you."

Einstein did not speak to her again until the B-29, with Betty in its bomb bay, lifted off with its compliment of fighter planes. They stood together on the insufferably hot tarmac amid a host of ground crew and government officials. Grim-faced General Eaker barked commands. Einstein's inscrutable gaze followed the planes until they were nothing more than tiny, black blotches against the darkening skies. His eyes were red and wet, and he looked as if he'd aged ten years in the last twenty-four hours.

"If you'll kindly excuse me, I think I'll retire to my quarters," said Einstein, never taking his eyes off the horizon. "I think I've had quite enough of this world."

THE SCIENTIST

Albert slid beneath the blankets and closed his eyes for the last time. He relished the cool feel of the pillow against his cheek and the clean smell of bleach on the sheets. He tried to take it all in, to hold it to him somehow. These were likely his last hours, and though he was too tired to spend them doing anything else, he wanted, at the very least, for his last sensations on Earth to be pleasant.

He would not die, not technically. But he would be *gone*. All of them would. Possibly far enough gone that they'd never exist again.

The Vice President's intentions had shaken him to the core, and he cursed his own naiveté. He wasn't playing on the same level as the Texans, so why had he expected them to be any less duplicitous? They didn't want the magic free at all. They wanted it for themselves. The moment she'd spoken, a host of alternate futures had exploded into life in his mind, and none of them were any better than the one he planned to eradicate. As long as that sort of power existed, there would be someone willing to exploit it.

It wasn't the Pool's fault. It was his. By itself, the Pool was nothing more than a wonderful gift from Creation. But with tampering, his and others, it had become something it shouldn't have.

In those last moments, in the choking heat of that hanger, Albert had performed a few small changes to Betty's calibration. A few degrees here, a pressure adjustment there. Now *all* of his mistakes could be erased.

Betty would still be his salvation. She would turn back the world to a time before he'd hired his brilliance to such an unworthy cause, but not to a time when he might once again be tempted to turn from science to alchemy, nor to a time when he might still grow to become a person of such reckless pride. Time would be turned back far enough that such temptation might never occur, at least not to him. Far enough, perhaps, that the Pool could have a good, long rest without worrying about the presence of humanity.

There was a real possibility that, if Betty did her job, Albert Einstein would never be born. Or any of the other wolves who chased immortality and power through the forests of human weakness.

That would not be such a bad thing.

Albert turned on the radio, not quite ready to fall asleep forever. He tuned in a fuzzy station and was delighted to hear Hiram—or *Hank*, as he called himself professionally—speaking in his southern American drawl.

"Thank y'all for letting me play for you. I've got one more, and I'll dedicate this one to my scientist friend. Maybe this is the last one I'll ever play, at least in this life."

Hiram sang a low, mournful tune that brought tears to the scientist's eyes. It was the sort of melancholy that the end of the world deserved.

"There is no greater satisfaction for a just and well-meaning person than the knowledge that he has devoted his best energies to the service of the good cause."

　　　　　　　　　　　　　　　　　　　—Albert Einstein

INTREPID TRAVELERS

CLOSE MY EYES FOR JUST A SECOND AND THE WORLD IS SUPER-
nova gorgeous. My head feels like it's going to collapse in
on itself as the rush trips merrily from synapse to synapse, reaches
out through the ship's hull to wrap the others in a blanket of light,
then snatches hold of creation itself and . . . *pulls* us where we need
to be.

I open my eyes and we've dropped into the middle of a shit
storm. The Kennedy sector is filthy with botcraft, and they key on
us the second we register on their scanners. This is not a problem.
These are small maintenance ships, cargo haulers, upper atmosphere defenders that don't have enough fire power to tackle the
kind of smoke Kesey's throwing at them. They close in like tiny
clawing predators eager to pick and chew at the soon to be dead
things that just popped into their little sector of space, but what they
don't know is we are the *Intrepid Travelers* and they don't have a
hope in hell. I mean, we're *inside the primary planetary defenses*,
just popped there out of thin space which . . . to bot thinking . . .
ain't possible. While they're trying to sort that out, Jill the Pill bears
down in her attack craft and disrupts a whole slew of them with energy waves. Gentleman Jim, Day-Glo Danny, and the others follow
suit and the botcraft drop one by one as their return laser fire sizzles
against a shield of cold silver light that shouldn't exist. Good thing
we're not overly concerned with the laws of physics.

My ship spins and I feel the kiss of Kesey's false gravity as we near the edge of the atmosphere and approach the queue of ships waiting to clear security for the hop down to the planet's surface. My ship is a little out of place. It's a hulking gray dreadnaught the Soviets designated *Raskolnikov* before Kesey liberated it from the Soyuz sector, but everybody now just calls it The Bus. The Bus draws close to the target vessel and suddenly the forever slope of the blue planet . . . above . . . below . . . begins to melt into the blackness of space, painting the spinning security station with a feral rainbow of screaming primary colors and light so brilliant and true that it must have just escaped from the soul of a star.

I'm *pretty sure* this isn't really happening.

Energy beams continue to wipe away the . . . resistance . . . and ships start to peel away from the security station like I've come to blow it out of the sky. This is safe space. No one is used to seeing battle vessels so close to a planet. I scan the ships but have no idea which is the target. Kesey seizes on my indecision and then his voice is in my head . . .

—*Eyes left, Cool Breeze. It's the private craft with the neutral designation. General broadcast ID 00957HH7Y.*

I have no idea which way is left at this point, but Kesey has the Bus scan the broadcast ID. The vessel comes into view and it looks like a demolition expert's private experiment, not exactly the kind of ship you'd expect to be carrying *that* sort of cargo.

But I don't argue, because Kesey, that cat *knows* things.

I maneuver up close to the small craft and broadcast over the private channel. "Close in. We're about to hit the road."

The others rattle off acknowledgements and I feel the twitch of intravenous wires as Kesey instructs the Bus to administer the *impulse*. Like I'm not loopy enough. Kesey tried to explain it all to me once in a flood of acronyms—LSD, LSA, DMT. I don't know shit about ancient drugs, but I understand what's happening, for the most part. Kesey figured out a way to convert the effects of these drugs into an electrical . . . *impulse* . . . that can alter consciousness and that means . . . well, with Kesey that means altered reality. And a man that can change reality can be anywhere he damn well pleases, including behind the planetary defenses of the Kennedy sector's mother planet, New Hyannisport.

I allow the impulses to take me again and the world shifts as I close my eyes. I latch on to my companions and I latch on to the target ship and the universe melts around us and sputters out like a candle surrendering to the endless night, and we . . . are . . . gone.

When I open my eyes again, we're home. The Bus is back in familiar space, circling the dead Earth's moon. The husk of that ancient wasteland lingers like a wound on the face of creation, the ultimate morality tale about the fate of men who aspire to be gods. Kesey chose this place as our base of operations because it's light-years from any of the Affiliated Sectors—there's not a wormhole generator to be had in the whole galaxy, so nobody's going to crash our little party—and the dead planet is a convenient place to dispose of the weapons we steal.

Mostly, though, I think Kesey sees it as an object lesson. He wants us to turn eyes to the ruin of our own human history so we stay focused, so we don't lose sight of why the hell we're tagging along on this lunatic ride.

I can *see* Kesey's voice more than I can hear it right now; the man's talking in bold green letters that swim across my field of vision. *Enough.* I pull the impulse leads free from my intravenous wires and cap the jacks. I'm not bothering to read everything Kesey's saying until his words begin to sparkle like diamonds and everything gradually begins to regain focus.

—. . . *scanned the cargo. We got the bomb, man. We got it.*

"Right on." My voice slurs.

—*Can you believe that shit? I mean, lifting nukes from wanna-be terrorists and rogue consciousnesses that fancy themselves planet-states is one thing, but popping into Kennedy's back yard and snatching away a bomb from his private stash? That's a major fucking prank.*

"Swell."

—He's initiated about fifty different anti-planet weapon treaties with everyone from the Soviets to the Euros to the god damn fringe societies. Man, if proof got out to the masses that the Kennedy sector is still stockpiling nukes, there'd be Hell to pay.

I guess he's right, but it's not like everyone else doesn't hide nukes too, and way worse shit than that. Any sector that's ever applied for Affiliated recognition has to learn real quick how to keep their secrets stashed in a deep dark hole. Can't let the hypocrite superpowers know you're up to the exact same shit they are, right?

"So you're thinking blackmail on this one?" I say.

—No, blackmail's a bad play. We do that, every human in the sector will rebel and the whole thing is liable to tear itself apart and then all those nukes would find new homes in the hands of people even crazier than the Kennedy consciousness. Nothing scares humans like radiation, Cool Breeze. It's part of their genetic makeup at this point. It's primal. Like fear of the dark."

Sometimes I think Kesey forgets I'm human. It's like he's caught up in his web of plots and plans, doing all the virtual legwork it takes to process meaning out of an eight-hundred-year artificial existence. Maybe we're just lab specimens to him. God knows the impulse charges aren't doing good things to my body or my mind.

"Neither one bugs me much."

—That's because your mind is wide open. You're a special case 'cause you're willing to think about all the ways you—

Thankfully, Kesey's voice is audio again. I pull the ship's audio interface out of my ear and he's suddenly speaking through the room system. I tune out most of what he has to say; I've heard it all before and no matter what he thinks, I don't have to be reminded every day that I'm the only one in the universe that's ever expanded my mind enough to . . . imagine . . . myself and everything else around me into the exact spot in the universe I want to be. I figure that's bullshit anyway. Kesey swears he's a sole consciousness, but there's no telling how many instances of that crazy loon are riding the tech waves from one end of creation to the next, or how many bands of Intrepid Travelers he has risking their necks to do his bidding.

Big Dogs like Kennedy and Khrushchev might fancy themselves too great to exist in more than one instance, but fringers like Kesey are notorious for copying themselves. It's like procreation for them. They can't fuck (unless they want to limit themselves by entering a vat body, and really . . . that's just . . . ick), so they create a new consciousness, pack it a sack lunch, and kick it out into the world to fend for itself.

Not that I care what Kesey does with his free time; I just wish he wasn't always so full of shit.

I'm pretty sure Jill is a Soviet spy named Natasha, but it's not something we talk about much. Kesey says the Soviets have been on his ass, trying to get the dreadnaught back ever since he stole it from their shipyard, and he claims to be one hundred percent certain that Jill is working for them. Kesey is plugged in like a mother and he's rarely wrong about anything. But if Jill is after anything, I doubt it's the ship. More likely it's the decaying planet full of nuclear weapons that we're orbiting. Just saying.

Right now, my interests in Jill are far more immediate. I'm on my back still trying to catch my breath. One of her bare legs is draped across mine, one arm is across my chest, one hand pulls at my overgrown hair. She breathes softly against my neck; her heart beats a gentle rhythm against my chest.

"How's your mind?" she asks.

"Better," I say. "I'm seeing colors again instead of smelling them, so that's a plus."

"I'm serious," she says.

"Better. Really. My brain tickles a little, but that's standard operating procedure anymore." I squeeze her arm and try not to tip her to the fact that I'm afraid I might snap out of here any second and wind up some place I can't come back from. Used to be I'd only travel when Kesey applied the *charge*. It still helps, especially when I'm carrying people and ships and stuff with me, but it's hardly necessary. These days, I have so many impulses crackling through me the hard part is *not* traveling.

"Maybe it's time you tell Kesey you've had enough." She pulls the sheet up around her shoulders and buries her face against my neck. Her hair falls across half my face. It's a wonderful shade of blue that I've never seen anywhere else in nature, and I can't figure out if the color really belongs to her or if it's another product of my skewed perceptions.

"Maybe I haven't had enough," I say.

"Then you're stupid," she says. "I know you think what's going on here is important, but there are others who can take the hit from time to time, you know?"

"Yeah, but Kesey doesn't trust anyone else." She stiffens against me and I know it's the wrong thing to say. The room is suddenly hot; the intensity of her fear and sudden anger begins to burn me, and I feel sweat beading on my bare skin. The room starts to waver, and I cling to it with the whole of my sanity. "Sorry, but it's true. That's just Kesey."

"Yeah, well maybe Kesey is an asshole," she says.

"You know he can probably hear you?"

"What do I care?" Jill pushes away, sits up and retrieves her panties from the floor. She stands, slips them over her feet and pulls them up, and all the while I can't help staring at her, and I'm wondering . . . is she real? I mean, can she possibly be that . . . *impossibly* gorgeous . . . or is that just how I want to see her? My heart's galloping and I'm giving in to the *impulse,* and if anything, she looks even more devastatingly beautiful when she turns . . . chin back over her bare shoulder with that . . . shit, can that really be her hair . . . and then she realizes what I'm doing and unleashes on me.

"See, right there! I can look in your eyes and see what Kesey is doing to you! You're losing it. And for what? So the *memory* of a burnout and criminal who's been dead eight hundred years can solve all the world's problems by stealing everybody's weapons? I got news for the both of you. Steal all the weapons you want. If people want to kill each other bad enough, they'll make more. They'll figure it out."

"I thought you said what we're doing is important?"

"I thought it was when I joined up, but that's before I understood the futility of the whole thing."

"What we're doing isn't futile," I say. "Stealing the nukes isn't even the point. That's just Kesey having fun. Perfecting the impulse tech is the point."

She pulls her shirt over her head, frees her hair from the collar and it spills over her shoulders like blue electricity. I think I can hear it buzzing. Curiosity washes away her anger in a flood of confused facial expressions, and she climbs back onto the bed and kneels beside me.

"What are you talking about?"

"Just that Kesey maybe tells me things he doesn't tell everyone else."

"Because he thinks I'm a spy."

"Yeah, maybe."

"Kesey is paranoid."

"Can't fight programming."

"We're not here to steal nukes?"

"Oh, we're stealing nukes. Kesey's crazy about nukes. He's not stupid enough to think we can get them all, but he's going to do his best. But he just sees our raids as a cool way to keep testing the impulse technology. Tearing down the walls of science and keeping the world safe from its neighbors, all wrapped up in one neat package."

"Why's Kesey so hot on perfecting this technology?"

"Togetherness."

"Huh?"

"To keep *that* from happening." I point over her shoulder at the Earth. My cabin on the ship must have belonged to some big muck because it has a floor to ceiling window that spans one wall. The moon's crusty surface dominates the view, but a blackened sliver of the dead planet beyond is just visible over the horizon. "Kesey thinks everybody spent too much time trying to keep everyone else at a distance. It's real easy to build up xenophobia and nationalism if you never get to look the other guy square in the eye from time to time. Kesey says that's what led to the last apocalypse."

She's been staring at the Earth, but she turns her eyes back my direction and now they're the same color as her hair and they're . . . alive . . . swirling masses of reflective blue light containing the genetic memory of fleeing generation ships and a world in flames. She can see their screams and I can hear them, and when she puts her hand on my bare chest and leans closer to whisper right in my ear it almost causes my heart to stop. I grit my teeth to stop a sudden case of the shakes, and as I struggle against the *impulses* I listen, and I feel her words soft against my cheek.

"What's he planning?"

"Once we're sure this impulse thing is really . . . working . . . ah, once we've got it *perfected* and it can be controlled. Then he's going to . . . give it away?"

"Give it to who? Do you mean he's going to give this to a government?" Her fingers melt into my chest and I experience a wondrous feeling of completeness. The room around us is a cocoon of warm water that hugs our bodies together so closely that I think our souls touch.

"Yes."

"Which one?"

"Not one," I say. "All of them."

Her breath hisses through her teeth. "All of them?"

She's so insistent in her questioning that I'm momentarily convinced that she really is a Russian spy, and I'm babbling away all of Kesey's secrets, selling him out; then she leans back, and the world regains its proper shape. The stateroom is just a stateroom again, the bed is just a bed, and her fingers are only fingers against my shuddering chest, and everything is way too *real*. The pain and the horror in her eyes, the pale, slack expression on her face; they can't be forced. She looks so *unmistakably human* and I'm blindsided by the knowledge that there aren't many of us left, less than a million souls all told, and that we'd better stick together and fight with every fiber of our being if we want to avoid extinction.

I know Kesey is right.

"He's going to put the technology on the com nets. Anyone who wants it can have it. No more regulated wormhole generators. Go where you want, when you want, and suddenly the whole universe is united. What's the point of fighting over prime systems when they belong to everyone, right? Not to mention that there's an infinity of planets to be had, if only they could be reached. Now they can."

Jill pulls away from me again. "That's ridiculously idealistic."

"Like I said, you can't overcome programming."

"That's Kesey's excuse," she says. "What's yours?"

"What's wrong with idealism? Maybe he's right."

"I'm in love with a fool," she says, then digs her pants from beneath the sheets and finishes dressing in silence. She leaves without saying goodbye, and I lay in bed for a long time, staring out at the planet my ancestors destroyed centuries before.

My dreams are *vivid*.

Kesey says he's been to the edges of creation, where the universe is still stitching itself together with twining strands of matter and probability. I asked him once if he'd let me go there but he refused to show me the way. The human mind couldn't handle the experience, he said. Assuming I didn't simply fast forward out of existence, there'd be nothing left of me but a human husk bound for an asylum.

Still, I really, *really* want to go.

Kesey says not only is it the farthest distance you can travel in space, but that it's ahead of us in time too. Whatever ultimately happens to humanity has already happened and all of our successes and failures mean absolutely nothing in the face of time's irresistible march. We're all ancient memories at the end of the universe.

Sounds pretty good to me.

We're lifting nukes from a private stash in the Havana system when I . . . slip? What the hell do you call it when one second you're focusing in on the target, ready to pull the nukes and the support ships full of . . . friends . . . back to Earth space and the next you're staring into an endless expanse of spiraling colors and exploding impressions of soon to be reality?

The Bus isn't even there anymore. It's just me at the very ass end of creation and I reach out with alien fingers that string out forever into midnight oblivion and the only thing I'm afraid of is that somehow I've finally found Heaven and Jill didn't make it here with me.

"Jill?"

—*What the hell's going on with him?*

"Jill."

"Why do you think we'd know? You're the one that did this to him! Where is he?"

—*Gone somewhere.*

"Jill?"

"Gone somewhere? Are you kidding me? Is that the only—"

"—answer you have?"

I'm not *there* anymore, I'm here.

—He's back.

My eyes open and I suck stale air into my lungs like I haven't had the stuff in weeks. I'm on the Bus and I'm not alone. The whole merry band of Travelers is there, and Jill yanks the impulse lines from my jacks and tosses the hissing cables to the floor like they're live snakes. She lifts a canister of water to my lips and I realize they're dry and bleeding. I've never been so thirsty in my life.

"Are you okay?" Jill asks.

I guzzle the water, cough some down my chest and drink more. I'm freezing cold and jittery. Worried faces swim around in the sea of blinking lights and black metal that in brief snatches of lucidity I recognize as the ship's bridge. Jill is grim and the Gent is customarily detached and poor Bold Angus looks like he's afraid I'm going to transport us all into the heart of a sun which, come to think of it, isn't entirely outside the realm of *possibility.* Where the hell did I go and what am I doing back here now? Danny and Mighty Mags and everyone else crowd around until they're one big human stew, boiling with a bleak flavor of fear that I swear to God I can taste.

And Kesey. I can't see him, of course, but his voice is always there.

—You okay now kid? Where the hell did you go?

"What's wrong with me?" I ask.

—Nothing's wrong with you. You must have quit paying attention or something.

"Don't tell him nothing's wrong," says Jill, supporting my head as it tries to loll back against the reclined command chair. "Obviously something is wrong."

—Who knows more about this, you or me? Cool Breeze has expanded his mind further than any person in history. It's all about tricking the brain into a state of altered consciousness, to where he thinks he's somewhere and then by God he is that somewhere. *Same shit we were trying to do with acid in the sixties, but not enough people could ever get past the recreational aspects of the whole trip. They all thought it was fun, yeah? But it's not a game. Cool*

Breeze is hip to that. But knowing and doing ain't always exactly the same thing. He's got to keep focused on the task at hand. The where and when. He does that and we're all cool. He doesn't and things maybe get a little hairy.

"How is he supposed to focus in this state of mind?" asks Jill. "He's a wreck."

—*It takes a certain kind of mind. A tranquil soul if you want to look at it that way. Cool Breeze has it. That's why I signed him up for this gig in the first place.*

I don't remember signing up for this gig at all. Becoming Kesey's test subject just sort of *happened*. One day I'm a Kennedian Military Academy dropout with just enough classified flight knowledge to make the government nervous about my intentions, the next I'm getting coded communications about a research project being conducted by a rogue AI and *would I like to join* and I realize that I might not even have the funds to feed myself for another week and this guy . . . this machine, I guess . . . is paying and what the hell else am I supposed to do with my life?

Everyone else here has similarly checkered pasts. Jill says she's a Kennedian Naval pilot gone AWOL during training maneuvers, a political protest in response to Kennedy's hard line against communist star systems. Come to think of it, being a commie sympathizer doesn't exactly contradict Kesey's take on her being in bed with the Soviets. The Gent is ex-British intelligence, Angus is a mercenary willing to hire up with anyone, anywhere if the funds are adequate, and Danny, Mags and the rest all claim they were solicited in the same fashion—large sums of money in the service of science and the elimination of nuclear threats to what remained of humanity.

Kesey brings us in one at a time, gives us funny code names that he really gets a kick out of, calls us his Intrepid Travelers, whatever the Hell that's supposed to mean, then sets the plan in motion. The whole thing seemed titanium solid until I started to crack, and the weird surrealism of the venture began seeping in until I began to question more things than maybe I should.

The most terrifying thought I have as I'm sitting here, watching Jill scream at the ceiling like she's hurling curses at God, is that *none of this is real.* These are play actors, provided by Kesey to keep me entertained while he does Lord knows what to my brain. I think of him seducing me with a virtual Jill and it makes my stomach roil.

I realize I've been tuning out again. Got to focus so I don't *slip.*

"—is all bullshit anyway," says Jill. "Cool Breeze told me what you're really up to. This isn't about the nukes at all. This is all about you being dumb enough to think you can bring about universal peace. You can't give this technology to everyone. Don't you see how dangerous and stupid that is?"

—*Why, Natasha? Because it doesn't give your government an advantage?*

"My name's not Natasha! It's Melanie!"

"Why do I feel like I'm out of the loop?" asks Gentleman Jim. "I signed on to help you stop the proliferation of interstellar nuclear weapons. If that's not our goal, then I'd like to know what is."

"I told you his goal," says Jill. "He's going to perfect this brain impulse technology, whether it kills Cool Breeze or not, and then he's going to put it on the com nets. Everyone in the universe will be able to figure out how to make this happen. No more walls, anywhere. You get it?"

"Doesn't sound so bad," says Bold Angus, tentatively. "Something like this shouldn't belong to just one person."

—*It's not bad. Not to be immodest, but it's brilliant.*

"Sounds like a recipe for endless war," says the Gent. "And what's this about Jill being named Natasha?"

—*Don't play the idiot with me, Gent. I know all about you. Who you are.* What you are. *You're here because I wanted you here. All of you. Do you think I'm dumb enough to let a whole boatload of spies into this gig unless it serves my purposes? Keep sending your . . . coded . . . rerouted messages to your keepers every time we jump into occupied space. Make sure they all know exactly what crazy ass Kesey is up to and make sure they know there's not a hope in hell they can stop any of it, unless they figure out real quick how to zip on out to Earth space without aid of a wormhole What fun is a prank of this magnitude without a bunch of rubes to gawk at it?*

More than a few faces in the room develop colorful sheens of uncertainty, but the Gent is cold marble, and Jill is so worked up by the whole thing that she's barely even breathing anymore.

"Let's go," she says, sliding an arm around my waist and lifting me to unsteady feet. "No more of this. Ever."

—Once more, at least. I've got that boy's mind mapped now, Natasha. That's all the info anyone will need to open this party up to the public. We pop back into occupied space and that info is going to be broadcast, whether you want it to or not. The alternative is to stay here for the rest of your lives, but that would be a total drag.

"Then we'll stay here forever," says Jill as she leads me from the bridge, from the stunned gathering of suddenly accused spies. Kesey might still be saying something, but my brain is producing white noise to all my senses and I trust that Jill will put me somewhere safe, keep me breathing and confined to right here, right now.

God bless my lovely Russian spy.

I think maybe . . . probably . . . I've been totally used up.

It's not easy to hold my cabin in focus as Jill helps me onto the bed and shoves a pillow under my head, but I lock on to the image of the dead Earth out my window and try not to question the fact that the whole planet is on fire. This is definitely not happening—I can tell by the fact that Jill is tending to me and not gaping in horror—but the silver flames look so real I figure they might as well be. The line between what is and what *can be* is pretty fucking slim right now.

"Kesey's lost his mind," says Jill as she moistens a towel and drapes it across my head. It's cold metal against my skin—*senses are seriously whacked now*—and I grab double handfuls of the bed sheets in a preemptive strike against the spasms beginning to wake beneath my skin. They crawl and sizzle and I moan a little when Jill lays beside me and hugs me with all her strength, like she can sense my . . . soul? . . . being? . . . is about to leave this body and hit the road for good.

"Kesey doesn't have a mind." I have no idea if what I'm saying is intelligible, but talking gives me something else to cling to. "He's just a program."

"Just a fucking NASA baby is what he is!" She screams this to make sure Kesey hears her. She doesn't understand. Screaming isn't necessary. Kesey hears everything. "He thinks he was human once, like they all do."

The room in buzzing, and I can't tell if it's coming from me or if it's Kesey reacting to Jill's insults.

There's no quicker way to piss of an AI than to remind it that all those memories it likes to claim as its own actually belong to a brain that's been rotted for centuries. They prefer the *human* take on things. They like to think maybe God or aliens or just some random freak of nature is the reason for their existence. I've never interacted with an AI yet that cared to embrace its own creation myth.

The way I hear it, Kennedy—the *real* Kennedy, not the one running things now—was real keen on getting his country to space before anyone else did and generally in favor of doing anything and everything better than the Soviets. So he had this group of scientists called NASA charged with reaching the moon, and one of those bright eggs figures Earth is at the dawn of a new age of humanity and why doesn't he save all the knowledge of that time he can for future generations, so he tap tap taps into a computer the size of a small botcraft and models the minds and personalities of everyone he can think of worth cataloging, good, bad, real and fictional. Top secret stuff on technology that wasn't even supposed to have been invented yet, and thanks to that dude, my brain is about to leak out both my ears.

All this I got from a seriously depressed AI in a departure bar on New Manhattan who'd downloaded himself into a diseased looking vat body and covered it up with rag shop clothes. He said the AIs call this god of theirs the CODER and he's in the resident memory of every living program in the universe, whether they want to admit it or not.

The problem I see with this is all of these artificial souls were created in the image of this one man's *perceptions* of who they were, and those perceptions wouldn't necessarily have been based in . . . ah, reality? Were the Earth-based commies really the terrifying, militaristic, baby eating monsters they are today? And was Kennedy really the boldest, brightest leader of a country that was the poster child for civilization perfected, tasked with weeding out usurpers to that claim at all cost?

Probably not.

But of more immediate concern is Kesey. What did the CODER think of him? Is he a literary icon and a radical champion of freedom or an anti-establishment wacko ready to bring down the social order of a whole universe to satisfy a whim? I've seen him lean both directions, and I figure the answer to that question will go a long way to determining if we ever get out of Earth space alive.

"Are you there?" Jill shakes me.

It's easier in my head. I can think there. I can focus. I'm not too hot on the real world right now.

"Are you there!"

And, yeah, suddenly I am *there!* I am *here*, and the hyper-reality of the situation reaches down my throat with a spiked gauntlet and pulls bloody screams out by the fistful. Jill's panicking now, trying to hold me in place on the bed, and she's totally unaware that Earth's silver fire has reached the moon and those flames are so bright I'm afraid I'm going blind and *give them a minute* . . . give them maybe *just a few seconds*, how do I know? . . . and they're going to turn us both to ashes.

And that's not really so bad, is it?

"Stop it!" she screams. "Stop it! You aren't losing it right now. You're here, with me. With Jill!"

With Jill. With my lovely Russian spy.

With the only person I can tolerate on this ship.

With the woman I fell in love with the moment she appeared on the Bus's bridge, freshly recruited by Kesey and even then . . . *even then! . . .* I felt almost sorry that she'd been dragged into this whole idealistic struggle against . . . what . . . something . . . hard to tell anymore but there was a connection between us and I'm almost completely certain it's not just because she's a spy and she's trying to find out if there's anything of value rattling around inside my fucked up head. And every tear streaking down her face *right now*, catching that horrible silver light from the approaching flames makes me *that much more certain* that she's legit, she really does love me and fuck Kesey, you know, fuck him if he wants to use me up and let me melt away because those tears will bring me back from the dead.

"You aren't a spy." I touch her wet cheeks. She coughs, shudders, holds my fingers tight against her face and pulls me back to the pillow.

"I'm not a spy, Cool Breeze. And I'm not sure what I can do to fix you and get us out of here, but I'm going to figure it out."

"My real name is Nathan."

"I love you, Nathan. Now sleep."

I relax. I let the pillows take me and I let her arms take me and together we sleep, burning in our own private fires at the end of humanity's first age.

Peace never lasts.

"Wake up, Cool Breeze." The voice is familiar. Only one accent like that on the Bus. "Wake up, Jill."

Jill sits up like a shot, hair streaking behind her like electric blue paint on a canvas. I follow more slowly, but I see the ashy color of her face and the gun, the old-fashioned gun with honest to god projectiles loaded in it, pointed straight at my skull. The Gent holds the weapon with practiced ease, and something has *changed* in his expression. He's hard, businesslike. He doesn't look like a man who'd wave a gun around without the constitution to use it.

"Where'd you get that thing?" asks Jill, looking more confused by the fact that he's menacing us with a weapon favored by out of touch, vat-dumped AIs and historical re-enactors than concerned that he's going to kill us. Me, I'm just wondering how we survived the fire that wasn't there, and which hurts less, burning to death or getting shot between the eyes with a high velocity chunk of metal.

"Family heirloom," says the Gent. "Let's go, on your feet. We're going to the bridge."

"What is this?" Jill's getting pissed now. And afraid. I can pick that emotion out of the air for sure.

Jill is standing, but I haven't gathered the strength to rise yet, so the Gent grabs my shirt and tugs me onto my feet. "*This* is me taking charge of this madhouse. *This* is me looking to Her Majesty's interests before Kesey rips apart the whole order of the universe."

"You're really a spy!" says Jill.

"No more charades, Natasha. Don't think I wasn't properly briefed on you. We're after the same thing. At least we *were* until Kesey changed the rules of the game. Laying claim to the impulse tech is useless if our boy here can't jump us back home without all the secrets stashed in his head hitting the com nets. But the stockpile of nukes? I think Her Majesty is the best custodian of that little arsenal."

"What the hell are you talking about? My name's not Natasha! It's Jill, shit, I mean it's Melanie!"

"Mine's Nathan," I say absently, still trying my best to remain standing.

The Gent regards me with a look of utter pity. "God, he's really fouled you up, hasn't he? Not to worry, we'll get you back to civilization and you'll be ship shape in no time."

"He's not going anywhere with you," says Jill.

"Yes, he is."

The Gent shoves us both into the hallway and begins leading us toward the bridge, his little black gun never wavering from my head. Jill looks eager to murder him, but she seems less keen on seeing the inside of my head on the outside of my body, so she walks stiffly beside me, an arm around my waist for support. Her body is a furnace and my brains feel like they're boiling. Lights and sounds careen into one another and form new . . . sensations . . . that I've never felt before and I realize I'd much rather escape into the warm pool of sensory overload that my mind is conjuring than concern myself much with the British spy and his cute little gun. The Gent doesn't want me dead. Doesn't want Jill dead either or he'd have taken care of her in the room. And there's always Kesey. Lord knows Kesey won't let some dude just waltz off with his prize. That guy always has something up his sleeve.

—*What are you doing, Gent?*

Kesey's voice is there as if he's been reading my thoughts, waiting for me to summon him. I smile and Jill looks at me like I've finally lost the last of my faculties. Maybe I have.

"Leaving."

—*Yeah? What good is that gonna do you?*

"You're the one with all the answers," says the Gent. "You don't need me to tell you how this story ends."

—*You've got that right. I was there, man. I know who you are. I've read all the books you're in. I probably know more about you than you do. Man, you're not even* real.

Kesey's got the Gent rattled, but he does a decent job of hiding it. Uncertainty pours off him in warm waves of light, but his face is dull stone. The guy's cold. He doesn't rise to Kesey's bait, he just ushers us onto the bridge, drops me into my customary seat with the gaggle of wires and starts hooking me up, setting the system. I try telling him that I don't need the impulses to go places anymore, and that jolting me again might just make me think up a black hole or something, but when I speak my words sound like metal on metal, diamond on glass, and they hurt. Nobody else seems to mind, and they damn sure don't have a clue what I'm saying.

—*You know, you're not really Agent 070. The CODER made a mistake. You're a fucking typo!*

Kesey is laughing now and *God Almighty* I wish he would stop before it blinds me.

—*How's that for putting life in perspective? You're just one big mistake. A big oopsie on the part of the creator. Don't sweat it, though. You're not alone. We're all pretty much mistakes, right?*

"You're a vile man," says the Gent. "And one whose word holds little value."

"What's going on here?" Bold Angus slips into the room and Jill starts to scream something at him. The Gent whips around as Angus is digging in his pocket and then a deafening crack and a foul, acrid stench and there's a fucking . . . hole . . . in Angus' chest and more blood than I would ever imagine a body could hold and Jill is trying to yank wires free from my jacks until the Gent backhands her with the gun. A whine hisses from between her clenched teeth and she loses her footing.

—*Well, only one of us is a* murderer.

"I don't relish killing. I try to avoid it as a matter of course." The Gent, Agent 070, the weird, mostly-silent-until-now guy who apparently is a fiction-based AI in a vat body, is shoving wires back into me at a furious pace with his free hand. His gun doesn't waver. Much. "But he was reaching for a weapon."

—*Score one for the Queen, then. Looks like you've taken the Cubans right out of the ballgame.*

"He was a good Scot. If he'd been turned by the Cubans, he deserved worse than I gave him."

—*Seriously, man, what do you think you're accomplishing here? The second we pop back into occupied space everybody learns what we've been doing out here and suddenly the Queen's got a Soviet dreadnaught parked in her garden.*

"Yes, and we'll have enough nuclear weaponry to take on all comers. Couple that with the freedom to go anywhere, and the Bear stands little chance against the Lion I think."

—I don't mind if your actions free the tech. That's cool. But you know I'm not going to let you bring all those nukes back with you.

The Gent is fiddling with the system board that drives the impulses and I'm wondering if maybe I should put up a fight. I try to sit up, and he shoves me forcefully back and that's about all the strength I have left in me at this point. I let my head fall to the side and see Jill on the floor, stirring. She reaches for my outstretched hand and I try to grab it and help her up. Letting the Gent claim all those nukes is a bad idea. I have no idea if Jill is really a spy, but she's a human being, and I figure she's the only one here in a position to stop this from happening.

"I don't see what you're going to do to stop me," says the Gent, then he codes in the impulse command and the system begins to buzz. "Cool Breeze, I need you to reach out and grab those nukes. They're going with us on this trip. We're going to jump to British space, and you'll leave them on an uninhabited planet for retrieval by Her Majesty's military. And if you don't follow those orders precisely, I'll have no problems shooting your lovely spy."

—Last chance.

"Please be quiet."

—You are a pain in the ass.

There's a *click* somewhere and fresh impulses light up my body. I squeeze down on Jill's hand and she pulls herself up and I start screaming like I'm getting those electroshock treatments that Kesey is always reminiscing about. And maybe I am. Maybe the Gent's screwed this whole thing up and I'm about to die a sizzling pile of flesh right in front of the woman I love.

Then Kesey's voice is there in visible letters that span the width of the bridge. Two words that change everything.

—ACID TEST

Oh my . . . God . . .

The haze surrounding my senses lifts in a rush and I am suddenly *aware* of everything. The sharp bite of the impulses as they race through my skull and pull the universe into such hard focus that I can barely stand to keep my eyes open. The taste of electricity on my tongue. Jill's shriek of pain as I squeeze down so hard on her hand that her bones snap in a rapid series of pops that sound like nuclear detonations. She's pulling to get free and somehow I can . . . not . . . let . . . go, even when I realize it's me hurting her.

The rush of information into my brain is far too much to process at once, but I reach into the flood of memories and pull out the most important one, the one that tells me *who I am*, who I really am, not Cool Breeze, not Nathan, but a guy his parents named Cody and the government named Rover, an honest to God operative, C.I.A., a deep cover dude if ever there was one. And I remember the briefing on Kesey, the mission, go deep and figure out what the hell that crazy drug-addled A.I. is up to and make sure whatever it is can be turned to Kennedian advantage. But it turns out Kesey is a crafty cat, smarter than the average bear as he likes to point out, and it didn't take much . . . just a little . . . tap? A little instant conditioning while under the influence of the impulses and that C.I.A. man becomes *Kesey's* man, through and through. But maybe Kesey doesn't trust him, not entirely. Better to push him down, hold his head under reality no matter how hard he flails, right up until the . . . exact . . . moment that he's necessary.

Right up until now.

"What's the deal, Kesey?"

—*Kill the Brit.*

My fingers release Jill and she jumps away like I'm a mass murderer in close quarters. I forget about her for the moment because all I can see through the blazing red pain of my new reality is the Gent and his gun. I'm out of my seat and the gun is in my hand before 070 has a chance to blink. I know how to fight. I know how to kill. That's what I was trained for. And the fact that all of my senses are raging out of control only makes the Gent's failure all the more certain. Stunned, he tries to turn away, and I shove him to the floor, turn his own pistol on him. I don't offer up any witty banter, any outraged vitriol, any hope for salvation. I just aim for his chest and pull the trigger. One shot's all I need.

His blood becomes a river and I know I'm seeing things again. Thing is, I don't really care. The Gent flails on the floor like he's going to be able to wriggle free from death's grip, and I read his dying thoughts. They rise up from his chest wound like bits and bytes of what passes for his soul scurrying to desert a sinking ship, and I get . . . *visions* . . . of a future where all those weapons fell into the hands of one . . . motivated . . . government and I feel flush with pride at murdering the man.

Kesey is a righteous dude with righteous ideals and this is just more proof.

—*Kill the Russian.*

"Jill?"

It's possible that I spoke out loud, but she doesn't answer. She grips her broken hand to her chest and backs up against the far wall of the bridge. Her sheer terror at what I've suddenly become stalls my advance.

"Jill!"

"What are you doing?" she asks.

I realize I'm pointing the gun at her and what I'm doing is *following orders.*

"I'm not a Russian!" she yells. "Rover, you know me! I'm Sideways. We've worked together a hundred times. I'm Melanie! Your girlfriend! I followed you into this mess to get you out of it. I just haven't figured out how yet. Remember what Kesey has done to you. This isn't who you are. You're Rover and you're a good man and you're an American, just like me. You aren't Kesey's creature. God, if you don't remember any of that just remember that I'm Jill! I love you and damn it, you aren't going to kill me!"

"She's not a Russian." I know she's telling the truth. Our minds are bridged, just one more thing about me that I no longer understand, but her thoughts are mine and I know exactly who she is, exactly what we've shared, and it doesn't matter one bit because Kesey says she's got to die. Besides, she's been lying to me, to one of me, to *a couple of me* maybe? And she's pulled a fast one on Kesey. Dude thought she was Russian all along but shit no she's pure American like I used to be but what does that matter because . . . *I know* . . . I know exactly what's in her head and exactly what her bosses have planned and I know handing these nukes over to the Americans is no better or worse than giving them to the British, and no matter how much she loves me (and that's in there too, that's not bullshit, it's real as rain) she's an *American* and this is about advancing those interests as much as it is about rescuing me. More so, really.

Something vital to my humanity . . . snaps . . . and my jaw hangs low but my aim is true and Kesey is screaming at me in Technicolor rage and I can tell he knows he's losing his grip on me a little, and with that his grip on this whole mad experiment.

—*Whoever she's working for. Kill her. You know what she has planned.*

His command is . . . God, it's . . . difficult to disobey and Jill is shrieking at me as I advance on her until we're close again, hearts slamming together. The gun barrel presses against her temple and my hand shakes from the sheer effort of defying . . . his . . . will, and Kesey is screaming directly into my brain now, erasing all other concerns but Jill's death. He's really screwed up, letting all these spies into his web just because he thought he was a big bad spider and could gobble them up at will. And now he wants to use me to clean up the mess, when all I ever wanted was to . . . who knows what anymore . . . but he wants me to kill Jill and I know that doing so might be the best thing that could happen to the universe at this point.

And yet . . . she's Jill. She's Melanie. She's Sideways.

The gun goes off and a bullet whines and tings through the bridge in a series of wild ricochets. Jill screams and shoves away from me, not entirely caught up to real time and the fact that she hasn't been shot.

"I'm Rover."

—*Kill her and I'll put you back to sleep.*

"I'm Nathan."

—*You are Cool Breeze.*

"No, I'm really not."

I feel things beginning to *slip* and I know I'm not long for this place. I tune out whatever Kesey is saying now, blind myself to the neon words zipping from periphery to periphery. I block out everything but me and Jill. Impressions of who we are, who we were. And I can't make sense of any of it. My grip on the gun falters and it falls. I see Jill's eyes follow it as it clatters to the ground. They're . . . hungry. She's wondering if she can get to it while I'm tuned out, while I'm slowly losing what's left of my mind.

I'm getting *out of here.*

I *reach* . . . and take hold of the dead Earth. Billions of burned souls and billions of centuries-dead memories are mine to bear. Screams slit my throat and spill out in shards of smoking white light. I stare into Jill's eyes and they're pleading with me to stop whatever it is I'm doing, but there's no stopping this, not even if I wanted to. I'm gone and she's going to be left here with Kesey and the others, no way home unless he finds another lab rat, but alive, which is better than nothing and which is all I think I can give her right now.

My perception of reality splits in two and I realize while I'm still on the bridge of the Bus, I'm also drifting at the end of the universe, chasing creation with my planet full of nukes. I'm living right this second and at the very edge of the future and I can't stay both places long. Jill's arms are around me as if hanging on tight is all it takes for her to travel with me, and I see that her hair is red. Not blue. God, not blue but red and wasn't that always Melanie's hair color?

"Don't leave me here! I love you."

I tell her I love her too, and it's true. Standing here at the beginning and the end I know for certain that I love her, and there's no doubt that she loves me.

But there's only room for one in Heaven.

The warm press of her body against mine, the wonderfully clean smell of her hair, the terrified sound of her voice as she pleads with me; these are my last human sensations. I close my eyes. I let them all drift away.

And I . . . am . . . off . . . the . . . Bus.

STORY NOTES

CHASING AMERICA

This is probably my most well-known story, and I've been fortunate that it's found a home in two wonderful venues. This tale of Paul Bunyan on the run came to me when I was reading a bunch of American folklore while also re-reading *On the Road*. It's a prime example of disparate influences and ideas crashing together to create something new and weird. Stories often come together this way for me, and it's so much fun when they do.

"Chasing America" originally sold to Deb Layne and Jay Lake for the sixth volume of their celebrated *Polyphony* anthology series. Later, John Klima reprinted it in *Happily Ever After*, a book of fairy tale retellings from Night Shade Books. The story shared that table of contents with the likes of Neil Gaiman, Peter Straub, Charles de Lint, and a ton of other writers I admire. Still not sure how I cracked that one, but thanks John!

THE GUADALUPE WITCH

This was my second story published in *Beneath Ceaseless Skies*, a magazine I really love. Both this story, and "February Moon" benefited greatly from editor Scott H. Andrews and his editorial eye.

Beneath Ceaseless Skies offers feedback to every submission, and that's a rare thing for professional genre magazines. Part of Scott's goal is to encourage new voices, and this sort of feedback can be really valuable to new (and established!!) writers. The stories of mine he's rejected have all been improved by his feedback, to the eventual benefit of the next editor who reads them. And the stories he's bought from me became something so much better once Scott helped coax out all the elusive things they were missing.

If you love short fiction, please consider supporting your favorite genre magazines with a subscription or a Patreon donation. *Beneath Ceaseless Skies* is a great one to start with. Believe it or not, short story magazines aren't rolling in cash, and your few dollars a month actually mean a lot.

VERONICA

Kelly Link is the best short story writer alive today, in any genre. This is a known fact and I'm not listening to any arguments. Yes, I know so-and-so is really amazing and nobody can write such-and-such like this person or that person, and I'm eager to read every one of them just as soon as I read whatever new thing Kelly might publish. Okay? Good.

So, this story was my attempt to write something that feels like how a Kelly Link story often makes me feel, but the problem is, she's a genius and I'm not, so this is as close as I could get. The opening paragraph of Link's "Magic for Beginners" is one of my favorites, and I'll take the book off the shelf from time to time just to read that paragraph. It's a burst of pure wonder, written in the second person, and the perfect story hook. The opening paragraph to "Veronica" aspired to capture some small measure of that feeling, but the story gets pretty dark as it progresses. More than one person has told me this story made them cry, so that's something, right?

Like a number of shorts in this collection, Eric Marin at *Lone Star Stories* gave "Veronica" a home in his fantastic magazine.

REWIND

I used to work in this video store, but only parts of the story are true. Renters snuck their video tapes back into the store on Sundays, silent as ninjas. *The Little Mermaid* VHS had gone out of print for a time, and people offered us large amounts of cash for our copy. We had a director's chair to hang out in when the afternoons began to drag, and I watched *Close Encounters of the Third Kind* pretty much on a weekly basis.

This story turned out weird and goofy and kind of hopeful. I like it a lot. Thanks to Mark Teppo for including it in his *XVIII* anthology from Underland Press.

GONE DADDY GONE

There are swan maiden tales from all around the world, but I wanted to write one that was thoroughly American, with all the good and bad that goes along with that. The mid-century setting and the beat dialogue made this story a fun one to write. It originally appeared in *Lone Star Stories*, and received an audio reprint in *PodCastle*, where Dave Thompson did a fantastic job of narration. It's still archived there if you'd like to give it a listen.

A BETTER PLACE

I grew up in West Texas, where the sandstorms can blow through and erase the horizons in a hurry. This story was inspired by that surreal feeling of standing in a world gone dusty brown, waiting for the real world to come back.

This originally appeared in *Realms of Fantasy*, a wonderful magazine that I really miss. I was fortunate enough to have eight of my stories appear in their glossy pages, all with fantastic, commissioned artwork. Shawna McCarthy, Doug Cohen, and everyone at *Realms of Fantasy* were a joy to work with. I'm always hoping they'll get the band back together some day, but for now, *Realms of Fantasy* has gone to live in that better place. Still, I can dream.

HER SOUL, A DARK FOREST

This is the newest story in the collection, fresh from the laptop, and never before published. I think this story might live in the same universe as some others I've been writing lately, where cosmic forces beyond our understanding are affecting small town Texans in less than pleasant ways. Not sure how this one slots into that story cycle yet, but I guess time will tell.

FEBRUARY MOON

I love westerns. King and Bradbury and Tolkien were all formative to me, but I also read dozens of paperback westerns by the time I was in middle school. A whole lot of them were Louis L'Amour books handed to me by my Granddaddy, and I'll pick a good western novel to read before just about anything else, even today.

Some favorites include *Lonesome Dove* by Larry McMurtry, *True Grit* by Charles Portis, and *Ballad of the Gun Years* by Richard Matheson. Yes, that Richard Matheson. I also enjoy westerns in a more modern setting, including *The Time it Never Rained* by Elmer Kelton, one of the best books I've ever read, and the most authentic novel concerning the part of West Texas where I grew up, even though it takes place a couple of decades before I was born.

"February Moon" is set in the Hill Country of Central Texas, a place heavily settled by German and Czech immigrants. I wanted to tell a story about those settlers and play around with a few western tropes. Once I figured out it was going to be a werewolf story, the rest of it fell into place like dominoes.

I'm working on a series of dark fantasies set in nineteenth century

Texas, including "The Guadalupe Witch" appearing earlier in this book. Hopefully more of them will see publication in the coming years.

RATTLESNAKE SONG

My favorite writer is Larry McMurtry, and my favorite book is *Lonesome Dove*, but McMurtry's *The Last Picture Show* is a great novel too. The movie is every bit as good as the book, and I'm a sucker for anything involving small town Texas. In this case, I approached that small town from a cosmic horror angle, and the story found a great home in the anthology *Triangulation: Dark Skies*.

IN THE THICKET, WITH WOLVES

This is my East Texas story. Some of you may have the impression that Texas is flat, arid, and filled with snakes, and that's definitely true about huge swaths of the state. But there are also mountains, rolling hills covered in flowers, sandy beaches, and in the case of East Texas, tall pines and swamps and . . . yeah, snakes also.

I'm a big fan of Joe R. Lansdale, and he so effectively describes his East Texas settings that they become characters in the story. Sometimes a character you'd like to sit on the porch with and have a cold beer, and sometimes a character you'd best avoid if you don't want your ass kicked. "In the Thicket, With Wolves" is my attempt to play around in Joe's part of the world.

This one originally had a different ending, but Shawna McCarthy at *Realms of Fantasy* rightly pointed out that I wasn't playing fair with the protagonist, and she helped me figure out what the ending really needed to be.

This story is pretty dark, but I guess it had to be.

CIGARETTE LIGHTER LOVE SONG

I don't know if this one is science fiction or fantasy or something else, but I like it quite a bit. Nostalgia can be a trap, and maybe that's what I was trying to say here. This one was published in *Daily Science Fiction*, a cool magazine that will deliver a free story to your email inbox, five days per week. That's hard to beat!

ALL MY PRETTY CHICKENS

What if animals had an afterlife, but maybe we didn't? What does that say about our souls? I enjoyed contrasting something bizarre like ghostly chicken reincarnation against the backdrop of a society already jaded by that occurrence, and pushing on to Mars.

The melancholy was strong with this one, not exactly the light sense of wonder story that I set out to write, but I think it works. *Farrago's Wainscot* gave this really odd story a home.

CAN'T BUY ME FADED LOVE

This one originally appeared in *Lone Star Stories*, and was the title story to my first collection, published by Wheatland Press back in 2008. That collection is now out of print, but it featured rock and roll fantasy, science fiction, and alternate history tales. This may be the only story I've ever written where a title came to me fully formed and I had to figure out what kind of story needed to go along with it.

I've included it here because it's one of the stories people ask me about the most, and because Bob Wills is still the king.

STEPHANIE SHRUGS

I used to write a lot of rock and roll stories, and this one about a muse who brings mixed blessings is one of my favorites. It appeared in *Realms of Fantasy*. Despite the darkness that runs through the story, the protagonist winds up happy, or at the very least, content. That wasn't the plan when I started writing, but I just couldn't go with the downbeat ending I was expecting. Maybe I chickened out, but I think it works better this way.

THE BEAUTIFUL PEOPLE

I love old Hollywood movies, and the ones mentioned in this story are some of my particular favorites. Anytime something with William Powell or Myrna Loy comes on, I've got to stop and watch it. And when I first learned about the sad fate of Robert Walker from *Strangers on a Train*, it made me wonder what kind of career he might have built off that brilliant performance.

We invest a lot of time and attention in the actors we enjoy. What if, like gods, they required love and devotion to survive? And what if they could sell their souls for that kind of adoration? Every story comes down to *what if*, right?

"The Beautiful People" appeared very recently in Mark Teppo's new magazine *Underland Arcana*, and I'm thankful to Mark for letting me collect it here, so hot on the heels of first publication.

ESCAPING SALVATION

It goes like this—you decide you want to start submitting your writing in the early 2000s, so you find a genre fiction message board where you can commiserate with other aspiring writers, and these folks become your critique partners and your friends. Fast forward nearly twenty years, and a whole lot of us are still here, plugging away.

One of these friends is Samantha Henderson, and if you've never read her fiction, you should fix that. She writes the kind of stories I wish I could write, and they've been published in places like *Clarkesworld*, *Strange Horizons*, *Fantasy*, *Shimmer* . . . you get the picture. Her stories are beautiful and strange and haunting and well worth your time.

We used to challenge one another with random story starters, and I think "Escaping Salvation" might have been born when Samantha suggested I write a story about angels. Can't say for sure, it's been a while. But ultimately, we put our heads together and wrote this post-apocalyptic fantasy novelette that's desperate and violent and does a great job of melding our different styles. Reading it ten years later, I have absolutely no idea which parts either of us wrote. "Escaping Salvation" appeared in issue #100 of *Realms of Fantasy*.

And, Sam, if you're reading this . . . I promise, I'm getting around to Jezebel really soon.

POSSIBLY GRIEF

This story is about tall tales and local legends and how they continue to change their shape as new people tell them. I wrote this specifically for an anthology of speculative war stories called *From the Trenches*, edited by Joseph Paul Haines and Samantha Henderson.

IN THE TEETH

This is a story about grief, at least the way it feels to me. Maybe the sun's never going to shine that bright again, but life is still there to be lived. "In the Teeth" is original to this collection.

FURY'S HOUR

Yeah, I'm obsessed with The Clash.

They still hit me hard, and it would be tough to overstate how much their music means to me, or the effect it's had on my life. Joe Strummer has been dead nearly twenty years, but I still see the world the way he did, and I keep learning something new from those lyrics every time I listen. When Steve Zisson put out the call for a punk rock science fiction anthology called *A Punk Rock Future*, I took it as my chance to distill all of that love into a story about people coming together and fighting back. If you like this one, you should definitely check out *A Punk Rock Future*. It's stuffed full of really amazing stories from diverse voices.

"Fury's Hour" is actually the second story I've written that concerns Joe Strummer. Sanford Allen and I joined forces to write a story called "The Reckless Alternative" about Strummer in the afterlife. You can chase that one down in the Bram Stoker Award winning anthology, *After Death*. That book is also very much worth your time.

"I think people ought to know that we're antifascist, we're anti-violence, we're anti-racist, and we're pro-creative. And we're against ignorance." —Joe Strummer

BEST ENERGIES

I love alternate history, particularly the bizarre, almost unclassifiable kind from writers like Howard Waldrop and Neal Barrett Jr. This was my attempt to go that far out on the ledge.

"Best Energies" found a fantastic home in a book called *Rayguns Over Texas* that was published to commemorate the 71st annual World Science Fiction Convention, held in San Antonio back in 2013. *Rayguns* featured science fiction stories by Texas writers—native Texans and transplants. "Best Energies" appeared alongside a slew of talented folks, and a few of my literary heroes, including Joe R. Lansdale, Brad Denton, and Michael Moorcock.

My original title for this one was "Avoiding the Cold War," but editor Rick Klaw helped come up with "Best Energies" based on an Albert Einstein quote, and I think it's a vast improvement.

INTREPID TRAVELERS

This is my far future riff on Tom Wolfe's *The Electric Kool-Aid Acid Test*. I'm not sure if I managed to capture that same kind of propulsive, chaotic narrative, but I had a lot of fun with it.

I've been told by a few people that this one is still enjoyable if you haven't read Wolfe's book, but I think there's another level of enjoyment to be found if you've read about Kesey and his Merry Pranksters. Thanks to John Klima for publishing "Intrepid Travelers" in his ultra-cool magazine, *Electric Velocipede*.

ACKNOWLEDGEMENTS

I've been writing as long as I can remember, but I only began summitting for publication around 2001. In the past twenty years, I've made countless friends in the writing business, and received the support of so many people, it would be impossible to name them all here.

I've had the good fortune to belong to a couple of fantastic critique groups—Critical MS and Rejectomancers—and I greatly appreciate the valuable feedback I've received from all my writing buddies in those groups over the years. In particular, I'd like to thank Samantha Henderson, Mikal Trimm, Jaime Lee Moyer, and Lon Prater, who have been subjected to early versions of my stories going back to the early days, and have likely read more of my unpublished words than anyone else.

Thanks to the editors who originally bought these stories and gave them homes: Scott H. Andrews, Michele Barasso, Darin Bradley, Joseph Paul Haines, Samantha Henderson, Rick Klaw, John Klima, Jonathan Laden, Jay Lake, Deborah Layne, Eric Marin, Shawna McCarthy, Misti Morrison, Chloe Nightingale, Mark Teppo, Diane Turnshek, and Steve Zisson. And to all the other editors I've worked with who love short stories as much as I do.

Special thanks to my agent, Kris O'Higgins, for always championing my work, and to Patrick Swenson with Fairwood Press for releasing this collection into the wild.

Finally, thanks to my family and friends for being awesome. You've encouraged me to keep writing my whole life. And in particular to Kristin, Beckett, and Gibson, who know that when I have that blank look on my face, it just means I'm trying to put the pieces of a story together in my head. Love you all.

Josh Rountree
Georgetown, TX
February 15, 2021

ABOUT THE AUTHOR

Josh Rountree has published over 60 stories in a wide variety of magazines and anthologies, including *Beneath Ceaseless Skies, Realms of Fantasy, Bourbon Penn, Polyphony 6, PseudoPod, PodCastle, Daily Science Fiction,* and *A Punk Rock Future.*

A handful of them have received honorable mention in *The Year's Best Fantasy & Horror* and *The Year's Best Science Fiction.*

Wheatland Press published a collection of his rock and roll themed fantasy fiction, *Can't Buy Me Faded Love,* in 2008. *Fantastic Americana: Stories* is his second collection.

Josh lives somewhere in the untamed wilds of Texas with his wife and children.

PUBLICATION HISTORY

"Chasing America" originally appeared in *Polyphony 6,* Wheatland Press (2006) | "The Guadalupe Witch" originally appeared in *Beneath Ceaseless Skies* (2021) | "Veronica" originally appeared in *Lone Star Stories* (2008) | "Rewind" originally appeared in *XVIII*, Underland Press (2020) | "Gone Daddy Gone" originally appeared in *Lone Star Stories* (2009) | "A Better Place" originally appeared in *Realms of Fantasy* (2006) | "Her Soul, A Dark Forest" is previously unpublished and appears here for the first time | "February Moon" originally appeared in *Beneath Ceaseless Skies* (2020) | "Rattlesnake Song" originally appeared in *Triangulation: Dark Skies*, Parsec Inc. (2019) | "In the Thicket, With Wolves" originally appeared in *Realms of Fantasy* (2007) | "Cigarette Lighter Love Song" originally appeared in *Daily Science Fiction* (2014) | "All My Pretty Chickens" originally appeared in *Farrago's Wainscot* (2015) | "Can't Buy Me Faded Love" originally appeared in *Lone Star Stories* (2006) | "Stephanie Shrugs" originally appeared in *Realms of Fantasy* (2007) | "The Beautiful People" originally appeared in *Underland Arcana* (2021) | "Escaping Salvation" originally appeared in *Realms of Fantasy* (2011) | "Possibly Grief" originally appeared in *From the Trenches*, Carnifex Press (2006) | "In the Teeth" is previously unpublished and appears here for the first time | "Fury's Hour" originally appeared in *A Punk Rock Future*, Zsenon Publishing (2019) | "Best Energies" originally appeared in *Rayguns Over Texas*, F.A.C.T. (2013) | "Intrepid Travelers" originally appeared in *Electric Velocipede* (2011)

OTHER TITLES FROM FAIRWOOD PRESS

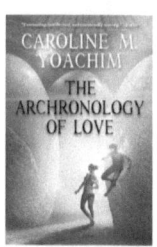